RECEIVED
NOV 1 8 2021
NO LONGER PROPERTY OF
SEATTLE PUBLIC LIBRARY

THE CHILDREN'S SECRET

Also available by Nina Monroe
(Writing as Virginia Macgregor)

What Milo Saw
The Return of Norah Wells
Before I Was Yours
You Found Me

And for Young Adults

Wishbones
As Far as the Stars

THE CHILDREN'S SECRET

A NOVEL

NINA MONROE

NEW YORK

This is a work of fiction. All of the names, characters, organizations, places and events portrayed in this novel are either products of the author's imagination or are used fictitiously. Any resemblance to real or actual events, locales, or persons, living or dead, is entirely coincidental.

Copyright © 2021 by Nina Monroe

All rights reserved.

Published in the United States by Crooked Lane Books, an imprint of The Quick Brown Fox & Company LLC.

Crooked Lane Books and its logo are trademarks of The Quick Brown Fox & Company LLC.

Library of Congress Catalog-in-Publication data available upon request.

ISBN (hardcover): 978-1-64385-875-3
ISBN (ebook): 978-1-64385-876-0

Cover design by Melanie Sun

Printed in the United States.

www.crookedlanebooks.com

Crooked Lane Books
34 West 27th St., 10th Floor
New York, NY 10001

First Edition: July 2021

10 9 8 7 6 5 4 3 2 1

For Willoughby Walden,
my son born on American soil.

Families & Characters

The Days
Eva, Will & Lily

The Wrights
Kaitlin, Ben & Bryar

The Carvers
Priscilla, Peter & Astrid

Avery Cotton
Abi & Cal Johnston

The Bowens
True, Skye, Phoenix & Wynn

The Sayeds
Ayaan, Yasmin, Hanif & Laila

There is no them. There is only us.

—Luis Alberto Urrea

DAY ONE

Sunday, September 1

PROLOGUE

NO ONE SEES the girl standing on the edge of the field. Hair the color of wheat, a green dress, legs so pale they disappear against the white sky.

The air is heavy with the heat of the day; the sun so low it's blinding.

The girl looks at the bounce house, lying in the backyard.

She watches the magician walking back to his car, his black shoes squeaking with each step. He throws his props into the trunk, unclips his bow tie and wipes the sweat off his forehead.

She sees a little boy running between the farmhouse and the stable, trying to keep up with the older children. His face is painted to look like a bear cub: the colors are melting into each other. A red balloon comes loose from his hand and floats into the high branches of a tree. He looks up, his eyes wide. The balloon pops.

The boy opens his mouth: a high-pitched, single-toned wail.

His older sister, a painted butterfly glittering on her cheek, scoops him up in her arms, dangles him upside down until he's laughing, and carries him to the stable.

The girl in the green dress knows that she should go back home. She's dizzy from the heat; her skin is burning.

It's not safe, Astrid, that's why I'm not letting you go.

But she's tired of being left out. And she's tired of her mom telling her what to do.

She looks up at the farmhouse. Through the front window, she sees the mothers. They lounge on chairs and sofas, their bodies cooling as the AC unit whirs.

She watches a man, the only father at the party, coming out of the kitchen with a pitcher of iced tea in one hand and a bottle of gin in the other.

She looks away from the adults to the stable. No one's watching the kids, she thinks.

She walks to the edge of the field. Soon, she's standing outside the stable.

There's a boy sitting in a tree, looking down at her, but she doesn't notice. Her heart's hammering too loud, beating out the same words over and over:

You shouldn't be here.

You shouldn't be here.

You shouldn't be here.

But she's come too far to turn back now. She leans in closer to hear what the children are saying. The top of her sandal catches a rusty barrel; it echoes across the valley.

She holds her breath, hoping that no one heard.

And then slips in through the back door of the stable.

On the porch, the mother places her hand above her brow to block out the glare of the sun. She heard a sound coming from the stable, a metal clang, and thought she should come out and check on the children.

She scans the front yard but there's no one.

Wiping the sweat from her top lip, she leans her head against one of the posts holding up the porch and sighs.

No one had prepared her for this heat.

A wave of nausea sweeps over her. She misses home.

She turns her gaze to the stable. *The children are fine*, she thinks. *There's nothing to worry about: they're just playing.*

But it's hard, at this age, to let go of their hands when their palms are still soft and fleshy from childhood.

The screen door opens behind her.

Why don't you come and join us inside? the man asks. He gives her a tumbler of iced tea. *A little cocktail.* He smiles. *For surviving the party.*

She takes the tumbler, even though she won't drink it.

The glass feels cool in her hot palm.

She looks over again at the stable.

The father follows her gaze.

Don't worry, he says. *My eldest is in charge, she'll keep them in line.* He hooks his arm under hers. *Come inside, it's cooler.*

He guides her into the farmhouse, where she settles into a chair. A blast of cold air hits her from the AC. She leans back and closes her eyes.

Better? the father asks.

Yes, better.

He sits beside her, takes off his hat and balances it on his knee.

Looks like the kids had fun today, she hears him say, but his voice blends into the chatter from the other parents in the room. Already, she's drifting off.

Darkness falls behind her eyelids. And she sleeps. Perhaps for a minute. Or an hour. She's not sure—the heat, the nausea, the tiredness, they make her lose track of time.

But she's sure of this.

The cells of her body know, a moment before it happens.

Her eyes fly open.

She cries out at the room: *No!*

And a second later—perhaps less—a gunshot rings out from the stable.

CHAPTER

1

2 p.m., three hours earlier

KAITLIN LICKS THE frosting off her thumb and stands back to look at the cake: it's not straight. She pulls a spatula out of a drawer and pushes the back of it against the uneven layers. The cake straightens but now there's a dent on one side.

Just leave it be, she whispers to herself.

She's always making things worse by fussing at them.

The recipe is easy, the blog had promised. But then Kaitlin found out that she needed six cake pans, one for each layer of the rainbow. She didn't have six cake pans. So she had to make it in stages, cooling and washing up the pans in between. And then the decorating. Kaitlin had gotten to bed just before 1 a.m., hot and frazzled, with a sugar headache from licking the frosting off her fingers so many times.

Do we really need a cake? Ben had asked, watching her disappearing under a cloud of confectioner's sugar. *I mean, it's not his birthday, Katie.*

No, it wasn't Bryar's birthday. It was much more important than that.

Officially, it was a Back to School party. That's what the invitations said. A chance for the new middle schoolers to get together before term started.

Unofficially, it was a help-Bryar-make-friends-so-that-middle-school-wouldn't-be-a-total-disaster party.

A cake will make it feel special, Kaitlin had answered. *It'll be something for the kids to gather around.*

Okay, my love, okay, Ben had said, kissing her cheek.

And despite the crazy, middle-of-the-night baking, Kaitlin was proud of it: her big, lopsided rainbow cake. *The kids will love it,* she tells herself.

She takes off her apron, steps out of the house, and looks around the front yard. Her heart gives a little skip. So what if the party was beyond their budget? She'd give a few more riding lessons in the fall; they'd pay off the debt soon enough. It would be worth it in the end.

To the side of the house, on a patch of dry grass, the bounce house sways in its yellow, red, and black skin. Next to it, the water slide. She'd gone through the safety precautions with the rental company. In case any families turned up with infants or toddlers, she'd child-proofed the whole property—the stable and the house and the front yard and the outbuildings. She'd checked with Angela, the face-painting lady, that her paints were allergen-free. She'd gone to Target and bought extra bottles of sunscreen, in case anyone forgot. And she'd set up coolers full of ice with juice boxes and water bottles next to each of the attractions.

Kaitlin Wright wasn't going to leave anything to chance.

She heads toward the magician setting up under the small gazebo she's rented for the day. The pictures of him online looked more impressive than the man who had showed up in a faded black suit and a clip-on tie. As Kaitlin walks toward him, she can smell it: sweat on nylon.

She panics, suddenly. Kids these days are smart. What if the old gold-coin-behind-the-ear and rabbit-from-a-hat doesn't cut it? What if they're disappointed?

A disappointed child could bring down a whole party.

Stop worrying, she tells herself. *It's going to be fine.*

"Have you seen my son, Bryar?" she asks the magician. "I told him to come down and help you set up."

"The birthday boy?"

"He's not the birthday boy—it's not . . ." She'd explained it to him. "Oh, never mind."

She really should have gone for the more expensive magician.

"He came for a bit and then left," he says, pulling out a black and white wand that looks like it came from a kid's magic set.

"*Left*? Where?"

"I don't know. He said he was hot."

Of course the party had to take place in the middle of a heatwave. And of course Bryar would find it too hot. His Irish coloring—red hair and pale, freckled skin, like hers—wasn't made for this climate. She suspects that life would have been easier if he'd inherited Ben's dark hair and olive skin.

Kaitlin looks up to her son's bedroom window. The curtains are drawn. She must not have heard him go back upstairs.

She sighs. They'd had a chat this morning about how important today was—that sneaking away to his bedroom to play with his rocks wasn't okay; not until all the guests had left.

She runs inside, straight up the stairs, and knocks lightly on Bryar's bedroom door.

She hears a faint "Come in."

He's sitting at his desk, looking through a magnifying glass. A lamp casts a hot light over his stooped shoulders. His ears glow; the hairs on the back of his neck are lit up.

She goes over and picks up a piece of granite that sparkles like silver. They drive her crazy, sometimes, these rocks cluttering up his bedroom—and all that time he spends digging them up and then polishing and classifying them. But they're beautiful, in their way.

"Your friends will be here soon," she says, putting the rock down.

"They're not my friends, Mom."

She feels a stab in her chest.

"Well, they could be," she says. "Remember what Eva said? When people spend time together, it helps them see how much they have in common; how they're more alike than they realized. That's how friendships start, Bry."

Kaitlin had taken Bryar to more therapists than she could count. None of them had gotten through to him. They wanted to give Bryar a label; she'd wanted someone who understood him for the amazing little boy he was. And then Eva, a music therapist, showed up with her soft English accent and, in only a few sessions, sitting beside Bryar at Ben's old piano downstairs, she'd won him over. As had her daughter, eleven-year-old Lily who was going to be in the same class as Bryar.

In fact, it was Eva who'd suggested having a few of Bryar's classmates over before school started. An opportunity for the kids to have some fun on the long Labor Day weekend, and a chance for the parents to get to know each other too.

Kaitlin had jumped on the idea. Anything to help ease the transition for Bryar. She'd sent out an invitation to every middle-school-aged kid in town. They could bring siblings too, she'd said. She'd even invited the Bowen kids, who don't go to school because their dad teaches them at home. No one was going to be left out of this party.

She pulls up a chair and sits beside Bryar. "It's your party, Bry. It would be nice to welcome them."

"It's not my party."

Another stab.

Willing herself to stay positive, she ruffles his hair and laughs. "Well, whose party is it, then?"

He places a different rock under the magnifying glass and leans over intently.

"It's your party, Mom."

His words hang between them for a moment.

"What?" She shakes her head. "No. This is for you, Bryar. That's why your dad and I have gone to so much trouble—"

He looks up at her, his pale eyebrows scrunched up.

"Where's Dad, then?" he asks.

"Sorry?"

"If it's such a special party, why's Dad not here?"

Kaitlin checks her watch. He's right. Ben really should be here already.

When they lived in Texas, he had an excuse to be late. He worked a difficult border; was always dealing with a crisis. That's why they'd moved here: to raise a family somewhere safe and peaceful. The Canadian border had its occasional incidents, usually drug-related, but it wasn't anything like El Paso.

They had it all planned. Their dream life in cozy, safe New Hampshire: a short drive to the border; regular hours for Ben; a stable where she could give riding lessons. A friendly small town in which to raise their little boy. A real community.

"He's probably handing over at the station. He'll be here." She gives him a nudge. "You know your dad—he'd never miss a party."

Ben Wright, her sociable, easy-going husband who breezed through life. How could their little boy have turned out so very different from him?

Bryar takes a small brush and works away a bit of dirt on the surface of a rock.

"Bryar?"

He stops brushing and looks up at her. "I just want to finish this. I'll come down soon, okay, Mom?"

She puts her hands on his shoulders and kisses the top of his head. "Okay, okay."

And then she leaves the room and closes the door behind her.

Kaitlin stands on the landing, her back against the wall, her eyes closed, trying to muster some energy.

Maybe the party was a mistake. Maybe she should find an excuse to cancel. Or maybe it won't matter because no one will come. People had been slow to respond. Some hadn't answered at all.

Before heading back downstairs, Kaitlin looks out through the window on the landing, across the valley to the next hill where Priscilla Carver lives with her daughter, Astrid, a girl Bryar's age. They even look alike: the same pale skin and hair, the transparent blue eyes. Despite everything that happened with Priscilla, Kaitlin had invited Astrid to the party. She'd thought that maybe Priscilla would let go of the past: they lived in the same town; they saw each other in church every Sunday, bumped into each other at the general store and the library. Surely, after three years, Priscilla could forgive them for what happened.

And she feels sorry for Priscilla, her husband walking out on her like that. Kaitlin doesn't know how she'd cope without Ben. She wanted to show her that she cared.

Don't get your hopes up, Katie, Ben had said when he saw her writing the invitation for Astrid Carver.

And Kaitlin had tried not to get her hopes up, but when Priscilla had been the first to reply, her heart had lifted right out of her chest. Maybe it was a sign that she was keen to come, she'd thought as she tore open the envelope. But then, as she'd pulled out the typed message on headed notepaper, Priscilla's name followed by a list of academic qualifications and her position at the Daniel Webster Law School embossed across the top, her heart had sunk right back down again.

Thank you for the invitation, the note read. *I'm afraid we will not be able to attend. Priscilla Carver.*

Kaitlin can't help but think that if Bryar and Astrid had been allowed to remain friends, things might have turned out better for Bryar. It would have helped, having a smart, confident girl like her at his side.

She looks back over at Bryar's door. It'll take a miracle to get him out of his room.

CHAPTER

2

2.15 p.m.

"YOU SURE YOU'LL be okay on your own?"

Priscilla looks at her daughter sprawled over the sofa, her green dress hitched up to reveal her pale legs. Astrid doesn't take her eyes off her phone, a gift from Peter before he left for his new life in California. *So we can do FaceTime*, he announced, as if a fancy phone was a replacement for a flesh-and-blood, sit-at-the-breakfast-table parent.

"Astrid?" Priscilla says.

"I'll be fine," Astrid says, not looking up from her screen.

"I won't be long," Priscilla says.

Astrid doesn't answer.

"If you don't want to be on your own, I could call someone—a babysitter . . ."

"I don't need looking after."

Blood rushes to Priscilla's cheeks. Before she went into academia, she was an attorney. She's argued in front of some of the toughest judges on the East Coast without her heart rate rising a notch, but a few words from her eleven-year-old daughter and she feels like she's unraveling.

Priscilla remembers the first time it dawned on her that she had no control over Astrid. A Sunday morning trip to the grocery store. Two-year-old Astrid had a meltdown about not being allowed to have a popsicle. *It's the middle of winter*, Priscilla had tried to reason with her. But reason didn't cut it with Astrid. She started taking items out of the cart and hurling them across the store in protest. A milk carton split open, sending a river of white down the aisle.

Priscilla had felt them staring, the mothers.

You're a terrible mom, she heard them thinking.

Ten years of legal training, and she had no authority over her own child.

Nothing had prepared Priscilla for motherhood. For Astrid.

Tentatively, Priscilla steps forward and kisses Astrid's cheek.

Astrid jerks her head away.

Priscilla feels guilty about going into the office on a Sunday. Tuesday is Astrid's first day at Brook Middle School. Maybe she should stay home and make sure she's ready. They could go shopping for new clothes. Get an ice-cream in town. Wasn't that what mothers and daughters were supposed to do?

Priscilla sits next to Astrid on the sofa. "I know it's going to be hard—starting at a new school . . ."

Astrid had been struggling at her private school. Cliques. Girlish rivalries. The teachers said she was socially isolated and underperforming academically. It had gotten worse when Peter left. Priscilla had decided that Astrid could do with a fresh start. Being in a public school might help ground her. And now it was just the two of them, it would be good for Astrid to have some local friends.

"I'm fine, Mom," Astrid says. "Just go and work."

Even before Peter left, their relationship wasn't great. But now, it's as though Astrid is punishing her for being stuck with the parent she doesn't like.

"Okay. But call if you need anything," Priscilla says.

She picks up her laptop bag, looks over at Astrid once more, and walks out into the blazing sunshine.

A wall of heat slams into her. It hasn't let up since July. Six weeks with temperatures hovering between 90 and 100 degrees Fahrenheit. Sweat runs along her hairline.

As she gets into the car, the leather seat burns her thighs. She puts the AC on full blast. Hot air rushes at her. As she fiddles with the levers, trying to angle the fans toward her, she notices the stack of mail on the passenger seat. The letter sitting on the top is from Peter's lawyer: another reminder for her to sign the divorce papers.

She'd been shocked—and hurt—at how fast Peter had processed the paperwork. He left in the middle of a snowstorm in February and a month later, before the snow had even melted, the first letter from his attorneys landed in her mailbox.

This isn't going to last, she's told herself, over and over. *He'll come back.*

That's why she's ignoring this letter, like she has the others.

As the car cools down, she looks across the valley to the other side of Middlebrook. On the crest of the hill, parallel to their house, stands Woodwind Stables, the Wrights' home. The town lies in the dip of the valley between her cottage and the stable. In the early days, before she fell out with the Wrights, she'd loved this clear line of sight between their homes. They were *meant* to be friends, she'd thought.

Not letting Astrid go to the party was the right decision, she tells herself. If anyone knows the damage that firearms can do to a family—to children—it's Priscilla.

When she'd had conversations about the party with the other Middlebrook moms—Tracey, her hairdresser who had a son Astrid's age; Sharon, the mom of four who she was in a barre class with on Friday nights; Zoe, whose daughter did ballet with Astrid; Yasmin, whose husband was building the new mosque—and a handful of others she'd bumped into in the days after Kaitlin mailed out the invitations—they'd listened earnestly. They trusted Priscilla's opinion. And they agreed: keeping your kids safe is a basic principle of motherhood, and in a country like America, keeping your kids safe means keeping them away from guns.

Naturally, there were some parents she could never persuade. Avery Cotton, the minister of St. Mary's, was close to the Wrights: she was bound to take those foster kids of hers to the party. And True Bowen, who walked around the Middlebrook woods with a hunting rifle slung over his shoulder, he'd go, no doubt. But the rest of them would stay clear. Kaitlin would be lucky to have more than a couple of kids show up to that party of hers.

Priscilla looks back at Woodwind Stables. She thinks she can hear music drifting across the valley. A picture flashes in front of her: eight-year-old Astrid and Bryar running hand in hand through the long sheaves of corn in the fields that separated their homes, Priscilla and Kaitlin walking behind them. She'd actually believed that they could be friends.

She blinks away the image, switches on the ignition and pulls out of the drive.

C H A P T E R

3

2.40 p.m.

BEFORE YASMIN HAS time to switch the incoming call to handset, Ayaan's voice comes through the car speakers.

"Hi, it's me. I'm going to be late again tonight. The damage looks pretty extensive."

Early this morning, Ayaan's project manager called to say there was a crack in the minaret; some kind of fault in the installation process. That, or the heatwave had made the materials expand. Ayaan had driven straight to the construction site.

"Will you be able to fix it in time?" she asks, trying to sound sympathetic.

The mosque was due to open in six days: this was the last thing he needed.

"Of course," Ayaan says. "I'll just need to work overtime to make sure it gets done."

Sometimes, Yasmin thought that these problems were a sign that the mosque was never meant to be. Not that she'd ever tell Ayaan that. They'd moved their whole lives here so he could build this mosque: taken the twins out of their international school in Lahore, left behind their friends and family.

"Yas? You still there?" Ayaan's voice floods back into the car.

Yasmin turns into the driveway of Woodwind Stables. Several families have arrived already. Kids are tumbling out of minivans and SUVs.

"I've got to go, Ayaan," Yasmin says.

"You driving?" Ayaan asks.

Yasmin swallows hard. "Just taking the twins to see some friends."

"Which friends?" Ayaan asks.

"Oh, just some friends from school—"

Laila leans in between the front seats and gasps, "Wow! I didn't think it would be a party like *this*!"

Yasmin switches the phone from speaker to handset and brings the cell to her ear. She hasn't told Ayaan about the party.

"What did Laila say?" Ayaan asks.

"Oh, nothing."

Yasmin looks at the house at the top of the driveway. "Sorry—I've got to go, Ayaan."

Before he has the chance to respond, she hangs up.

She should have told him that she was taking the kids to the Wrights' party; keeping a secret is as bad as lying outright, she knows that. But he would have tried to talk her out of it, especially after the fuss Priscilla Carver's been making. Priscilla and Ayaan are friends. She's helped him raise money for the mosque. And in Middlebrook, what Priscilla Carver said was law.

Ben Wright is a dangerous man, Priscilla had explained, making him sound like a criminal. *Better keep your twins away from his house.*

That had struck Yasmin as absurd. She knew that Ben and Priscilla didn't get on, but there was nothing in the least bit dangerous about Ben Wright. In fact, Yasmin had always been fond of him: one of those all-American guys from the movies she'd watched as a teenager back home in Lahore. The kind of man she'd dreamt of meeting when she set off for America as a seventeen-year-old student. But then, she'd met Ayaan and, despite herself, she'd fallen in love with him.

She'd tried to tell him that they needed to work harder to integrate. That people were suspicious of them, walking around in their traditional Pakistani clothes, building a mosque on their land. And they were the only family of color in town. If they embraced American ways a little a more, perhaps it would help. But he didn't listen to her. They should be proud of who they were and where they came from, Ayaan said.

She scans the driveway for Ben's massive red truck with its big LOVE YOUR NEIGHBOR on the bumper. Whenever she sees him driving through Middlebrook in his uniform, it reassures her that there's someone like him around, watching out for all of them. And he's kind to her. He always stops to chat. And he actually listens to what she has to say—more than Ayaan does, these days.

No. Priscilla was wrong. About the party. About the Wrights. About Ben. And her views were confirmed when she bumped into Eva Day, the English woman who had just arrived in town with her family.

It's a kids' party—it'll be fun! Eva had said, so lightly that Priscilla's warnings had dissolved.

So, without mentioning it to Ayaan, Yasmin had accepted the invitation. He never needed to find out: he was so busy these days, he hardly noticed her and the twins.

Yasmin twists round in her seat and looks at Hanif and Laila. "Ready for the party?"

"Ready!" they chant together.

She steps out of the car, lifts her salwar kameez so that it doesn't trail in the dust, and opens the door for the twins.

CHAPTER

4

3.20 p.m.

ASTRID WAITS FOR a while before leaving the house.

Long enough to make sure that her mother isn't coming back to check on her.

She glances at the pages she called up on her phone and then switches it off and places it on the arm of the couch. Her fingers brush the worn red fabric. She remembers lying here for hours with Dad, each of them at one end, their legs dangling off the edge, talking.

Now, whenever she calls him, he barely has the time to chat. Kim, his new girlfriend, is always telling him to get off the phone. Mom had given Dad space. Too much space, as it turned out. Perhaps that was the problem—maybe Dad *wanted* to be nagged.

Until six months ago, Astrid had taken it for granted that Mom and Dad loved each other. But now she realizes that maybe Dad was pretending; that all this time, he'd been waiting for someone better to come along. For a better life than the one he had with her and Mom. He left fast enough.

Astrid closes her eyes. Whenever she thinks about her parents and what happened between them, a sharp pain pushes up under her ribcage and she finds it hard to breathe.

She opens her eyes again, puts on her sandals and shoves her phone into a pocket of her green dress.

It takes a while for her eyes to adjust to the brightness outside. She stands there blinking.

The air hums with heat.

It makes her feel alive—the burn on her pale skin.

She walks to the front of the house and looks out across the valley.

Astrid remembers the afternoon, three years ago, when she decided to go for walk on her own. It was winter. She'd found Jake asleep in the kitchen. He was Mom's dog. Dad had gotten him for her as a present from a shelter in Colebrook. Put a red bow around his neck and tried to make him stand still under the Christmas tree.

Mom said that she'd wanted a rescue dog ever since she was little. Thinking back now at how Mom had hugged and kissed and fussed over Jake, Astrid wonders whether maybe she preferred having a dog to a kid. Some people were more dog people than kid people.

She remembers how, as she'd walked past him that afternoon, Jake had lifted his head from his paws, his ears pricked up.

I'm sorry, buddy, she said to him. *You're not allowed out. Not yet.*

The people at the shelter said that Jake had a bad time with his last owners. Barked and bared his teeth at the slightest thing. He'd wrecked Mom's fancy couch when he was spooked in a thunderstorm. No one had wanted him at the shelter—Dad felt sorry for him and thought that, with a bit of love and a bit of training from Mom, he'd get better.

Anyway, Astrid wasn't allowed to take him on walks, not while he was still getting used to them. But it had gotten to her, his sad, droopy eyes, his tongue hanging out.

Poor dog, she remembers thinking.

And he must have heard her thoughts because he let out a low whine, like he was agreeing with her.

I'll bring you a stick back from the woods, she'd said.

But when she walked past him, he'd whined louder. And then he'd got to his feet and thumped his tail and she hadn't been able to stand it. She'd taken him with her.

Astrid wishes that afternoon had never happened.

She blinks away the thought and walks to the bottom of the drive. And then she starts running through the fields and down the valley that separates her house from the stable. The long grass whispers against her legs. She closes her eyes and remembers Jake running ahead of her, fast and hard. He was so happy to have been let out of the house.

As she runs, she spreads her arms wide, swallowing gulps of hot air. For the first time in ages, she feels free.

But there's another feeling in her chest. The same feeling she had that afternoon three years ago.

That she'd been warned not to do this.

That something bad was going to happen.

And that it would be her fault.

CHAPTER

5

3.45 p.m.

Lily climbs off the bouncy castle and puts her shoes back on. Her hair sticks to her forehead and she can feel a patch of sweat at the base of her spine. It's so hot the rubber burnt her feet as she bounced.

Sometimes Lily wishes she were back in England where people moaned about the rain and not having proper summers. Everything here is too hot.

"Catch me!" squeals a voice from behind her.

She spins round. Before she has time to reply, four-year-old Wynn leaps off the bouncy castle and into her arms. He's a fireball of heat: red-faced and sweaty, his long blond hair tangled. He kicks his limbs in the air and laughs.

"I could have dropped you," Lily says.

She puts him down gently on the ground.

He shrugs and smiles and looks up at her with his fierce blue eyes and red cheeks. "There's grass," he says. "I'd have been fine."

She's not so sure. The ground is hard, the grass burnt by the sun, and there's a big gap between the top of the bouncy castle and the earth.

Lily looks around for Wynn's dad, True. She spots him standing on the porch chatting to some of the mums. He's got dreadlocks that are tied back with a kitchen-elastic. Mum said that his wife died a few years ago, just after Wynn was born, from something called ovarian cancer. Whenever Lily hears about other people's parents dying, it scares her. She can't imagine living in a world without Mum and Dad.

Wynn stands on tiptoes, looking up the valley at a dark clump of pines where the woods start.

"Do cubs like bounce houses, do you think?" he asks Lily.

She tries to unjumble the sentence in her head. "Cubs?"

"Yes, bear cubs. Maybe they'll want to come to the party too but then their mom will be angry—"

"Their mum?"

Wynn turns back to face her, his eyes wide. "Mama bears don't like their cubs to be near people. Daddy said."

"Oh, right. Yeah, I suppose that makes sense."

Lily starts to feel out of her depth. She looks around the front yard of the farmhouse.

"Where's your sister?" she asks Wynn.

He shrugs again. "Probably somewhere. Can I have some juice?"

Lily keeps looking around.

Finally, she spots Skye, sitting under the tree on a high stool; legs crossed, feet bare, one pointed toe skimming the ground, the top of her head brushing the leaves from a low-hanging maple. She's having a butterfly painted across her face: a rainbow wing shimmers across her cheek.

"I'd like some juice," Wynn says again, tugging at Lily's T-shirt.

"Okay, sure."

She grabs a juice box from one of the coolers, pierces the foil opening with the straw and hands it to him. While he drinks, she scans the front of the house.

Rev Avery's foster kids, Cal and Abi, are sitting in the dirt outside the stable, watching everything but not joining in. Cal keeps looking over at Skye. She's seen them sneaking into the woods, and once, when she went to the dock on Middlebrook Pond, they were swimming together. She reckons that just about every girl in Middlebrook must fancy Cal—and must be jealous that he chose Skye. He's got tousled, sun-bleached hair and misty green eyes, like sea glass, and skin that's so tanned it probably doesn't even go pale in winter.

From up in his tree, Phoenix, Wynn's older brother, picks up a stick, takes a small knife out of his pocket, shapes the end, and then pretends to shoot at a chipmunk as it skitters across the patch of yellow grass in front of the stable.

"Bang! Bang! Bang!" Phoenix yells.

"Bang!" Wynn copies and laughs. "Bang!"

"Hey! Cut it out!" True calls out from the porch.

The other day, True came by the house and gave Mum some deer meat to put in the freezer as a welcome-to-the-neighborhood present. He said that he goes hunting and that he finds everything his family needs to eat in the woods, so they never go to the supermarket. Mum and Dad said thank you, to be polite, but Lily could tell that they were just as freaked out by it as she was. Anyway, it strikes Lily as a bit odd—True telling Wynn and Phoenix off for pretend shooting when he goes around hunting things.

Phoenix drops the stick, jumps out of the tree, and runs off.

"Dad doesn't like bang, bang games," Wynn says, as if he's read her thoughts. And then he says: "I'm going to see Skye now," and runs off. Before he gets to Skye, Wynn looks over his shoulder and calls out. "Let me know if you see a bear!"

Lily laughs. "Okay!"

Maybe she will get to see a bear one of these days. Or a moose. Or a coyote. Something cool she can tell her friends about back in London.

Lily looks back up at the house and notices that the curtains behind Bryar's window are drawn shut. As she walks up the porch steps, she catches a conversation between Kaitlin, Bryar's mum, and True.

"I was going to do the cake before the magic show. But we're running out of time." She panics. What if Bryar doesn't come down?

Bryar's mum is always worrying about him.

"I just don't know what to do with him." Kaitlin's voice goes shaky.

True puts an arm around her shoulder.

"He'll be fine, Kaitlin, the kid just needs to find his way."

Lily pushes past them into the house. She goes through to the kitchen and sees the cake—it's so huge it could feed a whole army of kids. Lily's stomach groans. She hopes they still do the cake, whether Bryar likes it or not.

As she looks up the stairs to Bryar's bedroom, Lily thinks about how sad it will make his mum if he stays in his bedroom for the whole party.

She runs up and knocks on his door.

He doesn't answer.

"Bryar?" she calls out.

She hears a shuffling.

"Is it okay if I come in?" She pushes at the door.

He's sitting on his bed surrounded by those rocks he's always showing her.

"You coming downstairs?" Lily asks. "Everyone's here."

He takes a smooth, black rock and turns it between his fingers.

"Your mum's made this amazing cake. She'd be sad if you didn't come to have a piece with everyone."

Bryar puts the rock down, scoots off his bed, goes to his window and pulls the curtains back a little.

"There are too many people," he says.

"It's a party—people are kind of the point."

He shrugs.

"You know, you can ignore them if you like. They're all busy doing their own thing, anyway. You could pop down for a slice of cake and a go on the water slide. Then you can come right back up."

"I think I'll stay up here. No one will notice."

"*I* noticed."

He looks up at her. "Yeah, but you're different."

She feels a rush of warmth in her cheeks.

"I'm different because you know me. And because we've spent time together. If you got to know some of the others—"

He shakes his head. "I'm fine here, thanks."

Lily feels exhausted by their conversation. She feels exhausted by everything these days.

She turns to go. If he doesn't want to come down, she can't force him to.

But then something makes her turn back round. He's sitting at his desk now, his head bent low, a hollow between his shoulder blades. And she thinks about the kids that Mum's worked with as a music therapist. How she said that the main thing was never to give up on them—because they'd had too many people give up on them already.

"We can go down together," Lily suggests.

He doesn't say anything.

"Then it won't be a big deal," she adds.

His spine shifts a little.

"I mean, if you're with me, it won't be like you've been hiding away up here on your own—people will think that we've just been hanging out somewhere."

He's sitting up straight now.

Just turn around, she thinks. *Please, just turn around.*

"I'd like you to come down," she says. And then she wishes she hadn't said it, because it sounds kind of lame and needy. And because she's not even sure it's true. Being at the party on her own was hard but being down there with Bryar is going to be even harder, especially if the last few minutes are anything to go by.

But it works. Slowly, he turns to face her.

His voice is quiet. "You really want to go with me?"

Her breath catches in her throat. "Of course."

And this time she knows she means it. She doesn't know why, but she does. She wants him to be down at the party, with her, even if it's hard.

She takes a step forward and holds out a hand. He stares at her and she thinks that maybe she should take her hand back again, because he's probably never held a girl's hand before.

But then, he stretches out his arm and she wraps her fingers around his and pulls him to his feet.

CHAPTER

6

4 p.m.

SEVERAL FAMILIES HAVE gone home already, before even the cake or the magic show. It's been a long afternoon. The heat's gotten to them. Their children were starting to get tired.

Don't be disappointed, thinks Kaitlin as she carries the cake to the snack table. *They came, that's the main thing.*

She goes toward the group of children sitting cross-legged under the red maple. The magician walks around the circle, touching a head, a shoulder. And then he stops next to Bryar, cups his hand behind his ear, and pulls out a gold coin the size of a quarter.

Kaitlin worries that Bryar's going to crumple from having been singled out, but he's smiling.

She wishes Ben were here to see this: their little boy, happy at last, sitting among the other children, a lucky coin in his palm.

The children clap.

The magician had been a hit after all.

When the show is over, the kids run to the cake table. Kaitlin checks her phone once more to see whether Ben's answered at least one of her messages, but there's nothing. She knows that the reception isn't great on his bit of the border, but it makes her nervous that he's still not here.

At least the cake is a success. The children like the rainbow layers. She's glad she went to all that trouble.

After the cake, a few more kids go home with their parents. There are only a handful of families left now.

The remaining children run off in different directions around the property. The magician and the face-painting lady pack away their things.

And the grown-ups begin to relax.

Yes. Things are going to be better from now on. Better for her little boy. Better for all of them.

Eva comes out of the bathroom, walks through the living room and out onto the porch. A breeze sweeps through the wind chimes hanging from the porch. Gray clouds are sweeping over the sun. They could do with a good thunderstorm. And rain. God, she'd love some rain.

She gulps down some air. She's been hiding in the airconditioned house for so long, dry heaving over the toilet bowl, that she hadn't realized the party was winding down.

She spots Lily running intently around the back of the house with Bryar, like they're off to find something. Today was good for Lily, she thinks. Making new friends. Good for both her and Bryar. She's glad that so many people came. It will make a difference to the children, having had this time together before school starts.

Eva sits down on the porch steps. As she looks out across the fields, she thinks she sees a child running through the corn and wonders whether she should let someone know that one of the children has gone too far. But it's probably just the Bowen boy, the one who likes to climb trees and go off by himself.

She leans back and closes her eyes. No, there's nothing to worry about.

* * *

Sunburn pulls across Astrid's cheeks and the backs of her calves. Her throat is dry too. She'd forgotten how long the walk was from her house to Woodwind Stables.

Keeping close to the wall of the stable, she pokes her head around the corner.

From the top of the fields, it had looked as though the party was still in full swing, but there's hardly anyone left. The grown-ups are disappearing into the house. Some of the kids are running around in the front yard. Others are heading toward the stable.

Looking at her watch, she works out that, if she runs back home now, she might make it before Mom gets back from the office. No one would ever know that she'd come all this way on her own.

But her legs are tired. And she's got a headache.

And anyway, Astrid hasn't seen Bryar yet, the boy who used to be her friend. The boy who, three years ago, Mom said she could never talk to again. She's not going to leave without letting him know that she came to his party.

CHAPTER

7

4.30 p.m.

BY THE TIME the grown-ups have gathered inside the house, the few children who remain at the party have gone to the stable. Wynn said he wanted to pet the horses and the others followed.

Only Phoenix is off somewhere on his own. He's found a high tree from which he can see the girl with the green dress, the one who shouldn't be here, standing outside the stable. He knows why she came. Those places where you don't belong—the ones where you're not meant to go—they pull hardest on kids like them.

Inside the stable, Bryar guides the old mare out of her stall. Lucy is the horse Mom uses when a kid first comes for riding lessons. She's good with children. She'll be gentle with Wynn.

Bryar takes Wynn's hand and guides his open palm in a long, smooth stroke across the side of Lucy's neck. The old mare dips her head and leans in toward the four-year-old boy.

"She likes me." Wynn smiles, stroking the top of the horse's nose now.

"Yes, she does," says Bryar.

The other children stand around the old mare, watching.

"You can pet her too," Bryar says, looking around at the twins and the foster kids and the English girl who he likes even more, after today, than he did before. He's glad she persuaded him to come down from his room.

One by one, the children step forward and touch the mare. Lucy stands still, only her tail swishing lightly.

Bryar likes this feeling. Of sharing his world. Of not being so alone. Maybe Mom was right. Maybe this party wasn't such a bad idea after all.

As the younger children gather around the horse, Cal, the older of the two foster kids, goes over to Skye, the girl with the butterfly on her face. He has something he wants to show her, he says. She smiles and, when they think no one's watching, they reach for each other's hands and slip out through the stable door.

All summer, Cal and Skye have been stealing moments together. They like to talk. She tells him about her life in the woods with her dad and her brothers—and about her mom not being there any more. And then he tells her about the world he came from. His mom, who left him and his sister alone so often that she may as well not have been there at all. He tells her about the police sirens blaring outside his bedroom window through the night. And how when those sirens stopped by their house, the night his mom was taken away for good, they knew their lives would never be the same again.

As they walk out through the front of the stable, Astrid, the girl in the green dress, the one with the pale hair and skin and the sunburn, slips in through the back door.

It takes a while for the children to notice her.

It's the mare that gives her away, jerking her head up so suddenly that the little boy tumbles backward into the straw.

Now the children stare at her. They've all seen her, at one time or another. Walking through town with her mom. At church. In the back of the shiny white car. At the library or the general store. She has a way of looking at them that makes them feel small, like they don't have a right to be in the same place as her. But none of them really know her, not except Bryar, and that was a long time ago.

She whips out her phone. "Smile, everyone," she says, taking a picture. "Got to have a memory of your party, right, Bryar?"

Bryar's face flushes red.

"Now, how about we have some real fun?"

CHAPTER

8

5 p.m.

THERE ARE DAYS, especially in late summer, when the air is so thick with heat that time slows right down.

Sometimes, when the conditions are right, time stops altogether. For a moment, everything is suspended.

And in that gap, no one notices the shadows moving in.

The adults, who have lived through many cycles of the earth spinning around the sun, adults who should know better than to trust this trick of time, choose to forget that it's their job to watch over their children. They allow their bodies and their minds to go slack. They sink into themselves. They don't even see the boy with the red hair, tiptoeing down the stairs to the basement.

They don't see because they believe the trick: that for a second, the world will take care of itself.

As the boy's father pulls up the driveway in his truck, late from his shift on the border, he looks at the welcome banner flapping in the wind: one of its sides has come loose. He feels it—that something's not quite right. He's trained to notice these things. It's too quiet. Where are the children? And their parents? He asks himself all the questions but he's too late: he can't make a difference now.

Perhaps the only ones who notice in time are the horses, who kick their hooves against the stalls; and the dark, oil-slicked crows who sit in the trees, watching; and the clouds that are thickening overhead, preparing for a thunderstorm.

But they're not allowed to intervene in the human world.

All they can do is wait.

And watch.

And listen.

For the gunshot.

For the thud of a small body falling into the straw.

CHAPTER

9

5.15 p.m.

Priscilla pulls into the driveway, looks at the cottage, and takes a deep breath. She always feels the need to brace herself before going back to Astrid. She'd stayed at her office later than she'd planned to, working on a lecture series for the fall. And then she'd got talking to Will Day, the new law professor from England. These days, she feels more at home at the university than here, in the cottage she spent years renovating with Peter.

She steps out of the car and looks down the valley. The sun casts long shadows across the fields. The heat of the day still hangs in the air. Clouds are gathering; it's been building up to a thunderstorm for days.

"Astrid?" she calls out as she comes through the door.

The couch is empty. Maybe she's gone up to her room.

Priscilla climbs the stairs and knocks on her bedroom door. "Astrid?"

She walks in. It's empty.

She goes down to the basement, the coolest part of the house. Always too cold for her but Astrid likes it down there. Goosebumps flare along her arms.

"Astrid!" she calls out again, louder this time.

But she's not here either.

If Astrid were a different sort of child, Priscilla would assume that maybe she'd cycled off to see a friend in town. But the truth is that Astrid doesn't have any friends. She prefers her own company. And she has a way of rubbing other kids up the wrong way. Maybe that will change with her going to the local school.

She goes back outside and walks around the house to the vegetable patch that Astrid and Peter planted together last summer. It's overgrown with weeds now. When Peter left, Astrid lost interest.

She feels an ache in the back of her neck.

There's nothing wrong, she tells herself. Astrid will be around here somewhere.

"Astrid?" she calls out again.

Astrid is unpredictable. And angry—mainly at Priscilla. For Peter leaving. For Priscilla failing to be the mother Astrid wants her to be. But she wouldn't just take off, would she?

Where the hell are you, Astrid?

Her cell starts ringing. She grabs it out of her bag, relieved, for once, that Astrid has a cell too. But when Priscilla looks at the screen, she doesn't recognize the number.

"Hello?" she says.

"Mrs. Carver?"

"Dr. Carver—yes."

There's a pause.

"This is Lieutenant Mesenberg. I'm calling about your daughter."

CHAPTER

10

5.30 p.m.

"I NEED TO ASK you a few questions, Mrs. Wright," Lieutenant Mesenberg says.

Shortly after the ambulance tore up the drive, the police arrived. Two officers who secured the scene. A minute or two later, a senior lieutenant. A short, solid woman with frizzy gray hair.

She made her way straight to Kaitlin.

Kaitlin recognizes her from the papers and from TV reports. Ben has worked with her a few times: in this part of the world, law enforcement help each other out. Ben was one of the first they called: hard-working, reliable, ready to go the extra mile.

"You're the owner of this property?"

Kaitlin looks over to Ben. He's speaking to one of the other detectives. The front of his border patrol uniform is covered in blood.

"Mrs. Wright?"

She looks back at the lieutenant. "Yes. Yes, I am."

"Please could you tell me, as simply as possible, what happened?"

There's a pounding at the back of Kaitlin's skull.

"Mrs. Wright?"

"I . . . I don't know."

"A child was shot," the lieutenant prompts.

"Yes . . ."

"And another badly injured."

She nods.

"Did you see what happened, Mrs. Wright?"

"No. We . . . the adults . . . the parents. We were in the house."

"So, the children were on their own?"

Kaitlin closes her eyes. How could she have let this happen? She'd been so careful with everything.

"I know this is difficult, Mrs. Wright. But I need you to answer as clearly as you can."

"Yes. They were playing in the stable. My son—"

The lieutenant looks down at her notes. "Bryar?"

"Yes."

"So, while the children were in the stable, the adults were in the house—all of them?"

"Yes, that's right."

"So, no one saw what happened?"

"No. Only the children."

Kaitlin notices that the detectives and police officers have started separating the parents and children into groups to gather more information. One of the police officers goes over to Eva, Lily, and Bryar. Bryar stares down at his sneakers, not saying a word.

"And you're sure the children were on their own?" asks the lieutenant. "There wasn't anyone else?"

"Yes, that's what I said."

Lieutenant Mesenberg looks around. "This property is wide open—could there have been an intruder?"

"An intruder? No . . ." But then she hesitates. How can she know, for sure? How can she know anything any more? "I don't think so."

"When you got to the stable, you didn't see anyone suspicious? Someone who shouldn't have been there?"

Astrid Carver. That's the first name that comes into Kaitlin's head. She shouldn't have been there. But that's not what the lieutenant's asking.

Kaitlin shakes her head. "No."

"Tell me about your husband—Mr. Wright."

"My husband?"

"He wasn't at the party?"

"He arrived late. He was working. He arrived just as—"

If only Ben had turned up even a few seconds before, none of this would have happened.

"Just as?" the lieutenant prompts. "You said he arrived just as what?"

"He was getting out of his car as we were coming out of the house—when we heard the gunshot."

"So, your husband was outside when the gun was fired?" The lieutenant pauses. "You're sure of that?"

"I don't remember. It happened so fast. We were trying to get to the kids. Ben was the first to see that one of them had been injured. He's trained to notice—to help in situations like this."

"So, he was ahead of you?"

"Yes. I believe so. Why don't you ask him? He'll know—"

"My team is questioning him, Mrs. Wright. I need to hear it from you." The lieutenant holds Kaitlin's gaze. "Is it conceivable that your husband could have been in the stable when the pistol was fired?" She speaks slowly and deliberately.

"No—no. It wasn't like that." Kaitlin's heart hammers. The lieutenant is getting it all wrong.

The lieutenant closes her notebook and places a hand on Kaitlin's arm. "I'm just trying to get the facts, Mrs. Wright."

Kaitlin swallows again, pushing the fear down her throat.

"When you first came into the stable, did you see any of the children holding a firearm?"

"No. Not that I saw."

"Were *all* the children there—in the stable?"

"Yes." She thinks back. She has a vague memory of Laila running in after the adults. But maybe she was there already? And Phoenix. It was always hard to locate him. "I think so."

Lieutenant Mesenberg takes off her glasses and locks eyes with Kaitlin.

"Everything was happening so fast. It was confusing. Quite a few of the families had left already. But I believe the children who were meant to be there were all in the stable." She pauses. "Except—" She doesn't know whether or not she should say it.

"Except?" the lieutenant prompts.

She has to say it.

"Except Astrid Carver. She wasn't meant to be there."

CHAPTER

11

6.40 p.m.

PRISCILLA RUNS THROUGH the parking lot outside the ER, ignoring the police officers who are calling after her to wait. The ones who drove her here in their car, their sirens ringing out into the darkening sky.

It's started raining—thick, heavy drops. She wipes her face with the palms of her hand and pushes through the glass doors. By the time she gets to the nurses at the reception desk, she's so breathless she can barely get the words out.

"My daughter—" A sob rises in her throat.

She cried the whole way here. Hot tears streaming down her cheeks, like she'd been storing them up for years.

The nurses exchange a look.

They know. Of course they know.

She feels a nurse touching her arm.

"Why don't you take a seat," the nurse says, helping Priscilla into a chair. "Could I call someone for you?"

She thinks about Peter. She should have called him right away when she heard from the lieutenant: before she left the cottage—or from the car. Because no matter what a mess their relationship is in, they're still Astrid's parents. But she couldn't say the words: *our daughter's been shot.*

"No. It's just me."

As the nurse turns away, Priscilla notices a familiar face in the waiting room. The man with the pale blue eyes and the dreadlocked hair turns to look at her.

"True?" she says.

For a moment, she doesn't understand what he's doing here.

And then she sees the expression on his face, and suddenly, she does.

DAY TWO

Monday, September 2

Labor Day

CHAPTER

12

2 a.m.

BRYAR STANDS AT the window of the spare room in Rev Avery's house. He can't sleep. He feels like he's never going to be able to sleep again, not after this.

You can't stay in the house, Lieutenant Mesenberg had explained to Mom. *We need to gather evidence.*

It was past midnight when they let the kids and the grown-ups go, saying they'd do more interviews tomorrow.

They'd kept Dad at the police station for more questioning, though. Bryar keeps hoping he'll hear Dad's truck pulling into the church parking lot.

Sheets of rain pour from the sky. There are puddles and rivulets around the church; water rushes along the brook that runs through town. Far off, there's a rumble of thunder. And then a flash of lightning.

Bryar wonders whether they're still there; the police officers with the metal detectors who stayed behind at the stable to search for the gun. And the dog they brought in, the one who was trained to find things. Drugs. Guns.

Bryar's eyes drift up the valley. The ambulance would have taken Wynn and Astrid to Colebrook; Middlebrook was too small to have a hospital of its own.

Sounds and pictures flicker through his mind.

The gunshot.

Lucy bucking, knocking Wynn over and then running out of the stable.

And Astrid—lying in the straw, all that blood coming out of her body.

His throat goes tight.

When he saw her walking into the stable, he'd thought that her mom had let her come to the party after all. That maybe they could be friends again.

But that wasn't why Astrid Carver came. She came to make him feel small in front of the others. And he wasn't going to let her do that, not this time.

The Sayed twins lie awake, curled into each other, their brains spinning from all the questions the detectives asked them at the stable. They didn't want to sleep in separate beds, not tonight.

There's a clap of thunder. And a few seconds later, lightning blinks through the gap in their curtains. Their house is the tallest on the street. Whenever there's a storm, they worry that it will get hit and catch fire.

They squeeze each other's hands tighter.

Their bedroom door is open. Mom left the light on, on the landing, like when they were little and they lived in Lahore.

Dad went to have a shower while Mom was putting them to bed. He didn't even say goodnight.

When Mom phoned Dad to tell him what had happened at the party, he came charging into the police station, still in his fluorescent jacket and his big dusty boots from the construction site. They thought he'd hug them or hug Mom, like Mr. Day had hugged Lily and Mrs. Day when he showed up. But Dad just stood there, in silence, waiting for the police to say that they could go.

They left Mom's car at the station so they could drive home together in Dad's truck. The twins wish that Dad had let them go home with Mom on their own, because for the whole drive he kept asking Mom shouty questions like why she'd put their family in this position and why she'd gone against Dr. Carver's advice about the party and didn't she know that the mosque was opening in six days.

They drove past a bunch of people standing by the side of the road, bunched together with cameras and microphones and vans with satellite dishes and a police car guarding them. Dad thumped the steering wheel and said, *Great. That's all we need.*

And then he went on about how it was bound to get out, the twins being involved in this. And how it was bad timing for the opening of the mosque.

Mom said sorry, over and over.

But Dad didn't listen to her sorrys. He just drove too fast and kept shaking his head.

After a while, Mom said, *The twins are safe, that's the main thing, Ayaan.*

But that made him madder because he said that wasn't the point.

The twins had thought that maybe they should say something to make Dad less angry at Mom. They should tell him that none of this was Mom's fault. But they were scared of making it worse. So they stayed quiet.

Through the open door, the twins hear Mom pacing around the kitchen downstairs. And then they hear her open the closet where they keep their coats and shoes and after that, the front door clicks shut behind her and they know she's going out for one of her walks to the woods.

They think of Mom walking under dripping trees.

And of Dad, lying asleep alone in their big bed.

In Lahore, Mom and Dad used to do things together. They'd hold hands. And they'd kiss when they said goodbye and hello. But ever since they moved to America, it's like they're always finding excuses to be away from each other.

The twins have tried to get to sleep, but whenever they close their eyes, the pictures come back: of that pistol being handed round. Of Astrid getting shot. Of the horse screaming. Of Wynn lying against the side of the stall, his arm all twisted. And of Laila running out to Mom's car just before the grown-ups came out of the house.

"*Laila?*" Hanif whispers into his sister's ear. "*What did you do with it?*"

"*It's okay. You don't need to worry.*"

"*But—*"

"*It's best if you don't know, Hanif. Just trust me, okay?*"

"*Okay.*" He nods in the dark, and then curls in closer to his sister.

They thought that one of the detectives might ask questions about why Laila wasn't in the stable with the others, but so far, no one seems to remember that she wasn't there the whole time.

Maybe they'll ask tomorrow.

Or maybe, if the twins are lucky, they'll forget about it.

Maybe, if they're *really* lucky—maybe if they can keep quiet long enough—all this will go away.

And they'll stop feeling like this is their fault.

Deep in the Middlebrook woods, Skye lies awake, listening to the rain falling through the tall pines. The cabin has never felt so empty. Dad and Wynn are still at the hospital. It's only her and Phoenix and Lumen, their dog.

The cabin is just one big room. At night, Dad pushes together a bunch of mattresses for them to sleep on. He built the cabin when he found out Mom was pregnant with Skye: he said he wanted their family to live as close to nature as possible. And to each other. He said there was no need for walls and doors, not between people who love each other.

Lily's parents drove her and Phoenix home from the police station. Mrs. Day offered to make some food and to stay the night with them, but Skye said that they'd be fine on their own. She'd take care of things.

On the mattress beside her, Phoenix's limbs twitch under the sheets. He hasn't said a word since the accident. Not to the police.

Not to her. The last time he stopped talking like this was when Mom died.

Ever since Lily and her parents left the cabin, Skye's been desperate to ask Phoenix more questions about what happened in the stable while she and Cal were outside.

Cal had wanted to give her one of his drawings. And then she'd kissed him and the world around them had disappeared. She remembers the feel of his lips against hers. And then, she'd pulled back, jolted by a voice she recognized, shouting in the stable.

There was only one girl in town who spoke like that: as if she was better than everyone else. As if she was in charge.

Skye knew that Astrid Carver wasn't meant to be at the party. And from the raised voices, she knew that she was causing trouble.

So she jumped up and ran into the stable. She could feel Cal running close behind her, trying to catch her hand, but she pulled away from him.

And then it all went wrong. Horribly wrong.

She looks up at the wooden beams of the cabin and thinks of Wynn's small body, limp against hers. Of how twisted his little arm looked. Where was Phoenix when their brother got hurt? And what had happened while Skye was outside the stable with Cal?

She's seen Phoenix around Astrid. How he tries to show off. How he thinks they're the same just because they don't like being around other people. She's worried he did something to try and impress her. Something stupid.

She wishes she could call Dad to ask about Wynn, but the police took everyone's cell phones for evidence.

Her throat goes thick and she knows she's about to cry but she swallows hard so that the tears stay down. She clenches her fists under the sheet. She doesn't get to cry, not when she's the one who messed up.

She pushes away the bedsheets and stands up.

Lumen skitters toward her and presses her warm body against Skye's calves. She follows her out onto the deck.

They sit on the steps and look out into the dark woods.

Thick drops of rain fall onto her bare arms. Mist rises from the damp earth.

Far off, there's a rumble in the night sky. Rain clouds drift over the pines.

She thinks she sees something moving between the trees—a wild animal, perhaps; a deer or a bear. Only it looks more upright than an animal would be. Surely no one would be out here in this weather?

With Lumen beside her, Skye walks down the porch steps toward the stream. The riverbank has been dry for months because of the drought. But with all the rain that's fallen in the last few hours, it's filling up fast. For the first time in months, there's enough of a current to sweep the dark water through the woods into Middlebrook Pond.

She and Cal had planned to go for a swim here this afternoon, just the two of them; one last stolen moment together in the pond before school kicked in.

She pulls a scrunched-up piece of paper out of her pocket and smooths it out. He'd wanted to give it to her—that's why he'd asked her to go out of the stable with him. He'd painted her face. And, for the first time, looking at the picture, she'd seen what people meant when they said she looked like Mom. It had made her so happy, as if somehow Cal knew Mom, even though he'd never met her.

A lump pushes up her throat.

If Skye hadn't been so focused on Cal—if they hadn't left the stable together—none of this would have happened.

How stupid she'd been to think that she could have anything for herself. But that's over now. She'll let him know that they're finished. She won't let anything distract her ever again from taking care of her family.

She rips up the painting and lets it drop to the wet ground. The colors bleed out of the paper.

The rain falls more heavily now.

And there's a clap of thunder.

Lumen yowls.

She looks up too, rain falling on her face.

"*I'm sorry, Mom*!" she cries out to the dark, thundery sky.

* * *

In the rectory, the big house next to the church, Abi walks into Cal's bedroom. It's the first time they've had rooms of their own—rooms with name plates and nice furniture that matches.

She sits on the end of the bed.

"*Cal . . .*" she whispers.

His body is curled up, facing the wall.

He doesn't answer.

Abi reaches over and tries to take Cal's hand, but he shifts his body away from her.

Abi's eleven and Cal's thirteen. But they've never felt it, those two years. They don't remember a time when they weren't together.

It's the one thing they'd always fought for: that they wouldn't be separated.

She looks up at the rain smacking the skylight. Every few minutes, a flash lights up the room.

In Roxbury, the noises from the city were so loud that they drowned out the rain.

In Roxbury, everything was different.

Bad different.

Which is why they'd promised each other that, this time, they'd make sure they got to stay: they'd be so good that Avery would want to keep them for ever. They weren't stupid: they knew they'd never find a place as good as this again.

Cal was going to work on his painting. It's the one thing that everyone always focused on—how talented he was. How, if he applied himself, he could maybe go to art school one day. As soon as they came to Middlebrook, Avery had introduced him to the art teacher at Brook Middle School.

And Abi, she'd just work at staying out of trouble. Like not getting wound up if a kid asked about their mom or where they were from or why they didn't have a proper family like everyone else.

That girl who came into the barn, she'd tried to wind Abi up once. Her mom took her to church every Sunday and when Rev Avery introduced them, because they were the same age, Astrid had turned round to her mom and said, *Roxbury—isn't that where all the junkies live?*

She'd said it loud enough for everyone to hear.

Abi had wanted to punch Astrid in the face, but she'd held it together. And after that, she'd made a point of staying out of her way.

Yeah, until today, Abi and Cal had worked really hard to stay out of trouble. But now everything's gone wrong again, like deep down, she always knew it would.

Which is why Cal isn't talking to her. And why he won't hold her hand.

Because he's upset.

Because he knows it too.

People will think it's their fault.

The kids whose mom's in jail.

The kids who've never stayed in one foster home for more than a few months.

The kids who come from a place where trouble grows like weeds between the cracks on the sidewalk.

Lily sits on the landing outside her parents' bedroom, her back pressed into the wall. The walls are so thin, she can hear everything they're saying.

They've been going around in circles, arguing about the same things over and over, neither of them listening to what the other one is saying.

It starts with Dad asking Mum to go over what happened.

And Mum saying she doesn't know what happened, because she wasn't in the stable.

Then Dad asks Mum why she didn't tell him that Dr. Carver had warned her off the party. That if he'd known that she was against it, he'd never have let Lily go.

And Mum says that that's exactly why she didn't tell him. And then she says that Kaitlin is her friend and she'd wanted to support her. And that Bryar is Lily's friend, which is even more important. That Lily needs friends right now.

And Mum was right, wasn't she? Bryar *is* Lily's friend. Which is why it upset her so much when Astrid came into the stable trying to spoil the party—undoing the work Lily had done to make Bryar feel good about himself. *You don't have a right to do that*, Lily remembers thinking as she watched Astrid striding around the stable like she owned the place.

It had taken Lily by surprise: how angry she'd felt. How protective of Bryar. How, at that moment, she'd have done anything to stand up for him and to make that horrible girl go away.

Mum and Dad keep arguing.

Dad says that you don't put your child in danger just to support people. Or just because your kids are friends.

And when Dad says that—about putting Lily in danger—Mum goes quiet and Lily can picture her face: it's the same face she had when she saw Astrid lying on the ground, bleeding: confused and scared and guilty and like it was all her fault.

And after the quiet, Mum starts crying.

When Mum called Dad to say what had happened, he cycled straight from the university to the station. When they moved to America he said he wanted to get fit so he bought a second-hand bike and he's been using it to get around.

At least the roads are safer here, Mum had said as they watched Dad seting off on his bike on his first day of work.

And it wasn't only the roads. Everything in Middlebrook felt safer than London. That's what Mum and Dad were always saying when she asked why they'd moved here.

London isn't a place to raise kids, they'd said. *You'll have a proper childhood here. No traffic and noise and pollution. No gangs with knives. Just fresh air and trees and ponds to swim in summer and mountains to sled down in winter.*

They'd made it sound like nothing bad could ever happen here.

Lily listens to the water rushing through the brook at the bottom of the drive.

She closes her eyes and she feels the thunderstorm rising and falling.

She wonders whether, if the storm is big enough, it could knock the whole house down. Maybe it could wash her and Dad and Mum and all their things into the brook that runs through town and out into big rivers and lakes and finally to the sea. Maybe the storm could take them home to England.

In Colebrook Hospital, Wynn blinks open his eyes. The first thing he sees is his father, sitting asleep in the chair beside him.

Wynn tries to pull himself up but there's a sharp pain in his arm so he slumps back down.

He looks around the room. He doesn't understand where he is or why his body hurts so much.

There's a window to his right. It's dark outside. Raindrops hit the glass making hard *pop, pop, pop* sounds.

And then he remembers.

Being in the stable.

Finding it so fun, hanging out with the older kids with no grown-ups watching.

And how it had been the best feeling in the world—petting that horse: kind of strong and soft at the same time.

And then Astrid showed up.

And made Bryar take that pistol out of the safe.

And both those things—the gun and the angry girl who lives in the cottage on the hill—had made all the happy feelings in Wynn's body seep away.

Wynn had seen Dad's hunting rifle a million times, but not a pistol like this. Not unless it was on a police officer.

Whenever Wynn asked Dad to have a go with his rifle, Dad always said the same thing: *No, Wynn. Guns aren't toys. You'll have to wait until you're older.*

Dad hadn't even let Phoenix have a go yet, and Phoenix was much older than Wynn. It made Phoenix mad, that Dad wouldn't take him hunting—so mad that sometimes he'd threaten to take Dad's rifle when he wasn't looking and go off on his own.

At first, Wynn had thought that maybe the pistol Bryar took out of the safe was a pretend gun. But then he got to hold it and it was so heavy it hurt his hand, and he realized, suddenly, that it wasn't a toy. It was real.

Wynn blinks open his eyes and looks back at Dad, asleep in the chair. He doesn't want to be here alone with his thoughts, in this strange room that isn't their cabin.

"Dad . . ." Wynn whispers.

Dad shifts slightly, his mouth moving.

"Dad . . . ?" he says again, louder this time.

Dad opens his eyes and sits up stiffly. "Wynn!"

Dad's eyes get watery.

"Oh, Wynn—thank God." Dad gets up out of his chair and comes to stand above Wynn. He leans over and holds Wynn's face in his hands and kisses his forehead for a long, long time.

In the ICU, Astrid feels her chest pulling so tight she thinks that if she breathes, it's going to tear open.

Her arm burns where the needle presses into her vein.

Her skin burns too. The back of her neck. Her forehead. Her legs.

She feels Mom's hand in hers, gripping her fingers and then going slack as she cycles in and out of sleep.

Sometimes, she hears the footsteps of a nurse coming in. Leaning over her. Checking.

She tries to talk to the nurse, but the words won't come.

And when she tries to open her eyes, her lids stay shut like someone's pressing down on them.

And every time she tries to push herself up to sitting, her muscles go limp.

And then she gets tired again and drifts back into herself.

One moment she's running through the fields, her legs brushing the long, dry grass.

And then she's in the stable, falling, the horse screaming beside her.

And then there's whispering. Everyone's talking over each other in these hushed, panicky voices.

As her mind begins to slip, she hears one of them yell out, loud enough to shut everyone else up: *We don't tell anyone!*

She'd wanted to open her eyes to see who'd said it, but they were pressed shut.

No one, okay? the voice went on.

There was a beat of silence.

And then another kid whispers: *Okay.*

And the others join in. She hears them whispering above her: *Okay . . . okay . . . okay . . .*

And she knows they're making a pact. A deeper pact than any of them has ever made before in their lives.

And there's a brief gap, a space between when the children stand, looking down at her, having made their promise, and when the grown-ups come running into the stable.

And after that, everything goes black.

CHAPTER

13

9 a.m.

"I UNDERSTAND HOW SHAKEN up you must be by all this." Mrs. Markham, the principal of Brook Middle School, folds her hands on her desk.

Yasmin notices Ayaan's leg jiggling up and down with impatience.

"Rest assured that we're putting every provision in place to support the children. I've called a faculty meeting for later this morning."

It's Labor Day. A final day of fun before school starts. But no one in Middlebrook would pay attention to that, not after what happened yesterday.

Yasmin doesn't even know why they're here.

She twists her head round toward the door. The twins are sitting on chairs outside the office, waiting. This morning, when they came downstairs, their faces were gray with tiredness. They barely touched their breakfast.

"This is a small community," Mrs. Markham says. "We pull together in times like these—"

Ayaan interrupts her. "We would like to separate the twins from the other children."

Yasmin looks back round. They haven't discussed this. Ayaan has barely talked to her since last night.

Mrs. Markham furrows her brow and says, "*Separate* them?"

"Yes. From the children involved—in all this." He swipes his hand through the air.

Our children are involved in all this, Yasmin wants to say. In a few hours, they're taking the twins back to the police station for more questioning.

"I'm not sure I understand, Mr. Sayeed," Mrs. Markham says.

Ayaan holds up a hand and starts counting them off. "I would like you to make sure that our children are kept away from Lily Day, Bryar Wright and Abi Johnston." He pauses. "I gather the others are in different grades, though I'd appreciate your support in making sure that the twins don't come into contact with those children either. Perhaps you could relay this information to your teachers at the staff meeting."

Mrs. Markham clears her throat. "I realize this is still very raw, Mr. Sayed. But this is a complicated situation."

Ayaan stands up. "They're not to be in the same class. I think I've made myself clear."

Mrs. Markham's cheeks flush pink. She holds out her palms. "Mr. Sayed, there is only one sixth grade class."

"It seems obvious to me, then, that you should create two classes."

"I'm afraid we don't have the teachers—or the resources—to create another class. We're a small school—"

Mrs. Markham shoots Yasmin a look, hoping she might intervene.

Ayaan stands up and takes his rain jacket from the back of his chair, making it clear that the discussion is over.

Mrs. Markham comes out from behind her desk. "Mr. Sayed—maybe we could talk this through a little more. I hear your concerns, but—"

"I'm sure you'll work it out, Mrs. Markham. There must be other parents, like us, who are worried about their children. Creating a new class will, I'm certain, be welcomed. Like you said, your aim is to do everything in your power to support the children."

Mrs. Markham stands in the middle of the room, stunned.

Ayaan walks to the door.

She clears her throat again. "Mr. Sayed. If I may. Under circumstances such as these, we've often found that it's best to keep things as normal as possible for the children. Separating them out—creating barriers—sends the wrong message. They need to work through this together—"

Ayaan spins round. "Under circumstances *such as these*?"

"Yes—"

He takes a step back toward her. "You mean, when a child gets shot?"

Mrs. Markham shrinks under his words. Yasmin feels sorry for her. She wants to tell her that Ayaan does this—that he pushes and pushes until he gets what he wants. He's not a bad man, he's just stubborn and determined and isn't always good at listening.

"Are they common to you, these circumstances?" Ayaan asks, his gaze level with hers.

"No—of course not—"

"Well, then, perhaps you need to revise your methods. Tomorrow morning, my wife will be bringing our children to school. And I look forward to hearing about their new class."

He turns back around and walks to the door, opening it just wide enough for Yasmin to see the side of Laila's body. She wonders how much the twins heard.

"Mrs. Sayed?" Mrs. Markham looks at Yasmin.

She's giving Yasmin a final chance to say something. She should speak up for her children. For all the children who were at the party on Sunday afternoon. But instead, she looks down at the brown squares on Mrs. Markham's rug and stays quiet. Like she's stayed quiet ever since Ayaan stormed into the police station last night. She knows that she has to make it up to him: for taking the kids to the party without telling him; for going against Priscilla's advice; for not supervising them better; for drinking that gin-laced iced tea handed to her by True Bowen. For believing that she could be like the other moms and decide things for herself.

Eventually, Mrs. Markham turns away from her and says, "I'll see what I can do."

The four of them drive home in silence. Yasmin and the twins follow Ayaan into the house. He pulls on the high-vis jacket he wears on the construction site. If it hadn't been for the meeting—if it hadn't been for what happened yesterday—he would have left for work already.

The twins stand in the middle of the hallway, looking to their parents for instructions.

Yasmin waits for Ayaan to say something, but he just ignores them.

"Why don't you go to your room for a while?" Yasmin says.

"Will the police want to talk to us again today?" Laila asks, her eyes wide.

"Probably, yes. I imagine there's a great deal for them to sort out—"

"You're not going to the police station," Ayaan talks over her. "I'm meeting a lawyer up at the site. I don't want the twins involved in the investigation."

"I don't think it's up to us—" Yasmin starts.

Ayaan looks at her and blinks. "Our children can't be interrogated without our consent. And it's obvious they had nothing to do with this—"

"We don't know what happened, Ayaan. We need to help the police as much as we can—"

"Help the police?"

"Yes. To get to the bottom of what happened."

She feels the twins, staring at her.

"Please go to your rooms," Ayaan says to them.

The twins disappear up the stairs.

Ayaan turns to Yasmin. "We need to distance ourselves from this, Yas. You know that."

"For the mosque—"

"For our future here. As a family." He walks to the front door and starts pulling on his boots. "We're on a visa. If the USCIS find out that our children are involved in a criminal investigation, we can say goodbye to our lives in America. All my work here will have been for nothing." He's facing her squarely now. His voice is manic with tiredness. "The *Boston Chronicle* called my site manager last night and asked whether our twins were involved in the shooting. Do you realize how this looks?"

At first, Yasmin thought he was angry that she'd put their children in danger. But she knows it's not really that. The kids are safe. He's not even interested in their future here as a family. It's *his* future here he's worried about. *His* reputation. *His* work.

He opens the front door.

She calls after him. "Ayaan?"

He doesn't answer. She walks after him and catches his elbow. "About separating the twins from the other children—"

He turns to face her.

"I think Mrs. Markham's right. It might send a better message if . . . if we don't," she says.

"A better message? What's that supposed to mean?"

"I think it might be best to keep Hanif and Laila with the other children. To show some support—"

He stares at her, incredulous. "You want us to *support* the children who got the twins involved in this?"

"We were all there, Ayaan. The parents. The kids. We're in this together. We can't pretend—"

"The mosque opens in four days, Yas. Do you realize that?"

"Of course—I know. But isolating the twins—"

"We're not isolating the twins, we're protecting them."

"From what?"

"Bad associations."

"Bad associations? What happened was an accident. They're kids. They made a mistake. But they're *kids*, Ayaan. Good kids. And their parents are good parents. We all want the same thing for our children: for them to be safe and happy. To make the right choices." She stops for a second and then says, "But sometimes things go wrong."

"Things don't just go wrong. We let them go wrong—by the decisions we make. And we *are* different, Yas. We come from a different culture—a different religion. It's our duty to stay clear of anything that could taint us."

"But we live here—in America. If we're going to be part of this community, we can't keep removing ourselves—"

He holds out his hand like he's trying to block her words. "You got this one wrong, Yasmin. Now let me sort it out."

C H A P T E R

14

Midday

THEY KNOW, ALREADY, that today is different.

The dragonflies that brush their wings against the rain-soaked grass outside St. Mary's church.

The rainbow-green hummingbirds that flit between the pines by the cemetery.

The last of the monarch caterpillars that hang off the milkweed, weaving their cocoons.

The bullfrogs, their goggle eyes blinking above the water of the brook that swells and rushes along Main Street.

They know that on this Labor Day, Ben Wright won't pull his grill from the back of his red truck.

That True Bowen won't open his ice-box full of trout caught from Middlebrook Pond.

That the farmer who owns the field next to Woodwind Stables won't bring his bag of corn to throw on the grill.

That this year, the potato salads and the coleslaws and the peach cobblers and the slices of watermelon will sit in people's refrigerators, uneaten.

Most of all, they know that the children won't come out to play. There'll be no games of Sharks and Minnows behind the church. No hopscotch squares drawn in chalk on the sidewalk. No bike races around Main Street.

It would have been a beautiful afternoon for it. After a night of rain, everything is shining, like it's been made new. And it's cooler at last. It would have been a Labor Day picnic to remember.

But the children aren't coming.

Or anyone else from the town.

They know this, the dragonflies and the hummingbirds and the caterpillars and the bullfrogs.

Like the horses knew, in the heat of yesterday afternoon, that the girl in the green dress and the sunburnt skin was making her way through the fields to the stable and that she carried trouble with her like the storm clouds that were gathering overhead.

And they can see something else. That whereas the people from the town are staying inside, too scared to face this new day, there are new faces walking the streets. People from the big cities with notepads and cameras and recording devices. Already, they're parking by the church and the library; they're buying coffee in the general store; they're walking along the brook, muddying their city shoes; they're knocking on doors and waiting outside the gates of the middle school. And they're asking questions. These days, reporters get to the scene of a crime before the police do. News travels fast.

They're here because they want to understand why this girl, in particular, was shot—what the children had against her.

And they want to understand who fired the pistol.

Because when someone gets shot, there's always a reason, isn't there?

And there's always someone to blame. There can only be one person who pulled the trigger, right?

They'll keep asking questions until they find their story: a bright, colorful story that will carry their words around the world. The story of a small town, of a stable, of a hot afternoon in August, of a little girl who had no friends, of a gun, of a party that went terribly wrong.

Yes, they can see it coming, the dragonflies and the hummingbirds and the caterpillars and the bullfrogs. They know better than we do when the world is shifting. When the ground is cracking open.

CHAPTER 15

5 p.m.

THE MIDDLEBROOK POLICE Department, with its one full-time chief and its three part-time police officers, is too small to handle a case like this.

The parents have to drive their children thirteen miles away, to Colebrook.

There's a Children's Advocacy Center there. A place set up to handle cases involving minors.

It takes most of the afternoon. They're separated out. Each one taken to a room by a detective while, in another room, their parents, a police officer and a district attorney watch the interview relayed through a video screen.

You have to be careful with children. Not to frighten or overwhelm them. To ask the right questions. Questions that will get them to tell the truth.

Lieutenant Mesenberg sits back in her chair and folds her hands behind her head.

She's listened to the tapes over and over. The words swim in her head:

She came out of nowhere . . .
It was meant to be a game . . .

He told us to be careful with it . . .
It looked like a toy . . .
It wasn't anyone's fault . . .
We told him to be careful . . .
It happened fast . . .
I wasn't really looking . . .
We lost track of who was holding the pistol . . .
We took turns . . .
The girl, the one in the green dress, she wouldn't stop talking . . . It was like she . . .
I was scared, but I didn't say anything . . .
It wasn't anyone's fault.
I was sitting outside the stable . . .
I didn't see it happen . . .
She wanted us to play her game . . .
The shot came out of nowhere . . .
We were playing . . .
We were just playing.
It wasn't anyone's fault.

She should have gotten clearer answers by now. They were children, for Christ's sake. And she'd been doing this for over thirty years.

And they were tired.

And scared.

Scared about their friends being hurt: the girl with the bullet hole through her lung fighting for her life; a little boy with his twisted arm.

And scared about what might happen to them as a result.

Usually that was enough. The exhaustion. The fear. The awe at being interviewed by the police.

One of them, at the very least, should have given her something to go on.

But there was nothing. Just a blur of confused statements.

And only two of the children had phones: Skye Bowen and Astrid Carver. The detectives have already pulled apart Skye's phone: there's nothing except messages between her and her dad and some selfies of her and Cal Johnston. Astrid Carver's phone is missing, along with the pistol.

Damnit, this shouldn't be so hard.

She goes back a few seconds in the recording.

It wasn't anyone's fault.

Then she goes back a little further.

It wasn't anyone's fault.

And then further back still.

That same phrase. Different children stating it like they'd rehearsed a script. It was the only thing their statements had in common. Like they'd agreed, in advance.

She turns to a set of papers on her desk. Statements taken from the parents. Those who were at the party. Some who left early, before the shooting. Others who'd been invited but didn't come.

We didn't know there were firearms on the property or we wouldn't have come . . .

Bryar Wright was missing from most of the party . . .

We were in the house when it happened . . .

Ben Wright was meant to be at the party . . . No one understood why he wasn't there . . .

Aren't those foster children meant to be under some kind of special supervision? Should they even be allowed to go to parties . . . ?

My children would never touch a firearm . . .

There was alcohol . . .

We found it strange how those twins were wearing religious outfits to a kids' party . . .

We were hot . . . that's why we stayed in the house . . .

It was a long afternoon . . . everyone was tired . . .

He shouldn't have left his little boy alone without adult supervision . . . But he lets his children run wild . . .

And the one thing everyone seemed to agree on:

Astrid Carver was never meant to be at the party.

The lieutenant presses her eyes with the heels of her hands and then blinks them open again. As soon as the girl wakes up, she's going to have to question her. At least she won't have anything to hide.

And the little boy too. He's too young to know how to keep secrets. He'll give her something.

Lieutenant Mesenberg sits up, picks up her mug of cold coffee, takes a long swig, and replays the interview tapes one more time.

CHAPTER

16

7 p.m.

KAITLIN SWITCHES OFF the engine and looks through the rear-view mirror. She can still see them, parked at the bottom of the drive, their cameras set up. They've been waiting for her and Bryar to come home.

Part of her had wanted to jump out of the car and set them straight: that they should pack up their stuff and look else-where for their answers; that neither her husband nor her son were to blame in any of this. But the lieutenant had told her not to talk to the press. That it would make things worse for them. So she'd bitten her tongue and driven right past them, ignoring the questions they yelled out.

She looks away from the mirror and stares out across the front yard at the house. It feels like they've been away for a lifetime.

Kaitlin remembers standing here on Sunday afternoon, holding the rainbow cake, waiting for the children to gather around. How Bryar had run over with Lily, his face beaming. In that moment, she'd thought that maybe she'd done it. That, despite everything, her little boy was going to be okay: he was going to make friends; that middle school wasn't going to be the disaster elementary school had been.

Her eyes well up. She can't believe how stupid she'd been—to believe that she could fix her son's life with a cake and a few balloons.

She looks back at the rear-view mirror, at Bryar this time. He's staring at the stable, at the police tape stretched over the doors.

A crime scene, that's what they were calling it.

It's not a crime scene, she'd wanted to scream. *It's my home. My family. My life.*

"Will we have to go back to the station?" Bryar asks. "To answer more questions?"

"I don't know. Probably."

"But I've told them everything," Bryar says, his voice shaking.

"I know, buddy. I know."

For hours, Kaitlin had sat watching the video screen that relayed Bryar's interview with the police detective. She'd felt it in her body: how they pounded those questions at him, trying to wear him down.

But he just gave them same answers as yesterday:

Yes, he was the one who took the pistol out of the safe.

And worse than that: he'd gone back into the house without any of them noticing, to get bullets out of the safe in the basement.

No, no one had forced him to do it, he'd said. It had been his decision.

And after that?

He wasn't sure what happened.

They were playing a game.

Things got out of hand.

They were bunched up together.

They were passing the pistol around so fast.

Wynn was jumping up . . . he wanted to have a turn . . . Everyone was yelling at him to get out of the way but he wouldn't listen . . .

But no, he doesn't remember who was holding the gun when it went off.

He'd looked hollowed out after the interview, his shoulders hunched over. It had taken everything out of him: to sit there, answering questions without telling them anything.

She'd sensed the frustration in the detective's voice at the lack of new information. But Lieutenant Mesenberg didn't seem worried.

It's not like a bunch of kids can pull the wool over our eyes, she'd said after the interviews. *We're trained to do this. We'll find out soon enough who fired that pistol.*

Kaitlin wondered whether the lieutenant had children of her own, and whether she knew how strong children could be. Stronger, often, than grown-ups.

And how long they could keep hold of a secret. If they were scared enough.

If they had enough of a reason.

Kaitlin turns around to look at Bryar. His eyes are still fixed on the stable.

"Come on, let's go inside now, Bryar, it's getting late."

She gets out of the car and opens his door.

Bryar looks up at her. "Mom?" he asks.

She turns back round. "Yes, Bryar?"

"I want to go to school tomorrow."

"Oh, Bryar, I'm not sure that's a good idea."

"I thought you'd want me to go."

"I think it might be best to take a few days, Bry. We can do some work at home—"

"No." His mouth is set hard. "I want to go."

Her heart contracts.

If she'd been scared about him starting school before the party, what would it be like now? What happened on Sunday would be all over town. They'd have been talking about him. And they'd make him feel it: that he was the kid at whose party Astrid Carver got shot.

"It's going to be hard, my love," Kaitlin says.

"But they'll be there, won't they—the others?"

"The others?"

"The kids who were there today, at the station," he says. "My friends."

My friends. She swallows. How she'd longed to hear him say those words.

"I . . . I don't know, Bry. I think so . . . I haven't spoken to their parents. I guess everyone has to make their own decision."

"But Lily's going. She told me." Bryar looks Kaitlin right in the eye and she notices a new expression in her son's face: confidence. "So I'm going too," he says.

"Maybe I should talk this through with Dad—"

"Please, Mom."

She remembers what one of Bryar's first therapists had said to her: that mothers of kids with special needs often hold them back. She'd said that it was a natural impulse to want to protect your child. But that it didn't help, not in the long run. Kaitlin had been furious. Hadn't she spent her life trying to help Bryar move forward—to join in with the other kids? But maybe the therapist had been right. Because, right now, she'd do anything to keep him away from a world that, she feels, has already decided he's guilty.

As she tries to think of something that will persuade Bryar to stay home tomorrow, she notices a police car at the bottom of the drive. A moment later, Lieutenant Mesenberg is parking beside them.

"Why don't you go inside, Bryar? Grab something to eat."

Bryar stares at the lieutenant.

"I'll come in and check on you in a bit."

She picks up the bag of Bryar's clothing that one of the police officers gave her at the station. Kaitlin remembers how bewildered the children had been when, on Sunday evening, they were asked to change out of their clothes and hand them over. And how they'd all gone home in a bunch of ill-fitting sweatshirts and pants that the detectives had given them. The Sayed twins, especially, had looked so very different.

We have to test for gunshot residue, one of the officers had said to her when she asked why they needed the clothes.

It still doesn't feel real: that they're part of a police investigation.

Bryar takes one more look at the lieutenant and then walks off toward the house.

Lieutenant Mesenberg gets out of her car. "Good evening, Mrs. Wright. I'm here to take another look at the stable." The lieutenant's eyes follow Bryar as he walks up the porch steps. "My team still hasn't found the pistol." Her eyes settle on Kaitlin. "No idea where it might have gone?"

Kaitlin stares at her and blinks. "You think I might be hiding it?"

"I don't know, Mrs. Wright."

She's right, of course. If she believed it would make a difference, Kaitlin would do anything to protect Bryar.

"If I find it, I'll let you know," Kaitlin says.

The lieutenant cocks her head to one side. "And your son—he hasn't mentioned it?"

Kaitlin swallows hard. "No. He's told you everything he knows."

"It's surprising, don't you think? That the firearm should just disappear like that?"

"Yes, it is."

"My team used metal detectors. Brought in a German shepherd. Swept the whole area. And still nothing." She pauses. "It's unusual."

"May I ask a question?" Kaitlin says.

"Sure."

"What difference will it really make? Finding the pistol, I mean? You already know that the bullet they removed from Astrid's chest matches the gun that's missing from the safe in my office. And my son told you that he was the one who opened it. What else do you need to know?"

"We need fingerprints."

Kaitlin's heart contracts.

She thinks back to what Bryar said. About how the children passed the gun around, how they'd made a game of it. How he doesn't remember who was holding it when Astrid got shot.

"What if there's more than one set of fingerprints?" she asks.

"We can probably work out who pulled the trigger. There'll be dominant prints."

She sounds so certain that she'll work out who did this, thinks Kaitlin.

"Bryar must be comfortable with firearms," the lieutenant adds.

Kaitlin sees the light on in Bryar's room. She looks back at the lieutenant. "Comfortable?"

"Having grown up with guns. With his father. I gather your husband has quite a reputation at the range."

"A *reputation*?"

"He's a good shot."

"Yes—but he's in law enforcement. It's part of his job—"

"But for your husband, it's more than a job, right?"

Kaitlin feels sick. "More than a job? I don't understand."

"Did Bryar ever go with him—to the range?"

Kaitlin thinks back to the first time Ben took Bryar to the shooting range: it was a year ago. Bryar's birthday. He'd bought him a rifle as a present, like his dad had on his tenth birthday. He was passing on a Wright tradition that he hoped, one day, Bryar would pass on to his son or daughter.

But Bryar had hated every minute of it and begged to go home.

Kaitlin had been disappointed for Ben—by how Bryar had reacted at the range. And she'd been worried that it would cause a rift between them. They were already so very different.

Though, of course, Ben had taken Bryar back to the range. He couldn't force his son to like guns but he'd make sure that he knew how to handle them safely.

He taught him how to load and unload a gun.

How only ever to aim the weapon at a target.

How to keep the safety catch on until you were absolutely sure you were ready to shoot.

"Yes, they've been to the range together. But Bryar isn't interested in guns."

"I see."

Kaitlin looks back up at Bryar's bedroom window. He's drawn the curtains. "It's been a long day, Lieutenant. My son needs me."

"Of course."

Kaitlin turns to go but then she stops and looks back round at the lieutenant.

"What's going to happen next?" she asks.

"Next?" she asks.

"With the investigation."

"Well, we need to be thorough—I'll keep taking samples from the stable, and looking for the pistol. We'll have another around of questions for the kids—and the parents. In a homicide investigation like this—"

"A *homicide* investigation?"

"Yes."

"But Astrid's still alive—isn't she?"

"Yes. But in cases like this, we follow homicide procedures from the start."

Ben's still at the station. They haven't stopped asking him questions.

"So, my husband—" She swallows hard. "Might he be charged?"

Lieutenant Mesenberg's face softens.

"We're not there yet."

"But that's what you're looking at?"

"We have a long road ahead of us, Mrs. Wright. We need to take this one step at a time."

"Ben wasn't even there when the shooting happened."

"And yet the children got hold of his firearm. And the ammunition."

"You know that Ben would never put anyone in danger, least of all a child."

"Perhaps not willingly, no. But there might be a case for neglectful homicide."

"*Neglectful*? Do you have any idea how seriously my husband takes gun safety? I just explained how he taught our son—"

"We all make mistakes, Mrs. Wright."

"Ben doesn't make mistakes. Not like this."

"Well, that's why we need a thorough investigation."

"And what about the child—the one who shot Astrid? What would happen to them?" Kaitlin asks.

"That depends."

"On what?"

"On if there was intent."

"*Intent?*"

"Yes."

"You mean intent to kill?"

"Yes."

Kaitlin's heart jolts. They think that someone tried to shoot Astrid on purpose?

The detective takes a step forward. "Look, Mrs. Wright, I know that this has been a big shock. I'd recommend that you talk to your son and your husband, try to help us get a clear story. Now, if I may, I'm going to take another look at the stable."

As Kaitlin watches the lieutenant walking away, she listens to the wind pulling leaves off the maples, to the horses shuffling their hooves in the straw, their warm bodies shifting in the dark; she thinks about her oldest horse, Lucy, who was so scared by what happened that she ran from the stable, far out into the field. It had taken Kaitlin hours to coax her back.

Bryar's words from the police interview come back to her:

Wynn was jumping up and down next to Astrid . . . he wanted to have a turn with the gun . . .

And that's when it dawns on her.

It wasn't an accident—Lucy knocking Wynn off his feet like that. Kaitlin has known this horse her entire life: she's too much in control of her body to have made a mistake like this. No, there was nothing accidental about what happened to Wynn. Lucy threw him to the side of the stall intentionally. She was getting him out of the way of the gun. She saved his life.

CHAPTER

17

9 p.m.

"SO, YOU HAVE no idea what Astrid was doing at the party?" Lieutenant Mesenberg asks.

Priscilla looks down at the lieutenant's notepad, filled with scratchy handwriting. When the lieutenant had called to ask whether she could come to the hospital to interview her, a series of excuses had run through Priscilla's mind. She didn't feel up to seeing anyone. But in the end, she'd agreed. She needs to know whether they're any closer to finding out who did this to Astrid.

"No, I don't have any idea what Astrid was doing at the party," Priscilla says, gripping her cup of coffee.

The detective pushes a strand of frizzy gray hair out of her eyes and looks at her notepad. "And you weren't home at the time—is that correct?"

"I was at work." Priscilla feels her hackles rising. "Shouldn't you be focusing your resources on interviewing the families who were actually *at* the party—and the children who were involved in shooting my daughter?"

"My team is working on that. But we need to take a 360-degree view of the situation. It's important that we gather all the information we can."

"I'm not sure you need to go much further than Ben Wright and his son."

Lieutenant Mesenberg pauses for a beat. And then says, "I've heard that your relationship with the Wrights is strained."

Priscilla laughs. "Strained? You could say that."

"And yet your daughter still went to the party?" the lieutenant goes on.

"Yes."

"Against your wishes?"

"Of course, against my wishes."

"I see."

Lieutenant Mesenberg puts on her reading glasses and looks back at her pad and says, "So, back to Sunday afternoon. You left your daughter alone in the house."

"She's eleven. She's more than capable of looking after herself." Priscilla feels the hollowness of these words. She takes a breath. "I wasn't going to be long."

"You were away from the house for . . ." She reads from her notepad. "Four hours?"

Priscilla straightens the back of her neck. "Do you have children?"

The detective shifts in her chair. "No—"

"Because of the job?"

"Look, Dr. Carver—I understand that this is a difficult time for you. But I need to get the fullest picture I can of what happened on Sunday afternoon." She pauses. "And of what led to the shooting."

Her throat tightens. She doesn't want to be sitting here. She wants to be with Astrid. She never wants to leave Astrid again.

"Dr. Carver?"

Priscilla looks back at the lieutenant. She wants her to go now. To leave her alone.

"Coming back to your daughter. You said you have no idea why she went."

"I assume she was lured there."

Lieutenant Mesenberg's eyebrows shoot up over her glasses. "*Lured?*"

"Yes. By that Wright boy. Or one of those other kids."

"You believe they wanted her there?"

"What's that supposed to mean?"

The lieutenant will have been interviewing the other children; God knows what they've been saying to her.

"Astrid and Bryar Wright used to be friends," Priscilla says.

"How long ago was that?"

"Three years."

"And, what happened?"

"We decided that he wasn't a good influence."

"We?"

"My husband and I."

"Of course. It would be helpful to speak to him too."

"He's not here."

"Right. Well, maybe when there's a convenient time."

A wave of tiredness washes over Priscilla. She doesn't want to have to explain the details of her family life to this stranger. It's no one's business other than hers. And it has nothing to do with what happened to Astrid. She should never have agreed to this meeting.

"You said that you and your husband thought Bryar Wright wasn't a good influence. In what way?"

"We don't share the same values as the Wrights."

"And which values would those be?"

Priscilla looks straight at Lieutenant Mesenberg. "The Wrights have firearms in their home."

The detective sits back. "Many families have firearms in their home, Dr. Carver."

"And my daughter doesn't play in any of those houses. She knows it's dangerous."

"So, if I'm hearing this right, you're saying that you suspected a child could get shot at the party?"

"*Suspected?*" Priscilla shakes her head. "No. I didn't suspect. I knew."

"Could you be more specific?"

"Ben Wright is obsessed with guns."

The detective raises her eyebrows. "Obsessed? That's a strong word."

"He has firearms all over his house. Spends hours at the shooting range. What else would you call it?"

"He's a law enforcement officer, Dr. Carver."

She should have known it: they've all got each other's backs.

"Does being a law enforcement officer put you *above* the law?" Priscilla asks.

"No, certainly not. But it does come with certain responsibilities—"

"He killed my dog."

"Excuse me?"

"A rescue dog. Three years ago. Shot him, right through the heart, for no reason at all."

The detective opens her pad and makes another note.

"He probably has loaded firearms just lying around the house—" Priscilla goes on.

"I believe the pistol in question was taken from a safe."

"Do you have a gun safe in your home, Lieutenant?"

She doesn't answer.

"Okay, you don't want to say. I get it. I assume you have firearm safes at the police department?"

"Yes, that's right."

"And how many digits make up the code needed to unlock those safes?"

"Six."

"Do you own a cell phone?"

The detective shifts uncomfortably in her chair. "I'm not sure that this is relevant."

Priscilla laughs again. "Oh, believe me, this is the most relevant part of the conversation we've had so far. Do you own a cell phone, Detective?"

"Yes, of course."

"And does it have a code?"

"Yes."

"How many digits?"

Priscilla notices a pink blush seeping into Lieutenant Mesenberg's cheeks.

"Six," the lieutenant says.

"Do you know how old my daughter was when she first memorized the code to my phone?"

The detective waits for Priscilla to go on.

"Five years old." Priscilla leans forward, holding out her palms. "So it doesn't take a rocket scientist to work out that a kid could open a gun safe, does it? That Bryar Wright, watching his father opening and closing those safes of his several times a day—when he goes to work, when he comes back from work, when he goes to the shooting range, when he goes hunting—"

"I understand what you're saying, Dr. Carver, but there's a big difference between shooting a dog and shooting a child."

Priscilla thinks back to the case that made her leave her job as an attorney and turn to academia. The one that taught her that guns had no place in people's homes, especially homes with children. Human beings were too unpredictable—too emotionally unstable—to be trusted with anything as dangerous as a gun.

"You know as well as I do, Lieutenant, that when there are guns around, anyone can be a target. An animal. A child. A police officer, even."

"You have strong views on firearms, I understand that, Dr. Carver—"

Priscilla's done with this conversation. She puts down her cup of coffee, stands up, and walks toward the door.

"Is there any chance your daughter might know how to open a gun safe, Dr. Carver?"

Priscilla spins round. "Excuse me?"

"You said yourself how easy it was."

"I said that she *could* if she *wanted* to. That any child her age—or younger—could. But no, she doesn't know how to open a gun safe."

"Does your daughter have a phone?"

"I don't see what this has to do with—?"

"You said your daughter could unlock your phone easily. Does she have one of her own?"

"Yes."

"We didn't find it."

"Sorry?"

"We didn't find a phone on her—or in the stable. We took the phone of every child at the party—every child who had one. The media department at the station has been looking closely at everything from text message exchanges to Facebook profiles to internet search histories. It's often a shortcut to getting to the bottom of cases like this."

"Astrid would have had her phone with her. She refuses to go anywhere without it."

"Well, it's missing."

"Then I suggest you find it. One of the other children probably stole it."

"They were all stripped at the station."

"Well, then, it's probably still in the stable somewhere."

"We've looked."

"Okay. Well, whatever. It doesn't really matter, does it? What my daughter had on *her* phone, does it? Why don't you focus your energy on who did this to her?"

"Might your daughter have had a motive for getting hold of a firearm?" the lieutenant asks as though Priscilla hasn't spoken.

Priscilla looks up. "A *motive*? For Christ's sake, it's my daughter who got shot—who's lying in a coma with a bullet hole through her chest!"

"Okay. Let's turn the question round. Do you know why Astrid might have been a target?"

Priscilla stands on the spot, frozen, the question sinking in. "Are you suggesting it was her fault that she got shot?"

"No, but I'm saying there have been suggestions that she's unpopular."

"*Unpopular?*"

"That she makes the other children feel . . . inferior in some way. That she finds it hard to make friends."

Priscilla turns back to the door. "I've heard enough of this. I need to get back to my daughter."

"I have a few more questions," the lieutenant says, standing up. "It will help with the investigation. I need to establish the facts."

Priscilla walks back toward her, her chin jutting out. "The *facts*?"

"Yes."

"Let me give you some facts, Lieutenant." Priscilla holds up one finger. "On Sunday afternoon, at a children's party, my eleven-year-old daughter was shot. Fact."

She holds up a second finger. "On the Wrights' property. Fact."

She holds up a third finger. "And now she's in a coma. Fact."

She holds up a fourth finger. "And while we've been sitting here, whoever is responsible for shooting my daughter, is walking around free to shoot anyone else they please." Priscilla looks down at the detective. "Why don't you start with those facts?"

Priscilla thinks about the media contacts she has in her phone from her days as an attorney in Boston. Reporters. News anchors. TV presenters. Friends who feel like she does about gun laws. She's going to make sure that people around the country are talking about what happened to Astrid—maybe then Lieutenant Mesenberg will start taking this case seriously.

Priscilla walks back to the door. As she reaches for the handle, it opens from the other side. Her breath sticks in her throat.

He's standing in front of her. His skin a golden tan. An open white polo neck. Chinos. His blond hair bleached by the sun.

The lieutenant stands up. "I'm afraid that we're having a private meeting, sir—if you could give us a few minutes—"

"This is Dr. Peter Carver," Priscilla says, her voice cracking. "My husband. Astrid's father."

CHAPTER

18

10 p.m.

KAITLIN GOES INTO Lucy's stall and leans her head against the old mare's neck.

Lucy hasn't touched her food. And Kaitlin can tell, from the position of her head, and from how she's pressed up against the side of the stall, that she's still in shock.

"Thank you," she whispers to her. "For trying to help."

Kaitlin knows how much Lucy loves children.

She wishes she could reach out to True and tell him that Lucy was trying to protect Wynn. That it wasn't her fault. But when a child gets hurt, there's no knowing how a parent will react, even a parent as level-headed as True Bowen.

From this stall, she can see the back office. The open doorway. The empty safe.

She's walked past it a million times without giving it a second thought. Like the rifle cabinet in their living room and the biometric safe by their bed.

When had she agreed to have all these guns in her house?

On her parents' ranch back in Texas, she'd grown up with guns. But as a kid, you don't get a say in the choices your mom and dad make. Most of the time, you don't even question them. And it was Texas. Everyone in Texas has firearms.

But when you get married—when you have your own family—don't you get the chance to make a fresh start? To do things differently from your parents?

A knot of anger forms in her stomach. Anger at Ben for putting them in this position. But even more at herself.

Why had she gone along with it?

She'd never asked Ben to put a gun safe in the stable. She didn't need protecting, not like this. She hardly knew how to shoot a gun—what good would it have done, even if there had been an intruder?

He could keep his work pistols at the station. He could store the rifles he used for hunting elsewhere. There was no need for them to have guns in their home.

Why had she never told him that?

And how many other things in her life—in her marriage—has she gone along with, blindly?

"Katie?"

She spins round.

She hadn't heard Ben's truck pull up the drive.

"What are you doing here, standing in the dark?" he asks.

"I . . ." She looks away from the gun safe. "I was checking on Lucy."

He steps toward her and folds his arms around her. He smells of the police station: of dust and metal; paper and coffee. But underneath, she can still smell his skin: the smell of the earth warmed by the sun, a smell that makes her feel safe. Even when they were high school kids, Kaitlin knew that Ben wasn't just another human being, separate from her: he was her home.

She breathes in deeply until the smell of him floods her body.

"I was worried they'd keep you overnight again," she whispers into his thick, dark hair.

"Me too," he answers.

They hold on to each other a little longer.

Lucy takes a few steps from the corner of the stall. She seems calmer too, now that Ben's back.

He sits down on one of the bales of hay, slumping his torso. "It's been a hell of a day."

She sits down beside him. “Yeah.”

“Bryar okay?” he asks.

“I don’t know.”

Ben looks around. “Did he say anything about what happened in here?”

She shakes her head. “Not really.”

“You think he’s got something to hide?”

“I don’t know.” Her throat goes so tight she feels she can’t breathe.

He puts his hand between her shoulder blades and rubs her back. “It’s okay, Katie. It’s okay.”

She takes a breath. “It’s just that he usually talks to me—when things are really bad. You know?”

“Things are more than really bad, Katie. None of us know how to handle this. He’s a kid. He’ll open up when he’s ready.”

“He wants to go to school tomorrow,” she says.

“Really?”

“Yeah.”

“Is that a good idea?”

She shrugs. “I don’t know, Ben. I don’t know about anything any more.”

They sit in silence again.

“What about you?” she asks. “What did they say—at the station?”

He looks down at his hands: the thick knuckles, the lines, the tanned skin.

“I’m not allowed to work, Katie.”

“What?”

“Not until the investigation’s over.”

He looks up at her, his eyes glassy. “I can’t be involved in law enforcement and be a suspect.”

“A suspect? But you weren’t even here when Astrid got shot.”

“Well, maybe that’s the problem. I should have been. Or maybe it’s that I arrived at just the wrong time. They’re still establishing a timeline of events. I don’t know. They’re not telling me anything.”

She swallows hard. "Why were you late, Ben?"

They haven't had the chance to talk since the accident, not properly.

"There was a search and rescue—a couple got lost in the mountains with their kid—"

"We needed you here."

It was a battle she'd fought when they lived in Texas and he worked a difficult border: persuading him not to put himself in danger, to remember that he had a family and that being there for them—alive and healthy—mattered more than his work.

"I was doing my job, Katie. I tried to call you but there was no reception—I was too far out."

"And no one else could have done it? One of your colleagues?"

He takes her hand. "Come on, Katie, don't do this."

She pulls her hand out from under his. "It was a lot, you know—to manage on my own?"

"I told you that you should have kept the party smaller."

She feel stung. "I wanted it to be special—for Bryar."

"But it was too much. We can't afford parties like this—we're not that kind of people, Katie—"

Tears push up behind her eyes. "Why are you saying this now?"

"I was responding to what you said, Katie—about finding it too much to manage." He reaches for her hand again but she folds her arms. "Come on, let's not do this now. We're both tired. We need to get some sleep."

She looks past him, out across the barn. She feels their relationship splintering in a way it never has before. He's right: it was stupid to hold such a big party. To invite so many people. To think that she could pull it off. But holding a party they couldn't afford—getting carried away because she wanted to make things better for Bryar—those things aren't crimes, are they?

It catches her eye again, the gun safe. She turns back to Ben. "The party wasn't why Astrid got shot."

He stares at her.

"The fact that Bryar got hold of that gun—" she goes on. "And the ammo."

"What are you implying?"

"Bryar's seen you open and close our safes a million times. And you know what he's like. He's good with numbers. He remembers *everything*."

"He knew not to touch the safes. Not without me there."

"But he did, didn't he? Kids do stuff their parents don't want them to do all the time. We should have been more careful—"

"If Bryar wanted to shoot Astrid—"

"If Bryar *wanted* to shoot Astrid?"

"I'm just saying that if a kid gets it in his mind to hurt another kid, they'll find a way."

"You actually think that Bryar did this?"

"No. I'm just saying—"

"Do you even know our son? He wouldn't hurt anyone, Ben. Not intentionally."

She'd felt it ever since Bryar was born. How she was somehow tuned into him in a way that Ben wasn't. And now it was clearer than ever: when it came to their son, they were on different sides.

"It's not about Bryar." Her voice is cold and steady. "None of this is on him."

They stare at each other, trying to find their footing again.

"We need to get some rest, Katie," Ben says gently. "Come on, let's go inside."

She keeps staring at him. There are dark circles around his eyes. He came straight off his shift to the party. And then the hours of questioning at the station. He hasn't slept in over twenty-four hours. He's right, they need to get some rest. But she can't let this go.

"We shouldn't have had them in our home to begin with. The safes. The guns." She gulps.

"Katie . . . ?"

She stands up. "I don't want us to have guns in our home any more."

For a long time, he doesn't say anything. He just stares at her, confused, like he doesn't recognize her any more. And then, slowly, he shakes his head.

"You're blaming me for what happened."

"No—no. I didn't say that."

"It's what you implied."

"I'm saying that if we hadn't had guns in the house, none of this would have happened."

He stands up. "You *are* blaming me."

He turns away and walks to the stable door.

"Ben—please," she calls after him.

But he doesn't turn around.

She hears him cross the yard and walk up the porch steps and into the house.

And she thinks of going after him—of trying to explain—but she knows she can't. Because she meant it: she doesn't want to see a firearm on their property ever again.

CHAPTER

19

10 p.m.

PRISCILLA CAN'T TAKE her eyes off Peter.

How many times has she wished for this moment? For him to rush back to her—to realize that he has a wife and a daughter that he loves.

And how many times had Astrid pleaded with her to find a way to get him to come home?

He's not coming home. Just get used to it, okay! she'd yelled at Astrid once, unable to handle the weight of her grief for her father, coupled with her own.

"I'm sorry," the lieutenant says. "Of course you can be here, Mr. Carver. My name's Lieutenant Mesenberg. I'm heading up the investigation concerning your daughter's shooting."

Priscilla watches the words hit Peter. Words he never thought he'd hear: that his little girl has been hurt. Badly hurt. That she might not make it.

"In fact," Lieutenant Mesenberg goes on, "I was saying to your wife that it would be good if I could ask you a few questions too."

Priscilla waits for Peter to correct her. Ex-wife, isn't that what she is now?

But he doesn't say anything.

"He's just flown in from California," Priscilla says. "And he hasn't seen Astrid yet. I'd appreciate it if you could give us a little privacy."

The detective begins to pack up her things. "I'm sorry. Of course. I'll come back later."

"Maybe you can come back when you have some actual answers," Priscilla throws back.

Peter steps toward Priscilla. His eyes are bloodshot. He's struggling to take it in. The hospital. The fact that there's a police detective here. That their eleven-year-old daughter has been shot.

The lieutenant pulls a card out of her pocket and hands it to Peter.

"Maybe once you've settled in, you could give me a call."

Settled in? She makes it sound like he's here on vacation.

Peter takes the card and puts it in the pocket of his chinos. "I will. Thank you, Lieutenant."

The lieutenant turns to Priscilla. "Thank you for your time, Dr. Carver." Then she hesitates. "If you think of anything else—"

"Anything else?"

"Maybe something that Astrid told you before she went to the party—something that might shed light on this situation."

Priscilla digs her nails into her palms. *Astrid doesn't tell me things,* she wants to say. *And even if she did, it wouldn't reveal anything. Astrid's not to blame for any of this.*

When Priscilla doesn't answer, the lieutenant gives her a small nod.

"I'll be in touch," she says. And then she catches Peter's eye, as if she's decided that he's the reasonable one, the one who might give her the information that she needs.

When Lieutenant Mesenberg has gone, Priscilla and Peter stand in the family room, a gulf of silence between them.

"Thank you for coming," she says to him.

He steps toward her.

And then she starts crying. He hesitates for a second and then walks toward her and puts his arms around her.

She should push him away—let him know that he doesn't have the right to do things like this any more, not after he walked out on her. But something inside her comes loose and her body falls into his chest.

He strokes the back of her head, like he used to. As they stand there leaning into each other, she wants him to keep holding her. Because it's the first time in twenty-four hours—it's the first time since the day he left, seven months ago—that she doesn't feel completely alone.

But then she forces herself to remember why he's here. That it's not for her. That he's come all this way because their little girl has been hurt.

She musters all the strength she has and pulls away from him.

"I'll take you to Astrid's room," she says.

He nods.

And then she guides him out of the family room and down the hall, to the room where their little girl lies unconscious, tubes covering her small body, fighting for her life.

DAY THREE

Tuesday, September 3

The First Day of School

C H A P T E R

20

8.15 a.m.

EVA WATCHES A news van with a satellite on its roof parking behind the yellow school bus. Her stomach churns. The cooler weather had eased the nausea but standing here, surrounded by kids and parents—and journalists—it's come flooding back.

"What are they doing here?" Lily asks.

They're here because Priscilla wants them to be here, Eva thinks. Will had all but said as much over breakfast: that Priscilla had the media contacts she needed to make a big story of this—that she'd make sure the shooting got national attention.

"They're just trying to get a story," Eva says.

"About us?" Lily asks.

"Yes."

A woman with a video camera, a man with a microphone and a presenter walk toward the school yard. They have the creased look of people who've been travelling for hours—and the determined look of people who aren't going to leave until they've got what they've come for: a good story.

Eva squeezes Lily's hand. "It's okay, they won't be allowed into school."

Not that she'd put it past them. The press has been crawling all over town. Local. National. Everyone wanting the lowdown on "the Playdate Shooting." That's what they're calling it.

The police are no closer to finding a culprit. The children's stories simply don't add up, read the front-page article in yesterday's *Boston Chronicle. Meanwhile Astrid Carver is fighting for her life at Colebrook Hospital.*

Without a clear conclusion to the investigation, the press was weaving its own narrative:

Children left unsupervised.

A gun at a party.

A child with a motive.

And a cover-up.

They made it sound like one of the kids had shot Astrid on purpose.

Yesterday afternoon, Eva and Will took Lily to the Children's Advocacy Center, where the kids were questioned again. The only ones she didn't see were Hanif and Laila, the twins. There was a lawyer throwing his weight around, saying that he was representing the Sayeds. She'd wondered whether maybe they should get a lawyer too, for Lily, but Will said that it was best to cooperate with the police.

All Lily has to do is tell them the truth, he'd said. *It's not like she'd have fired the gun.*

Eva didn't believe that Lily had shot Astrid, not for a second. But she'd worked long enough with children to know that they shouldn't be underestimated. If Lily was keeping quiet, there was a reason for it.

She wishes Will were here, but he's covering for Priscilla at the law school. It's his way of making it up to her: that his wife brought their daughter to the party where her daughter got shot. Worse: that the party had been her idea.

"Why are they so interested in us?" Lily asks, staring at one of the cameramen setting up.

"People find it exciting to read about bad things happening to other people," Eva says.

"They do?"

"Yes, sadly, they do. Especially when children are involved."

And guns, she thinks. Children and guns—what journalist wouldn't jump on that story?

"I wish they'd leave us alone," Lily says. She stares wide-eyed at the group of journalists camped outside the school gates.

"I'm sure they'll move on to another story soon, my love," Eva says.

But Eva knows that they're not going anywhere. Not the press or the police. Not until they get to the bottom of what happened on Sunday afternoon.

More children and parents pour into the school yard.

There are tables with coffee and doughnuts and sign-up sheets for the PTA.

Teachers are buzzing around, welcoming parents and kids, pretending that this is just another beginning of term.

Mums are taking photographs of their kids by the sign for Brook Middle School.

Before this happened, Eva had planned to bring flyers with her to advertise her music therapy lessons: the first day back at school was the perfect time to get parents to sign their kids up. But with everything going on, she'd decided to leave them at home.

She feels dizzy at the noise and people.

Lily shrinks beside her.

"It's okay to change your mind about starting school today," Eva says. "We can go home. Give it a few more days."

The truth is that it's Eva who's beginning to change her mind. Maybe it would have been better to have kept Lily home until the dust settles.

"I promised Bryar I'd be here," Lily says.

That was something else Eva knew about kids. How loyal they could be. To each other. To anyone they loved—no matter what those people had done.

After the police interviews, yesterday, while Eva and Priscilla talked, Bryar and Lily went off to get a snack from the vending machine. On the way home, Lily announced that she wanted to go to school the next day. That she and Bryar had decided they were going to face it together.

Eva crouches down so that she's level with Lily.

"You don't *have* to do anything, Lily. Bryar would understand."

"We have to show them, Mum."

"Show who?"

"Everyone." She looks around at the children and their parents and the journalists. "We have to show them that it's not Bryar's fault." Her tired eyes fill with tears.

"Oh, Lily. That's not your job—"

Lily sniffs. "If we come to school, they'll stop talking."

Eva knows it's not that simple, but she doesn't say anything.

"Okay. But remember to tell your teachers if you're struggling, and I'll come right away and get you."

Last night, they'd received an e-mail from Mrs. Markham. Words of reassurance. The teachers had been briefed about the sensitivity of the situation. She'd given out the number of the school counselor in case any of the children needed support.

Lily's trying to be brave. But from the way she's staring at the playground filled with kids and parents and teachers—and from the way she's gripping Eva's hand—Eva knows that her little girl is hanging on by a thread.

She's scared. They all are.

Scared that Astrid might not wake up.

And scared about what's going to happen when the police find out who shot her.

Eva notices Yasmin and Ayaan Sayed walking the twins over to Mrs. Markham. Eva tries to catch Yasmin's eye but her head's down.

When Avery turns up with Abi and Cal, Eva hears a couple of mothers whispering behind her. They were some of the first parents here. Their daughters are the ones sitting on the bench with the new dresses.

"Reverend Avery shouldn't be allowed to bring kids like that into Middlebrook," one of the mothers says. "It's asking for trouble."

The ambivalence Eva felt, a second ago, about being here, is replaced by a rush of anger.

"I suppose they brought the gun with them from Roxbury," the second mother replies.

Eva's so angry, now, that even the nausea disappears.

Lily looks up at her, wide-eyed. "What are they talking about, Mum?"

"It's nothing, Lily. They don't know what they're saying."

"They shouldn't be allowed to mix with our kids," the first mom says.

"I thought that at least she'd keep them away from school—they could be a danger to our kids," the second mom says.

That's it.

Eva lets go of Lily's hand, spins round and walks toward the mothers.

Lily follows her. "Mum—where are you going?"

Eva stops right in front of the two mothers.

"They're children," Eva says, looking from one woman to the other. "Yes, they've had a tough start to life, which means that they need our support." Her body is shaking but she keeps going. "And they haven't been charged with anything. None of the children have."

The women stare at Eva. She recognizes, now, that one of them stopped her at the library a couple of weeks back to ask about music therapy lessons for her son.

After a few seconds, the first mother says, "We didn't mean any harm—we were just staying—"

"Well, don't," Eva jumps in. She's on a roll. "Don't *just say* anything. Not if you don't know what you're talking about."

The second mother blinks. Then she puts on a forced smile and holds out a hand. "You're new in town, aren't you? I'm Zoe. Pleased to meet you."

Eva stares at Zoe's hand but doesn't take it. The mother lowers her hand back to her side.

"I think we met—didn't we?" the other mother says to Eva.

"Yes," Eva says weakly. "We did."

The mother leans in and smiles at Lily. "And this must be your daughter. I'm sure our daughters would love to play with you, wouldn't they, Zoe?"

They don't know yet, Eva thinks. That Lily was there when Astrid got shot.

Lily takes a step back from the two women.

"It must be so very shocking—that this has happened when you've just got here," Zoe says to Eva. "I mean, we're shocked too, aren't we, Sharon? Middlebrook isn't the kind of place where things like this happen."

"And poor Priscilla." Sharon shakes her head. "What she must be going through."

Zoe looks up at Eva. "Your husband works with her, doesn't he?"

Before she has the chance to answer, Lily cries out: "He's here, Mum, look!"

And then she's off, running across the playground.

Sharon and Zoe suck in their breath.

"Wait up!" Lily's voice bounces off the tarmac and the brick buildings of Brook Middle School. "BRYAR!"

Bryar turns around. He stares at her, confused. And then she takes his hand and his face softens.

The two mothers look at each other.

Lily throws her arms around Bryar.

"Oh!" says Zoe.

"Your daughter . . ." Sharon starts.

". . . and Bryar are friends, yes," Eva says.

As Eva watches Lily standing in the playground, holding Bryar's hand, she feels a rush of pride.

Try to make some new friends today, Will had advised Lily over breakfast, adding emphasis to the word *new*. It was his way of telling her to stay away from the kids involved in the investigation.

Will's a good man. A good husband and father. And a brilliant academic: he specializes in legal ethics. If anyone knows right from wrong, it's Will. But he doesn't understand that what happened on Sunday will make Lily feel closer to the very kids he wants her to avoid. Because in this way, Lily's like Eva: she understands that some things are more complicated than simple right and wrong.

Eva hears the children and the parents and the teachers fall silent around Lily and Bryar, like a spotlight's fallen on them.

If those two mothers were gossiping about Abi and Cal's involvement in the shooting, it was obvious that they—and the rest of the Middlebrook community—would have even more to say about the Wrights. The shooting had taken place on their property, in all probability, with Ben Wright's pistol. It wouldn't take much for them to make the next logical leap: that Bryar had pulled the trigger.

Kaitlin stands beside Lily and Bryar, her head low, like Yasmin's.

Eva turns back to Zoe and Sharon.

"I hope your daughters have a good first day of school," she says.

And then she walks across the playground toward Kaitlin.

Eva feels the other parents moving their gaze from Bryar and Lily, holding hands, to her and Kaitlin.

If they didn't know that Lily was involved, they would now.

Kaitlin looks at Eva. "Thanks for coming over," she says.

"Of course."

Eva had wanted to call Kaitlin to ask how she was doing, especially with Ben being held back for more questioning, but Will had told her to give the Wrights some space. He'd said it in the same tone that he'd used when advising Lily to make new friends.

At first, Eva had thought that maybe he had a point. After all, if she hadn't got so caught up with Kaitlin and Bryar and the party, Lily wouldn't be facing all this on her first day of school.

But standing here, looking at Kaitlin, she knows that blocking her out of her life isn't an option. They're in this together. And more than that: Kaitlin's her friend.

"I should have kept Bryar home," Kaitlin says.

Eva doesn't know what a right decision looks like any more, but hiding from what's going on isn't going to do any of them any good. "I thought the same, about Lily, but I've changed my mind."

She glances over to Zoe and Sharon, who are still staring at her. "I think it's good that they're here."

"It's just . . ."

"Hard. I know."

"Yeah."

"But guess what?" Eva asks.

Kaitlin looks up at her.

Eva nods over at Bryar and Lily, who have taken off toward the main entrance to the school.

"I reckon they're better at this than we are," Eva says. "They'll be fine."

The school bell goes. A long, shrill ringing that shocks the children and parents and teachers out of their focus on Lily and Bryar. The children disappear into the school building. And then there's no one left in the school yard but the parents.

How different it would have been if things had gone smoothly on Sunday, thinks Eva. They'd have been worried about all the ordinary things mums are worried about when their kids start school: which friends and teachers they'd come home talking about; which activities they'd signed up for; whether they'd eat their packed lunches.

The parents head back to their cars.

A few of them stop to talk to the journalists. Anger sweeps over Eva again: as if those parents have any kind of valid insight into what happened on Sunday.

When they get to Kaitlin's car, Kaitlin turns around. Her eyes are watery. "I wanted to say that I understand if you don't want to give Bryar music lessons any more—or have the kids over to play. There'll be no hard feelings."

"I don't ever give up on my students," Eva says. "And Lily doesn't give up on her friends, either. I'm afraid you're stuck with us."

Kaitlin's eyes well up. "Are you sure?"

"Yes, I'm sure."

Kaitlin's tears spill out now, down her cheeks and onto her sweatshirt.

Eva takes both of Kaitlin's hands. "You haven't done anything wrong—you know that, don't you?"

Kaitlin sniffs and looks up. "I don't think many people would agree with you."

"What people think doesn't equate to the truth, Kaitlin."

"It does in Middlebrook," Kaitlin says.

Eva squeezes Kaitlin's hands. "Well, then, we'd better prove them wrong."

Kaitlin bites her bottom lip and nods. Eva can tell that she wants to believe that the gossip will die down; that people will come around to seeing things more reasonably; that Wynn's arm will heal; that Astrid will wake up and be okay; that no one will be charged; that the investigation will conclude that it was just a terrible accident, a party gone wrong. And that, with time, people will forget.

And Eva wants to believe it too. She has to believe it. Otherwise she's not going to be able to cope with it all. The pregnancy. Supporting Lily. Navigating this crazy situation she's in with Will, who seems more concerned with what Priscilla Carver thinks about him than with how his own family is doing.

Otherwise, she might as well pack her bags and go back to England.

CHAPTER

21

9.30 a.m.

YASMIN SITS ON the bottom step of the staircase that runs through the middle of the house and feels the emptiness around her.

She hugs her knees and looks out through the window at the empty swing set.

I've arranged for them to be taught separately, Mrs. Markham told them when she greeted them in the playground.

It was too complicated, she explained, to create two classes.

The twins had looked at each other, mortified.

Yasmin had been desperate to intervene. To say that this wasn't the kind of education she wanted for her children. That it was important that they should be with their friends. That separating them off like this would do nothing but draw more attention to them.

But before Yasmin could say anything, Ayaan had shaken Mrs. Markham's hand and thanked her for her trouble and said that was precisely the outcome he'd been hoping for.

They'll get one-to-one attention, he'd said in the car on the way home. *What could be better?*

She hadn't answered. Because if she had, she'd have told him that she didn't want them to have one-to-one attention. She wanted them to be with the other children. Including the children who were at the party.

So, again, she'd stayed quiet.

Because she didn't want to upset him.

And because she was afraid. Not of him, but of her own feelings. About how this gulf was opening up between them and how she felt like she was the only one who was seeing it.

Or worse. How maybe the gulf had been there from the beginning.

She thought back to how it was when she first met him as a young architecture student at Columbia. He'd remained so steady in his faith; he dressed and spoke and walked as though he'd never left Pakistan; he didn't touch a drop of alcohol; he stayed away from parties. She, on the other hand, had thrown herself into student life. She'd loved wearing jeans and T-shirts and cutting her hair short and partying through the night.

And yet they'd been drawn to each other. Because there's something powerful about meeting someone who comes from home, when that home is far away—someone who understands where you come from, even if it's the place you longed to escape. Being with Ayaan made Yasmin feel safe. In fact, having him at her side gave her the courage to embrace her new life. The steadier he was, the freer she felt to cast off her past, knowing that he would be her anchor: she could stray as far as she wanted because, in him, there was always a way home.

Back then, when they were young, they'd embraced each other's differences.

She'd been impressed by how devout he was—how he prayed five times a day, no matter what else was going on. She'd been touched by his shyness, by how hard he worked and how faithful he was to their homeland. And, she believes, he'd admired her. For being so outgoing. For casting off her old life in Pakistan and adapting so easily to American life and for helping him step out into this new world.

They'd admired the very things in each other that now seem to separate them. And, she supposes, they'd both kidded themselves that, in time, they could change each other.

If they were more courageous, they'd face the truth head-on: that they've drifted apart. That the dynamic they had doesn't work any more. But instead, they've both kept up the pretence. Because it's easier. And because she can't bear the thought of splitting up her family.

Ayaan has thrown himself into his work: building the mosque has become an obsession that allows him to ignore anything that's happening in his personal life.

And, in the meantime, she hides away in this big house, unable to embrace her life in America in the way she longs to—in the way she had as a student—for fear of disappointing him.

She feels trapped.

Which is why she takes longs walks at night when the others are asleep.

Which is why she'd gone to the Wrights' party. Because, for once, she wanted to make her own decision. Because the Wrights were exactly the kind of people she wanted to be friends with when she moved to America: kind, open-hearted people. Because Priscilla Carver and her way of hovering over Middlebrook, pressuring people to adapt to her views, was what she'd wanted to escape when she left Pakistan.

The walls of the house press in on her. The house that Ayaan bought and set about renovating as soon as they decided to move here. He wanted to give her a place that reminded her of home, he'd said. By the time he was finished, it was the tallest, showiest house in town.

She hates it.

She doesn't want to be reminded of home.

And she doesn't want to stand out. It embarrasses her.

If she could choose, she'd live in a wood frame house with an American flag hanging outside the front door—the same kind of flag that hung outside the Wrights' house.

But wanting those things was obviously wrong: she'd taken the twins to the party and now Astrid was lying in hospital, in a coma. And her children are caught up in a criminal investigation. And no matter how much money Ayaan pays that lawyer, he can't make it go away: the fact that they were there when Astrid got shot.

Yasmin stands up.

I need to be outside, she thinks. *Away from this house. I need air and sky.*

She runs upstairs, gets changed out of the blue salwar kameez she'd worn to take the children to school and throws on an old pair of jeans. She finds one of her old sweatshirts from Columbia at the back of the closet. She stops at the landing mirror and ties up her long, dark hair in a messy bun, like she's seen American women do. And then, barely recognizing her reflection, she smiles. She feels lighter already.

Laila's feet would be too small for Yasmin!

She leaves behind her purse and her phone and goes outside.

She walks down to the brook at the bottom of their drive, the brook that runs alongside Main Street and heads up through the woods to Middlebrook Pond. It had all but run dry through the summer drought but after a few days of rain, it's filling up again.

She keeps walking.

Past Eva's house.

Past St. Mary's church.

Past the old white clapboard house with the wrap-around porch that's been standing empty, a for sale sign in the yard, for over a year now.

Past the reporters in front of the general store, clutching paper cups of coffee and talking into their phones. She's glad that she's changed out of her formal clothes, that nothing will draw attention to her.

Yasmin keeps going, up the steep incline of the valley until she gets to Woodwind Stables.

Even from the bottom of the drive, she can see the police tape; the lieutenant's car parked in front of the stable next to Ben's red truck.

She imagines Kaitlin and Ben sitting in their house, trying to get their heads around all of this. She wishes she could tell them something—anything—to make them feel better. She wants them to know that she doesn't blame them.

Of course, everyone's focusing on Priscilla and Astrid. God knows what Priscilla must be going through. But Yasmin can't help thinking that it must be worse for Kaitlin and Ben, the parents who hosted the party where a kid was shot. And, of course Yasmin had picked up on the rumors that were already beginning to circulate around the village and the school playground. Bryar was a strange kid, they said. On the spectrum. And he didn't have friends, not like normal kids. As if these facts automatically made him the shooter.

The shooter.

Yasmin hates the phrase. Bryar is eleven years old, the same age as her twins. A child, still.

Yes, it would be kind to show them some support.

But then Ayaan's words rush back to her: *We can't afford to be caught up in this, Yas.*

If he found out that she'd been to see the Wrights, he'd be furious.

She turns to go but as she does, she notices a copy of the *Boston Chronicle* sticking out of the Wrights' mailbox. Even though it's curled up and wrapped in plastic, she knows that the front page is filled with news about the shooting on Sunday.

She pulls the paper out of the mailbox, tears open the plastic and shakes it out until it's straight.

Along the banner at the top of the front page, there's a picture of Reverend Avery, and next to it the words:

Turn to p10 for an insight into the Playdate Shooting from Middlebrook's minister.

Avery gave the press an interview?

Yasmin's about to turn to the article when her eyes scan down the rest of the page. And that's when she sees them: the series of headshots; the faces of the kids who were in the stable that afternoon. Their faces have been blurred out but it's obvious who they are.

Bryar's face is in the middle, his picture larger than the others.

And next to him, there's a photograph of Hanif and Laila, with the caption: *Muslim twins involved in Playdate Shooting.*

The Boston Chronicle
The Playdate Shooting
Lydia Richards: Chief Editor

On Sunday, September 1, an eleven-year-old girl was shot in the chest at a children's party in Middlebrook, NH. She's currently in a coma in Colebrook Hospital, fighting for her life.

You might be forgiven for not having heard of the small town of Middlebrook. Drive a little too fast along US-3 on your way to the Canadian border, and you'll miss it. As one of the locals, eighty-seven-year-old Judy Creech, proudly puts it: "Nothing ever happens here." Which makes the shooting all the more shocking.

This wasn't a high school massacre. No drugs were involved. And it wasn't an act of terrorism—not that we know of, anyway. What's more, the firearm used wasn't one of the controversial semiautomatics that lie at the heart of the gun control debate. The weapon used to shoot Astrid Carver was an everyday handgun. And it's the ordinariness of this crime that makes it shocking.

This is the kind of shooting that the mother of the victim, Dr. Priscilla Carver, refers to as "the real crisis in the story of American gun-control." When asked to expand, Dr. Carver explains that: "The everyday exposure of children to firearms is a crime, one that Americans should wake up to and legislate against." Dr. Carver, a law professor at the Daniel Webster Law School, is known for her strong views on gun control.

The screenshot from a Facebook page Dr. Carver set up (pictured right), shows the photographs (blurred out to protect the privacy of the suspects) of the nine children who were in the stable where the shooting took place. Any one of them, it would seem, could have shot Dr. Carver's daughter. Why Astrid was made a target is still unclear. Lieutenant Mesenberg, the detective in charge of the investigation, says that all the children and families concerned have been interviewed. "We are doing everything we can to find out what happened on Sunday afternoon," she told one of our reporters.

Which is not enough, according to Dr. Carver. In a heartfelt phone conversation from her daughter's bedside, she told us that she believes that the criminal justice system is failing Astrid: that more should be done to uncover her daughter's shooter.

Over the coming days, our team of investigative reporters will be taking a closer look at each of the children—and families—involved in the shooting. Our first interview was conducted by Fern Spencer, who spent time talking to Reverend Avery Cotton, the Middlebrook minister. Reverend Cotton's foster children—both from a troubled background—were present at the shooting. For more, turn to page 10.

CHAPTER

22

10 p.m.

"PLEASE TELL ME you didn't?" Peter says, scanning the front of the *Middlebrook Monitor*.

He turns the front of the paper round to face her.

She looks at the article.

THE PLAYDATE SHOOTING.

It's a good headline, she thinks. It will get attention. The strapline, underneath, reads:

Distraught mother releases pictures of child suspects on Facebook.

There's a screenshot of a Facebook page she made shortly after her interview with Lieutenant Mesenberg: *Justice for Astrid*. It already has over 400 likes.

"Priscilla?" Peter asks again.

"I had to do something," she says. "The police aren't taking the investigation seriously."

Peter shakes his head.

They're sitting in the hospital café. Peter forced her to leave Astrid's side for a few minutes to get some food. He doesn't understand that she can't eat. Or do anything else—sleep, work, wash, change her clothes. Just sitting here, watching her little girl fighting for life, is taking every ounce of energy she has.

Sometimes, she finds it hard even to breathe.

And he doesn't understand how him being here is making it harder.

Harder because she likes him being with her.

Harder because it reminds her of how things used to be when they were still a family; when he still loved her.

Harder because she knows that, sooner or later, he'll leave again.

Peter goes back to reading the article.

She notices that he's taken his wedding ring off.

I want us still to be friends, he'd said when he announced that he was leaving her. *I don't want us to be one of those separated couples who fight—or who don't even talk. We need to get on—for Astrid's sake, at least.* Then he'd paused and looked her in the eye and said: *I'll always love you, Cil, you know that.*

She'd wanted to yell at him that she didn't want to be his friend. She didn't want them to just get along for the sake of their kid. She wanted them still to be married. And if he still loved her, why didn't he want that too?

More than that, she'd wanted to yell at him that he didn't get to come off as the calm, reasonable one when he was the one who put a bomb under their marriage and went off to California with his graduate student.

But she'd been too stunned to find the right words. And by the time she had found the words, he was gone.

"I know how raw you're feeling about all this, but releasing photos of the kids for anyone to see—on a public Facebook page . . . there are other ways to do this," Peter says.

She swallows hard. She's not going to let him question her judgment.

"I haven't done anything wrong, Peter. The photographs have already been published in the public domain." It had been easy to find the pictures. A picture of Avery's foster kids in an article on the online church newsletter, welcoming them to the community. The Bowen kids on the town website celebrating the Fourth of July last year. An old article about the building of the mosque which had a picture of the Sayeds, and a family photo Will sent in for the university website. A bit of cropping and she'd gotten decent headshots of each of the kids who were in the stable when Astrid got shot.

"Getting the press involved always makes things worse, I thought you knew that." He closes the newspaper and pushes it away.

"Raising public interest will help put pressure on the investigation," Priscilla says.

"I don't think the investigation needs any more pressure. Lieutenant Mesenberg assured us that she and her team are going to get to the bottom of what happened."

"Astrid got shot, that's what happened. And one of those kids shot her. We need to find out who that was. And unless we take this investigation seriously, unless we draw attention to the shooting, it's going to happen again. And again. Every day, kids in America are getting shot and no one's doing anything about it." Her voice is getting louder and louder, but she doesn't care. Peter has to understand.

"I know that you're sensitive around this subject. Because of what happened back in Boston . . ."

"*Sensitive*?"

"Come on, Cil, you lose it whenever anyone so much as mentions guns."

When Priscilla decided she no longer wanted to be a practicing attorney, he'd stood by her. He'd understood how the case had left her so shaken that she couldn't put herself on the front line again, not in a country where guns destroyed entire families. And now he was calling her *sensitive*?

"I thought we were on the same page," she says.

"We are. I just think that we have to be reasonable. Being emotional—"

"Emotional? Our daughter's in a coma—*because she got shot*—but I guess that's nothing to get upset about?"

"That's not what I meant."

"It's been over forty-eight hours and they haven't even found the gun, Peter."

"I know." He holds out his palms. "But lashing out against people—and getting the press involved—isn't going to help us. Or Astrid."

"Help *us*?" Her heart contracts. "You lost your claim to *us* the day you left."

She feels herself sabotaging the very thing she longs for: them being together again as a family. But she's so angry at him for not understanding her when it's now, more than ever, she needs his support.

He stares at her. "I'm sorry."

For a long time, they stay there in silence, Peter standing, holding his paper coffee cup, Priscilla in her molded plastic chair.

Then she looks up at him, her neck stiff, her eyes hard. "Why are you here, Peter?"

"Excuse me?"

"If you're not going to be supportive, why are you here?"

"I'm here for Astrid—and for you, Cil. I know it hasn't been easy for you but I still love you. We've shared so much—"

"If you loved me, you would never have left."

His shoulders drop. "Come on, Priscilla."

"Come on, what? How do you want me to respond, exactly?"

"I think you should trust Mesenberg and her team to do their work and focus on Astrid."

Priscilla looks at Peter, incredulous. "Wow, California really has made you go soft. We're lawyers, Peter. Since when do we trust the police not to fuck things up?"

"I'm just saying that you're wasting your energy on this—energy you don't have right now."

He reaches out to her but she pulls away.

And then she sees him: True Bowen walking down the corridor toward the café. Peter sees him too. He stands up and walks toward him, holding out a hand.

"True, good to see you."

True looks at Peter, not sure how to respond. Eventually, he takes his hand.

When Peter still lived in Middlebrook, the two of them were friends. They were an unlikely pairing: the stay-at-home dad of three and the law professor. But it worked. They'd go fishing together in the White Mountains and True would show him how to find morels in the woods. Priscilla and Peter both knew that True went hunting—that he owned a rifle—so they'd never allowed Astrid to go over for playdates. But hunting was different, wasn't it? True would never shoot a human being. And he hunted to feed his family. They'd both been able to get their heads around that.

And then, when news got out of Peter's affair, True had broken off the friendship. After Peter left for California, True came to see Priscilla to tell her how sorry he was—and how angry. *I'd do anything to have Cedar back—even for a second,* he said. *And he's just walking out on his family. It's not right.*

For a moment, it had made Priscilla feel better—that someone was on her side. But it didn't bring Peter back.

Skye stands a few paces behind True, avoiding Priscilla's gaze. She's pale and there are dark shadows under her eyes. She's carrying Wynn, his face buried in her neck. His right arm is locked in a purple cast, and there's already writing scrawled along the plaster—long, loopy sentences alongside pictures of bears.

A little way behind Skye and Wynn, Phoenix is playing with a water cooler, pressing the tap over and over. There's already a puddle of water on the floor.

True lets go of Peter's hand and walks toward Priscilla. "I'm so sorry," he starts.

Priscilla's spine whips up. "*Sorry*?"

"About Astrid. You must be beside yourself with worry. We've been in such a state over Wynn but he's going to be okay . . ." He stalls.

"Where were you, True?" she asks.

"Cil . . ." Peter starts.

"I'm just asking a question, Peter." She keeps staring at True.

A deep line forms between True's eyes. "I don't understand."

"Where were you when the kids were playing in the stable—with a fucking handgun?"

Everyone around them goes quiet.

Peter steps forward. "I'm sorry, True," he says. "We're going through a lot right now." Then he turns to Priscilla. "Come on, Cil, let's get back upstairs."

"No. I want him to answer. I want him to tell us—as the father of three small children—what he was doing when a gun went off and blew a hole through my daughter's chest."

True's shoulders drop. He takes a step back from her.

A week ago, they'd bumped into each other on Main Street. She'd asked him directly whether he was going to Bryar Wright's party. He'd laughed. *You still haven't buried that old hatchet, Priscilla?*

"I'm just asking where you were when my daughter got shot." She looks over at Wynn, sleeping in Skye's arms. "And when your four-year-old son got hurt."

"I . . ." he starts. "I . . ."

She looks over at Phoenix, who's managed to break off one of the plastic taps on the water cooler. "And Phoenix was in the stable, wasn't he?"

If it wasn't Bryar who shot Astrid, the next kid she'd put her money on was Phoenix. He was always looking for trouble. And he probably knew how to shoot a gun too.

"What are you implying, Priscilla?" True says.

"I think you know," Priscilla says.

Skye steps forward, her face blotchy. "It was my fault. Dad put me in charge. I was meant to look out for them."

Wynn stirs in her arms and looks up, confused, his eyelids heavy.

"It wasn't your fault, Skye," True says, his voice so loud and hard that Wynn opens his eyes for a second. "None of this is your fault."

Skye strokes Wynn's head to soothe him. "It was, Dad. You told me to watch the little ones." She swallows hard. "If I hadn't gone out of the stable with Cal, I could have stopped things getting out of hand."

Priscilla lets out a laugh. "You put a thirteen-year-old child in charge? Wow, forgive me for questioning your judgment."

"I know you're upset, Priscilla . . ." True says.

Priscilla ignores him. "Well, at least your daughter has some sense of moral responsibility. That's something for you to be proud of, I suppose."

Slowly, True looks up at Priscilla. "Moral responsibility? What are you talking about? This was an accident, a terrible, terrible accident."

"Is that what Wynn told the police?" Priscilla asks.

She'd watched Lieutenant Mesenberg and her partner come into the hospital early this morning. She knew that they were there to question Wynn. He might be four years old, but he saw what happened—at the very least, he's old enough to identify who fired the gun.

"Wynn's really shaken up," True says. "He's been through a lot. He needs some time to recover—physically and emotionally."

"And some time to conveniently forget what happened," Priscilla says. "The Bowens stick together, right?"

True shakes his head. "I don't know what you want from us, Priscilla. I'm sorry for what's happened. Really, I am. But this isn't doing anyone any good—"

"Dad?"

They all turn around to look at Phoenix. He's moved on from the water dispenser to a newspaper rack on the wall of the café.

"Not now, Phoenix," True says.

Phoenix picks up a newspaper. "Come and look, Dad," he says. "We're in the paper."

"What?" True says.

"Me and Skye and Wynn—and the other kids. They've blurred out our faces but they're saying that someone's been sharing pictures of us—"

True walks over to Phoenix, takes the paper from his hand and studies the front page. Then, slowly, he puts the newspaper back on the stand.

"Come on, Skye, Phoenix, let's go," True says, his voice low and steady.

Skye goes over and grabs Phoenix by the hand.

True turns round to look at Priscilla. She's rarely seen him angry at anyone. He makes allowances for people. For their tempers and their irrationalities and their mistakes. It's why he's friends with the Wrights—and why he went to the party. But the way he looks at her makes her feel like she's the one in the wrong in all this.

He turns back around and then the four of them walk away down the hall and out through the main doors of the hospital.

"He was trying to be kind, Cil," Peter says. "He must have been through a lot—with Wynn . . ."

"He was at the party, Peter. And he let this happen." She swallows. "And that son of his—"

"You can't go around blaming everyone you see for what happened to Astrid—"

"Yes. Yes, I can. And I will—I'm going to blame every single child and every single parent who was at that party until I find out who did this."

Peter holds his hands up. "Okay, Cil, okay."

"*Okay*? What does that mean?"

He stands up and puts on his jacket.

"Where are you going?"

"I think you need some space. My being here is obviously not doing you much good right now."

He zips up his jacket.

"Fine!" Priscilla says. "Go. It's what you're good at, isn't it, Peter? Walking out. In fact, why don't you book a flight back to California. Leave me to deal with this." Her voice chokes. She looks down into her coffee, forcing herself not to cry.

He walks up to her gently and puts his hands on her shoulders. The familiarity of the gesture overwhelms her. It's what he'd always done when she was spiraling—pressed down lightly on her shoulder blades, as if anchoring her. It's what he'd done on the night of the shooting that ended her career as an attorney.

"She's going to be okay, you know that, right?"

She looks up at him through blurry eyes. "How do I know that, Peter? Tell me."

He looks right into her eyes and says, "I know because she's a fighter, Priscilla. Like her mom."

They keep looking at each other and she wants to tell him to stay—that she needs him here, with her. And that she's sorry for lashing out at him. But the words stay stuck in her throat and instead, she watches him turn away from her and walk out of the hospital doors under the heavy gray rainclouds.

CHAPTER

23

10 a.m.

AVERY DOESN'T UNDERSTAND, at first, why everyone goes quiet when she walks into the general store on Main Street. Or why everyone's staring at her.

And then she realizes that they must all know about Astrid getting shot—and that Cal and Abi were at the party. She wishes she could explain it to them. That she'd do anything to go back and stop Astrid and Wynn getting hurt.

As she walks to the counter, she hears a whisper from behind her.

"Shame on you."

It takes her a moment to realize that it's Hillary, who does the flower arranging for special occasions in church. She's worked for the church her whole life. Prides herself on keeping the cemetery looking beautiful throughout the dry summers and the cold winters. She does the holly wreaths at Christmas and the floral arrangements on Easter Sunday. She does the weddings too. She's the most loyal member of Avery's church: she supported Avery from the moment she arrived in Middlebrook.

"Hillary?" Avery asks. "Is everything okay?"

Hillary shakes her head. "Those poor children."

"I know, it's awful." Avery reaches out to take the old woman's hands.

Hillary pulls her hands away. "I mean, *your* poor children. How could you do this to them—after everything they've been through?"

Avery feels a thud in her chest. "I don't understand—"

Hillary thrusts a newspaper she'd been holding at Avery. "Well, maybe you need to read it again—those things you told that reporter." Hillary's voice wobbles. Her cheeks are flushed pink.

Avery looks down at the newspaper. There's a piece on how Priscilla's released pictures of the kids on Facebook. She'd heard people talking about it. But there's another article too.

It comes back to her now. How, late yesterday afternoon, she'd sat on the bench under the oak tree in the church garden and that kind young woman had come to talk to her.

Her hands start to shake.

She turns to the article on page 10 and it feels like the world slips away from under her.

It will be good for the community to hear from their spiritual leader . . . the reporter's words come back to her. *Your voice is important to people at times like this.*

A young woman. Big, open blue eyes. An empathetic smile. A chain with a small cross around her neck. Avery had trusted her.

Avery looks around the store at the people from her congregation, people she knows so well, who've supported her and confided in her—people she's come to see as part of her family. None of them will meet her eye.

She pushes the newspaper into her bag and walks across the general store and out down the front steps, and then breaks into a run. And she keeps running, past the church, through the cemetery, with the beautiful flowers Hillary planted, and then deep into the woods.

Interview Special: Reverend Avery Cotton, Middlebrook Minister
The Dark Side of Fostering
By Fern Spencer

Rev Avery, as she's fondly known to the Middlebrook community, is as wholesome as apple pie. Rosy cheeks. Sparkling eyes. A ready smile. A popular, loveable local with a liberal theology. Rumors have it that her appointment to St. Mary's caused quite a stir—but not for long. As a local says of her: "The minute you meet Rev Avery, you're smitten. You kind of feel lucky just for bumping into her."

Which is what her latest two foster kids must have felt when they were dropped off on her doorstep by their social worker at the beginning of the summer: lucky. Because, until Sunday afternoon, you'd have believed that there couldn't have been a better foster parent for those kids than Reverend Avery Cotton.

Born in Roxbury, to a mother with a heroin habit and a long line of abusive boyfriends, the thirteen- and eleven-year-old siblings must, indeed, have seen a great deal in their short lives. Rev Avery confided in me that, not long before their mother was sentenced to jail on a drug trafficking charge, the girl, then nine, took a .38 caliber (the same type of pistol used to shoot the young victim at the party on Sunday) from one of her mother's particularly unpleasant boyfriends and threatened to shoot him if he didn't leave their mother alone. That was the first time the siblings were taken into foster care.

So, yes, these new members of the Middlebrook Community must have felt that their lottery ticket came up when they landed on Rev Avery's doorstep.

As we sat outside the church in the fall sunshine, she pointed out the basketball hoop she had put up on the back wall of the rectory to encourage one of her foster kid's passions. She went on to explain how she'd bought a set of paints for the girl's brother to encourage his love of art. "I wanted to show them that they belong here, and that they're loved and appreciated for who they are," she told me.

She promised to give them a good life. There was talk of adoption. And it was going so well. Until the party.

"Rev Avery would have known that there would be guns around," says Tracy, who had turned down the invitation to the party. "Priscilla warned us that it wasn't safe to go up to Woodwind Stables, not with our kids."

But Reverend Avery went all the same.

And now, these two kids from Roxbury, already scarred by a childhood filled with violence and neglect, find themselves at the heart of a criminal investigation.

There's still disagreement as to where the older boy was at the time of the shooting, but locals confirm that there had been an upset between him and the victim of the shooting earlier in the summer. As for the boy's sister, as we know, she's no stranger to handguns.

"Is there not a risk in bringing vulnerable children into a community like Middlebrook?" I asked Reverend Cotton.

She was quick to defend her actions: "It's precisely children like this who need to experience communities like ours—kind, warm-hearted, welcoming places where kids get to be kids and where everyone looks out for everyone else. They need to see that the world can be different. It's healing—"

"But it didn't work, did it?" I said, interrupting her. "They wound up in trouble—again."

"Bad things can happen anywhere," Reverend Avery was quick to answer. "And we have to work through them. That's life. And we're going to work through this together."

It's obvious that Reverend Avery is an optimist. Perhaps too much so for her own good.

Before we parted, I asked her one last question. The question that everyone's been asking, in one form or another, since the shooting on Sunday.

"Could your foster kids have fired the gun?"

She remained silent for a long time, looking up into the branches of the tree under which we sat, as if in prayer. And then she said, “I don’t know.”

“But you believe that you know these children—and what they’re capable of?” I replied.

She paused again. Even longer this time. And then she said, “Do we ever really know anyone else? I mean, truly? Completely? Human beings are mysteries. And most of us are capable of doing bad things. But we have to believe in the essential goodness of children, don’t you think? Otherwise, what hope is there?”

Sunday’s shooting has left the local community reeling and at times like this, a community turns to its minister for guidance. But when that minister may herself be implicated in that shooting, what happens to a town like Middlebrook?

All this raises questions, not only about gun control but also about who should be allowed to foster and whether there should be tighter monitoring of foster parents.

The investigation continues.

CHAPTER

24

12.30 p.m.

Lily watches Bryar standing outside the cafeteria, gripping his lunchbox. Everyone's staring at him and whispering, like they've been doing all morning.

He's frozen to the spot—which is making him even more of a target.

She takes his clammy hand. "Come on," she whispers, "let's go outside."

He doesn't move.

"Bryar—we need to go."

She pulls at him. At last, he starts to shift.

When they get outside, she guides him to a tall birch tree in the corner of the school yard. It's been raining all morning; the trees are dripping. But Lily and Bryar don't mind. It means the other kids are less likely to come outside.

Lily thinks about being back in London in a school where she had a best friend she'd known since she was three. If anyone had stared at Lily like they've been staring today, Amanda would have marched up to them and told them to stop.

But Amanda isn't here.

Lily's on her own. And she has to take care of Bryar. In the playground this morning he seemed okay but he's got worse through the morning. She's worried he's going to shut down altogether. So, she has to be the strong one. And she doesn't feel strong, not one bit.

She looks at Bryar's lunchbox. "You should eat something," she says.

He just stares, not moving. Then, in a really quiet voice, he says, "You don't have to do this."

"Do what?"

"Hang out with me."

It had crossed her mind a few times—how not hanging around with Bryar would make things easier for her. How the other kids wouldn't stare as much. How maybe she'd be able to make new friends. But then she felt guilty. Bryar had it much worse. Everyone blames him for what happened. Being there for him was the least she could do. And he was her friend. If there was one thing Amanda had taught her, it was that friends don't let each other down—no matter how bad things get.

"I like hanging out with you," she says.

"Even after what happened?"

"We're in this together, Bryar."

"But . . ." His voice trails off.

It's been playing over and over in her head, those few seconds before the grown-ups came rushing in, just before Astrid lost consciousness. They'd sworn that they wouldn't say anything. And it had felt right—or it had, then. Anyway, it was too late to back out of it now.

"But nothing." She takes his hand and threads her fingers through his. "Like I said, we're in this together."

Cal sits outside with his back pressed into the wall of the main school building with his sister, Abi. They'd both been to enough schools to know that cafeterias are the worst kind of hell for kids like them. It's like other kids can smell it on them: that they don't belong.

"How was this morning?" Cal asks Abi.

She shrugs and looks down at her feet.

Ever since Sunday, she's gone into herself again. She won't talk, not even to him.

Cal looks over at the school gates.

He wonders how long it would take to walk into town, to the church, through the woods, to the cabin where Skye lives. He needs to tell her that he's sorry for asking her to go out of the stable with him. But that he's not sorry they kissed. And that he'll do anything he can to make things better again.

When he saw Skye being taken into the Child Advocacy Center for a police interview yesterday afternoon, he'd tried to catch her eye, to make sure she was okay, but she'd looked away. He was worried that she blamed him for her little brother getting hurt. Just like he blamed himself for not having been there to protect Abi. They were the oldest kids at the party. They should have known better than to leave the younger kids on their own.

But whatever Skye's thinking, he has to find a way to talk to her.

To set things straight.

And to let her know he can't bear not seeing her again.

Because in the entire thirteen messed-up years of his life, he's never met anyone like her. Someone who makes him feel like maybe he's worth something. Like if he sticks it out, if he tries to be good and make a go of things, life could be okay, after all.

That's why he'd brushed away Astrid Carver earlier in the summer. He didn't want anyone like her to spoil things for him.

"Abi—Cal!"

It takes him a second to work out where the voice is coming from.

The English girl, Lily, is standing on a mound of earth on the far side of the playground, waving. Bryar, the boy whose party it was, is sitting beside her.

"Over here!" Lily says.

Abi and Cal look over at them and he knows they're both thinking the same thing: *Stay away.*

Because wasn't that what they did whenever something bad happened in Roxbury? Heads down. Mouths shut. Stay away from the kids who could bring them down.

But these kids felt different from the kids back home.

Just like Skye felt different from any girl Cal had ever met.

And, deep down, Cal and Abi feel something else too: that if anyone should be avoiding anyone else right now, those two kids sitting under the tree should be avoiding them, not the other way around. Because didn't everyone here know that Cal and Abi were the foster kids whose mom was in prison? The kids who'd grown up with guns. The kids who brought trouble with them wherever they went.

Cal looks over at Abi. Ever since Sunday, he keeps getting flashbacks of that night two years ago when she got hold of Mike's handgun. It had looked so big in her nine-year-old hands but she'd held it steady, like she knew what to do with it, even though no one had ever shown her, not properly. Mom was sleeping. Her boyfriend, Mike, was sitting on the sofa smoking and drinking beer. He'd had a fight with Mom. Pushed her so hard against the kitchen counter that she fell and cut her head open on the side of the dishwasher.

When Cal had heard Abi arguing with someone, he'd stumbled out of his bedroom.

I want you to leave! Abi was yelling, waving the gun around.

And, before Cal could grab the gun from her, it went off. Hit Mike right in the leg.

Cal had blamed himself for not watching Abi more closely. She should never have gotten hold of that gun. And he blames himself now, for leaving her on her own in the stable on Sunday afternoon.

When Abi gets angry, she loses control. When he and Skye got back into the stable, he'd seen it in Abi's eyes: how wound up she was by Astrid.

He has to find a way to protect her. To take the attention of the investigation away from her. From both of them.

The English girl waves them over again.

Cal knows that if they're going to get through this, they have to stick together.

"Come on," he says to Abi.

And before she has time to object, he grabs her hand and they walk over to Lily and Bryar.

The Sayed twins look over at Bryar, Lily, and the foster kids having lunch together. They feel it: the thread that ties them together. How, ever since the gun went off in the stable on Sunday afternoon, and in the moments that followed, when everything was so quiet, when they looked each other in the eye and then nodded, slowly, agreeing that there was only one way they were going to get through this: by keeping quiet. And by sticking together no matter what.

They were part of them now, those other children.

Behind them, they can see the top of the minaret above the trees. Dad had explained that he wanted it to be so big that everyone would see it from miles around.

Standing out. Making everyone see that they're different. Ever since they left Lahore, that's been Dad's focus. He doesn't understand that they just want to fit in with the other kids: to wear the same clothes and play the same games and mess around—even if that means getting in trouble. Even if that means doing something really bad. That's why they'd been so excited when Mom agreed to take them to the party. And it's why they'd gone into the stable. And joined in with the game. For the first time in their lives, they felt part of something bigger than just the two of them. And they liked it.

All morning, they had to sit in that room outside Mrs. Markham's office, filling out worksheets rather than being in a classroom with the other sixth graders. Because Dad didn't want them to mix with the other kids.

He thinks it's the other kids' fault, what happened on Sunday.

Because he'd never for a second believe that Hanif or Laila could have done anything wrong.

Lily spots them and waves them over.

The twins wave back and, as they walk over to the yellow birch tree where the other kids are sitting, they have the same thought: Dad's not here. He'll never know who they had lunch with. Just like he'll never know what really happened in the stable on Sunday afternoon.

CHAPTER

25

3.30 p.m.

AVERY WAITS FOR them on the bench outside the church, clutching the newspaper. She didn't dare go to the school gates—all those parents staring and whispering about how she could have done this to the children put in her care. So, she's waiting for them here, praying that they haven't seen the article yet.

And she's ignoring Bill's calls. He would have seen the article, obviously. But she wants to talk things through with Cal and Abi before their social worker gets involved.

For God's sake don't talk to the press. That was one of the first things Bill had said to her when they talked on the phone on Sunday night.

And she hadn't meant to. But then she'd bumped into that young woman, just outside St. Mary's, and they'd sat under the tree, talking so easily. The reporter said she wanted to present what had happened in a more nuanced way than the other reporters. That her article would help the community.

Naïve. Stupid and naïve. That's what I am, Avery tells herself.

When Abi and Cal spot her, they shoot each other a look. It's the look they used to give each other all the time when they first got to Middlebrook. A look that said: *Don't trust her. Don't trust anyone.*

Keep your distance. It had taken them two months to let her give them a hug before turning off the light at bedtime.

Did they blame her for taking them to the party on Sunday?

Was that reporter right when she said it was her fault for putting them in a vulnerable position?

She stands up and walks toward them.

They look at each other again.

"We need to have a chat," she says.

Their bodies tense up.

"It's okay—you haven't done anything wrong." She swallows hard. "It's actually me—I've done something I need to tell you about."

Cal's brow furrows.

She has to tell them before they find out from someone else.

While she explains about the article, Cal and Abi stay really quiet. They don't touch the cookies she made for them.

"Can we read it?" Cal says, looking at the newspaper sitting on the kitchen table.

Avery's throat goes dry. She nods. "Sure."

She watches Cal's eyes scanning the reporter's words. Abi doesn't even bother to look.

"The reporter left so much out," Avery tries to explain. "She only used some of what I said—the bits that weren't important. And then she twisted things and put them out of context . . ."

When Cal's finished reading, he looks up and says, "What about the bit where you said you thought we could have shot Astrid. Did you mean that?"

"I didn't say that."

He points down at the newspaper. "You said that most people are capable of doing bad things. So that includes us, right?"

"I was making a bigger point—about everyone—"

"But you didn't tell the reporter that you believe we didn't do it."

"I wasn't blaming you, Cal—"

But he doesn't hear her.

"And what about the bit where you said you don't know us? That we're . . ." He looks back down. "A mystery?"

"Everyone's a mystery, Cal. You, me, Abi. Everyone. It takes a lifetime for people to really get to know each other—and even then . . ." She pauses, knowing that her words are coming out wrong. "Look, I just wanted the reporter to understand that people are complicated."

She realizes how stupid she's been. How the words of her theology books, of the sermons she writes, are a world away from the words used by reporters. She may as well have been speaking to Fern Spencer in a different language.

Slowly, Cal stands up. "But you didn't defend us, did you?" He turns to go.

Avery stands up. "Please, Cal. I blame myself. I shouldn't have taken you to the party. And I shouldn't have talked to the reporter. I don't blame you—or Abi. Not one bit."

But Cal's already walked out of the kitchen. The front door bangs. Through the kitchen window, she sees him making his way to the woods.

She comes and sits back down in front of Abi.

Her phone buzzes again. Another message from Bill.

Abi looks down at Avery's phone. "I guess you're going to get rid of us now." Her voice is flat.

"No—of course not."

"Bill won't let us stay."

"I'll fight for you. You know that. You belong here, Abi. You and Cal. You guys have done so well—we can't give up now."

"But you think we might have done it, right?"

Avery's shoulders drop.

"Right?" Abi says.

"I think it was an accident, Abi. A terrible, terrible accident—"

"An accident that was our fault."

For a while, Avery goes quiet. Then she looks up. "Why don't you tell me what really happened, Abi? Then I can help you. You know you can trust me—"

Abi laughs and stands up. "*Trust* you?"

"Of course."

Abi shakes her head.

"Please, Abi." Avery reaches out and tries to catch Abi's hand.

"I'm going to see if Cal's okay."

"But—"

Abi turns and runs out of the kitchen.

Avery slumps over the table and puts her head in her hands.

The truth is, she doesn't know whether or not Abi or Cal fired that gun. Were they capable of it? Probably. Did they have a reason to shoot Astrid Carver? Not that she can think of—except that Astrid has a way of winding other kids up. No. She doesn't know for sure that they didn't do it. That's why she couldn't tell the reporter, right out, that they weren't to blame. But she does know this: that she wants them to stay. That hasn't changed. And she's going to fight to keep them, no matter what they did.

CHAPTER

26

9 p.m.

"It would be a shame to cancel—she's been doing so well." Eva sighs down the phone. "Okay . . . well, get in touch if you change your mind."

She ends the call and slumps into a chair at the kitchen table.

Will looks up from his computer. "Who was that?"

"Another family's cancelled."

It's been less than forty-eight hours since the party and already three mums have called, making excuses for why their kids can't have music lessons with Eva.

When they decided to move here from London, Eva had thought it would take a miracle for her to keep working as a music therapist—surely demand would be limited in a town as small as Middlebrook. But she'd underestimated the power of word of mouth. Kaitlin, in particular, had shared with other families how Eva had managed to get through to Bryar. Except that was the problem, wasn't it? No one wanted to be associated with Kaitlin Wright, not after Astrid got shot—and not being associated with Kaitlin meant not being associated with Eva either.

"They'll come around," Will says.

"Come around?"

"They'll realize that you're not to blame for any of this. Just give it some time."

She swallows hard. He doesn't know that the party was her idea. And that she'd gone out of her way to persuade people to go. And he doesn't seem to have registered that Lily—their daughter—was right there when Astrid got shot: that she's one of the suspects.

Will shuts his laptop and picks up a bottle of wine from the counter. He goes to pour Eva a glass but she puts her hand over the rim.

"Not for me, thanks."

He raises his eyebrows. "Really?"

"Really."

She wants to tell him about the baby—that this is the longest a pregnancy has lasted since she had Lily. That after ten years of waiting, they might finally get a chance to be parents again. But with everything that's going on, it never feels like the right time.

He sits down in front of her and pours himself a glass of wine." He leafs through today's paper. They'd both seen it: how Priscilla had made that Facebook page with the kids' photos. And there was the article about Avery's foster kids. They made it sound like Avery thought Abi or Cal might have shot Astrid.

Eva doesn't know what to think. The kids' stories aren't adding up. None of them are coming out with anything concrete. Maybe it was Abi Johnston. Eva hates herself for thinking it, but part of her would be glad if it did turn out to be her. It would be easier. A girl who grew up around violence—it would make sense to people. Then they'd stop blaming Bryar and his family. And her and Lily. Then maybe this horrible witch hunt would end.

Her phone buzzes. It's a message from Kaitlin.

See you at the meeting?

Detective Mesenberg has called a town meeting at the library for tomorrow morning. *To address the community's concerns,* she'd said.

Even she must be surprised that her small-town investigation had made national headlines. But then, with Priscilla Wright involved, this was never going to be a small investigation.

She texts back, Yes. See you there.

Then she adds, Hope you're doing okay.

"Who was that?" Will asks.

"Kaitlin."

"Oh." Will looks down at his glass.

They sit in silence. Things have been awkward between them since the party.

Will takes a sip of wine and then puts down his glass. "Look, Eva. I've been thinking."

She feels her body squirm. "Okay."

"I know you're trying to be a friend to Kaitlin." She waits for him to go on.

"But . . ." He pauses. "Is it wise?"

"Wise?"

"All I'm saying is that maybe you should take a bit of distance. Maybe that's why those families are cancelling."

"Those families are cancelling because they're idiots, Will."

"Come on, Eva, you know better than that."

"Do I?"

"They're scared. When something happens to a kid, people worry—"

"They're not scared. They're self-righteous, like Priscilla. They think that by scapegoating Kaitlin and her family—and by blaming the parents and kids who went to the party—it somehow makes them superior."

"But Priscilla was right, wasn't she?"

"Excuse me?"

"She was right to warn people off."

"It was an accident, Will."

"We don't know that, not yet."

"*I* know that."

They sit in silence for a bit. Eva looks out of the kitchen window at the dark night.

"Do you?" he asks after a while.

"What's that supposed to mean?"

"Do you really know what Bryar Wright is capable of? You said it yourself—he's got issues."

"All the kids I teach have got issues; that doesn't make them capable of shooting their friends."

"But Astrid wasn't Bryar's friend, was she?"

"Come on, Will."

"Come on, *what*? I don't think you're taking this seriously enough."

"Oh, I'm taking it seriously. I just don't believe in blaming kids for getting caught up in something that was way out of their control."

"American children are different."

"Different?"

"They grow up around guns. Bryar would have seen his dad handling firearms. Priscilla understood that it was dangerous—that's why she warned everyone." He pauses. "That's why she warned us. Put yourself in her place, Eva. She's the one who brought us over here from England—who persuaded the board to hire a new professor. And then you explicitly ignored her advice—"

"No one gets to decide who I'm friends with—or who our daughter is friends with."

"That's not what I'm saying."

"Do you have any idea how hard it's been? Getting used to living here in this God-ugly bungalow, trying to make friends for me and for Lily, rebuilding my business—rebuilding our whole lives in a new place?"

"I know it's been hard, Eva. I don't take any of that for granted." His voice softens. "This has just put us in an awkward position. Maybe you could apologize to her—"

"Apologize? For what, exactly?"

"For having gone against her advice. You could tell her it was an error of judgment—because you're new here."

A ball of anger pushes up Eva's throat. Like any couple, they've had their share of arguments, but Will's never patronized her like this before.

"It wasn't an error of judgment, Will."

He takes another sip of wine and then puts down the glass and looks at her. "What was it, then?"

The anger pushes back up Eva's throat and this time she can't stop it from coming out.

"I went to the party because Kaitlin invited us. And because I wanted to support her. And because Lily and Bryar are friends." She pauses. "I went to the party because it was my idea."

He looks at her, stunned. "What?"

"I suggested Kaitlin get together a few kids before school started, so he'd feel more comfortable." She pauses. "Kaitlin got a bit carried away."

For a while, he doesn't say anything, as if waiting for his mind to recalibrate this new piece of information: that not only did his wife take their daughter to a party where his boss's daughter got shot but, if it hadn't been for his wife, there wouldn't have been a party to begin with.

He puts his head in his hands. "Christ, Eva. Do you always have to—"

"Have to what?"

He looks up. "Save the fucking world!"

She stares at him, hard. And then, as calmly as she can manage, she says, "I wasn't trying to save the world. I was trying to help a friend. There was a time, Will, when you believed that standing up for people who were having shit thrown at them for no reason was the right thing to do. What's changed?"

He shakes his head.

"What?"

"I don't want to argue with you."

"It's a bit late for that, don't you think?"

"Look, I know you don't mean any harm—"

"*Harm*?"

"Priscilla warned you. This isn't England. People have guns in their houses. And she's right: it's bloody dangerous." He tops up his wine. "And you didn't listen."

"So, it's my fault that Astrid got shot—that's what you're saying?"

"No. Of course not. I'm just saying that you've put us right in the middle of a hugely sensitive situation and we need to make sure that Priscilla feels our support. She has to know that we're on her side."

Eva looks at Will and blinks. She's always been amazed at how quickly love can seep away when you're having an argument. How the person you thought you knew—the person you loved, the person you had a child with—can suddenly look like a total stranger.

"It's not about sides."

"You're doing it again."

"Doing what?"

"Being fucking naïve. There *are* sides, Eva. And right now, you're on the wrong one."

When he's gone, Eva stands up. Her body is shaking.

She walks over to the open window and tries to swallow some air but it's so humid it makes her feel worse. She thought that the storm might have cooled things down a bit, but it's as bad than ever.

At the bottom of the drive, the brook rushes past, swollen with rainwater.

Then she looks out across town. In England, it stays light so much longer. It's barely gone nine and already, it's dark. Squares of light shine out from the houses. Across the road, Ayaan's car is missing again from in front of the Sayeds' house. At the far end of the front garden, she thinks she sees Yasmin walking through the dark maples.

Eva imagines the fault lines running through Middlebrook.

Will's right, people are taking sides.

And that's exactly why she can't stay out of things. Because if she does, those fault lines are just going to get bigger.

DAY FOUR

Wednesday, September 4

CHAPTER

27

8.30 a.m.

KAITLIN TURNS OUT of the driveway and switches on the car radio.

"And now we have a special guest on the program. Dr. Harriet Glazner, a child psychiatrist from Johns Hopkins who has spent ten years studying the psychology of child shooters. Dr. Glazner is going to give us an insight into what it takes for a child to aim a gun—and pull the trigger—on his peers . . ."

It takes Kaitlin's brain a moment to register what they're talking about. She loves the radio. She has it on all the time: when she's driving or mucking out the horses or cooking or taking a bath. The voices of the presenters feel as familiar as friends. She's always loved these special reports by Amy Sandborne: how she goes deep into the subjects. How she's uncompromising about digging down to the truth of things.

"Dr. Glazner is going to give us her professional take on what she thinks happened in Middlebrook, New Hampshire, when an eleven-year-old girl was critically injured at a children's party . . ."

Kaitlin swerves the car to the side of the road and stalls.

Lieutenant Mesenberg's words come back to her. She'd dropped by last night to take another look at the stable. *I'd recommend you stay away from the news. For some reason the story's caught national attention.*

Media speculation is getting a bit out of hand . . . she'd added. *You might find it upsetting.*

As if anything could be any more upsetting than it was already, Kaitlin wanted to say.

But now this. *This* was worse. It felt like the radio station she relied on to teach her about the world—to keep her company on those long nights when Ben was out working the border—was attacking her.

Turn it off! her brain warns her. But she can't. She has to know what they're saying because everyone will be listening—and they'll believe what they hear, just like she's always done.

"*You wrote an article for the* New York Times *in the wake of the Marjory Stoneman Douglas High School shooting: The Profile of a Shooter . . .*" Amy Sandborne goes on. "*Your research gives us an insight into the type of kid who's likely to do this . . . to turn violent—to shoot his friends?*"

"*Yes.*"

"*Could you share those findings with us now?*"

Kaitlin closes her eyes.

The *type* of kid. How many times has she clenched her fists when she'd heard those words. She doesn't care what this doctor says or how many letters she has after her name: there's no such thing as a type of kid. Kids are all different. And some of them do bad things and sometimes there are reasons for why they do those things—but you can't lump them in categories. And you can't just look at them and predict which ones are going to kill their friends.

"*It's common for a child shooter to be lonely . . . to have few, if any, friends . . . to have obsessive tendencies . . . to prefer spending time alone, inside, rather than socializing with others,*" Dr. Glazner explains.

"*It's been said that the boy whose party it was might match this description. Any thoughts?*" Amy Sandborne asks.

Kaitlin feels like she's been punched in the stomach.

"*We don't yet know who shot the girl,*" Dr. Glazner says.

"*No—but people are speculating. And it's clear that one child stands out.*"

Bile pushes up Kaitlin's throat. They can't do this. Not when millions of people are listening.

"*I understand that the boy who had access to the firearm had some social problems, yes . . .*" Amy Sandborne prompts. "*Might these kinds of problems have predisposed him to this kind of violence?*"

Kaitlin leans back in the car seat and screws her eyes shut. How dare they speculate about Bryar like this? How dare they pass judgment on him? They haven't got a clue who her son is.

Damn the party.

Damn those stupid guns that Ben keeps in the house.

Damn all of it.

"*Now, there's been a lot of discussion about the role of the parents in all this. Is there a particular parent profile we should be looking for when trying to identify potential shooters?*"

Kaitlin's stomach clenches.

"*Well, the children are often troubled. They might be on the spectrum. Have learning difficulties or difficulties adapting socially. It's hard to parent kids like that. Many parents will fall into the pattern of ignoring what's going on.*" She pauses. "*Oftentimes, in the aftermath of a shooting, the parents of the shooter will say that they hadn't spotted the signs, that they didn't think in a million years that their child would be capable of something like this.*"

Kaitlin snaps off the radio.

She winds down the window to get some air. Then she looks down the road to the town. She doesn't know if she can face it: walking into a room full of people she knows, people who will be judging her and her family—her son—for what happened. Maybe she should turn around and go home and lock the door behind her.

But then she hears the sound of a car engine. She glances in the rearview mirror. It's Priscilla's white Audi—the only car like it in town. And it's pulling up so close that she can see Priscilla sitting in the passenger seat, Peter driving.

Kaitlin scoots down in her seat, hoping that Priscilla won't see her. But then she realizes how stupid she's being: if she recognized Priscilla's car, then Priscilla's going to recognize Kaitlin's beaten-up Jeep too.

And then it happens. Peter slows down to overtake. And Priscilla looks to the side and locks eyes with Kaitlin. Through the open window, Kaitlin hears the low hum of voices coming from the speakers in their car. They're listening to the radio; the same station as she was. She could recognize the presenter's voice from a mile away.

Kaitlin turns away. When she looks back out through the windscreen, Priscilla's car is disappearing round a bend in the road.

She leans back and closes her eyes again.

A picture of Bryar flickers behind her eyelids: Sunday afternoon, sitting next to Lily under the big maple outside their house, the yard flooded with sunshine. Bryar's looking up at the magician, smiling.

He's my son, she thinks. *I have to stand up for him.* If she stays home and hides away, they'll think Bryar's guilty.

She switches on the engine, puts the car in gear and drives toward town.

CHAPTER

28

9 a.m.

IN FRONT OF the library, a two-story white clapboard that sits at the crossroads leading out of town, the street is lined with news vans and trucks. Eva recognizes the logos: Fox News. CNN. ABC News. NPR.

A couple of articles in *the Boston Chronicle* and all the news networks jump on the bandwagon.

She notices Phoenix sitting on the low branch of an oak tree in the cemetery. He's got his back turned to her, but she can see what he's doing: raising his hand in the air, curling his fingers into the shape of a pistol, pretending to shoot at the sky. Is he doing it on purpose? To rile up the reporters?

She had taught a kid like him in London. Wild. Tough. Walked to his own beat. Liked to attract negative attention—to make people think the worst of him just for the hell of it.

Well, whatever he's trying to do, it works: a reporter takes a picture of him with one of those long, telescopic lenses.

Eva's throat goes dry.

She wishes she could run over and tell Phoenix to get down off the tree and go back to his cabin and stay there. She wishes she could gather up the children and protect them from this.

Lieutenant Mesenberg said that she wanted to call the meeting to calm rumors following an unexpected level of press interest. She said it would be helpful for her and her team to offer a few clarifying comments to calm everyone down. Only, right now, it feels like this meeting—getting the whole town together, and these reporters—has done nothing but stir things up more.

People pour through the doors to the library where the meeting is taking place. Reporters. TV crew. Locals. A few faces Eva recognizes from the town and many others she doesn't. An open meeting like this was bound to attract a crowd.

Eva checks her watch. Kaitlin should be here by now; the last thing she needs is to draw attention to herself by rushing in late.

The Sayeds walk past her and then stand awkwardly in one of the far aisles, looking for a place to sit.

When Eva asked Lily how the twins were doing at school, she said that they weren't in their class, which was strange. Eva had wanted to reach out to Yasmin, to ask her how she was doing. Maybe she could catch her after the meeting.

At the front of the room, behind a row of microphones, sit a line of men and women in suits and police uniforms. Lieutenant Mesenberg is standing up, overseeing it all.

Priscilla and Peter are sitting in the front row. There are a few seats with reserved signs beside them. Priscilla's wearing a baggy sweatshirt and leggings. Her hair is greasy and tied back. Eva thought that she'd make an effort for the meeting: that she'd be holding her head up high, wanting the world to see her as the successful law professor, determined to find someone to blame for what happened.

Although they're sitting next to each other, Priscilla and Peter aren't talking or even looking at each other.

Eva thinks about the row she had last night with Will. The coldness between them this morning. She's seen couples break apart over less than what they were going through right now. She couldn't bear it if she and Will ended up like the Carvers.

"Eva!"

Kaitlin rushes in, her cheeks flushed, and gives Eva a hug.

"Thank goodness you're here," Kaitlin says. Her eyes are puffy: it's obvious she's been crying.

Late last night, Kaitlin had called Eva. She'd told her that Ben wasn't coming to the meeting. Apparently, Lieutenant Mesenberg advised against it, saying *It would be too inflammatory*. What she'd meant, of course, was that it wasn't a good idea to put Ben in the same room as Priscilla.

Over Kaitlin's shoulder, Eva sees Priscilla turn around in her chair. She scans the room and then her gaze falls on Eva. They lock eyes.

Eva wishes she could tell Priscilla that this isn't what it looks like. That she isn't taking sides, she's just trying to be there for the people who need her. That she wants to be there for her too.

Priscilla turns back round.

Eva kneads a knot at the base of her neck.

Lieutenant Mesenberg picks up a microphone and taps it to check that it's working. An electronic whine sweeps over the room and everyone falls silent.

Eva and Kaitlin find a seat a few rows behind Peter and Priscilla.

Detective Mesenberg starts speaking. Eva lowers her head. Out of the corner of her eye, she sees Priscilla at tapping her phone and then looking back across the room at the door, like she's waiting for someone.

Over the next half-hour, various detectives make statements. The reporters ask questions. A few members of the public do too.

Why is it taking you so long to find out what happened?

Where's the gun?

Have the Carvers brought charges against the Wrights?

Is Astrid Carver going to make it?

Has Ben Wright been charged?

Could you confirm the severity of Wynn Bowen's injury?

Is it true that the children were left unsupervised?

Has the President responded to the request for tighter gun control?

The President? Christ. The last thing this community needs is for him to weigh in, thinks Eva. And aren't there shootings that take place all over America, every day? Why would this one be on his radar?

The questions keep coming:

Is it true that the Wrights gave their son access to a firearm?

Could you confirm reports that the adults were consuming alcohol on the afternoon of the shooting?

Is it true that Bryar Wright has been undergoing psychological treatment?

She hears Kaitlin sucking in her breath.

Eva thinks about the tabloids back home in the UK. How they target people. How they have no qualms about printing half-truths or untruths for the sake of a good story. She supposes it's the same the world over.

She reaches out and puts her hand over Kaitlin's.

Eva looks at the back of Priscilla's head as she feels Kaitlin sinking into herself. Priscilla's head is bowed, her hands folded in her lap. Then Eva hears the screech of a chair behind her. Everyone turns around.

True's standing up in the middle of the room. "Pointing the finger isn't going to do anyone any good," he says.

Eva notices Skye sitting beside True, Wynn on her lap, his cast covered in words and pictures.

Usually, True is a picture of health. But not today. Today, he looks tired. Eva would be surprised if any of the parents who were at the party on Sunday have been sleeping.

On True's other side, Phoenix sits cross-legged on his chair. He's ripping one of the information flyers from the police into little pieces.

They're the only three children in the room; the others are at school.

Then Eva looks back over at Priscilla. Her eyes are dark and wide and angry. She notices that Peter is holding her hand now, but not out of support. He's pinning her down.

"This was an accident," True goes on. He has a deep, deliberate voice. "A terrible accident. And we need time, as a community, to heal." He pauses. "This isn't a show. All of you . . ."—he sweeps

his hand across the reporters at the back of the hall and then to the police and officials sitting on stage—" . . . should go home and leave us alone."

Then he sits down.

The room falls quiet.

Lieutenant Mesenberg clears her throat. "The purpose of this meeting is to keep the public informed about the investigation. We're aware that it's a highly sensitive case, especially in a small community such as this. No one is blaming anyone, sir."

Priscilla pulls free from Peter's grip and stands up.

"I am!"

It hits Eva again: what a state Priscilla's in. The greasy limpness of her hair. The bitten-down nails on the hands she's holding out in accusation. Her bloodshot eyes.

"My eleven-year-old daughter was shot." Priscilla voice trembles. "And now she's in a coma. And it wasn't an accident." She gulps. "Someone's to blame."

Behind her, Eva notices the Sayeds. Yasmin's eyes are wide with fear.

If anyone is innocent in all this, it's the twins. They're too well behaved and kept too strictly in line by their dad to have gone anywhere near that gun. But Eva knows that Priscilla doesn't care about that: she's going after everyone who was at the party on Sunday afternoon. In her eyes, simply being there makes them guilty.

"Someone shot my daughter," Priscilla goes on. "And I'm going to find out who it was and make sure they pay for it." She looks around the library, as though if she looks hard enough, she'll work out who's responsible for hurting her child.

Peter tries to pull Priscilla back into her seat, but she shakes him off.

She keeps staring out at the room.

And then her face crumples. She lifts her head. "And it's not only the shooter who's to blame. Every one of you who thinks it's okay to have guns in your home is guilty. Every one of you who thinks you have a God-given right to own guns. You're the ones who put my daughter in danger. Who put *all* our kids in danger."

She wipes her eyes on the sleeve of her sweatshirt and then runs down the aisle between the chairs and out through the back doors. They bang shut behind her.

Everyone's talking now. Whispering and asking questions and looking around, including the officials on stage.

Slowly, Eva stands up.

Kaitlin looks up at her. "What are you doing?"

"I'm going to go after her."

"After Priscilla?"

"Maybe I can talk to her—help her see that being angry at everyone like this isn't going help Astrid."

And she shouldn't be alone right now, Eva thinks. Not with all that grief and anger. Maybe they're not natural friends; and maybe Priscilla's wrong, lashing out against everyone like this, but she's still hurting more than any of them will ever understand.

"Okay."

Eva wants to be here for Kaitlin but, right now, she feels that Priscilla needs her more.

"I'll call you," Eva says.

Kaitlin nods but she's not looking at Eva any more. Her eyes are far away. Something inside her is giving up.

"We're going to get through this, Kaitlin. I promise."

Eva doesn't know what she's promising or whether she even has the right to promise anything when she doesn't know how this is going to turn out, but she has to get to Priscilla.

She runs down the aisle. But as she gets to the back doors, they swing open and a moment later, reporters are pushing past her, cameras flashing, and then a woman walks in: a bright blue suit; a short blonde bob, hairspray-stiff; red lips; charcoal eyes. She recognises her from somewhere. She feels the familiarity that comes from staring into the face of a stranger over and over. It clicks into place.

The New Hampshire governor is surrounded by men and women in sutis with badges bearing her name.

Whispers ripple through the library.

Lieutenant Mesenberg comes to the front of the stage. "Governor Warnes," she says. "We weren't expecting you—"

The governor strides down the aisle, walks up the steps to the stage, picks up one of the microphones and looks out across the crowd. She pauses to smile and then she says, "I've come to express my deep, deep sympathy for what happened to your community on Sunday afternoon." She holds her right hand to her heart. "I would like to thank Dr. Carver for inviting me to this local gathering. It's clear that Middlebrook is a very special community." She takes the time to scan the faces sitting in front of her. "I would also like to take this opportunity to announce that, as your governor—and as a candidate for the US Senate—I will make gun control a cornerstone of my campaign." She leans into the microphone. "That's a promise."

Eva stands at the doors, stunned. And then, something catches the periphery of her vision. Priscilla, looking back through the open doors of the library, past Eva, past the reporters and the people gathered in the library, to the governor, the woman leaning into the microphone, the one person in this room who she knows is on her side. The woman she invited to the town meeting.

Eva was wrong. Priscilla doesn't need her. And she isn't alone. Not even close.

CHAPTER

29

11 p.m.

YASMIN GETS INTO the driver's seat of Ayaan's black Suburban, his work truck that's always full of tools and samples and architectural drawings. That and his prayer mat. Designing buildings and his devotion to Allah: the two things that drive his life.

She asked him once if she could drive his car.

He'd laughed at her. *Stick to the Subaru,* he'd said. *It's more manageable.*

But Yasmin didn't want manageable. She wanted to feel the weight and the size of the car. The power of the engine. The space around her. She loved the height of the seats: how it made her feel taller and stronger, like she was floating above the world rather than being swallowed up by it.

This was America, she thought. A country that invited you to fill up its vast spaces.

She looks out through the windscreen at the house.

Ayaan came in late again, threw his clothes on the floor and collapsed on the bed. She'd put the comforter over him and tried to cup her body into his, hoping he'd put his arms around her. But his body was too limp with sleep to respond to her. He hasn't touched her in days; he's barely looked at her. She can feel it: that he's punishing her for taking the twins to the party. The information meeting at the library had made him even more angry.

She switches on the ignition. The truck roars to life; the sound sends a thrill through her body.

It's the same feeling she got when she heard the engines of the plane that took her to New York when she was seventeen. As the plane climbed into the sky, her old world fell away: Lahore, her parents, the endless overlapping circles of relatives who filled her house and the mosque.

It wasn't that she didn't love her family, or her life in Pakistan. She just kept thinking that there must be another place or another life—somewhere that didn't expect her to stay small and quiet; and there must be someone else inside her too, someone strong and brave and free. Someone who could do and be anything.

She'd glimpsed that person, briefly, at Columbia. But then, when she went home and married Ayaan, she fell into the same old patterns: the shy, obedient daughter, the compliant wife. The person who'd do anything to avoid conflict. And the person she was, when she was in New York, disappeared.

As she sits behind the steering wheel, she pictures herself driving through town and then turning out onto the highway—she imagines keeping going; driving long enough until all this begins to fall away. The life she had with Ayaan and the twins. Her routines. The patterns of faith that Ayaan kept so strictly—if anything, more strictly since moving to America.

She looks at the clock on the dashboard: 11.02 p.m. She knows she won't be able to sleep, so there's no point going back into the house.

She reverses the car out of the driveway.

As she pulls out, she looks across at the Days' bungalow. They don't have drapes on the windows, so you can see right in. Eva is leaning over the sink, and Yasmin longs to reach out to her, to let her know that she doesn't blame her for encouraging her to go to the party; that it was her own decision. And she's sorry for not being braver. For not being a better friend.

Eva raises her head and Yasmin thinks that maybe she sees her but then she turns away from the window and the kitchen light goes off.

As Yasmin drives down Main Street, she notices how yard signs with WARNES FOR US SENATE have sprung up all over town.

The governor had never paid much attention to Middlebrook, not until today when she marched through the library, climbed onto the stage, grabbed the microphone and made this town her cause.

Ayaan doesn't like her—says she's too loud and too opinionated. But he needs women like her to support his mosque. Priscilla had advised Ayaan to reach out to Governor Warnes when they were fundraising, and she'd been right, of course—she'd mentioned the mosque in a number of her speeches, got it some positive attention. And so, regardless of his personal views, Ayaan had invited her to cut the ribbon at the opening on Sunday.

What if she finds out that we're involved in this? Ayaan had whispered as they listened to Wendy Warnes talking about her newly found passion for gun control.

Yasmin hadn't bothered to reply. He didn't want to hear what she thought: that there were more important things at stake than what Governor Warnes—or anyone, for that matter—thought about them.

I'll explain it to her, he'd said, answering himself. *I'll tell her that the twins had nothing to do with this.*

A few times, over the past few days, Yasmin has walked into the twins' bedroom and found them whispering. As soon as they notice her, they go quiet. When she suggested to Ayaan that maybe they should sit them down and talk to them about what happened on Sunday, he told her to leave it alone.

She thinks back to the program on the radio this morning. How that psychiatrist had said that parents didn't ever truly know their children. How parents are in denial about what their kids are capable of.

Yasmin keeps driving. Past the closed storefronts. The library. And then the church. A boy sits on one of the branches of the old oak tree in the cemetery; he swings his legs against the night sky.

She slows the car to get a better look, but the boy jumps down and disappears through the trees.

The rain starts up again. Thick, heavy drops. If it doesn't ease up, the stream that runs through town will burst its banks.

She drives past the old house that's been for sale for over a year now. And then past Brook Middle School. The twins looked miserable when they came home this afternoon. She wishes she'd put her foot down about them staying in the same class as their friends.

The rain falls harder. She increases the speed on the windscreen wipers.

She keeps driving up the steep incline of the valley toward Woodwind Stables and, suddenly, a shadow darts across the road in front of the car.

She slams on the brakes. The car skids off the road. Yasmin's heart thuds.

A deer ducks into the undergrowth, its white tail lit up by her headlights.

A second later, two fawns skitter after their mother.

Yasmin releases her breath.

She sits there for a while, letting the adrenaline drain out of her body. She could have killed the deer—the mother. Or its baby. Ayaan's right: she's not able to manage a car as big as this.

There's a knock on the passenger seat window. She jumps.

Ben Wright looks in through the glass. Rain drips off his baseball cap.

She opens the window.

"You okay?" he asks.

She glances in the rearview mirror and sees Ben's red truck, parked a little way off on the road behind her.

"Yasmin? Are you okay?" he says again.

She nods, blood still rushing in her ears.

And then she finds her voice. "Why don't you come in out of the rain?"

She's not sure where the invitation comes from. Except that she likes how he makes her feel—and that, right now, she wants him next to her.

He looks at the empty passenger seat beside her. "Sure."

He runs around to the other side of the car and jumps in. His warm breath steams up the window. He's drenched.

They both look out through the windscreen at the night sky, at the rain.

"It's a shock, isn't it?" he says.

She looks at him. His face is soft and concerned.

"How the deer just comes out of nowhere," he adds.

She nods and looks over at the clearing through which the deer and her fawns disappeared.

"It was my fault. I wasn't paying attention," she says.

That's what Ayaan would have said. Sometimes his voice in her head is louder than her own.

"You can pay all the attention you want, and they'll still run out in front of you without any warning," he says.

He's kind, she thinks. He finds excuses for people's shortcomings.

"They're a pain in the backside but they sure are beautiful," he says.

"Yes," she says. "They are."

She knows that Ben and True go hunting together. And yet he seems to have a love for these creatures. Is it possible, she wonders, to love something and then to destroy it?

"I've noticed them in this area for the past few weeks," he goes on. "I wish they'd stop crossing the road—that they'd learn it's not safe."

She looks into Ben's kind, open face. His strong jaw. His big smile. His neat, brown hair with its old-fashioned side parting. An all-American guy, that's what she'd thought the first time she met him. The kind of American guy she remembers from the movies she watched back home in Lahore. The kind of guys she saw all around her at Columbia. She'd dated one of them for a while, before she met Ayaan: Tom Adams. He was on the football team.

"You're out late," Ben says.

"I couldn't sleep." She feels a rush of embarrassment about her clothes: pyjama pants and an old sweatshirt. No one in town has ever seen her in anything other than her salwar kameez.

Ben tilts his head to one side and gives her a smile. "I do that too," he says. "Take drives when I can't sleep. It helps clear my head."

She likes how normal he makes her feel, as if maybe she's one of them after all.

And there's a gentleness to him. An easiness. He accepts people the way they are. She supposes that's why he and Ayaan have never really hit it off.

She's seen how Ben is with Kaitlin. How he holds her hand, like they've only just started dating. How they go on walks together around Middlebrook Pond. She's seen him at the grocery store, taking time to talk to the older people who live in town. How he'll stop and bend over to pet a dog or squat down to talk to a child.

How he'll stop and make sure that someone's okay when they've been startled by a deer shooting across the road.

Neglectful homicide, wasn't that the charge everyone was throwing around? But they're wrong: there's nothing the least bit neglectful about Ben Wright.

At times like this she almost wishes that she did believe in Allah—or any god—then she could at least pray to someone to make things right again.

I'm sorry, she wants to tell him. *I'm so, so sorry for what you're going through.*

"Well, I'm glad you're okay," he says.

"Thank you."

The way he looks at her, the warmth and kindness in his brown eyes, makes something come loose in her chest. Her eyes well up.

He moves closer to her and puts a hand on her arm. She can feel the warmth coming off his skin.

"You okay to get home?" he asks.

She sniffs. "Yes. Of course. I'm sorry."

"You say that a lot," he says gently.

She looks at him, confused.

"That you're sorry," he explains.

"Oh—I'm sorry—"

He laughs. She laughs too.

"That's better," he says.

"You're kind," she says, her tears thickening again.

And then she forgets herself. She leans forward and collapses into his chest, the gearstick and the handbrake sitting awkwardly between them.

"Oh . . ." he says. Then he puts his arms around her and pats her shoulder blades gently.

She feels his flannel shirt under her cheek and breathes in. He smells of woodchips and hay and engine oil. She hears his heart, beating under his ribcage.

She looks up at him and when he looks at her, she leans in and kisses him.

He jerks his head away. His baseball cap falls onto his lap, nudged out of place by her kiss. He picks it up, pulls it back on his head and reaches for the door handle.

"I'm sorry!" She flushes. "I'm so sorry. You were just being so kind. I didn't mean to do that—"

He looks at her, confused.

"Please forgive me—I forgot myself," she says.

"It's okay, Yasmin."

"No, it's not okay. You're married—I'm married. I got carried away. You were so kind. I didn't mean anything by it. Really, I'm sorry."

"I know you didn't mean any harm. It's okay, really it is."

Her throat goes tight. She wishes he would hold her again. Because even now, when she'd done something so wrong, he doesn't blame her.

He pushes open the car door. "I'd better be getting back."

"Of course."

"See you around, then." He steps into the rain.

"Thank you. For stopping," she says.

He touches the brim of his baseball cap. Then he walks back to his truck and drives off.

When he's gone, Yasmin opens the window and, for a few minutes, she sits there, on the side of the dark, quiet road, the pines bowing overhead, and breathes in the night.

She should drive straight home. It's late. Ayaan might wake up and worry, not seeing her in bed beside him.

But she can't, not yet.

She needs to pull herself together.

And she needs to find a way to appease her guilt at having felt more at home in Ben Wright's arms than in her husband's.

So she drives out of town and along the interstate to the junction that leads to the mosque.

She hasn't been up to the construction site in ages. Ayaan keeps telling her she should come and see the progress they've made. He's so proud of it. He wants her to be proud of it too: this amazing building he's created.

But she kept finding excuses not to come.

Because she can't bear it. The sick feeling that settles in her stomach whenever she thinks of the mosque—and about how she's been lying to Ayaan this whole time.

About sharing his vision for the mosque. About sharing his faith.

She steps out of the car and looks at the pool through the glass doors and then up at the minaret: the part of the mosque everyone's been talking about. Behind it, the moon shines, full and white.

Whatever she believes, Ayaan has created something beautiful. And he's right: she should be proud of him.

When she goes back home, she'll tell him that she drove out here to see the work he's done. Maybe it will help things between them. Maybe it will make him less angry at her for taking the twins to the party at the Carvers'.

She walks closer to the mosque, her eyes adjusting to the moonlight.

At first, she doesn't see it. She sees the scaffolding on the walls. Cranes and trucks that are perched around holes in the ground. Piles of bricks and timber. Big drums of concrete.

But then they leap toward her. The fresh paint sprayed across one of the white marble walls. Thick, jagged letters.

It must have happened tonight; maybe she's only just missed them.

The world around her spins. She tries to read the words again but they swim in front of her.

She rubs her eyes until they hurt and then looks again.

But the words are still there, sprayed over the glass doors, the dark pool shining behind the jagged letters:

TERRORISTS GO HOME.

DAY FIVE

Thursday, September 5

CHAPTER

30

4.30 a.m.

PRISCILLA RUBS HER eyes and glances up at the clock.

She curses herself for having fallen asleep.

Astrid is so pale she disappears into the white hospital sheets. Now that her sunburn has faded, there's no color left in her skin at all. Priscilla takes her little girl's hand and holds it to her cheek.

"I'll never leave you alone again." Her eyes swim with tears. "You're going to get sick of the sight of me, Astrid."

There's a flicker behind Astrid's eyelids; Priscilla wills herself to believe that she can hear her.

"If you wake up, things will be different," she whispers. "I promise."

Priscilla wonders how many people have done this in ICUs: prayed, not to God, but to their sick children, begging them—bargaining with them—to get better, as though they were just lying there, waiting for their parents to say the magic words, and they'd wake up.

"And I'm going to make damn sure that whoever's responsible for this doesn't get away with it."

She hadn't been certain that Wendy Warnes would show up at the meeting. Sure, they'd both been to Yale Law, but they'd been a year apart—nowhere close enough to consider each other friends. She'd be surprised if Wendy even remembered her. But Wendy must have seen the press coverage and worked out that getting involved on a local level could help her campaign. Priscilla didn't care what Wendy's motivation was, as long as she made some noise and got Lieutenant Mesenberg and her team to sit up and start taking this case seriously.

Priscilla strokes Astrid's pale arm. "What happened to you isn't going to get swept under the carpet, Astrid, I promise."

People shouldn't have firearms in their homes. Period. Priscilla was going to get that message out into the world once and for all. And this time, people would listen.

She stands up, stretches and walks around the room. "God, I'm sorry it's so horrible in here, Astrid."

Everything is beige and gray. The only splash of color is the peeling decal of a giraffe on the wall next the bed.

Priscilla had thought that maybe someone would send flowers. A card. A balloon. A note from a friend or a teacher from her old school.

But nothing came.

She'd failed to see how lonely Astrid was. Failed to listen to her when she said she had no friends. Failed to acknowledge how much their lives had shrunk since Peter left.

Maybe she should have let her go to the party. Maybe then Astrid wouldn't have felt the need to sneak away without telling her. She and Priscilla could have gone together. And Priscilla could have kept her safe.

A headache pulls across Priscilla's forehead.

No. Whatever the circumstances, Astrid should never have been on the Wrights' property. No child should have been there that day. It wasn't safe. And if those other parents had only listened to her advice, no one would have gotten hurt.

Priscilla walks over to the window that looks out onto the parking lot of the hospital: only a tiny strip of gray sky is visible. It's started raining again.

She feels the hospital room pressing in around her.

I have to do something, she tells herself.

She goes back over to the bed and kisses Astrid's forehead. "I'll be back soon."

She gathers up her handbag and her raincoat and heads out into the hallway of the ICU.

Thirty minutes later, she's standing at the checkout in the 24-hour Walmart, a trolley full of balloons and cards and flowers.

"You're up early," says the checkout assistant. She has a peace tattoo on her forearm. "Planning a party?" she asks, scanning through the items.

"Sort of. It's for my daughter."

"She's lucky," the woman says. "You're a good mom."

Priscilla's heart pulls under her ribs. She gathers up the plastic bags, dumps them in the trolley and steers toward the exit.

"Hope the party goes well!" the woman calls after her.

By 6.30 a.m., Priscilla is back at the hospital. She pushes through the doors of the ICU, dripping from the rain, plastic bags digging into her palms.

When she gets to Astrid's room, Peter's there, sitting on the chair she spent the night on. He's staring at his phone, his brow furrowed.

He looks up. "Hey—where have you been?"

"Just out."

He glances down at the phone again. "There's been some vandalism at the mosque." He shakes his head. "It's awful."

Priscilla holds up her palm. "Not now, Peter."

She doesn't have the headspace for any news.

He switches his phone to silent and puts it in his pocket. Then he stands up and walks toward her. "You're soaked. What are you doing with all those bags?"

She feels foolish again. How could she think this would make a difference?

"I couldn't bear it any longer," she says. "This terrible room. I didn't want Astrid to wake up to this." Her eyes scan the beige walls. "I didn't want her to think that no one cares about her."

Peter takes another step toward her. She waits for him to tell her she's crazy. Or to make fun of her. But instead, he takes the bags out of her hands and puts them down on the floor. Then he eases off her dripping raincoat and hangs it over the chair. And after that, he comes toward her again and puts his arms around her and draws her in close.

He feels dry and clean and warm. He feels familiar, more familiar than anything else in her life right now. And, in those few moments, she lets her body collapse into his.

www.GoodMorningBoston.com
THE PLAYDATE SHOOTING: AN ACCIDENT OR AN ACT OF TERRORISM?
Special report by Ellen Armstrong

Graffiti on a new local mosque: a shocking act of vandalism or an insight into the background of the Middlebrook playdate shooting?

Up until the playdate shooting on Sunday afternoon, the most interesting thing about Middlebrook, NH, a small town near the Canadian border, was the fact that it was about to become the home of a new mosque.

The building of the mosque has been uncontroversial which is surprising, considering the conservative nature of Northern New Hampshire. Locals have largely supported the project, guided by their minister, Reverend Avery Cotton, who has been vocal in proclaiming it as a place that will bring different faiths together. Only a month ago, she told one of our religious affairs reporters that "the mosque will be a symbol of tolerance, respect and neighborly understanding."

The mosque was designed by talented Columbia-educated architect from Lahore, Ayaan Sayeed, whose family lives in Middlebrook and whose children attend the local school. It seems that they, too, have until now been largely welcomed into the community.

But then, on the afternoon of September 1, the eleven-year-old daughter of a local law professor was shot by a group of children playing in a stable. Among those children were the Sayed twins.

At first, it was suspected that the shooter was Bryar Wright, whose party it was. He had access to his father's gun safe and ammunition and it is widely known that there is animosity between his and the victim's family. Evidence has also pointed to the involvement of a couple of foster children with a violent past, who moved from Roxbury to Middlebrook at the beginning of the summer. The girl, in particular, looked to be a likely suspect.

Although those children are not off the hook, attention has now turned to the mild-mannered Muslim twins.

The graffiti reveals a greater antipathy toward the building of the mosque than Middlebrook led us to believe. Antipathy that the Sayeds—and the Sayed twins—may well have become aware of.

"They live in that big showy house on Main Street," the resident added. "They don't fit in here."

Not fitting in isn't a crime, you might argue.

But still. The shooting on Sunday. The graffiti discovered by police in the early hours of this morning. All of this points to a worrying unrest in the Middlebrook community, and might make us take a second look at what the motives were for the shooting—and who the shooter might have been.

CHAPTER 31

7 a.m.

FROM THE SECOND Mom comes into their room, Hanif and Laila know that something's up.

She's wearing sweatpants and a baggy sweatshirt; her hair is tied up in a messy bun at the back of her head and without make-up on her face looks like it's fading away.

And when they ask if they can wear jeans and sneakers to school, like the other middle schoolers, she doesn't fight them.

And when they get downstairs, she hands each of them a granola bar, saying there isn't time for breakfast. Mom always goes on about them having a proper breakfast to start their day right.

And she gives them lunch money instead of their lunchboxes. Then she ushers them outside. "Your dad will be here in a minute."

"*Dad's* taking us to school?" Laila asks.

"No," she says. "You're not going to school this morning."

The twins' eyes go wide. "We're not going to *school*?" She doesn't answer.

Dad swerves into the driveway.

The twins stare at him through the windscreen. His hair's sticking up, like on the days when he hasn't had time to shower before heading out to the site. His mouth's set in a tight, thin line.

Hanif and Laila inch closer to Mom.

"Is this because of what happened on Sunday?" Laila asks.

Before she has the time to answer, Dad's pulled up beside them. He winds down the window and says, "Get in, quick."

Mom goes to stand by Dad's window. "Are you sure this is a good idea, Ayaan?"

She whispers it, but they hear her anyway.

He turns on the ignition without answering. Mom steps back from the car.

"Buckle up," he calls over his shoulder and pulls the car out onto Main Street, leaving Mom standing alone in the middle of the driveway.

As they drive through Middlebrook, the twins see them—the children who were there on Sunday afternoon, like they were.

Across the road from their house, the twins watch as Lily puts on her helmet and her backpack and climbs onto her bicycle. She's probably going to Bryar's house so they can ride to school together, they think. She's always with him.

A little further along, Skye and Wynn sit on the bank of the stream. Skye's writing long sentences on Wynn's cast. Phoenix is sitting on a tree, above them, throwing stones into the water. They notice a line of reporters sitting on fold-up chairs in the grass, looking down at their phones. Others are walking around, taking pictures. A woman takes a picture of their car as it drives past.

Hanif's breath sticks in his throat. It feels like everyone's waiting to catch them out.

Laila squeezes his hand.

She's told him over and over that it's going to be okay, that no one's going to find out what happened. But he knows that she's scared too.

He keeps looking out through the car window.

On the doorstep of Reverend Avery's house, the man with the bald head and the black beard who brought Abi and Cal to live here at the beginning of the summer knocks on the door.

Outside the library, reporters set up their equipment on the grass.

More yard signs have popped up along Main Street: WARNES FOR US SENATE.

At the crossroads at the end of town sits a police car, its lights flashing blue.

Laila squeezes Hanif's hand tighter.

At the top of the hill, not far from Astrid's house, Dad takes a left and that's when the twins know where they're going.

Maybe he wants to show them the progress he's made on the mosque, they think. He's always saying how proud he wants them to be of it. That a bit of Lahore—and of their faith—is on American soil.

"Did you fix the crack in the minaret?" Laila asks.

Dad doesn't answer.

And then his phone goes off.

"Hey, Ayaan."

A man's voice comes through the car speakers—it's Jimmy, the attorney Dad got for them so they don't have to talk to the police about what happened at the party. He came to speak to them on Monday afternoon and when they told him that they didn't know what happened, he said, *Good, stick to that story. The less we give them, the better.*

Which had seemed like a strange thing to say. But the twins were glad they didn't have to speak to the police again. And they were glad they'd kept their promise to the other kids. It was better not to say anything. The grown-ups wouldn't understand.

"Did you see what they did?" Dad asks.

"Yeah."

"I want this kept out of the papers."

"I think it's too late for that. I saw some reporters taking pictures when I drove past. And there's an article online already."

Dad thumps the steering wheel. "I want to issue a statement, then," he says. "A direct response from me."

"I'm not sure that's wise—it might come across as defensive—"

"Defensive?" Dad laughs. "Of course I'm defensive. My family's being attacked. The mosque's being attacked. People here know me, Jimmy. It's a small community. They trust me. They'll want to hear something directly from me."

Jimmy goes quiet for a bit. Then he says, "Look, Ayaan, the graffiti was probably just some kid messing around. It might not be related to the shooting."

The twins exchange a glance.

"Oh, it's related," Dad says.

"Okay. But people do this kind of stuff all the time. We're seeing it throughout New Hampshire. You've been lucky up to now. Building a mosque was bound to attract some negative attention."

"Just get on top of it," Dad says. "We open on Sunday. I need this to go away."

And then, before Jimmy gets to say anything else, Dad ends the call.

The twins try to work out what Jimmy meant about the mosque being related to the shooting. And what he meant about their family and the mosque being attacked. None of this is making any sense.

Dad pulls into the parking lot of the construction site.

And that's when they see what Dad meant. Someone's spray-painted big red, yellow and black words across one of the marble walls.

They wait for Dad to say something—to explain—but, like them, he keeps staring at the graffiti.

Hanif squeezes Laila's hand, prompting her to speak. Dad takes things better from her. Whenever Hanif tries to speak, it irritates his dad.

"What does it mean, Dad?" Laila asks, her voice small.

"It means what it says," Dad says. "They think we're terrorists."

The twins learned about terrorists in fifth grade: that they were people who did bad things to make others feel scared. Really bad things.

"Who thinks we're terrorists?" Laila asks.

"The people who wrote it. And probably other people too," Dad says.

"But why would anyone write that about *us*?" Laila asks.

Hanif shoots Laila a glance, like she's meant to understand. And then she gets the sinking feeling that comes over her every time she thinks about the party and what happened at the stable.

"Because they blame us," Dad says. "As a family. For Astrid getting shot."

The twins look down at the yellow sand of the construction site. They wish it would swallow them up.

"What do they mean by *go home*?" Laila asks.

"Pakistan," Dad says.

"But Pakistan's not our home," Hanif says. "Not any more. We live here, now. In Middlebrook." His voice goes shaky.

It had taken them a while to adjust. The cold in winters. The bland food. The way people stare at them, sometimes, just because their skin is darker than theirs. But they like it here, now. They have friends.

"We're Muslims," Dad says, his voice hard and impatient. "And that makes us different."

Laila presses Hanif's hand. They should stick to her doing the talking.

"Who do you think did it?" Laila asks Dad.

Dad shrugs. "It doesn't really matter."

"But won't they get in trouble? When you tell the police?" Laila asks.

Dad turns around in his seat and looks from one twin to the other. "There's only one way we can put an end to this," he says.

The twins' hearts speed up.

"You're going to come with me—to the hospital," Dad says.

"To the hospital?" the twins say at the same time.

"Yes. We're going to see Dr. Carver."

"How will talking to Dr. Carver help?" Laila starts.

"Dr. Carver is our friend—and we offended her. And she's the only one who can make this go away."

"But didn't Jimmy say—" Laila goes on.

"Screw Jimmy," Dad says.

The twins suck in their breath. Dad never curses. Not in front of them, anyway.

"But what do you want us to tell her?" Laila asks. "We've already said everything we know to the police—"

Dad keeps staring at them, hard. It feels like ages before he starts talking again. So long they hope that he might change his mind and just take them to school—or better, back home to Mom.

But then he leans in closer. "You're going to apologize for being in the stable when Astrid got hurt—"

"But—" Laila starts.

He holds up a hand. "And you're going to tell her the truth about what happened. No more keeping secrets. No more protecting your so-called friends. You're going to make it clear to her that you had nothing to do with what happened." He pauses. "And then, you're going to tell her exactly who shot her daughter."

CHAPTER

32

1 p.m.

PRISCILLA SITS AT the table, watching Peter walking around the kitchen they designed together. He makes them each a mug of tea. He'd always been more domestic than her. Better at cooking and entertaining. At making sure everyone has a drink in their hand.

Every now and then, she catches herself forgetting that he left her: that he doesn't live here any more.

"I can't believe Ayaan," she says, putting down her mug.

"Come on, Cil, let's give it a rest."

"After the support I showed him with the mosque—getting his kids to say that it was Astrid's fault—"

"Ayaan looked mortified at what the twins said. And then he couldn't leave fast enough, he was so embarrassed. Remember what he said when he brought them in? He wanted them to apologize. And he wanted them to tell you the truth about who shot Astrid, to help with the investigation—to put an end to the speculation."

"But they didn't apologize, did they? They blamed Astrid."

"They were scared—couldn't you see that? It was the only thing they could think to say. And they didn't exactly *blame* her."

"They said it was her idea to take the gun out of the safe—that it was her idea to *load* the gun—that she should never have been at the party to begin with: I'd call that blaming." She takes a breath. "The point is, Peter, they *didn't* apologize—and they *didn't* tell us who pulled the trigger. Even when their dad pushed them to tell us the truth, they just kept repeating that it was Astrid's idea. They may as well have said that she pulled the trigger on herself."

Laila, who did all the talking while her brother stood, shrunk with fear, at her side, kept focusing on the fact that everyone was playing happily until Astrid showed up. The implication being that, take Astrid out of the equation, the shooting would never have happened.

"I think that they were—that Laila was—trying to say that it was a confusing situation for all of them," Peter says. "They were frightened when the gun came out. They didn't know what to do. And then some of them got over-excited. Stood too close to each other. Started passing the gun around. It happened fast. Astrid is one of the pieces of the puzzle, that's all she was saying."

"That's all, is it?"

"Maybe the children really didn't see what happened. Maybe they're not covering anything up. These things can happen so fast. They're confused. It must have been such a shock—"

"Can you imagine how confusing—how shocking—it must have been for our daughter to have a gun pointed at her? To see someone pulling the trigger?"

"Of course, Cil—I was just saying—"

"Those children know exactly what happened, Peter. And they're deliberately twisting things to avoid getting in trouble." She tops up her glass and takes a long, slow gulp. Then she goes on, "And Astrid's never held a gun. She knows not to go near them."

Peter catches Priscilla's eye.

"And she knew not to go near the party, too," Peter says. "Yet she did."

"What's that supposed to mean?"

"It means that we can't pretend that Astrid is innocent in all this. She went to the party. And, knowing Astrid, she probably had an agenda."

Priscilla gets up, walks over to the window. She looks out across the field toward the Carvers' house and pictures Astrid running through the long sheaves of corn.

"It wasn't her fault," she says.

Peter comes over and puts his palm on her shoulder blades.

"No one's saying it was. Ayaan was just trying to do the right thing. You know how principled he is. And how he raises those children of his—they're not allowed to step a foot out of line. All this must be devastating for him, having them involved. And then how they embarrassed him today."

Yes, Priscilla knows. The perfect twins with their perfect clothes and their perfect manners who live in their perfect white mansion with their perfect mother—the perfect wife, who's managed to keep hold of her husband.

And then Ayaan: elegant, eloquent, charming Ayaan Sayed who'd persuaded a conservative Board of Selectmen to let him build a mosque in the middle of rural New Hampshire. Who'd persuaded Priscilla to join the board—to be his ally.

"You saw how they vandalized the mosque," Peter goes on. They'd watched the news report together on the TV in the family room this morning. "He must be beside himself."

"He was trying to get his kids off the hook, Peter. That's why he came to the hospital. And it backfired. Because the way they blamed Astrid—in my book, that just makes them look even more guilty."

"You really think the Sayed twins shot Astrid?"

"I think they're just as capable of having done it as any of the other kids."

Priscilla walks over to the radio she keeps on the kitchen counter and switches on to the local station.

"After the August heatwave, fall has finally arrived. Temperatures dropping to the mid-40s tomorrow. Coming up, the latest on the Playdate Shooting, which has taken an unexpected twist with the vandalism of a local mosque . . ."

Peter walks over to the radio and switches it off.

"I was listening to that."

"You're going to drive yourself crazy, listening to what those reporters are saying."

"I need to know what they're saying, Peter—because it's obvious that they're doing more investigating than the police. They might have found something out." She pauses. "And maybe the reason the Sayed twins made that stuff up at the hospital is because they do have something to hide."

"The media's not investigating, Cil, they're chasing stories. And it's getting out of hand—"

"*Out of hand?* Our daughter's in a critical condition in the local ICU, Peter—how much more out of hand can it get than that?"

"Have you seen that picture they took of Phoenix? It's everywhere."

She nods. Every time the news feed opens on her phone, there it is: a boy, his back to the camera, sitting in the high branches of a tree next to St. Mary's church. He's holding his arm up in the air, his fingers curled into the shape of a gun.

"It could be any kid, Peter. The picture's symbolic of what's going on. It's making a statement. They haven't even named him."

"Everyone in Middlebrook will know it's him."

"So what?"

"So what? He's a kid."

Facebook finally took down her *Justice for Astrid* page. They'd received complaints. Priscilla knows the rules about using pictures of kids involved in a criminal investigation. But when it's your kid who's gotten hurt, the rules change. So what if Phoenix Bowen is in the paper? Astrid is in hospital, fighting for her life: she got shot at a kids' party. The rules no longer apply.

"Poor True—" Peter says.

"*Poor True*? Seriously, Peter. He took his three children to a party where he *knew* there'd be guns."

"For goodness sake, Cil, we can't keep turning on our friends. If we pit ourselves against the rest of the community, we're just going to make things worse—"

Priscilla looks back out through the kitchen window: a streak of purple slashes the sky just above Woodwind Stables. The lights are already on in the farmhouse. How she wishes she could just blot that place out of her life.

"When people took their kids to that party, they chose their sides," she says.

For a long time, Peter doesn't say anything. Then he comes and folds his arms around her and they stand there, by the window, holding on to each other. Her body collapses into his, her limbs too tired to move. The anger seeps away and all she feels is tiredness—and sadness. At the broken promises. At how they'd failed to be there for each other, and for their daughter, when it mattered most.

"I really think a rest would help. You could get a couple of hours in before the service."

"Oh God, the service."

Avery had sent her a text last night: she was putting together a family prayer meeting after school this afternoon. *To bring the community together,* she'd said.

Priscilla hadn't replied. She couldn't face another town meeting. And anyway, what good was praying going to do? But then Wendy Warnes had called her and said that one of her aides had got wind of the prayer meeting. *It will be good for us to appear together, don't you think?* Wendy had said, with an intimacy that suggested they might have been friends in college, after all.

And then she'd reiterated her promises:

To fight Astrid's cause every step of the way.

To make gun control the heart of her campaign for US senator.

To put pressure on the investigation until they got to the bottom of who fired that pistol.

So, Priscilla had said yes. Of course she'd go.

"I'll wake you in good time," Peter says gently.

He takes her hand, pulls her up the stairs, holding her weight, guides her into their old bedroom and sits her on the edge of the bed. He takes off her shoes and pulls off her socks. Then he lies her back on the bed and eases off her jeans.

Closing her eyes, she lets her limbs sink into the bed.

She feels his fingers brushing her skin as he covers her body with a sheet.

And then, before he steps away from her, he leans over and kisses her forehead.

"Peter . . ." she calls after him.

He stops.

She blinks open her eyes and musters all the strength she has to pull her body up against the pillows.

She pats the space beside her. "Will you stay with me for a bit?"

She feels his hesitation. She shouldn't have asked him. But she doesn't want to be alone right now.

He's at the door already and when he turns away from her she's sure he's going to leave. But instead, he closes the door and walks back to the bed.

He takes off his shoes and lies down.

The weight of his body presses down on the mattress beside her. How many times, since February, has she reached over in the middle of the night, expecting him to be there, only to find empty space?

He moves toward her and as she turns onto her side, he slips his arm under her body and pulls her back against him.

He kisses her shoulder.

She'd promised herself that she'd show him that she didn't need him any more. That she'd moved on, like he had. But they both knew that would be a lie.

So she lets her body rest into his.

And it feels right. Being here with him. More right than anything has felt in a long time.

"Thank you, Peter," she whispers. "For being here. Not just for Astrid . . . but for me too."

He pulls her in closer and kisses her neck, his breath warm against her skin.

And then she closes her eyes and lets go.

Public Radio: New Hampshire FM
Close-Up

Reporter: Nature or nurture. The age-old debate. What really influences how our kids turn out? Is it how they're parented? Where they grow up? Where they go to school? Or is it just down to genes? Is there nothing we can really do to affect what kind of people our children become?

This is the question that many of us are asking in the aftermath of the Playdate Shooting which took place on Sunday afternoon in Middlebrook. Today, we take a closer look at how different modes of parenting—and schooling—determine the behavioral outcome of pre-teens. I have with me the principal of Brook Middle School, Mrs. Sophie Markham. Most of the children involved in the shooting attend Mrs. Markham's school. Good afternoon, Principal, and thank you for taking the time to talk to us.

Markham: Of course.

Reporter: I imagine you've seen the photograph—the one taken by that freelance reporter.

Markham: Yes. It's an unfortunate picture.

Reporter: For those listeners who might not be aware, the picture of a young boy who, we suspect, attended the party at which the shooting took place, has become an internet sensation. The boy in question is sitting in a tree, fingers curled into the shape of a handgun.

Markham: Children like to play-act like this. It's not unusual behavior—

Reporter: Sure. But if he was one of the kids who was at the party on Saturday, he's part of a criminal investigation: shouldn't he know better than to be messing around—to be play-acting?

Markham: I don't believe we know the identity of the boy in the picture.

Reporter: But still, a child his age would know what's going on. It seems like a strange way to behave at this time, don't you think?

Markham: Kids behave unpredictably. And they like to show off. Sometimes, they enjoy getting negative attention. I'm not sure the picture really tells us—

Reporter: Okay, okay. Let's rewind a bit. Get some back story. There's a substantial home-schooling community in New Hampshire—is that right?

Markham: Yes, but I don't see how this is relevant—

Reporter: As the principal of a middle school, home-schooling is not a practice you would advocate, am I right?

Markham: It's not the way I would go, no, but parents have a right to choose how they want to educate their children.

Reporter: Isn't it often the difficult children who end up being home-schooled? Kids who wouldn't fit in well at a normal school?

Markham: Not necessarily. There are many reasons—

Reporter: And it's not just the home-schooling, is it?

Markham: I'm not sure what you're asking.

Reporter: Some children come from difficult backgrounds. They witness violence at a young age.

Markham: Not every kid has an ideal childhood, no.

Reporter: And others are raised unconventionally. In the woods, for example . . .

Markham: Some parents have strong views on the environment: they like their children to experience nature. That's no bad thing—

Reporter: Some of these children have parents who hunt for food—parents who have rifles in their homes.

Markham: Many people in our state do, especially up here in the north country.

Reporter: Children raised in the woods without any formal schooling. Perhaps it's not surprising that one of them should go off the rails.

Markham: We have no real evidence that children raised unconventionally turn out any differently—any worse—

Reporter: But in your—what is it, twenty years of experience as an educator—you must have noticed a pattern. How children brought up outside our societal norms sometimes go awry.

Markham: And sometimes they thrive. Every child responds differently to his or her environment.

Reporter: The magician hired for the party went on record to say that one of the boys at the party was pretending to shoot a gun at his brother. Clearly there's a firearm obsession there.

Markham: Small boys often fall in love with the idea of weapons: guns, knives. Even those who aren't really exposed to them. Like I said, they like to play-act, which is an important part of a child's development.

Reporter: But role play can quickly get out of hand: from shooting a pretend gun to pulling the trigger on a real gun—

Markham: There's a world of difference. Research shows us that children are acutely aware of the difference between make-believe and real life.

Reporter: Changing tack a little then, Principal Markham. Do you have any personal views on gun laws in our state?

Markham: It's a sensitive issue.

Reporter: But you must have some thoughts of your own on the subject.

Markham: I don't believe that guns have any place in a child's life. But it's not that simple—like I said, many people hunt in New Hampshire. There are law enforcement officers who have firearms in their homes as part of their profession. Most gun owners are very responsible when it comes to gun safety.

Reporter: Do you believe that children exposed to firearms are more likely to commit gun crime—either as children or later on, as adults?

Markham: I'd have to look into the research.

Reporter: But it would be a fair assumption, right?

Markham: Perhaps.

Reporter: Would you ever allow your teachers to carry a firearm—for protection, say?

Markham: I don't see how a firearm could protect my teachers—or our students.

Reporter: So, if you could wave a magic wand, you'd do away with guns altogether, Principal Markham.
Markham: [Pause] Like I said, it's complicated.
Reporter: But in an ideal world, you'd like to see them banned.
Markham: [Another pause] In an ideal world, yes.
Reporter: I'm afraid we're just about out of time. Thank you so much for joining us. For more on the Playdate Shooting, go to our website, where you can join the discussion thread on this important subject of whether a young shooter is born or made.

CHAPTER

33

4 p.m.

NO ONE CAN quite remember whose idea it was to leave the grown-ups behind at the prayer meeting. But somehow they agreed: they didn't want to be cooped up in that church with people staring and whispering, wondering which of them shot Astrid Carver.

They won't be long, they tell themselves.

They'll be back before their parents even notice.

One by one, they follow each other.

Through the cemetery.

Under the tall pines, into the thickest part of the forest.

Along the overgrown path and then out into the clearing by the dock that, on this misty September afternoon, seems to float out across Middlebrook Pond.

Lily and Bryar are first. They run straight to the end, holding hands, and then sit down and kick off their shoes and socks.

Lily draws circles in the water with her toes. It feels cool after the rain.

Bryar puts his feet in too and soon they're both sending small stars out across the pond.

Not long after, Wynn, running awkwardly with the big purple cast on his arm, comes up behind them. Skye catches him and scoops him in her arms and holds him tight.

"Not too close to the water . . ." she whispers.

She's decided: she's never going to let him get hurt again.

Phoenix walks past them both and balances his toes over the end of the dock. He pulls some stones out of his pocket and throws them into the water: *Plop. Plop. Plop.* He likes to watch them disappear to the bottom of the dark pond.

Then he takes out another stone, a bigger one, smooth and flat, and skims it across the surface. Light splinters across the water.

A moment later, Lily notices Cal and Abi by the clearing that leads to the dock. They seem to hesitate, like they always do—scared that maybe the children will change their minds and decide they don't want them to be here.

Lily stands up and waves them over.

As they walk over, Cal tries to catch Skye's eye but she looks away. He looks down at his paint-streaked hands and wonders whether she'll ever talk to him again.

Phoenix lies down on his belly and leans over the dock. He cups his hands under the water and tries to catch the darting minnows.

The twins are the last to arrive.

Mom and Dad had said they should wait outside the church for them: that the prayer meeting was for grown-ups. And Dad warned them to stay out of trouble.

They'd nodded, knowing they had to make things up to Dad after embarrassing him at the hospital. They feel guilty for saying that it was Astrid's fault for coming to the party, but they didn't have a choice, did they? How could they ever tell Dr. Carver—or Dad—what really happened?

Anyway, they'd tried to stay out of trouble. Really, they had. But when they saw the other kids running into the woods, they knew they had to follow them.

CHAPTER

34

4.15 p.m.

WENDY WARNES LEANS in and whispers to Priscilla, "You look perfect."

"Perfect?" Priscilla looks down at her jeans, her sloppy gray sweatshirt and her dirty white sneakers.

Wendy smiles. "We can't have you looking too polished. You're a mom who's going through hell, Priscilla: if we're going to change hearts and minds, the world needs to see that."

When Priscilla woke up from her sleep, she'd pulled a gray pant suit out of her closet—out of habit, more than anything. Up until last week, she'd lived in her work clothes. But as she'd looked at herself in the long bathroom mirror, she hadn't recognized herself. That person—the one who set up the law faculty at Webster, who published influential articles on family law, the person who had some semblance of control over her life—was gone.

So she'd gotten changed again. Put on the clothes she's been wearing to the hospital.

Wendy turns to Peter and looks him up and down but doesn't say anything. Clearly Peter is *not* presenting the right image of the suffering father. But then it's hard to look like you're suffering with a California tan and sun-bleached hair.

Peter shifts uncomfortably under her gaze.

"Thank you for coming." He attempts a smile, but it doesn't reach his eyes.

Priscilla can feel it: he doesn't like Wendy. But this isn't about liking her—it's about using every resource they have to get justice for Astrid.

"Well, it will be good for people to see you together—a united front." Wendy looks from Priscilla to Peter as though her gaze were powerful enough to yoke them back together.

When Priscilla woke up, he was taking a shower. They haven't talked about what happened this afternoon. Not that anything really *happened*. But for those few hours, as they were sleeping, as they held each other, they were close again.

"I'm going to do some interviews and then I'll join you both inside," Wendy says. "My team has made sure we're sitting together."

"Oh—okay, thank you."

Priscilla's grateful for Wendy's efforts. She's putting pressure on Lieutenant Mesenberg and her team; she's making sure that Astrid's cause doesn't get forgotten. But still, it doesn't feel quite right, being swept into her campaign like this.

"Wow, she's intense," Peter says when Wendy's gone.

"She was the same at Yale," Priscilla says.

Priscilla looks back through the crowd: Wendy's aides, reporters, police cars. And then, parked on the private bit of Avery's driveway, Ben's red truck.

It shouldn't surprise her: Avery and the Wrights had always been friends. But still, she was the minister, she could at least pretend to be neutral. Only, she wasn't neutral, was she? She'd taken her foster kids to the party. And they were in the stable when Astrid got shot. Either one of those damaged kids could have pulled the trigger—Avery basically said as much in that interview for the *Boston Chronicle*.

Peter touches her elbow. "Ready to go inside?"

"Not really. I don't even know what we're doing here. As if praying is going to make a difference."

Priscilla had always respected the ritual of religion. How it gave shape and order to human life. How it brought people together, giving them a shared moral framework. That's why she'd kept taking Astrid to church, even after Peter left. But right now, it feels pointless. What kind of God lets an eleven-year-old child get shot?

"Come on, Cil, you know it's important that we're here. Avery has organized this service for Astrid—and we're her parents. We need to acknowledge people's support."

This is how it had always been between then. She was the prickly one, the one who spoke her mind and got people's backs up. He smoothed things over for her. They balanced each other out, like that. And then he left. Was that why everyone had pulled away from her? Because, in truth, they never really liked her, not without Peter?

"We don't have people's support," Priscilla says.

"That's not true."

"Have you received any calls? Gotten any sympathy cards? Seen any pies show up on our doorstep?"

Peter goes quiet.

"Well, have you?" she asks. "Because I haven't. I haven't seen even the tiniest sign that anyone in Middlebrook cares about what's happened to us."

The only gestures of sympathy had come from Wendy Warnes and a bunch of editors from national newspapers. And that didn't count; they were in it for themselves.

Peter opens his mouth, ready to speak, but then closes it again.

"Say it, Peter."

"I don't think you want to hear it."

"Try me."

"They're scared," Peter says.

"Who's scared?"

"People from Middlebrook—our—" He pauses. "Your friends and neighbors."

"*Scared*? Of what?"

"Scared of you, Cil. They don't know how to show their support because you're so—"

A hot flush pushes up under her skin. "I'm so what?"

He holds out his hands. "You're angry. And that's totally understandable. But you're pushing them away—like you . . ."

"Like I what?"

"Nothing."

"*Like I what*?" She's speaking too loudly. People are looking. But she can't help herself.

"Like you push away everyone who doesn't agree with you."

Peter closes his eyes. He rubs his forehead.

The thing is, he's right. Even though she's been locked up in that hospital room with Astrid for days, she's felt it: that people in Middlebrook are avoiding her. That they're taking sides with the Wrights—and the other parents who were at the party. Worse than that. In some crazy, twisted way, she's felt that they blame *her* for what happened at the party.

Priscilla feels like she can't move. She doesn't want to be here any more. Coming to the prayer meeting was a stupid idea. She wants to go back to Astrid.

But then Peter touches her elbow again. "I'm here for you, Cil." He puts his hand in hers and she's overcome again, like she was lying next to him on the bed—by that feeling of closeness she's missed so much.

She relaxes her fingers into his and they walk into the church together.

Avery walks toward them.

"I'm so glad you came. How are you holding up?"

Priscilla considers the question. When she doesn't answer, Peter steps in. "Thank you for organizing this."

"It's good to see you, Peter," Avery says.

Peter gives her a nod.

After Peter left, Avery had alluded to herself and Priscilla being single parents. Priscilla had thought it a bit much. Avery's never been married. Her kids are foster children. And she doesn't have a clue what it feels like to have your husband walk out on you.

"Well, I hope you like the service," Avery goes on, filling the silence. "I wish it could have been a bit more private." She looks around at the reporters. "All of this has drawn quite some attention to our little community."

"All of this?" Priscilla asks.

The two women lock eyes.

Priscilla wishes Avery would just say it out loud*: The shooting. Of a child. Of your daughter.* That's what's drawn attention to Middlebrook. And rightly so. No child should ever get shot without everyone knowing about it.

"Well, I believe Governor Warnes has saved you a seat—one of her aides came in early. Let me know if there's anything you need, I'm here to help."

"Thank you, Avery, we're very grateful," Peter says.

It drives her crazy. It always has. How Peter feels the need to smooth things over—like he's apologizing for her.

Avery and Peter wait for Priscilla to say something.

But again, she keeps quiet. Because she knows that if she doesn't, she'll lose it. She'll tell Avery how she really feels about her and her foster kids and her pointless prayer meeting and the fact that she reserved a special parking spot on her driveway for the Wrights. And Priscilla knows she can't lose it. Like Wendy said, she has to keep a good public face.

So instead, she looks down and says the words in her head, the words she wishes everyone could hear: *You want to help, Avery? Really? Well, why don't you use that hotline you have to God or whoever it is up there who you think has control of things right now, and find out who shot my daughter? Or better. Why don't you get those foster kids of yours to tell the truth? Because they saw what happened. They must have. Just like the kids who were there that afternoon. Chances are, one of them did this.*

Kaitlin feels everyone pressing in, staring at her and Ben. She wishes they hadn't come.

She glances back at the doors of St. Mary's, hoping that Bryar might have decided to come in after all. He'd refused to get out of the car. It had scared him, seeing so many people crowded outside the church.

She turns around and scans the church. Her eyes fall on Eva and Will, sitting across the aisle. Lily's not with them either. Maybe she went to find Bryar.

If there's one good thing that's come out of this horrible mess, it's their friendship. For the first time in his life, Bryar's got someone at his side—someone who isn't his mom or dad. Under different circumstances, Kaitlin would allow herself to feel happy, but right now, she can't focus on anything besides the sick feeling she has in the pit of her stomach, sitting here, knowing that everyone is judging her son. She hasn't been able to get the radio interview out of her head. The one where that psychiatrist made it sound like it was inevitable that Bryar would do something like this.

And an even worse feeling lies under it all: about her and Ben. How they've barely talked in days.

She looks at Priscilla and Peter sitting in the front row, Wendy Warnes nestled in beside them. She's pretty sure that a few days ago, Wendy Warnes didn't even know that their small town existed. She'd seen it before, when they lived in Texas: politicians sweeping in for the elections, making promises they'd forget as soon as they'd gotten their votes.

Ben, no doubt sensing her anxiety, tries to take her hand. He's always been so good at reading her emotions. But she reaches for the prayer sheet to avoid the contact.

She feels him flinch but pretends not to notice.

Her whole life, Kaitlin's trusted Ben's judgment: his moral compass that never fails. His goodness. But now, she can't stop questions from crowding into her brain. About whether they've been wrong this whole time to let guns be part of their lives. Their home. Their family.

And now, every time she looks at one of those safes in her home, she feels like she can't breathe.

Kaitlin bows her head. She doesn't know if she can do this. Be here. Pretend things are okay with her and Ben. Pretend she doesn't blame him for what happened on Sunday—for putting his son through all this.

Avery walks past, barely making eye contact with Kaitlin.

They'd always been there for each other, but they haven't spoken since Sunday.

She blames us too, Kaitlin thinks. For inviting Cal and Abi to the party. For putting them in danger when they were already so vulnerable.

And maybe she's right. Maybe all of them are right.

"We shouldn't have parked on her driveway," Kaitlin says.

Ben looks up. "What?"

"The truck. We should have parked on the road."

He looks at her, confused.

"We can't go around pretending that things are the same, Ben."

"I don't understand what you're saying, Katie."

"People blame us for what happened."

Avery's voice comes through the speakers at the sides of the church. "Welcome to you all," she says. "It's important, I believe, that we come together in times like these . . ."

"Maybe it *is* our fault," Kaitlin goes on.

"Let's not do this now, Katie."

She swallows hard.

"I'm so glad to see so many of you today . . ." Avery says. "It's been a tough few days for our little community . . ."

There's a murmur. Some people nod their heads in agreement. Others just stare or shift uncomfortably in their seats. Everyone's felt it: how they're being watched; the articles and the TV and radio reports. How they've been talking to strangers about each other. How their community is slowly cracking open.

"I want to go and check on Bryar," Kaitlin says.

"He'll be okay. Let's not make a fuss," Ben whispers.

"No. I can't do this . . . I can't . . ."

She feels it breaking apart. The life she's always known. Her marriage to Ben. Her place in this community. Being a mother to Bryar. How can she sit here and pray, knowing that she's failed everyone?

"Look, we'll talk about this later, my love. Okay? Let's not draw attention to ourselves now."

She looks around her. At all these people. At Lieutenant Mesenberg, sitting across the aisle. At the reporters, hovering in the doorway.

"We come here, united before God . . ." Avery goes on.

Kaitlin swallows again, pushing down the thoughts that have been crashing around in her head for days now.

That she's been asleep her whole life. That she's gone along with things without questioning them. And that it's this weakness, this inability to think for herself, that put Astrid in hospital. That put her son and her husband at the heart of a police investigation.

I'm the one who should be locked up, she thinks.

Wendy Warnes spends most of the service scrolling on her phone. When they get to the actual prayers, she makes a show of putting it down beside her and bowing her head, but Priscilla can still see her sneaking glimpses at her screen.

To be honest, she's never really liked her, not even back at law school. But Wendy has influence. And she's supporting Astrid's cause. That's all Priscilla should be thinking about right now.

Most of the prayers, so far, have been general. Prayers for the community. Prayers for healing. Prayers for empathy and understanding at this difficult time. Prayers for children and families. Just when Priscilla thinks that no one's even going to mention Astrid, Avery clears her throat and says, "Before we close, we should bring to mind, once again, the very special young girl who's in Colebrook Hospital, fighting for her life."

Priscilla's throat goes tight.

"It's very hard to watch a child suffer, especially one of our own," Avery says. "And we must give our special prayers to Astrid's parents, Priscilla and Peter, who, very courageously, are with us today."

Priscilla feels people turning toward her and Peter. The silence in the church deepens. Peter laces his fingers through hers.

Priscilla and Peter. She remembers how, when they first started dating, she'd get a rush of joy whenever someone said their names together like that, as though the alliteration was a sign that they were meant to be together.

She tightens her fingers around Peter's and bows her head.

"We pray that God might give them strength at this difficult time. A child is the most precious gift from God . . ." Avery goes on. "And when something happens to our children, we are often tested beyond what we think we can bear . . ."

Priscilla digs her nails into her palms. She has to hold it together.

"We pray that you might be with them at this time . . ." Avery says.

Wendy Warnes's phone buzzes.

The hairs on the back of Priscilla's neck fly up. Couldn't she turn off that damn phone for a few minutes?

Wendy turns around and whispers to one of her aides. Then she stands up, right there, in the middle of the prayer meeting, and walks out of the church.

CHAPTER

35

9 p.m.

AFTER THE PRAYER meeting, Priscilla looked everywhere for Wendy Warnes, but she'd left already.

And then, when she and Peter got back to the hospital, she'd tried to call Wendy, left three voicemails. But she hadn't called back.

"Something's probably come up," Peter says. "You know how it is with people like her."

"But why did she just get up like that and leave? And why's she not answering her phone?"

Priscilla looks back at Astrid. She knows it's stupid but she'd hoped that maybe, all those prayers—everyone coming together to support her—might have made a difference. That Astrid would have felt it, somehow.

"What if she doesn't wake up," Priscilla says, quietly.

"She's going to wake up, Cil."

"How do you know that? Everything I've read says that the longer she's in a coma, the less likely it is that she'll make it—"

"Then stop reading that stuff and remember who our daughter is. She won't give up without a fight."

Priscilla wants to believe him. But she's starting to lose hope.

They settle back in their chairs on each side of Astrid's bed. Peter closes his eyes. It's been a long day for both of them.

Priscilla's phone rings. She puts it straight to her ear.

"Wendy?" she says.

There's a silence down the line.

And then, a man's voice comes through.

"Dr. Carver?"

"Yes."

"This is Chris Barker—from *Rise and Shine America*."

It takes a second for the words to sink in. For days she's been reaching out to him and to the other major TV networks. If only she could get on one of those shows, the ones watched by millions of Americans all over the country, then she could rally support for Astrid's cause and put real pressure on Mesenberg to start taking this investigation seriously.

"I'm sorry I didn't get back to you earlier," Chris Barker says.

Peter opens his eyes and mouths, *Who is it?*

Priscilla flutters her hands, stands up, and goes out into the hall.

She's surprised that he's called her directly: she'd expected it to be one of his producers.

"I realize this is a difficult time. I'm so sorry for everything you're going through." From listening to so many of his shows, there's a familiarity to his voice.

"Thank you."

"So, you're keen to come on the show to talk to us about what happened? Give us your version of events?"

"My version?"

"Of what Astrid might say if she wakes up."

"When she wakes up."

"Yes."

Priscilla thinks back to what Peter said yesterday. About things getting out of hand. About there being a witch hunt. How the kids were being profiled. She was the one who'd caused it. Who'd made people speculate and point the finger. But it was for the right reasons, wasn't it? It was because she wanted people to realize, once and for all, how dangerous it was to have guns in people's homes—in children's homes.

Through a window, Priscilla watches a bunch of fallen leaves dancing across the floodlit parking lot. The summer already turning to fall.

"We're running a special on the Playdate Shooting. It would be wonderful to have you on the show."

Priscilla's cheeks flush. Millions of Americans watch his show every day. And he gets to decide what they hear.

"Dr. Carver—you still there?"

"Yes."

"We've got a slot in tomorrow morning's show. We could send a car over to you later tonight. We've booked you on the last flight from Boston to JFK. And we made a reservation at a hotel near the studio. There's huge public interest in your story."

Priscilla's mind races. Leaving Astrid feels wrong. She hadn't even wanted to go home with Peter. But maybe this is what she's been waiting for: the opportunity to put real pressure on the police investigation. To share her views on gun control. To make sure that innocent kids like Astrid stop getting hurt by guns. And with Wendy going quiet on her, she has to find another way to keep Astrid's story alive.

"Dr. Carver—shall I give my team the green light?"

Through the window of the door to Astrid's room, she looks at Peter, asleep in the armchair. At Astrid, lying in the hospital bed, her pale hair spread over her pillow, her sunburn faded now.

Priscilla closes her eyes and takes a deep breath.

"Okay," she says. "I'll be there."

DAY SIX

Friday, September 6

CHAPTER

36

7 a.m.

Yasmin stands at the door to the twins' bedroom: clothes hang out of their drawers and wardrobe and books and dirty laundry cover the floor. With everything that's been going on, she hasn't had the energy to nag them to tidy up.

From downstairs, she can hear the television. School doesn't start for another hour but the twins got up early have done since the shooting, anxious, every day, to find out whether Astrid has woken up.

After the prayer meeting ended abruptly with Governor Warnes rushing out, Yasmin found the twins coming out of the woods with the other children: they said they went for a walk to the pond. Ayaan had gotten angry: he pulled them away and drove them straight home.

He was still furious at them for what they said to Priscilla at the hospital, putting the blame on Astrid like that. And now they'd gone against his will by running off with every kid on Ayaan's blacklist. Secretly, Yasmin was glad that the twins had spent time with their friends: that they had the courage to follow their hearts.

Looking back at the twins' room, Yasmin notices that Laila has stuffed things under her bed: school books, a deflated soccer ball, a hairbrush, old birthday and Christmas cards. She doesn't like to throw anything away. Yasmin kneels in front of her bed and reaches for the old trunk Laila has kept since she was five years old. It's always been stuffed so full that it's impossible to close the lid but, this time, the lid has been pressed shut. And she's put a lock on it too.

"Mum! What are you doing?"

Startled, Yasmin bangs her head on the bedframe and looks round. Laila's standing at the bedroom door.

"I was only tidying—" Yasmin starts.

Laila's face is red. She darts into the room and pushes past Yasmin, grabs her trunk and shoves it deeper under her bed.

"We're old enough to tidy ourselves, now," Laila says.

Yasmin feels struck by the fierceness of Laila's tone. She's never spoken to her like this before.

Yasmin stands up. "I wanted to help," she says. "You've had a lot on your plate. I thought you'd be pleased to have a tidy room."

Laila stands up too and looks at Yasmin. "Well, don't."

She definitely hasn't seen this side to Laila before.

"What's going on?" Hanif comes through the door.

"Mom's been going through our stuff."

"I haven't!" Yasmin protests.

Hanif shrugs and goes to sit on his bed. "What's the big deal?"

For a second, she thought that he would turn on her too. But he's her boy. He's always defended her, just like she defends him when Ayaan criticizes him for not living up to his impossible standards.

Laila stares at Hanif like he's betrayed her by not taking her side. "This is our room, Hanif. And we're not kids any more. We get to have some privacy."

Yasmin holds up her hands. "Okay, okay. I'll stay out of your room. Just tidy up, okay?"

"Sure," Hanif says and starts packing his school bag.

Laila walks toward her and holds the door.

She wants me to leave, thinks Yasmin. My eleven-year-old daughter wants me to get out of a room in my own house.

"We'll be out in a minute, okay, Mom?" Laila says.

Her face is still flushed, her eyes glassy. She may have crossed some line into teenage defiance but it's more than that too: it's not like Laila to over-react like this.

"I'll wait for you downstairs," Yasmin says.

Laila nods and closes the door on her.

True lights a cigarette and sits on the top step of the porch.

Sorry about this, Cedar . . . he whispers to the dawn sky. *I'm finding things a bit hard right now . . .*

He sees her emptying his packet of cigarettes into the sink and switching on the faucet.

I'm not going to watch you smoke your way to an early grave, she'd said, grabbing the sodden packet and throwing it in the trash.

She hated him smoking. Said that it was selfish to destroy your body when there were people who loved you—and that it was inconsistent with how they were trying to lead their lives. Cedar had such fucking high standards and now that she was gone he felt like he had to work even harder to live up to them.

Okay, you win. He stubs out the cigarette. *You always win.*

He stands up from the porch steps and pushes through the swing door back into the cabin.

His body aches with tiredness; he wasn't able to sleep last night.

He can't get it out of his mind: that awful picture of Phoenix that's been going around, making it look like he shot Astrid—and worse: like he enjoyed it. The reporter might have tried to disguise who it was, but there was no mistaking it was Phoenix.

True looks over at the mattresses pushed into a corner of the room. Wynn's curled up against Skye, his cast sticking out at an angle to the side of his head. Skye's small, loopy writing covers every inch now. By getting Wynn to focus on the story of a mother bear and her cubs who come to live in an abandoned cabin in the woods, Skye has taken her little brother's mind off what's going on in the real world. She'd learned this trick from Cedar—deflecting attention when a worry set in. Cedar would do it with Phoenix too. She was the one who taught him to climb trees.

True walks up to the mattress and leans in toward his daughter. He brushes her dark hair out of her eyes and kisses her forehead.

Then he turns to Phoenix, lying off to one side, pressed up close to the wall of the cabin. Lumen lies at his feet. Ever since Cedar died, Lumen's followed Phoenix around, as if knowing that he was the one who'd feel Cedar's absence most.

He looks at his son's hands resting, palm up, on the sheets, thick calluses on his skin from climbing trees, his forearms scratched by branches and brambles. His hair is a tangle of matted knots. He can't remember the last time he saw Phoenix taking a bath or running a comb through his hair.

Is all this my fault? True whispers to the night sky. *Have I failed them?*

Lieutenant Mesenberg had brought Phoenix in for questioning more times than any of the other children. Even Skye commented on it. He was worried that they suspected him above the other children: that his monosyllabic answers, his shrugs, the way he slumped in his chair, avoiding eye contact, made it seems as if he was asking to be found guilty.

Wasn't that what that photographer had tried to show in the awful picture he took? That Phoenix was letting the world know he was the one who'd done this?

True remembers Cedar lying in the birthing pool holding their firstborn son, his small body slick with blood and mucus, his umbilical cord still connecting them.

As True leant over to get his first good look at his son, Phoenix had looked right back at him, his eyes wide open. Only a few minutes old and his brow was full of knots, as if he knew already that there was something wrong with the world.

We're going to have to keep you out of trouble, little guy, Cedar had said, kissing the top of his head.

And she'd been right, of course. As he grew up, Phoenix found his own path. He battered down the thorns and brambles; stuffed his pocket with sharp stones; whittled sticks into spears; asked True to take him hunting when his arms were still too small to hold a rifle.

Cedar was never worried about him, though. *We just have to remind him to use that energy for good*, she'd say.

But she was the one who did that—who, time after time, steered Phoenix away from the shadows and back to the light. True had never been able to get through to him like she had.

And after she died, it felt like the distance between him and Phoenix had grown.

He strokes the back of his son's tangled hair.

Had Phoenix done it? Had he taken that gun? Been overwhelmed by the shadows and pulled the trigger—and had True failed to see it coming?

He tries to master his breathing, like he teaches his yoga students to do, but it doesn't work—he's snatching at the air, his breath ragged and forced.

I'm sorry, Cedar, I'm so sorry, he whispers.

And that's when he sees it. Just a corner, sticking out from under the mattress. He lifts it out.

"What the hell . . ?"

It's a cell phone. Had Phoenix found it somewhere in the woods—or worse, stolen it? And why was he hiding it?

Kaitlin stands on the porch watching Bryar cycling down the driveway, red and yellow leaves falling around him in the morning breeze.

For the past few days, he and Lily have been meeting at the crossroads in town and cycling into school together. Never in her wildest dreams could she have imagined her son going off like this, early in the morning, to meet a friend. It should have made her glad, but all she can think about is the police investigation hanging over them.

Kaitlin also has a nagging feeling that the reason Bryar keeps going off with Lily is so he can avoid answering her questions about what happened at the party.

She walks back into the kitchen and pours herself a black coffee. Ben comes down the stairs, his hair still wet from the shower. She still can't get used to seeing him hanging around the house all day in his home clothes. It's driving him crazy, not being able to work.

"I'm going out to chop some wood before it rains again," he says, heading to the door.

"Don't you want some breakfast?"

"I'll get some later."

He's been avoiding her. Working for hours outside. Sleeping on the couch.

"We need to talk, Ben," Kaitlin says. "About Astrid—about Bryar." *About us,* she thinks.

"We can talk later," he says, putting on his jacket.

She walks toward him. "Please, Ben."

He looks at her and his eyes seem to soften. "Bryar didn't do anything wrong. Neither did I. You know that, right?" he says.

She waits a second before responding. She doesn't know if their relationship is strong enough right now to weather another argument. But she can't keep swallowing it down.

"Whoever shot Astrid used your pistol, Ben."

His eyes cloud over. He pulls a cap over his head and opens the door.

She reaches for his arm. "You can't walk away from this."

"If you think this is my fault, Katie, there's nothing to talk about."

"I don't think it's your fault. I know you'd never hurt anyone—not intentionally."

He turns around. "*Not intentionally*?"

"We have firearms in our home. We have to take responsibility for that."

"So you're on Priscilla's side now?"

"Priscilla? No. Of course not. I'm not on anyone's side."

"Well, you sure as hell aren't on my side, Katie."

He turns back around and steps out onto the porch.

"You're not listening to me," she says. "I'm allowed to question the way we've been living. I'm allowed to ask myself whether we were right—"

He keeps walking, down the porch steps and across the yard to the stable.

"Just tell me one thing, Ben," she calls out.

He stops walking.

"Was he any good?" Her heart is hammering.

He doesn't move.

"When you took Bryar to the shooting range—when he was ten—was he any good?" she asks again.

Slowly, Ben turns around. "What?"

"I know he didn't like it. That he didn't want to go again. But you still taught him to shoot, didn't you? You wanted him to understand how guns work."

"Yes."

"So, I'm asking . . ." Her voice is shaking. "Was he a good shot?"

Ben looks at her as though he doesn't recognize her.

Then he goes quiet. His shoulders drop.

"Ben?"

"Yeah, Katie. He was a good shot."

Avery sits in front of Bill at the kitchen table.

"I've been watching the news," he says.

She can hear the agitation in his voice.

"What a mess," he adds.

Over Bill's shoulder, Avery looks out through the window at the steeple of St. Mary's. She wonders if he showed up early to catch her off guard. She hopes that Abi and Cal are still asleep—and that she can get Bill out of the house before they wake up. The last thing they need right now is to bump into him.

"To think it was meant to be a prayer meeting," he goes on. "Looked more like a political rally. Couldn't you make it—I don't know, more private?"

"Vetting who comes to a prayer meeting kind of defeats the point, Bill."

As soon as Bill found out about the shooting on Sunday, he called to say that he wanted to place Abi and Cal in a new foster home, at least until after the investigation. And then, when he read the interview she gave to the reporter, he hit the roof. But she'd done everything she could to persuade him that they needed stability—and that meant staying with her. Bill knows they've been doing better with her than with anyone else. He knows she's a good foster parent, and that this is Abi and Cal's chance of a better life. Reluctantly, he'd agreed.

But then the media storm just got worse. The attacks on the mosque. The involvement of Governor Warnes. And he's right, the prayer meeting didn't turn out as she'd hoped.

If Avery could magic Abi and Cal away to some wonderful, safe place where they didn't have to deal with any of this, she'd do it in a heartbeat. But the truth of it is that this is as good as it gets for them. They have a home here. And she loves them. She wants them to stay with her for good.

"At least you kept Abi and Cal away from the prayer meeting," Bill says. "That was wise."

Avery couldn't take credit for that. She'd wanted them to attend but they refused to come. And then they must have left the house without telling her because, the next thing, she knew they were walking back through the woods with the other children.

And they'd looked happy, which had felt incongruous, given the circumstances. But it had offered her a moment of relief, seeing them with their new friends. She wishes she could make Bill understand that despite what's happened in the past week, Abi and Cal are better off here.

"Avery—are you listening to me?"

"Yes, of course."

"We're going to have to make a decision about their future. We have to think about what's best for them."

"I know."

"They still haven't said anything?" Bill asks. "To you—or to the police?"

"No, they haven't."

"Look, I'm getting pressure from above. All this attention hasn't been doing our cause much good—"

"Your cause?"

"The Fostering and Adoption Agency depends on positive press coverage. Success stories. I know it sounds crass but if we're going to keep finding families for our kids, we need to make sure that our image is clean as possible. Foster families and prospective adopters know that these kids come from difficult backgrounds—but a shooting in a foster placement . . ." He whistles through his teeth. "It doesn't look good, Avery."

"Cal and Abi are happy here, Bill. I know that things look bad right now, but they like living with me. They like going to school. Abi's made the basketball team. Cal's really hit it off with his art teacher. You should see his hands, they're always covered in paint." She smiles. "And they're making friends."

He raises his eyebrows. "You mean the kids from the party—the ones involved in the shooting?"

"They're good kids, Bill. All of them."

"How do you know?"

"Because I live here. Because I'm their minister. Because kids aren't bad."

"But one of them shot Astrid Carver."

She takes a breath. "Please, Bill, we need more time. I can make this work."

Bill drops his shoulders and sighs. "Look, let me cut to the chase. Do you think there's any chance that Abi or Cal are involved?"

"Seriously?"

He holds out his palms. "Could either of them have pulled the trigger? Because if they did, this going to be one hell of a shit storm—"

"One minute you're complaining about them being involved with kids who might have shot Astrid Carver—and now you're suggesting Abi or Cal might have shot her themselves?" Not for the first time, Avery feels that Bill's priorities are off. "They're good kids, you know that, Bill."

"You keep saying that, but good kids do stupid stuff. Especially kids who've had a lifetime's worth of bad role models." He pauses. "You said it yourself to that reporter. We don't really know them. All we know is that they've been exposed to a whole load of crap—"

"You know Abi's background." She shakes her head. "Abi loves it here. She wouldn't have gone near that gun—*especially* after what happened with her mom's boyfriend. Come on, Bill, they deserve a chance."

"I'm sticking my neck out for you—you get that, right?" he says. "If I were following strict protocol, those kids would be in a new foster home already."

"I understand. And I'm grateful. But we're doing this for the kids. When you brought them to me, you thought this could be their last stop. We talked about adoption . . ."

His eyes go wide. "You're still considering that?" he asks.

"Of course."

He shakes his head. "You get that it'll be a long shot—after all this."

"Yes, I know." She pauses. "But they belong here, Bill. They just do."

He stares at her, blinking. Something seems to shift in him. "Look, I'll try my best."

"Thank you, Bill."

"Just keep them out of trouble, okay?"

"Of course."

"And don't get their hopes up."

"Okay."

"And don't get *your* hopes up."

"I won't," she lies. Because she can't help it. She wants them to stay with her—more than she's ever wanted anything.

He stands up and pushes in his chair. "I'll be in touch after the weekend. And if there are any developments, let me know."

"Of course."

She leads him out to his car and watches him drive away. She remembers the day he brought Abi and Cal here: how she'd stood outside the church for ages, just in case they arrived early. How tentatively they'd stepped out of the back of Bill's car, looking around as though they'd landed on the moon. And the truth was that Middlebrook might as well have been the moon compared to where they came from. It would take them a while to trust her, she knew that. But she'd felt it in her gut: that they were here to stay.

She's bought them a bit more time; it's not much, but it's something.

When she goes back inside, she heads up to the bathroom and bunches up their towels and the dirty clothes from their hamper and brings them down to the laundry room. She remembers a mother in her congregation telling her, once, how laundry defined her life: how the endless cycle of cleaning her children's clothes shaped the patterns of her days and weeks. And how, when they left for college, it was the empty washing machine, more than anything, that made her heart ache.

Avery pushes the white towels into the drum. And then she stops and takes one of them out again.

It's streaked with paint. Which isn't unusual: Cal's things are always covered in stains from the art room. She loves that Cal has a passion for art; it gives her hope that he'll find his way in life, one that makes him happy.

But the streaks of color on the towel trigger something in her mind.

Before she's aware that she's given her legs the instruction to move, she's running through the house, clutching the stained towel to her chest, and she keeps running until she gets to the kitchen, and then to the recycling bin. As she lifts an old newspaper from the pile, she knows why her legs took her here—and why there was a flash of recognition in her mind when she saw the marked towel.

The red, black, and yellow stains on the towel—they're the same colors that were used in the attack on the mosque.

CHAPTER

37

7.30 a.m.

Show: Rise and Shine America
Title: "The Playdate Shooting"
Date: Sep. 6, 2019, 7.30 a.m.
Topic: Gun control

Barker: Thank you for coming in, Dr. Carver, especially at this difficult time.

Carver: [Nods]

Barker: Let's get straight to the heart of this debate. You've called this "A Crisis in Modern American Parenting"—could you expand on that?

Carver: Yes. A crisis that no one seems to be willing to talk about. The high school shootings, sure, they get the big headlines. The debates about lockdown drills. But the real crisis is happening in our everyday lives. In our homes—at the playdates we blindly take our children to. The parties . . .

Barker: Like the one that took place last Sunday afternoon?

Carver: Exactly.

Barker: And you'd warned your friends—parents from the Middlebrook community—that it would be dangerous to take their children to this party?

Carver: Absolutely.

Barker: And they didn't listen?

Carver: One of the parents—she's new to the community—persuaded them to go. Said it would be a bit of harmless fun. [Stares into the camera] She has no idea what it means to live in a country where guns are part of people's everyday lives: it was naïve—more than naïve, reckless—to encourage parents to take their children to a party on that property.

Barker: A property on which firearms are kept, is that right?

Carver: Yes.

Barker: Lieutenant Mesenberg has gone on record to say that the gun in question was locked up in a safe.

Carver: Do you know easy it is for a kid to memorize a six-digit code?

Barker: You believe that the child whose party it was had access to the safe—that he knew the code?

Carver: It's more than likely, yes.

Barker: And you believe that he may be responsible for shooting your daughter?

Carver: He admitted to removing the gun from the safe—and to getting the ammo from the house—so he's *directly* implicated.

Barker: But there's no evidence to suggest that he *actually* fired the pistol? [Looks at his notes] The firearm itself hasn't yet been located. The investigation is still open. What makes you so sure that he's the shooter?

Carver: He was raised with a gun. It was his home.

Barker: But why would he have *wanted* to fire the gun?

Carver: To show off. To get attention from the other kids. Because kids like him are unpredictable.

Barker: Kids like him?

Carver: He has problems.

Barker: You've spoken out openly against the boy's parents. You believe they're to blame in this?

Carver: Yes. They brought families with small children onto their property.

Barker: [Looks down at his notes] Lieutenant Mesenberg has gone on record to say that the children don't remember who shot your daughter.

Carver: Children are good at keeping secrets, Chris. Especially if they're scared. Especially if they're trying to protect someone.

Barker: You think the children are trying to protect the boy whose party it was?

Carver: That's most likely, yes. But it could have been any of them, really. Once that gun was out of the safe—

Barker: So let me get this straight: you believe that any one of the children at the party could have shot your daughter?

Carver: Children who've experienced radicalization. Children who are raised without clear boundaries. Children who've witnessed gun violence. Children who don't understand the danger of guns. There are all kinds of motivations that might have prompted one of the kids at the party to shoot my daughter. If those children had decent parents, they wouldn't have been at the party to begin with.

Barker: You're making some big claims here.

Carver: Given the right circumstances, most human beings—including children—can be driven to do just about anything. It would be foolish to rule any of them out. Which is precisely why I believe that guns should never be kept in a family home. In any home.

Barker: [Turns back to his notes] You're a law professor, Dr. Carver, is that right?

Carver: I am.

Barker: And you used to be a practicing attorney.

Carver: [Pauses] Yes. I don't see how this is—

Barker: Your last case—it made quite some waves.

Carver: You could say that.

Barker: A multiple homicide. There were children involved. A shooting. That must have had a huge influence on your professional life. And your views on firearms.

Carver: [Visibly shocked] I really don't think we need to—

Barker: It's understandable, Dr. Carver, that you should feel strongly about guns—after what you witnessed.

Carver: It was shocking, yes.

Barker: That case was the reason you gave up your legal career, am I right?

Carver: I really don't see how this is relevant.

Barker: I suppose it's just interesting—in light of your current situation. And your feelings about gun control.

Carver: My feelings about gun control have always been the same. It's quite simple: good parents don't have firearms in their homes. Good *people* don't have firearms in their homes, *period*. New Hampshire has some of the most relaxed laws on gun control in the United States—and because it's legal, people think it's okay.

Barker: I believe that Governor Warnes has taken a personal interest in your story.

Carver: [Nods] She's put gun control at the heart of her campaign for the US senate. We're working on this together.

Barker: [Raises his eyebrows] You're willing to take on the NRA?

Carver: We're willing to take on anyone who puts our children in danger.

Barker: So, you really believe that what happened to your daughter might move the needle on the debate?

Carver: It has to. Like I said, every day, parents all over America are walking their children into death traps.

Barker: Many Americans believe that owning firearms is their constitutional right.

Carver: Well, then, the constitution is wrong.

Barker: That's quite a statement—especially coming from a law professor.

Carver: It's a big issue. Perhaps one of the biggest our country has ever had to face. [Looking straight into the camera] Chris said that I'm a law professor. He's right, I am. But that's not why this case matters to me. It matters to me because I'm a mom. If you're a parent who cares about the life of your child, you need to act now. What happened to Astrid could happen to any one of your children.

Barker: Thank you for that, Priscilla, I'm sure my viewers will take your words to heart. Before we close, I'd like us to tackle one more aspect to this story.

Carver: Sure.

[Images come up on the screen behind Carver: screenshots from a cell phone. The audience gasps]

Barker: Would you mind taking a look at these images?

Carver: Okay . . . [Carver twists in her chair to see the screen] What are these . . . ?

Barker: I believe they're screenshots from your daughter's phone.

Carver: What? No, they can't be.

Barker: They were released early this morning—

Carver: Released?

Barker: I gather that someone handed your daughter's phone to a reporter working on the case. The reporter believed it was in the public interest to release the images into the public domain. [Pause] There are links to videos in her search history—

Carver: Who found the phone?

Barker: We're not at liberty to say. But the person in question thought it might broaden the debate.

Carver: This doesn't make sense. Astrid wouldn't—

Barker: There's actually more evidence from her phone that we can't release right now, but these images are enough to show us that your daughter's involvement—

Carver: My daughter's *involvement* was that she got shot! My daughter's *involvement* is that she's lying in the ICU fighting for her life.

Barker: I understand how distressing this is. But you must see how this looks. Two days before the shooting, your daughter was looking up YouTube videos on how to open gun safes. [Pause] And on how to load a firearm.

Carver: [Stares at the screen] I don't understand . . .

Barker: So, you weren't aware?

Carver: These images can't be from Astrid's phone. [Shakes her head] They *can't* be.

Barker: They can't be—because?

Carver: Because she knows how I feel about firearms. She knows they're dangerous. She understands. She's never . . . [Her voice breaks off]

Barker: We're so grateful to you for coming on the show, Dr. Carver. This is an important issue, one that I'm sure we'll return to.

Carver: [Keeps staring at the images on the screen]

Barker: Dr. Carver?

Carver: [Slowly turns back in her chair]

Barker: Thank you for coming in.

Carver: [Looks down at the floor]

Barker: [Into the camera] It's clear that this is going to be a big talking point for those of you watching at home. The Middlebrook shooting has brought the gun control debate back to life for all of us. But we're also being challenged to ask bigger questions. Like how we parent our children. And how much we really know about them—and what they're doing on their phones. Thank you for tuning in.

[Lights dim.]

CHAPTER

38

7.45 a.m.

EVA PUSHES THE mute button on the TV.

She'd come down to find Lily watching *Rise and Shine America,* a program they often had on over breakfast. Except, this morning, the person filling the screen was Priscilla Carver. Eva hadn't been able to persuade Lily to switch it off, not until the interview was over.

Lily barely touched her cereal. She just kept staring, wide-eyed, at the screen as Priscilla savaged the families who were at the Wrights' party. She may not have mentioned them by name, but it was obvious who she was talking about. And then the presenter turned on her by showing those pictures from Astrid's phone.

All those articles speculating about the shooter, the radio interviews, the TV reports—it was obvious now that Priscilla had been behind them. No doubt with support from Governor Warnes. And now Astrid too was being put in the spotlight.

When Will came down and sat with them in front of the TV, Eva had thought that maybe he'd finally see that Priscilla had gone too far, but all he did was shake his head and mutter, *Poor Priscilla.* And then he carried on getting ready for work.

But you saw those images—from Astrid's phone. Eva had argued.

He'd just shrugged. *That doesn't mean much. So, she looked up some websites. It's not like she shot herself, is it?*

Eva and Will had always prided themselves on being on the same wavelength, but since they moved to America, she didn't feel like she could get through to him any more.

The TV interview had been overlaid with pictures high-lighting Priscilla's points. Woodwind Stables covered in police tape. Ben Wright in his border patrol uniform, with a close-up of his holster and the pistol he carried when he was on duty. The wall of the mosque, covered in graffiti. The image of Phoenix, sitting in that tree, shooting a pretend gun at the sky.

And then there was what Priscilla had implied about Bryar in the interview: that he had problems. That he was the most likely shooter.

Eva presses her hands against her stomach. The nausea has been easing over the past week but she's been feeling off all morning. It must be the stress of everything that's going on right now. She picks up the glass of water in front of her and drinks slowly.

Then she reaches across the table and places her hand over Lily's.

"Lily," Eva says gently.

Lily pulls her hand away.

"Do you think we could talk?"

Lily shakes her head. She gets up and stuffs her lunch box into her backpack. "I'm meeting Bryar before school."

"This is more important right now, my love."

Lily raises her eyebrows. "More important than school?"

"Yes, more important than school."

Lily hitches her backpack onto her shoulders, avoiding Eva's gaze.

"I know you're scared, Lily. I wish you hadn't watched that interview with Dr. Carver—and I know you don't want to get anyone in trouble. But I think it's time you told me what happened on Sunday: some real facts. You must have seen something—"

"I've told you everything I know, Mum."

Lily doesn't look at her when she says it.

A wave of tiredness sweeps over her. She's pressed Lily as much as she can. She's either telling the truth—that she really doesn't know who shot Astrid—or there's something she's hiding that's so bad that she'll never open up. Either way, Eva feels at a loss.

"You heard what Astrid's mum is saying about us, my love. She's doing a great deal of damage. Damage to your friends. To all of us. Damage that could be averted if we simply got to the truth about what happened."

Lily walks toward the front door. "I really have to go, Mum."

"Lily?"

Lily looks round. Every day, it seems to Eva, her little girl's skin has turned a shade paler; those circles under her eyes have deepened. This is getting to her more than she's been letting on.

"If you do think of something, you'll tell me, won't you?"

Lily hesitates and then nods.

"Promise?" Eva says.

She nods again.

And then she disappears through the front door.

Eva looks back at the TV. The interview's over but they're rerunning highlights. Priscilla's words run along the bottom of the screen: Good parents don't have firearms in their homes. Good *people* don't have firearms in their homes, *period*.

She snaps off the TV and goes to lie down on the sofa, but just as she rests against the cushions, her mobile rings. It's Yasmin. She wants to let it go to voicemail; she doesn't have the energy to talk to anyone right now. But then she thinks about what that poor woman and her family have been going through. And God knows what she must be thinking if she saw that interview. *Radicalization*, wasn't that the word Priscilla had used?

"Hi?" Eva says.

"Hi—it's me, Yasmin. I think we should meet. All of us. You, me, Kaitlin, True—Avery." Her voice is shaky. It's not like Yasmin to initiate a social gathering.

"You saw the interview?" Eva says.

"Yes . . . but it's not just that . . ."

What else is there? Eva thinks. Priscilla's gone on national television and attacked every child and parent who was at the party on Sunday.

"I was tidying the twins' room . . ." Yasmin says.

"Sorry?"

"I—I think I found something." There's a manic edge to Yasmin's voice that makes Eva sit up.

"Found what?"

"I think we should get everyone to come over," Yasmin says again.

"To your house? Will Ayaan be okay with that?"

There's a pause on the line.

"Ayaan's not here," Yasmin says.

"Okay."

"Can you call round a bit? Invite people?"

"You want me to invite the other parents to your house?"

"Yes."

Naïve and reckless. Those were the words that Priscilla had used about her getting involved in the Middlebrook community.

"They'll listen to you," Yasmin goes on.

And that was the problem, wasn't it? That people were so ready to listen to her. That's why they'd gone to the party.

"I don't know, Yasmin . . ."

"Please, Eva. We have to do this—for the children."

The determination in Yasmin's voice sways Eva. If she's found something that could help the kids, she's right, they need to pull together.

"Okay—I'll call them."

Eva ends the call and lies back down on the sofa.

A framed picture on the bookshelf catches her eye: Eva, Will, and Lily sitting in the garden of Eva's parents' house in Dorset. The same picture Priscilla had posted on her *Justice for Astrid* Facebook page. Eva remembers the day, last February, when she sent it to Priscilla: she was sitting in their home in London, exchanging messages with the American woman who would be Will's boss—and, she'd hoped, her friend.

Priscilla's right. Eva doesn't understand how this country works. And maybe she was wrong to get so involved—to persuade people to take their kids to the party. But what Priscilla's done is far worse: she's betrayed her neighbors and her friends—she's vilified their children. And you don't need to be a therapist to know where that kind of behavior comes from. Priscilla Carver said that the children were scared, that that's why they were keeping quiet. Well, she's scared too. That's why she's blaming everyone. Scared because maybe, deep down, she knows that she doesn't have any handle on her daughter—that she might turn out to be as much to blame as any of the other kids.

CHAPTER

39

8.30 a.m.

PRISCILLA SITS IN JFK airport, looking up at the departures screen: she would pick any of those places over going home right now. Chris Barker set her up—and she fell for it. How could she have been so stupid? Like he cared about Astrid and what had happened, and then he turned it on her.

Why the hell did Astrid look up those videos? Was it to spite her? Was it because she actually wanted to learn how to open a safe?

Her phone vibrates again. She hasn't taken it off silent mode since she left the studio. Peter's been trying to get in touch but he's the last person she wants to talk to right now.

He warned her not to go on the show. He warned her not to rile up the media. And he warned her, most of fall, not to underestimate Astrid. But looking up a few videos doesn't prove anything, does it? Kids are curious. Kids look up all kinds of shit. It doesn't mean that they're going to act on what they see. And didn't Bryar confess that he opened the safes?

Her phone vibrates again. A message this time:

For Christ's sake, pick up, Priscilla—I need to talk to you!

She takes a breath, calls his number and brings the phone to her ear.

"Thank God, Priscilla."

"Please don't lecture me, Peter."

"I'm not—"

"Everything you're about to say to me right now, I've thought it already. You were right, is that what you want to hear? Right about all of it."

"Cil, none of that matters right now—"

"'None of that matters?' Did you see what the show—"

"Of course I saw—"

"How the hell did he get hold of those pictures? Astrid's phone was missing!"

"Priscilla, I need you to stop talking and listen to me."

Priscilla goes quiet.

"She's woken up, Priscilla—that's why I've been calling you." His voice is shaking. "Our little girl opened her eyes."

Priscilla feels the world spinning around her. "What?"

"They're running tests but it looks like she's going to be okay—I mean, they're not making any promises, but Dr. Kittler say it's looking good."

Tears run down Priscilla's face. She is shaking.

"Cil—you still there?"

She looks back up at the departures screen—at her flight to Boston. She wants it to leave this second. She has to get back to her daughter.

"Cil?"

"I heard you," she says, her voice broken through the tears.

"Just get back here as soon as you can, okay?"

"Okay."

"Cil?"

"Yeah?"

"Whatever happened today—whatever's been going on all week—it doesn't matter any more. Astrid's going to be okay. That's what 's important now."

"I know. I know."

There's a pause. She thinks he might have ended the call, but she can still hear his breathing.

"I love you."

There's another beat of silence between them.

"I love you too."

She switches off the phone and puts it down on her lap and, through eyes blurred with tears, she looks out through the window of the departure lounge at the planes taking off into the blue September sky.

CHAPTER

40

8 a.m.

LILY AND BRYAR wheel their bikes down Main Street toward school.

She can tell from Bryar's stooped shoulders, and from the fact that he won't look at her, that he must have seen the TV interview too.

She wishes she could erase all those things that Dr. Carver said about him. About all of them.

And then those pictures from Astrid's phone—like she'd planned it out. At least they didn't show the video.

Part of Lily wishes she could erase the whole of that Sunday afternoon. But then she keeps getting a feeling that maybe, if it hadn't been for the party, she and Bryar would never have got so close. And maybe she wouldn't feel like she does about the other children either—even Astrid: that they're bound up together in this thing that's bigger than any of them.

She remembers how they'd stood on the dock during the prayer meeting. It was the first time they'd all been together again, just them, since Sunday afternoon.

Lily had suggested that they have their own prayer meeting, like the grown-ups.

Skye had gathered a bunch of leaves from a maple whose branches hung over the dock. She'd handed them out to the children and they'd taken a moment to look across the pond and then, one by one, they'd thrown their red leaves into the water.

Lily remembers standing there, watching her leaf floating away—how it had felt good, whatever it was they were doing. Better than anything had felt for days.

She'd reached out her hand to Bryar and curled her fingers around his and then he'd reached out his hand to Laila. Soon, they were standing in a circle. Even Phoenix joined in.

As they stood there, holding each other, Lily knows that they'd all felt it: that she was missing; the girl who was never meant to be at the party but who was one of them now.

Lily remembers how a picture flickered behind her eyelids:

Astrid running down the dock toward them, a red leaf in her hand.

Astrid placing her leaf in the water.

The leaf floating out along the current to join the other leaves.

And then Astrid coming back to the circle of children, her hand outstretched, her fingers reaching for theirs.

For a few seconds, standing on that dock, holding hands, imagining Astrid joining them, it had felt as though maybe everything might be okay after all.

"What Dr. Carver said, it's not true, you know that, right?" Lily says to Bryar.

He shrugs.

"She's mad at us for what's happened, that's all."

He doesn't answer.

"And she blames herself. Because she wasn't there when Astrid ran away."

Lily had overheard Mum saying this to Dad. That she thought the reason Dr. Carver was acting so crazy was because she felt like she'd messed up and it was easier to blame other people than to blame herself.

"We're going to make this right, Bryar, I promise," Lily says.

Bryar looks up at her. "How are you going to do that?" he asks.

"We're going to tell the truth."

His eyes go wide.

"What? But we agreed—we said—"

"We have to, Bryar."

"What about the others?"

"We're going to get everyone to agree. And when they do, we're going to find a way to say it." She squeezes his hand. "We don't have a choice, Bryar. But it will be okay. It has to be okay."

Bryar hangs his head again and starts wheeling his bike up the road. She can't tell whether it's because he's scared or sad or because he's thinking hard about what she just said. But he must know that she's right: they don't have a choice any more. Mum's right: it's gone too far.

When the twins spot Lily and Bryar, they walk straight to them. After Dad went off to work and Mom went to do the breakfast dishes in the kitchen, they'd gone to sit on the sofa and Hanif had gotten out his laptop and they'd watched a rerun of the interview on YouTube.

It had made them feel sick to their stomachs.

And then Laila had thought about Mom snooping around in their room. The box was locked but, sooner or later, Mom was going to find something out. They had to tell people first.

When they reach Bryar and Lily, Laila says, "We should get everyone together."

"I was thinking the same." Lily looks across the playground. "Have you guys seen Abi and Cal?"

The twins shake their heads.

"Okay. Let's see if we can find them. Then we'll go to the woods."

They know what going to the woods means: it means finding Skye and her brothers and getting them on board.

"I don't know about this," Bryar starts. "Maybe we should wait."

"Yeah," Hanif says.

Lily and Laila exchange a look.

"It's going to come out," Lily says. "We have to have a plan. And now that they have Astrid's phone, it's not like we can keep things a secret any more."

The boys look at each other.

"Lily's right," Laila says.

Slowly, the boys nod.

"Okay," Bryar says.

Laila turns to her twin. "Hanif?"

He stares at her. She tries to tap into what he's thinking but lately, they haven't been as in sync as usual.

"Okay," he says at last.

Abi walks out of the school building onto the playground and notices Lily, Bryar and the twins standing by the gates.

Lily waves her over.

"Where's Cal?" Lily asks when she gets to them.

"He's in the art room with Avery and Mrs. Tillman. He was called in early for a meeting."

The kids exchange a look.

"A meeting about what?" Lily asks.

Abi shrugs. "I don't know."

At first, Abi had thought the meeting was a good sign. Maybe Mrs. Tillman wanted to tell Avery about the amazing art Cal had been doing. Good reports from school might help convince Bill to let them stay with Avery. But when Mrs. Tillman had told Abi to go and wait outside on the playground, that she wanted to talk to her brother and her foster mom alone, Abi's heart had sunk into her stomach. When her brother was in trouble, she could feel it in the air.

"Did you see the interview?" Lily asks Abi.

"A bit of it."

They'd had the show on over breakfast. Avery had shut it off as soon as she came into the kitchen, but they'd seen enough to know it was bad.

"We're going to the woods," Laila says. "To talk to Skye and the boys."

The school bell goes.

Children start leaving the playground and heading inside.

"We have to go now," Lily says. "Before the teachers notice us."

"What about Cal?" Abi says. "He's still inside."

"You can tell him what we decided later," Laila says.

Abi looks back toward the school buildings. She and Cal don't do things apart, especially stuff like this. But she knows that the others are right. They've got to make a plan. And anyway, things are so awkward between Cal and Skye—maybe it will be easier without him there.

"Okay," she says.

Skye sits on the steps of the cabin, writing the story about the mother bear and her cubs on Wynn's cast.

"The mama bear would really do anything to protect her babies?" Wynn asks.

Skye nods.

"Even eat people?"

"Well, maybe not eat them—but she'd try to scare them off."

"Would she kill them?"

"If they got too close, yeah, she might."

They're so focused that they don't hear the children walking toward them.

Or Phoenix dropping out of the tree beside them.

"What are you all doing here?" Phoenix asks, standing in front of the cabin, like he's guarding it. Lumen comes and stands at his feet.

"We need to talk," Lily says.

Skye puts the pen away and looks at the children. "Aren't you guys meant to be at school?" she asks.

"Have you seen the TV interview?" Lily.

"We don't have a TV," Skye says.

Lily, Bryar and the twins exchange a look.

"What is it?" Skye says.

"Dr. Carver's been saying bad stuff about us," Lily says.

Skye shrugs. "As if that's news."

"She did it on national TV," Laila adds.

Skye rolls her eyes. "Of course she did."

"And the police got hold of Astrid's phone. So now they've got real evidence."

"What did you say?" Phoenix asks.

"They showed screenshots of her phone. Not the video, thank God, but evidence that she was looking stuff up about guns," Lily says.

Phoenix goes off to a corner of the deck and stares out into the dark woods.

Lily turns back to Skye. "I think they should hear the truth from us—before they come up with their own theories."

"They've already come up with their own theories," Abi says.

"Well, it's only going to get worse if we don't say something," Lily says.

Skye scans the children again. "Where's Cal?"

"He and Avery had to stay back and talk to the art teacher," Abi says. "I think he's in trouble about something. School stuff—not our stuff."

Our stuff, Lily thinks. Abi's too scared to actually say it, even when it's just them.

There's a gust of wind. The wind chimes play a tune above their heads and a bunch of small yellow leaves fall from the birch trees.

Lily remembers how they stood on the dock during the prayer meeting, watching their leaves floating away across the pond. How it had felt like they were doing something important. Something good. And they'd wanted her to wake up, hadn't they? To get better? Only, now that she has, everything's just got worse.

Skye stands up and brushes down her jeans and says, "You know that once we say it, there's no going back?"

The kids look at each other.

Lily steps forward. "Yeah, we know that. But we don't have a choice any more, do we?"

Skye stares at her. "I guess we don't."

She takes Wynn's hand and walks down the porch steps. One by one, the other kids follow her along the path, through the woods, back to town.

CHAPTER

41

10 a.m.

IF SHE HADN'T ignored what Laila had told her and gone back to the twins' bedroom; if she hadn't kept tidying their things; if she hadn't pulled the trunk out from under Laila's bed and smashed the lock—maybe Yasmin could have kept up the pretence that her kids weren't involved in the shooting. But pretending is no longer an option.

As soon as she found it, she knew she had to bring the parents together, those whose children were involved in the shooting of Astrid Carver. She couldn't make a decision about this without them.

"Priscilla made it sound like we wanted this to happen . . ." True says, shaking his head.

"She's angry," Kaitlin says gently. "And scared."

"That doesn't excuse what she's doing," True says.

"No, no it doesn't. But she's been through so much . . . more than any of us could ever imagine," Kaitlin says.

Yasmin wishes that Priscilla could hear Kaitlin now: defending her despite all the things she's said about her and Ben and her son.

Eva stands up. "True's right: Priscilla's gone too far."

She pours herself a glass of water from the sink. Yasmin notices that Eva's fingers are shaking.

"I just don't understand how they got hold of those images," Kaitlin says.

True takes a breath. "I found Astrid's phone," he says. "I didn't know it was hers. It had run out of battery."

They turn to him.

"Where did you find it?" Kaitlin asks.

"It was under Phoenix's mattress."

"Phoenix? But why—?" Kaitlin starts.

"You know how Phoenix is. God knows why the kid took the phone—or why he was hiding it. Anyway, I saw a reporter walking around with a similar-looking phone and asked if he could charge it for me. That's when we worked out it was Astrid's. It had a picture of her and her dad as a screensaver."

"And you thought that letting a reporter look through Astrid's phone was a good idea?" Kaitlin asks.

"Look, I wasn't really thinking. He helped me. And he seemed like a decent guy. He promised he'd hand the phone in to the police after he was done looking at it—and that's what he did."

"After he *released the images*, True," Kaitlin says. "I don't believe any of them are decent, not any more."

"They're just doing their job. And you know what? With all the stuff that Priscilla has been feeding the press about our kids, it didn't feel like the worst thing in the world for someone to take a look at what Astrid might have been hiding. She wasn't even meant to be at the party. We all know that there was something off about her being in the stable with our kids."

"But Astrid's the one who got hurt, True," Kaitlin says. "Nothing changes that."

"Yeah, but that doesn't make her innocent, does it?"

Kaitlin looks at him, her eyes wide, clearly trying to take in what he's saying. "I guess not."

Yasmin thinks about what she has to share with them too. And how it's much worse than a cell phone. She notices Eva bending over and pressing her hand to her side. She goes over to her.

"Are you okay?"

"I'll be fine." Eva gives her a weak smile. "Just feeling a bit wobbly today." She takes her glass of water back to the table and sits down. Yasmin joins her.

"That presenter said there was more on the phone—things they couldn't share on TV. What do you think he meant?" Kaitlin asks.

"I guess we'll find out soon enough," True says.

For a while, the parents sit there in silence, drinking their tea. Then True asks, "So, why did you get us all to come over, Yasmin?"

Yasmin thinks, again, about Laila's trunk. Her little girl who loved to store up memories. The lupines she'd pressed during their holiday in Maine. Birthday cards. Letters from her grandparents in Pakistan. A soccer certificate.

It hadn't taken much for the lock to snap open; it was small and flimsy.

"I called you over because there *is* more," she says quietly.

"More? More than what?" True asks.

"More than all those things that Priscilla said in the interview."

"How can there be any more?" True says. "She's attacked us all. There's nothing left."

"You're not the only one who found something, True," Yasmin says.

"You found something—where?" Kaitlin looks worried. She's waiting for another bomb to drop. For something else to be her or her family's fault.

"I found the gun," Yasmin says.

She can feel her words hitting each of the parents in turn. How the air changes in the room. It's what they've been waiting for—and dreading. Along with the phone, it's a real piece of evidence: something that will tell them what happened on Sunday.

"You found the gun?" True shakes his head. "Christ."

"Yes. The one that was used to shoot Astrid. Or I think it is. It must be." She looks round at the parents, trying to hold her nerve. "I found it under Laila's bed. It matches the one from the police reports. The one from your house, Kaitlin."

"Oh, God," Kaitlin says.

True stands up. "What have you done with it?"

"I wrapped it in a towel and put it in the laundry room. I didn't know what else to do with it, not before I'd talked to you."

Nothing could have prepared Yasmin to share information like this. Before this morning, she'd never even seen a gun in real life.

"Why do you think Laila had the gun?" Eva asks. "It doesn't make any sense."

"I—I don't know . . . I think she wanted to hide it. Like Phoenix—" Yasmin's voice cracks.

"Christ, those kids—what the hell are they hiding from us?" True says, shaking his head. Then he turns to Yasmin. "Show me where you put it."

Yasmin stands up. "Yes, yes, of course."

She takes him to the laundry room behind the kitchen and, a few moments later, they're back.

True unravels the towel and places it on the table.

They stare at it in silence. The small black pistol that their kids played with. That one of their kids used to shoot Astrid Carver.

"It's Ben's," Kaitlin says. "It's the one that's missing from the safe in the stable."

None of this feels real, thinks Yasmin. But then nothing's felt real since that Sunday afternoon when they heard a gunshot ringing out from the stable.

"We have to prepare ourselves," True says. "Once we hand the gun in, they're going to look for fingerprints . . ."

Yasmin knows that Kaitlin is right: they have to brace themselves for what the police are going to find. *She's* going to have to brace herself for what the police are going to say about why her dear, sweet Laila was hiding a gun under her bed.

They stand in silence. Then Eva says, "Have any of your children said anything to you—anything at all that might clarify what happened in the stable?" Eva juts her chin out toward the gun. "Something that might explain why Yasmin found this under Laila's bed?"

One by one they shake their heads.

"Lieutenant Mesenberg thought one of them would have caved by now. She said she and her officers are experts at getting people to talk. But the kids have stayed quiet. Every one of them," Eva says.

It had amazed and frightened her, this resolve the kids had to keep what happened that afternoon a secret. Lieutenant Mesenberg had underestimated them. They all had.

"What the hell do these kids have to hide that's so bad?" True says.

"Kids have complex motivations," Eva says. "They feel things deeply. They get scared."

"If they're scared then they need to come to us to ask for help," True says. "I've always taught my kids that they can tell me anything. It's how Cedar and I raised them."

Everyone falls quiet again. And then Eva's phone rings.

"Sorry," she says and turns it off.

But then Yasmin's phone goes off. She feels sweat gathering at the base of her spine.

The words BROOK MIDDLE SCHOOL come up on her screen.

"Hello?" she says.

"Mrs. Sayed?"

"Yes."

"This is Mrs. Markham. The principal."

She waits for her to go on.

"Did you send your children into school this morning?"

"Yes—yes. I brought them in myself."

"Well, they didn't show up for registration."

"I don't understand—"

"Hanif and Laila are not at school. And some of the other children are missing too."

"Missing?"

"The children involved in what happened . . . at the Wrights' party. None of them showed up to class today."

CHAPTER

42

10.45 a.m.

THROUGH THE BATHROOM door, Eva hears the others putting on their boots and coats and discussing where they should go to look for the children.

The mothers are going to split up and sweep the town. In the meantime, True is going to take the gun to the police.

Eva had convinced herself that Lily didn't have anything to do with the shooting. That, at worst, she was a bystander who saw what happened and agreed to keep it a secret. But if Laila Sayed, a girl who's never put a foot wrong, was hiding a gun, doesn't that call all the kids into question?

She folds her hands over her stomach to ease the cramps.

She'd thought that she could make a difference here. Even after everything that happened, she'd wanted to support the parents and the children. She'd tried so hard to do the right thing. But it turned out that Priscilla was right all along: she was stupid to have got involved in any of this.

She was foolish to have come to America at all.

She hears the front door opening and closing as the parents go off to look for their kids.

For the first time, she regrets not having given in to Lily's requests for a mobile phone. She'd wanted to protect her from that distraction; to let her be a kid for a bit longer, but right now, Eva would do anything to be able to get in touch with her.

She has to get to her but she doesn't have the strength to move.

When I find you, Lily, we're going home, she says. *I'm going to tell Dad he has to give his notice. That we have to go back to London. We're not meant to be here; we never were.*

The strength of her feelings—her certainty that this is what they're going to do—gives her a moment of relief from the cramps.

And then she feels something warm and wet rush between her legs.

Oh, God.

She rips off a wad of toilet paper and wipes herself. Bright red spots spread across the paper.

Her legs start to shake.

She pulls her underwear up and stumbles over to the sink.

There's a knock on the door.

"You okay in there, Eva?" It's Yasmin.

She grips the sink and stares at herself in the mirror but her eyes won't focus.

Please no, please, please, no . . .

"Eva?"

Eva stumbles toward the door. She unlocks it. Yasmin stands in front of her. "Are you okay, Eva?"

Eva shakes her head.

Yasmin looks past Eva, at the blood-spots on the paper dissolving into the water of the toilet bowl.

"Oh—oh, Eva . . ."

Eva tries to take a step forward but her legs give way.

Yasmin puts her arm around her. "I'm here," she says. "I'm here."

C H A P T E R

43

10 a.m.

THE CHILDREN STAND under the pines, rehearsing what they're going to say.

They've decided not to go back to school: they have to talk to their parents before they lose their nerve.

The twins are the first to leave, walking back to their big white house on Main Street. Mom's always there, waiting for them to get home from school.

Abi drags her feet back to St. Mary's. She wishes that Cal had been with her when they went to see Skye. She knows that he wouldn't have agreed with the others about coming clean to the grown-ups. It was too risky. The other kids don't have as much to lose as they do.

Early this morning, they'd heard Bill talking to Avery in the kitchen. She knew that it was just a matter of time before he took them away.

Skye and Wynn sit on the front steps of the cabin and wait for Dad to come home. Phoenix runs off into the woods without saying a word.

Bryar and Lily pick up their bikes at the edge of the woods. They give each other a hug, knowing that the next time they see each other, everything will be different. And then they cycle off to their homes. As Lily watches Bryar cycling up toward Woodwind, her body feels hollow. *Please may he be okay,* she whispers to herself.

On her way back to the bungalow, Lily hears a honking behind her. She looks round and sees Dad driving their car. Which is weird; he should be at the university. He must have cycled back and collected the car from home. But then why isn't Mum with him?

She'd banked on telling Mum before she told him—Mum would have helped her find the right words.

Dad winds down the window.

"Dad—" Lily starts.

"I need you to get in the car, Lily."

"Why aren't you at work?"

"Please, Lily, just get in."

She leaves her bike on the pavement, gets in the car next to Dad and they drive along Main Street.

Through the car window, she watches the brook rushing past, the water so high that it looks like it's going to burst its banks.

Dad's really quiet.

Maybe he's found out what happened. Maybe he's angry. Even more angry than he was before.

"Where are we going, Dad?" Lily asks.

"To the hospital."

"What? Why are we going to the hospital?"

"Mum's not well."

Lily's heart starts racing.

"What? Mum? I don't understand."

Dad flicks on the indicator and turns into the hospital car park.

"Your mother's expecting a baby, Lily." His voice is choked.

The words hit her right in the chest.

"A *baby*?"

He nods.

Lily thought Mum was too old to have a baby. She didn't know Mum *wanted* to have a baby, not any more.

"Why didn't you tell me before?"

Dad goes quiet.

"Dad?"

"Because I didn't know, Lily."

Lily's mind races. None of this is making sense. "But why is she in hospital?"

"Because there's been a complication."

"What kind of complication?"

Dad turns into one of the parking spaces and switches off the ignition. "I've only had a brief conversation with Mrs. Sayed—I don't know any more than I've told you."

"Mrs. Sayed? What does she have to do with Mum being at the hospital?"

"She took Mum to the ER."

"You mean you haven't spoken to Mum directly?"

Dad stares out through the windscreen. "No, I haven't. She was visiting Mrs. Sayed and she wasn't feeling well so Mrs. Sayed thought it was best to get her checked out."

"At the hospital? Why didn't she just take her to the doctor?"

"I don't know, Lily."

Everything feels jumbled in Lily's head. One minute she's cycling home, ready to tell Mum and Dad about what happened at the party, and the next Dad's driving her to the hospital because Mum's pregnant—and because something's wrong with her.

"Is Mum going to be okay?" Lily asks, her voice shaky.

"I don't know, Lily."

"And the baby?"

Dad leans over and takes Lily's hand. "I'm sorry, Lily, I don't know that either."

CHAPTER

44

2 p.m.

ASTRID LOOKS AROUND the room.

The bedside table with cards on top.

A single foil balloon floating by the ceiling.

Beside her bed, on the monitor, her heart beats out a jagged green line. Next to it, the IV drip that's connected to her arm.

Her eyes close again, tired from taking in so much. And then she feels someone stroking her head. And then a voice that sounds like Dad's, but isn't Dad meant to be in California?

We're going to take good care of you, Astrid . . . we're so glad you've come back to us . . .

She tries to look at where the voice has come from but her eyes feel too heavy.

Mom will be here soon . . .

Beyond her room, she hears footsteps, rushing; trolleys and gurneys being pushed down the hallway. Someone, somewhere, is crying.

She blinks again but her eyes won't open. A picture flickers behind her eyelids.

She's outside. She can see herself at a distance, standing on a patch of cracked earth. She can smell hay. Hear the horses kicking in their stalls.

She blinks again.

Now she's inside the office at the back of the stable. A boy she used to be friends with kneels in front of the gun safe. Others press in through the door behind him.

It's easy . . . she tells him. *Anyone can open it . . .*

He looks up at her. *I don't want to do this,* his eyes say.

But she knows he'll do it. For her. For all of them, watching.

She hadn't planned this—or not exactly. To make him get out the gun and then to sneak in through the back door of his house to get the ammo—*it won't feel real if it's not loaded,* she'd said.

At first, she'd only wanted to see what was happening at the party; she didn't want to be left out. But once she was in the stable and saw all those children there, having fun without her; once she saw Cal holding hands with Skye when she was the one who'd been the first to talk to him at church, right at the beginning of the summer—when she'd made it obvious that she liked him; and once she saw that English girl standing next to Bryar, like they'd known each other for ever, the voice had come into her head, the one that she tries so hard not to listen to because it pushes her into doing bad things:

Make him do it! You need to show him! To show all of them!

And then another voice, the one that made her come to the party to begin with:

You have to show Mom, the voice had said. *You have to show her that she can't stop you from doing what you want. That she's not in charge.*

And there was a third voice too, one that had been going around and around in her head since February:

Find a way to make Dad come home . . .

She'd tried to make the voices go away but the harder she tried the louder they shouted at her. And then, all of a sudden, she was the one doing the shouting—yelling at the boy who used to be her friend, making him feel small, pushing him into doing something he never wanted to do.

What are you waiting for? she'd yelled. *Open it!*

She remembers hating herself for speaking to him like that, but she couldn't make herself stop.

She blinks again.

It's cold outside now. Everything's frozen. There's snow on the ground and she's younger. She wasn't meant to take him for a walk; Mom gave her clear instructions that Jake should be kept inside for another few weeks.

And then, when she turned up with him at the stable, Bryar had warned her to keep the dog away from the horses.

He'll scare them . . . he'd said. *He's too jumpy . . .*

But she hadn't listened.

A horse screamed.

The dog barked.

A shot rang out through the stable.

And then silence.

She blinks again.

Lying in the hospital bed, her heart speeds up. Her chest hurts; every breath hurts.

Beside her, the machine starts beeping.

A nurse runs in.

And then a doctor behind her.

And then Mom. She's breathing hard, like she's been running. Her face is flushed.

And Dad's here too, leaning in, stroking her head again.

And then Mom starts crying and Dad puts his arm around her and the picture doesn't look right. Why is he touching Mom like that? He lives somewhere else now. Far away. He said that didn't love her any more.

Mom leans in and kisses Astrid's forehead; she feels Mom's warm tears against her brow.

Astrid tries to push a word out of her throat but her voice comes out broken. "Mom . . ."

She coughs.

A nurse tries to give her some water but she chokes on it; she feels it dribble down her chin.

"Mom . . ." she tries again. "I need to tell you something—" She coughs, a ragged cough that burns her throat.

"You need to rest, Astrid," Dad says. "We can talk later."

Astrid takes another breath and musters up all the strength she can.

She blinks.

Bryar is standing in front of the safe, staring at her, his eyes pleading. She's holding up her phone, telling him that it shouldn't be taking this long, that the YouTube video she'd watched made it look easy.

Now Jake's lying in the hay, bleeding out.

The pictures blur into each other but one day is hot—so hot that she can feel the sunburn on the back of her legs—and in the other picture, it's snowing outside.

More doctors and nurses crowd in. There are too many people in the room. But she has to keep trying.

"It was my fault . . ." she says.

"What? No, darling. No. None of this is your fault . . ." Mom says.

"I let him out . . ." Astrid pushes the words through her lips. "It wasn't a mistake . . . It was me."

She'd blamed Jake, said that he'd escaped on his own. And they'd believed her. Her story made sense. Jake came from a bad home. He was unpredictable—he would get mad when something spooked him. He'd found a way to get out by himself.

She'd never owned up to the fact that it was her fault that Jake had been shot. That she'd taken him to the stable. That he'd bitten one of the horses. That that's why Bryar's dad had taken out his rifle.

"Let who out, darling?" Mom says.

"I wanted to be with Bryar . . . I didn't want to be alone . . ." She feels the emptiness of the house without Dad in it; how it made the inside of her body feel empty too.

"You're confused, darling, please, please rest . . ."

Astrid thrashes her head violently against her pillow. Her thoughts spin. She has to get this right.

"I *made* him do it . . ." Astrid says.

She hears that horse kicking at the stall. Crying out.

She sees Wynn stepping too close—waving his arms about, getting in the way of everything.

She sees Mr. Wright holding the rifle, snow on his coat.

She sees Dad driving away, his car packed with all the things he wanted to bring to his life without her or Mom.

And then Bryar is looking up at her again.

Mom squeezes Astrid's hand. She's crying.

"Shhhh, Astrid—you don't need to worry about anything any more. You're back with us. That's all that matters now . . ."

A doctor's shining a light into her eyes. It's too bright.

She blinks.

"It was my fault, Mom . . ." she says again. "It was all my fault."

CHAPTER

45

7 p.m.

IT TAKES A while for the children to tell their parents. For them to be in the right place and to find the right words. The grown-ups are so busy talking about Astrid waking up that it's hard to interrupt them and make them listen. And the kids are scared about what Astrid will say too, now that she's awake. And about what will happen to them when everything's out. Some of the kids think that maybe they shouldn't talk after all; that they should go back to being quiet. But they promised each other.

I learned the codes to the safes, Bryar tells his mom and dad. *The safe in the stable, with the gun. And the one in the basement with the ammo. I saw Dad opening and closing them so often, the numbers sank in . . . It wasn't like I was planning to open them . . . but Astrid asked me to . . . She said I had to . . . I know it was stupid, but I thought that maybe, if I did something to make her happy, we could be friends again . . . like we used to be . . .*

It was Astrid who asked him to get the gun out of the safe, Abi says. *But we all wanted to see what it looked like . . . and to know whether he could shoot it . . .* Her voice echoes between the church walls.

And then, when Cal comes home with Avery, when she gets a phone call to say that the others are missing from school, he tells

Abi about how the red, black, and yellow paint got on his hands. How he got so scared by what was happening, by the news attention and the fact that Bill would probably pull them out of their new home with Avery. He'd wanted to do something, anything, to take the attention away from them.

I knew it was the wrong thing to do—to attack the twins and their family. But I thought that if people focused on them, then maybe they'd stop suspecting us and we'd get to stay. Their parents are rich. Their dad got them a lawyer. I didn't think they had anything to lose.

Cal had another reason too, one he doesn't tell them. He hoped that maybe Skye would be proud of him for taking attention away from her brother too. He'd heard people were whispering about Phoenix. Cal thought it might be a way to make it up to her for asking her to leave the stable that afternoon. That maybe then she'd like him again.

After Cal had had his turn, Abi told her story.

I took the safety catch off, she says. *Mom's boyfriend taught me how to do it—the one I shot in the leg. I wanted to see if I could remember. And I thought the others would think it was cool, that I knew how the gun worked . . . I thought it would make them like me . . .*

Avery puts her arm around Abi's shoulders, but that makes her feel even worse for letting her down. She'd promised herself that she'd do everything to make sure they could stay. But she'd messed it up. They both had.

As Lily sits beside her mum's hospital bed, she whispers, *I tried to make it into a game, Mum . . .*

Dad's getting them snacks from the vending machine. It's the first chance she's had to be with Mum alone.

I thought that if we all took it in turns to hold the gun, then we could get it away from Astrid and back into the safe . . . it was a stupid idea . . . I know that now . . . but I couldn't think what else to do . . . And Astrid went for it. She said it would be fun if we all held the gun. She even dared us to point it at her—like we were in a movie. For the first time, she seemed to like me—you know how she ignored me every time we went over to their house. And I thought that maybe it could work . . .

I wanted to have a go too, Wynn says, looking up at his dad, his eyes wide. *I didn't think it was fair. I never get to do anything that the big kids do. I wanted to touch it . . . So I jumped up and down and tried to reach it—but then the horse got in the way . . .*

The reason I was outside the stable when they were playing with the gun was because I was talking to Cal, Skye says. *I wasn't watching Wynn—or the other kids, like you asked me to. And then, when I did go back in, they wouldn't listen to me. They were so wrapped up in their game that they refused to hand over the gun. I couldn't stop them. And then Astrid got hurt. And I made them agree not to say anything. Because I was scared. I felt like it was my fault.*

The twins sit at the kitchen island in front of their parents. Mom and Dad are waiting for them to start speaking.

It took so long for Mom to get home from taking Mrs. Day to the hospital that the twins nearly changed their minds about coming clean. Especially Hanif.

"But you said you weren't involved," Dad says.

"We never said that," Laila says. "You just assumed, Dad. But we had an idea—"

"An idea?" Dad's voice is fierce.

"To take the gun—after Astrid got shot."

"Why on earth did you even touch the gun?" Dad asks.

"We had to hide it," Laila says. "That's why I took it to the car—I ran out of the stable, just before Mom and the other grown-ups ran over from the house to see what had happened."

Dad stares at her and she can feel the disappointment flooding his body: she was his little girl, the one he trusted to get things right.

"I found the gun," Mom says.

The three of them look up at her. She hasn't said a word up to now.

"What?" Dad stares at her.

"The gun that was used to shoot Astrid. I found it and gave it to True. He's handed it in to the police. They're checking it for fingerprints."

"What's True got to do with anything?"

"I invited him over with the other parents. I told them that I'd found the gun. I wanted their advice."

"You're not making any sense," Dad says. "You found a gun—where?"

"I was cleaning the twins' room. It was in Laila's trunk."

"You kept the gun in our room?" Hanif bursts out. "You said you'd gotten rid of it. That no one would ever find it!"

"I didn't know where else to put it." Laila's voice is shaky. "I found a lock. I thought that was enough. I didn't think that Mom would break into it. She wasn't even meant to be in our room. I told her—"

"Why would you want to hide the gun, Laila?" Dad says.

"We thought that if the police couldn't find it, then maybe no one would get in trouble," Laila says. "That maybe it would go away and that no one would be blamed for what happened."

"Oh, Laila." Mom sighs.

"And you went along with this plan, Hanif?" Dad stares at him.

Hanif's bottom lip begins to tremble.

"Hanif?" Dad says again.

Laila takes Hanif's hands and makes him look up at her. "We have to tell them, Hanif."

Hanif nods. He takes a breath. "I thought that maybe . . ." Hanif starts. "Maybe . . ."

Laila finishes his sentence. "He thought that he could get the gun away from Astrid. So, he grabbed it."

"You grabbed the gun!" Dad's yelling now.

"Ayaan . . ." Mom presses Dad's hand. "Let him talk."

Dad stares at the granite counter and shakes his head.

"Astrid wasn't going to let the gun go," Laila says. "She was waving it around at everyone. We were scared that it was going to go off. And then Skye and Cal came in and Skye tried to stop what was happening but no one would listen to her. It was Hanif who talked Astrid into handing it to him. He said he wanted a turn with the gun, to make her think he was playing the game, but really he wanted to scare her. He thought that if she saw how dangerous it was—that it wasn't a toy—that he could persuade her to hand it to Skye or to put it back in the safe."

But Dad's still shaking his head. The twins can feel it: how disappointed he is in them. Especially Hanif.

Hanif takes a breath and says, "I shot the gun." He looks right at Dad. "I wanted to shoot in the air—away from everyone . . ."

"But the safety catch was off," Laila says.

"It went off before it was meant to . . ." Hanif says.

"And Astrid was in the way," Laila explains. "The bullet hit her straight in the chest."

Mom and Dad sink into themselves.

"And the horse got so scared that she bucked and then stumbled backward and knocked Wynn off his feet. He was thrown against the side of the stall," Hanif says. "We were all so busy focusing on Astrid that we didn't realize he'd been hurt too."

"That's when we agreed—all of us—" Laila says.

"When you *agreed*?" Dad says.

"Not to tell anyone about what happened. It was Skye's idea but we knew we'd be in trouble if you found out. Especially Hanif."

"But Hanif didn't mean to do anything wrong," Laila says quickly. "He was trying to save everyone. He was really brave—"

Slowly, Dad stands up.

"You think what your brother did was *brave*?" He looks straight at Hanif. "It wasn't brave. It was stupid." He clenches his fists. "Do you realize what you've done to us, Hanif? *Do* you?"

"It was my fault too, Dad," Laila says. "It was all our faults. We all joined in."

But Dad's not listening.

They should have expected him to take it badly. To blame Hanif. They'd hoped that this time, Dad would understand. But he's never understood them, not really.

"I'm sorry, Dad—" Hanif's voice breaks.

Dad won't look at him.

"Don't be sorry, Hanif." Mom gets up off her stool. She's standing really tall. "And don't listen to your father."

Dad looks up at her.

Don't listen to Dad? The twins have spent their entire lives hearing the exact opposite: that they *had* to listen to him, to take his advice, to follow his example—to please him.

Mom faces Dad, square on.

"Our little boy wasn't stupid, Ayaan. Like Laila said, he stepped in when he saw that something bad was going to happen. He was trying to do the right thing." The words tumble out of Mom's mouth. She catches her breath and then keeps going. "He was trying to be a hero, like you're always telling him to be. To be strong and brave." She pauses. "For God's sake, can't you see it, Ayaan? He did it for you."

The twins stare at Mom. She's never stood up to Dad like this before.

And they've never seen Dad like this either: his whole body stooped over as he sits down on the stool at the kitchen island, unable to move or to say a word.

There's only one piece of the story that the kids leave out: the bit that will change everything—more than anything they've told their parents. But right now, none of them feel like it's for them to tell. The police have Astrid's phone. They'll have seen the video. It will come out soon enough.

CHAPTER

46

7.30 p.m.

KAITLIN GRABS HER keys and her handbag and heads to the front door.

"You don't need to do this, Katie," Ben says, following her out into the hall.

"I do. It's only a matter of time before Priscilla finds out what the children have been saying to us. I don't want her to hear it second-hand."

They watched the talk show together this morning, listening to Priscilla blaming them and their son for shooting Astrid. Bryar sat at the kitchen table between them.

When the show ended and Bryar set off for school, she'd gone to the stable to muck out the horses and Ben had driven off somewhere in his truck. They hadn't talked about the show. They haven't talked properly about anything, not in days.

"You really think Priscilla is going to want to see you?" Ben asks. "After what she said about us?"

"I don't know. But I have to try."

He looks up at her. "You want me to come with you?"

He's making an effort, she thinks. He wants to remind her of how things used to be between them: how they'd be there for each other no matter what.

"No. I think that would confuse things—"

"Because she hates me?"

Kaitlin waits for a beat.

"No. Because we're not on the same page, Ben."

"What's that supposed to mean?"

"She'll feel it, that you're not sorry."

"Of course I'm sorry—what happened to Astrid is terrible."

"That's not what I meant."

"You heard what Mesenberg said. There are no grounds for a criminal charge. The pistol and the ammo were both locked up—in separate places. The fact that Bryar memorized the codes isn't on me. And you saw those pictures from Astrid's phone: that's concrete evidence that she was the instigator. That she planned all this."

As soon as Bryar told them what had happened, Ben called the lieutenant. She went straight to interview each of the other kids, to corroborate Bryar's story. But she said that Bryar's version of events stacked up with the evidence: multiple finger-prints on the pistol, gun residue on the children's clothes. Hanif's direct involvement in the shooting.

"We're in the clear, Katie," Ben goes on.

She shakes her head. "You really don't get it, do you, Ben? It's not about who shot Astrid. It's about the guns being in our home. In our stable."

He looks at her, like he did when they were having that argument a few days ago. Like he doesn't recognize her any more. Like she's trying to hurt him on purpose.

"None of this is about the guns, Katie. They were locked away. They were safe."

"It's *all* about the guns, Ben. It is for Priscilla. And it is for me too. And it's precisely because you don't understand that that you shouldn't come with me."

She turns and walks toward the door. At that moment Bryar comes down the stairs. He's wearing his jacket, as if he's about to go out. He's been in his bedroom all afternoon, his curtains drawn.

"I'm coming with you, Mom," Bryar says.

He must have overheard them arguing.

"Oh, Bryar—" Kaitlin starts. "I'm not sure that's a good idea."

He shakes his head. "I'm coming. I've made up my mind."

"Your mom's right—this isn't going to help," Ben says. "And Mesenberg will have filled her in, anyway. She doesn't need you turning up—"

"I think he should go," Kaitlin says, talking over him. "He feels responsible. By telling us the truth, he's taken the first step. He now needs to speak to Priscilla. It will help him."

"Help him how?" Ben says.

"To work through this."

Ben sits down on the bottom step. He looks defeated. Kaitlin wants to tell him that she still loves him: that nothing will change that. But she has to do the right thing, even if it hurts him. Even if it hurts their marriage.

Kaitlin and Bryar drive through the dark September evening. Night is falling so much faster these days. Soon it will be winter: snow on the ground; the pond frozen over; a different world from that sweltering Sunday afternoon of the party.

She keeps looking over at Bryar. He's quiet, his eyes fixed on the road. She should be relieved that he wasn't the one who pulled the trigger. But there are still a million things wrong with what happened in the stable. And no matter how she looks at it, she always reaches the same conclusion: if she hadn't invited those children into their home, a home with guns, no one would have gotten hurt.

"Mom?"

"Yeah."

"I'm sorry."

"I know."

"If I hadn't—"

"It wasn't your fault, Bryar."

"But I was the one who got the gun out. And the ammo."

"It's more complicated than that."

If there was anything the children's story had showed them, it was this: that life's messy. That when things go wrong, it's rarely about clear-cut guilt or innocence. Most of the time, we're all to blame in some way.

They keep driving. Then Bryar says. "I don't want you to do the talking—with Dr. Carver. I want to tell her myself."

"Oh, Bryar, I know you mean well, but you don't have to do that—"

"I think it would be better coming from me."

She'd tried to get a diagnosis for Bryar. Gone to endless psychologists. It would have been easier to have a label for him. Something more specific than "*on the spectrum.*" A label meant there was a chance that she could find some kind of treatment. But then Eva had come along and said: *You don't need to put him in a box, Kaitlin. So what if he's a little different from the others? It might make things harder for him, but then life gets hard for all of us at one point or another, he'll just have a head start on understanding that.* Then she'd looked Kaitlin right in the eye and said: *Don't ever forget that Bryar is wonderful—just as he is.*

It took a while for Eva's words to sink in. But now she sees it too: her complicated, wonderful son for whom life would be hard. She couldn't protect him from that but she could believe in him—in the fact that he was strong enough to get through it. That maybe, just maybe, he could do more than just get through; he could do something good, like he was trying to do now.

"Remember that she might not be ready to hear what you have to say. What matters is your honesty and your courage. How she reacts isn't your responsibility, Bry. That's on her, okay?"

He nods. "Okay, Mom."

As they reach a red light, Kaitlin leans over, pulls Bryar's face toward her and kisses his cheek. "I love you, Bry, you know that?"

Bryar wipes the kiss off and smiles.

She laughs. "Well, at least that hasn't changed."

"Mom?" Bryar asks.

"Yes, buddy."

"Is Dad going to move out, like Astrid's dad?"

"Move out? No—"

"You keep arguing." He swallows hard. "And I know it's because of what I did."

"No—no, please don't think that." She takes her hand in his. "Let's focus on today—and on this brave thing you did by telling us what happened."

Bryar leans back in his seat. She wishes she could tell him that she and Ben are going to be okay, but right now, things feel so broken between them that she can't make that promise.

When Kaitlin and Bryar get to the reception desk of the pediatric ward, Peter comes up behind them. He's carrying a bag of clothes for Astrid.

"Kaitlin?" he says, surprised.

She hesitates. They haven't talked in close to three years, but, after a few seconds of awkwardness, astonishingly, he steps forward and gives her a hug.

"It's good to see you again, Kaitlin," Peter says. "And you too, Bryar."

Kaitlin and Bryar stare at Peter, floored by his warmth. But then she remembers that Priscilla was the one who'd taken against them. Peter had stood by her but he'd never attacked them about what happened to their dog, not like Priscilla had.

"We're so glad that Astrid is going to be okay," Kaitlin says.

Peter nods. "It's been a hell of a week for all of us."

She doesn't know how she's going to go through with this. This kindness or tolerance or whatever it is that Peter's showing right now—it's not going to last. Not when he finds out what happened at the party.

But that's why they're here. To tell him—and Priscilla—the truth. Maybe now that Astrid has woken up, she'll be ready to hear it. Maybe something good can come out of this after all.

Bryar steps forward and says, "Would it be possible for me to speak to Dr. Carver?"

Kaitlin's heart swells. At how polite he's being. And how brave. And by how scared she is that he's going to be knocked back.

Peter raises his eyebrows. "You want to talk to Priscilla?"

"Yes. I'd like her to know what happened in the stable—and how Astrid got hurt."

Peter stares at him. "Well, that's very good of you, Bryar. But I'm not sure that's the best idea." He looks at Kaitlin, clearly hoping that she'll agree with him. "Cil is still pretty raw about all this . . ." He clears his throat. "I guess you saw the TV interview."

Kaitlin nods. "We understand."

"And Lieutenant Mesenberg has been by already. She's given us an update on what the children have said. There's really no need—"

"I'd still like to talk to her," Bryar says. "So she can hear it from me."

Peter looks from Kaitlin to Bryar. "I see. Well, I suppose you can try. But don't say I didn't warn you. She's not in a good place."

"Thank you," Kaitlin says. "We appreciate it."

Before Peter guides them into the family room, Kaitlin glances down the hallway and catches sight of Priscilla; the door to Astrid's room is cracked open. Has Astrid spoken to her mother? Has she told her the truth?

Peter opens the door to the family room. "Take a seat here, I'll go and get her," he says.

When he's gone, Bryar squeezes Kaitlin's hand. "It'll be okay, Mom."

Kaitlin looks at her son, who suddenly seems so much older than the little boy he was, even a few days ago.

CHAPTER

47

8 p.m.

When Priscilla walks into the family room, Kaitlin stands up. Bryar stands up too and comes to her side.

"How is Astrid doing?" Kaitlin asks.

Priscilla's eyebrows shoot up. "How's she doing? She was shot, Kaitlin, how do you think she's doing?"

"I'm sorry . . ." Kaitlin mumbles.

"You're *sorry*?"

Ben was right, Kaitlin thinks. So was Peter. Priscilla's not ready to see them—let alone to hear what they have to say.

Bryar takes a step forward.

"I would like to tell you something, Dr. Carver."

Priscilla's head snaps up and she looks him right in the eye. He looks back at her, not flinching. "Lots of things happened in the stable—both before and after Astrid got shot. And I'm sorry that we haven't told you before now. We were scared—"

"*You* were scared?" Priscilla bursts out.

"Give the kid a chance," Peter says.

"I know what I'm going to say isn't going to make what happened to Astrid go away, but I still think you should know and then Mom and I will leave and you don't have to see us ever again."

Bryar says it all in one breath, as though he's worried that if he hesitates, he won't be able to finish.

Priscilla sits down in one of the chairs. "Okay, but I don't have long."

She looks toward the door and Kaitlin knows that she wants to get back to Astrid. If it was Bryar, lying in that hospital bed, Kaitlin wouldn't want to leave his side either. In the end, they're both mothers—they share that, and that's something, isn't it? More than something. Maybe it's the most important thing of all.

Bryar sits down in the chair next to her. Kaitlin and Peter take a seat too. And then Bryar starts to tell the story. About how he was the one who took the gun out of the safe and then the ammo too, and how, in the minutes that followed, each of the children, in their own way, made mistakes—or misjudgments. Things that they couldn't undo. But he keeps coming back to the fact that he was the only one who knew the code to his dad's safes. That if it hadn't been for him, the gun would still be in there now. Unloaded. That no one would have gotten hurt. That Astrid would be okay.

Not once does he put the blame on Astrid. He doesn't talk about how she'd stood in the stable, taunting him, or how she'd turned holding the gun into a big, dangerous game.

Priscilla listens. Or she seems to. Sometimes her eyes drift off, like she's being tugged back to Astrid's room. Or maybe she's just tired. Kaitlin hopes to God that she's at least taking in something of what Bryar is telling her. Nothing is going to take away the pain of the last few days, but *please,* Kaitlin prays, *please may Bryar's words make a difference.* Maybe even allow her to let go of some of her anger.

"I'm sorry, Dr. Carver," Bryar says. "I should never have opened the safes—the one with the gun and the one with the ammo. If I hadn't, then none of this would have happened."

And then he hangs his head and looks down at the floor, like she's seen him do a thousand times.

Priscilla sits there, her eyes still far away. Then, slowly, she stands up and walks toward the door.

"Cil?" Peter calls after her.

She turns around. "What?"

"It's taken a lot for Bryar to come here. To talk to you like this. Say something to the kid."

She stares at Peter, incredulous. "You want me to *thank* him, is that it?"

"Come on, Cil, don't be like this."

"There's nothing to say, Peter. Because nothing's changed."

Peter shakes his head.

Priscilla turns her head and catches Kaitlin's eye. "Has it, Kaitlin?"

Beside her, Bryar slumps into himself. He really believed he could get through to her. Kaitlin would do anything to take away his disappointment, to help him see that, regardless of how Priscilla is responding, what he did today was good and brave.

Priscilla turns to leave. She puts her fingers on the door handle and then stops.

"Where's Ben?" she says, not turning around.

"Ben?" Kaitlin says.

"Your husband."

So, this is what this was about: Ben. Maybe it's what it's been about all along.

Bryar looks up. "Dad's at home. He thought it was best . . ."

Priscilla turns around. "Best?" she asks.

"To give you some space," Kaitlin says.

Priscilla looks straight at Kaitlin. "Still loves his guns, does he?"

Kaitlin stares back. "*Loves* guns? No, no. It's not like that—it's never been like that. They're part of his work—they're—"

But then she isn't sure what to say. She can't defend him. Not any more.

Peter stands up and walks toward Priscilla.

"Come on, Cil," he says.

Kaitlin thinks about how she's tried to get through to Ben about having firearms in their home—to help him understand how others see it. And how she's come to see it too. She wants to tell Priscilla that, for the first time in their marriage, it's created a distance between her and Ben, one that neither of them knows how to bridge.

"It's complicated for Ben," Kaitlin starts. "The gun question . . ."

Kaitlin feels her words bouncing off Priscilla; she's not ready to hear it.

"So, in other words, nothing's changed," Priscilla says.

And with that, she leaves the room.

CHAPTER

48

8.15 p.m.

EVA'S EYES BURN with tiredness. Every bit of her body aches.

And then it comes back to her.

Standing in Yasmin's bathroom. The cramps. The blood. Yasmin driving her to the hospital.

She brushes her hand over her stomach.

How could she have pinned her hopes on this? She's over forty. She had Lily eleven years ago and every attempt at getting pregnant since then has ended in a miscarriage. Her body isn't meant to have a baby—Lily was her miracle. Why couldn't she just accept that?

The door to her room flies open.

"Mum!" Lily runs over to her bed. "You're awake!" She throws her arms around Eva.

Will comes in behind Lily. He sits down on the side of the bed and takes Eva's hand and kisses it. Then Lily draws him into a hug and, for a moment, the three of them hold on to each other and she breathes them in: their hair and their skin and the feel of their breath against her neck.

Will sits back and looks at her in a way that he hasn't done in ages. Not since the shooting. Maybe not since they left England.

Lily tightens her arms around her.

"I want to go home," Eva says.

"The doctor needs to run a few more tests," Will says. "Then we can head back to the house."

"I don't want to go back to the house. I want to go back to England."

Lily pulls back. She looks at Eva, her eyes wide and sad. "You want us to leave Middlebrook?"

She nods, her chin trembling. "Yes, my love."

"But I thought you wanted us to make a go of it here?"

"We don't belong here, Lily."

"But Mum—" Lily starts.

Will puts an arm on Lily's shoulder and then turns to Eva. "Let's take this one step at a time. You've been through a lot, my love, but everything's going to be okay now."

"*Okay*?" Her eyes fill with tears. "How can things be okay?"

"We're here for you, my love. And we're going to make this work."

Eva looks up at Will through blurry eyes.

"Yeah, Mum, Dad's right. And I'll help—I'll be the best big sister ever—"

"And I guess I'll get used to the idea of being a geriatric dad! Christ, Eva. I could have done with some warning."

Eva's heart jumps.

"But the baby—after what happened at Yasmin's—"

Will squeezes Eva's hand. "The baby's going to be fine."

"It is?"

"You had a placental abruption. You lost a lot of blood. And you're going to have to take it easy—bed rest from now on." Will's eyes go glassy. "But the doctor is confident that we're finally going to have that sibling for Lily."

"I guess I'll have to forget those lectures you gave me about only children rocking the world." Lily looks from Eva to Will, smiling.

"Big sisters rock the world too," Will says.

Lily and Will's words fly around Eva's head. She still can't quite take in what they're saying.

"So, the baby's okay?" she asks again.

"Yes, my love, the baby is okay."

Eva touches her stomach again. When she woke up alone in the hospital room, she'd felt it—the dark, empty space in her womb. She was sure that the baby had gone.

She looks out of the window and thinks about the last few weeks. The move to America. Trying so hard to be part of this community. Putting up with the horrible brown bungalow. The party at Woodwind Stables. The terrible accident—and then what happened afterward. And all the time, keeping the baby a secret from Will and Lily.

"I still want to go home," Eva says.

"But Mum—"

"I don't think I can live here, Lily. Not with everything that's happened. I don't understand how life works here."

Will takes her hand in his. "None of us understand how life works, my love. It doesn't matter where we're from. The best we can do is to be there for each other when things get hard." His voice chokes up. "And that's where I messed up. I'm sorry I haven't been there for you more."

"But Astrid's still fighting for her life . . ." Eva says.

Lily exchanges a look with Will. "Astrid woke up, Mum."

It takes a while for Eva to react; her brain is too foggy to take in this news.

"She's going to be okay," Lily says.

Something in Eva's heart comes loose. Thank God.

"And there's something else too, Mum." Lily takes a breath. "We told the truth about what happened," she says. "Like you wanted us to."

A vague memory comes back to Eva. Lily sitting next to her and talking to her in the middle of the night. She'd wanted to answer her but she had felt too weak.

We were all to blame, Mum . . .

There's a light knock on the door. Will stands up to open it.

Yasmin walks in.

"I'm sorry, I can come back later," she says.

"No . . . no, come in," ~~Peter~~ Will says. "I've been meaning to call you to thank you for bringing Eva in."

Yasmin steps forward.

On the way to the hospital, Eva had told Yasmin about the pregnancy. And it had felt like such a relief—sharing it at last. And then so unbearably sad because she'd been certain that she'd lost the baby.

"The baby's going to be okay," Eva says, reaching out her hand for Yasmin.

Yasmin rushes forward. "Oh, Eva."

The two women hold hands and look at each other. Eva thinks about the graffiti on the mosque and the things Priscilla said about her children on the TV show. They're both outsiders here.

"Why don't we leave Mum and Mrs. Sayed to have a chat," Will says. "We'll go and find one of the nurses and let them know that Mum's awake. They'll want to come and check on her. And maybe we can go and grab a bite to eat."

Eva looks over at Will and gives him a grateful smile. Something has changed between them. He's listening to her again. And not just to her words: he sees her.

Lily comes over and gives Eva a kiss on the cheek and then goes out of the room with Will.

Yasmin pulls up a chair.

"Will's right," Eva says. "Thank you for taking care of me. If you hadn't got me here so fast, I don't know—" She chokes up again.

Yasmin puts her hand on her arm. "You'd have done the same for me, Eva." She pauses. "You're my friend."

Eva nods. She grabs another tissue and blots it against her face. "I can't stop crying."

"Crying is good, Eva. You should cry as much as you want," Yasmin says.

Eva props herself up against the pillows. "I want to go home, Yasmin. I want to raise this baby in a country I understand."

Slowly, Yasmin takes Eva's hand again. "Bad stuff happens at home too, Eva."

"I know—but at home we're not outsiders. At home, we understand the rules."

"Do we?"

"I think so, yes."

"I don't think knowing the rules makes it any easier. In fact, it can make it harder. There's something to be said for being on the outside. It helps you see things more clearly."

"But those awful things Priscilla said about the twins—and what's happened to the mosque—doesn't that get to you?"

"Of course it gets to me. But look at what Priscilla said about True and Kaitlin—and Ben and their kids. She'd have found a reason to blame us, even if we were American. It's not about where we're from or whether we belong. We're all as guilty or innocent as each other." She pauses. "There is no them, there is only us."

"Maybe." Eva looks out of the window. The sky is gray. Thick raindrops hit the windowpane. "But don't you miss home?" Her eyes well up again. "Even the rain feels wrong here."

Yasmin follows Eva's eyes to the window. "Missing things is a kind of gift," she says.

"It is?"

"You get to appreciate the life you had: it becomes part of you in a way that it never would if you still lived there." She pauses. "And being somewhere else means that you get to start over. And that's a gift too."

Eva thinks about this. Yasmin's right. Being away from it all—the cool grass under her feet; the white roses nodding their heads over the door at her parents' cottage in Dorset; the way the traffic moves around London; the rain—it feels more real since she's been away from it. And more beautiful too.

But she's not sure about starting over. She tried that, hadn't she? To make a place for herself and her family in this town—in this country. And it had all gone wrong.

"And you know what else?" Yasmin goes on, as if sensing Eva's questions. "We get to live two lives. We get to remember and we get to become part of something new. And here, we can decide who we want to be. It's taken me a while to realize that. For a long time, I thought that I was locked into a role here: that Ayaan got to determine who we were going to be as a family—who I was going to be as a wife and a woman; that I had to show the world that I came from Pakistan; that I had to wear my heritage and my religion like a badge; that doing anything else would be some kind of betrayal. But you know what the greatest betrayal is? It's not having the courage to be the people we want to be. No one gets to decide that but us, Eva. You, and me. All this—" Yasmin sweeps her hands through the air. "Everything that's happened in the last week—it's made me realize that: *we* get to decide."

Eva looks at Yasmin. She's never heard her say so many words at once. Or so confidently. She can see it in her body too—the way she sits up straight, her eyes lifted and shining, the jeans and the sweatshirt and the sneakers: something's changed. She hasn't been broken by what happened, she's stronger.

"I wish I could see things like you do," Eva says. "But I'm not as brave as you are, Yasmin."

Yasmin squeezes Eva's hand and leans in. "Yes, you are. You're one of the bravest people I've ever met. You go out into the world and you try to make it better. That's the bravest thing a person can do."

A nurse knocks gently on the door and comes in. "Is it okay if I check your vitals now?"

Eva nods.

The nurse wraps a blood-pressure cuff around Eva's arm.

Yasmin puts on her raincoat.

"Call me as soon as you're back home," Yasmin says.

Home. The word makes Eva's heart lurch. She doesn't know where that is any more.

Yasmin walks to the door.

"Thank you—for bringing me to the hospital. For being there for me," Eva says.

Yasmin smiles. "Like I said: we are friends, Eva."

And then she leaves.

Eva lies back against the pillows. Friends. She feels herself welling up again. It's what she'd longed for most when she came here: to meet women she could share things with—be mothers with. Wasn't that why she'd wanted to help Kaitlin with Bryar? And why she'd persuaded Yasmin to bring her twins to the party? What Yasmin said was right: Eva had always prided herself on helping people, on being a good friend, on making a difference. But that's all it was, wasn't it? Pride. Because look at what happened. Everyone had turned against each other. The kids and their families had been attacked by the media. People in Middlebrook had betrayed each other.

Priscilla saw this. And she saw Eva even more clearly than Yasmin. She'd announced it on public television: that Eva had done nothing but cause trouble. That what she thought was kindness was in fact naivety—a naivety that put a child in hospital.

It doesn't matter that Astrid's woken up. She was shot in the chest. And Eva could have prevented it. She doesn't deserve to be here any more.

DAY 6

Saturday, September 7

CHAPTER

49

8 a.m.

PRISCILLA CALLS WENDY Warnes again but her cell goes straight to voicemail. She hasn't heard from the governor since the night of the prayer meeting.

"Hi, it's Priscilla. Astrid's doing well. Peter and I are so relieved. There have been other developments too. The children have been talking about what happened, you probably caught wind of that. I thought I should make a statement. Maybe you could get in touch with Chris Baker again—so I can respond to what he said in the interview. I was caught off guard—it obviously wasn't Astrid's fault. Anyway, when you have a moment, call me and we can make a plan."

As she puts away her phone, she feels a hand on her shoulder.

"Cil?"

It's Peter. He's just arrived from home. Freshly shaved. Showered. Clean clothes. It baffles her, how he's been able to keep functioning through all this. But at least he's here; she can't wait for the three of them to be back home together. Surely, after everything that's happened, he'll want to stay. He'll realize the mistake he made when he walked out on them. End things with Kim. Hand in his notice at UCLA. Move his things back into the cottage.

As terrible as all this has been, maybe what happened to Astrid was what they needed to save their marriage.

"I think you should let it go," Peter says, looking at her phone. He must have overheard her leaving the voicemail.

"Let it go?"

"Astrid's getting better. That's all that matters now, right?"

"We owe it to Astrid to keep fighting for this. We have to push for gun law reform, otherwise more kids will get hurt. This is our chance, Peter."

He looks at her for a long time.

"Aren't you tired of fighting?" he asks.

"What? No. Don't you get it, Peter? If we don't fight for change, Astrid will have gone through all this for nothing." Priscilla stands up and grabs her car keys and her coat.

"Where are you going?"

"To Concord." She puts on her coat. "If Wendy isn't going to answer my phone calls, I'm going to her office to speak with her directly."

Peter stands up. "Are you sure that's such a good idea?"

"You might be giving up on this, but I have to do this—for Astrid."

Peter raises his eyebrows. "For Astrid?"

"Yeah, for Astrid."

She walks to the door but then turns around again. "We have the attention of an influential politician at a key moment in the election. If Wendy gets a place on the US Senate, she could make real progress on this issue. You know as well as I do that we're not going to get another chance like this one. There's no other way, Peter."

"Okay, do what you have to, Cil." He settles in the chair next to Astrid.

In that moment, she hates him for being so weak—and for making her feel like she's in the wrong.

She walks out of the door, through the pediatric ward and out into the parking lot.

She's going to fight this, even if it means doing it on her own.

On the way to Concord, Priscilla dials Lieutenant Mesenberg's cell. Priscilla had hoped that the detective would have reached out to her already, but she supposes she's been busy, dealing with the ridiculous story concocted by the children.

"Lieutenant Mesenberg? It's Dr. Carver."

"Oh—hello." There's a pause. "How's Astrid doing?"

"I'm calling to get an update on the investigation," she says. "I gather the firearm was handed in.

The lieutenant wouldn't question why she was calling about the investigation so I cut that piece of speech. And that you've had the chance to talk to all the children again."

"We've done some preliminary interviews, yes."

A pause.

"I've actually been meaning to call you—to organize a visit with Astrid."

"With Astrid?"

"Yes. It would be good to have her corroborate what the children have been saying. And to shed light on one key element in the series of events that happened in the stable. We've had some more evidence come to light."

"*Corroborate*? What could Astrid possibly tell you that you don't know already?"

"I know this is difficult, Dr. Carver—but we do have to talk to Astrid. To tie up loose ends."

"Loose ends?"

"To determine her involvement."

"Her involvement is that she was shot. That she nearly died. You know who got hold of the gun and who fired it. Isn't it time you started pressing charges?"

"We have no cause to charge anyone, Dr. Carver—"

"My daughter was shot on the property of Ben Wright—with *his* pistol—"

"It was locked in a safe. As was the ammunition."

"But his son opened those safes, didn't he? And the other children played with the gun. And Hanif Sayed fired it—at my daughter."

"Children make bad decisions. All we can do is—"

"Keep guns away from them, Lieutenant—surely you can see that. And make an example of those who put children in danger. Men like Ben Wright. And children like Hanif Sayed who thinks he can fire a gun without any consequences."

There's a beat of silence. "I understand that you're upset."

"This isn't about me being upset. It's about justice—"

"And that's what I was trying to explain. We have no legal cause to detain anyone, Dr. Carver."

"So—that's it? You're going to close the investigation?"

"Like I said, we need to tie up some loose ends. Talk to Astrid. And of course, we all need to draw some lessons from what happened. But if no crime was committed—"

"An eleven-year-old was shot and *no crime was committed*?"

"I don't make the laws, Dr. Carver."

"Obviously." Priscilla hangs up and throws her phone down on the passenger seat.

Talking to Lieutenant Mesenberg is pointless.

She looks at her GPS: another hour and she'll be in Concord. If the police can't do anything to keep their communities—their children—safe, then it will have to be the politicians. One politician in particular: the one who made her a promise that, no matter what, she wouldn't let this go.

When she gets to the state offices in Concord, Priscilla goes straight to reception and asks to see Governor Warnes.

"I'm afraid she's not here," says a young man with gelled-back hair.

"I saw her car outside."

The black SUV that drives Wendy to her official events. The one she parked outside the library that day when she walked in on the town meeting, promising that she would support Astrid's cause.

"She's busy," the receptionist says.

"I realize that. But this is important. Just call her and say that Priscilla Carver is waiting to speak to her—she'll understand. We're friends."

"There's a great deal going on right now. You might have seen the news." He jerks his head at the television to the right of his desk. It's showing an aerial shot of a burnt-out building in Manchester. "The governor has a lot on her plate."

Priscilla doesn't want to play some kind of one-upmanship game, but a child getting shot—*that* was meant to be *on her plate*. Or it was until last night, when she stopped answering Priscilla's calls.

Priscilla recognizes one of Wendy's aides walking through the lobby and goes up to her.

"I need to see Governor Warnes."

"Mrs. Carver, it's good to see you." The aide smiles at her like Priscilla's come to pay a social visit.

"Could you show me to her office? She'll be expecting me."

The aide shifts her weight from one foot to the other, embarrassed. "The governor is busy today."

Busy? The aide was there when Wendy made her promise about putting gun control at the heart of her campaign. What could be more important than that?

"Fine," Priscilla says. She pushes past the aide and walks up the large staircase of the state offices. Wendy Warnes's office can't be that hard to find.

The aide runs after her. "You can't go up there, ma'am . . ."

She ignores her and speeds up. She needs to speak to Wendy in person.

She scans the name plates on the doors. She feels the aide following close behind.

"Mrs. Carver—please."

Priscilla spins round. "It's *Dr. Carver*."

"I'm sorry—Dr. Carver, you need to go back downstairs . . ."

And then Priscilla sees her, surrounded, as ever, by a group of aides and speech writers and other members of her campaign team. They're taking notes.

"I'm going to give a speech right at the site of the fire—maximum impact."

"Wendy!" Priscilla calls out.

Wendy stops walking and looks up. "Priscilla!" She gives her a forced smile.

"I've been trying to call you—"

Wendy mumbles something to her team and they disperse.

"Have the car ready for me," she says to the man who Priscilla recognizes as her personal assistant.

Then they're standing there, just the two of them. Priscilla expects Wendy to invite her into her office but she doesn't move.

"I'm so glad that Astrid is going to be okay." Wendy presses her hand down on Priscilla's arm in the way she did the first time they met. Like she genuinely cares.

Priscilla feels a rush of relief. She can't have forgotten the importance of Astrid's case. She'll listen to her.

"We need some media coverage," Priscilla says. "We need to talk about the fact that an eleven-year-old boy opened two gun safes in his own home and that another child of the same age fired a gun at my daughter. We have to talk about how these children came to be playing with a firearm. And we have to make sure that we put an end to gun violence, once and for all. We have to—"

Wendy presses on Priscilla's arm again and this time, it feels more like an act of restraint than reassurance. "We've made good headway, Priscilla. But we have to accept that this is as far as it goes. For now, anyway."

"As far as it goes? You said gun control was going to be a cornerstone of your campaign. That when you were senator, you were going to push hard for gun law reform—"

"That was before I received evidence of Astrid's involvement in the shooting."

"Astrid's involvement? What? She was shot, *that* was her involvement!"

There's a long silence.

"I've seen evidence that points to the contrary."

"What's that supposed to mean?"

"I gather she might have been the mastermind behind the shooting."

"The *mastermind*—that's crazy."

"The pictures from her phone. Her search history—days before the party."

Priscilla remembers, suddenly, how Wendy had kept looking at her phone during the prayer meeting. And how she'd left without saying anything. And then the phone call from Chris Baker a few hours later. Wendy must have seen the pictures before they got out.

"Look, Priscilla, why don't you go back to Astrid. She needs you right now—"

"I'm doing this *for* Astrid. We have to keep pushing on this, Wendy."

"There isn't a story any more."

"I don't understand."

"If Astrid had died—"

Priscilla stiffens. "You're saying that my daughter had to *die* for things to change?"

"All I'm saying, Priscilla, is that the water has been muddied. Now that—thank goodness—Astrid is going to be okay, there's no longer a narrative—"

"*A narrative*?" Priscilla feels her legs giving way. She needs to find a place to sit down.

"Look, I know this is hard. But I can't be seen to be defending an eleven-year-old child who loaded a firearm—"

"What? *Loaded* a firearm? Who are you talking about?"

Wendy looks right at her. "Surely, Priscilla—you must know."

"Know *what*?"

"That your daughter loaded the firearm. That there's video evidence on her phone. Evidence that couldn't be shown on the television."

Mesenberg's words come back to her: One key element in the series of events that happened in the stable.

"Astrid hasn't confirmed any of this—"

"She doesn't need to. We have enough evidence." Wendy tilts her head to one side. "And I'm told that, when she woke, there was an admission—"

"How the hell do you know that?"

"Look, it's my job to stay on top of these things. I have to know what I'm getting involved in."

All those doctors and nurses in Astrid's room. One of them must have said something.

"Astrid's still on medication. She's waking up from being in a coma for five days. She doesn't know what she's saying."

Wendy gets out her phone, swipes at the screen and then presses play on the video. "Just look, Priscilla!"

Priscilla leans in. Her mind's shooting off so many thoughts it takes her a while to focus.

But then Wendy turns off the mute button and Astrid's voice comes out of the speakers, clear as day:

You hold the phone, Bryar—since you're having such a hard time loading the gun, maybe I should do it.

Having a hard time loading the gun? What does Astrid mean?

The screen wobbles as the phone changes hands between Astrid and Bryar. For a while, all you can see is the floor of the stable.

Hold it up, Bryar! Don't you know how to take a video? Astrid says. *You can play it back next time you get stuck.*

Slowly, the phone focuses back on Astrid.

In one hand, she holds the black pistol; in the other, a couple of bullets.

Priscilla's heart pushes up under her ribcage. She can't watch this.

"Looks to me like she knew what she was doing." Wendy's voice interrupts the video.

And then they both watch.

How Astrid slots the bullets into the chamber of the gun, her small, pale fingers quick and nimble.

I learned this on YouTube, Astrid says as she loads the gun. *It's easy.*

*Maybe you shouldn't—*A girl's voice comes in from off screen. An English accent.

What's a gun if it's not loaded? Astrid says. *If we're going to have fun, we have to do this properly, right?*

And then it's done. The gun's loaded.

Astrid smiles into the camera and gives a little bow.

The video breaks off.

Priscilla stares at the black screen for a second and then Wendy Warnes takes away her phone and puts it back in the pocket of her jacket. She glances at her watch. "I'm sorry, Priscilla, but I've got to be somewhere."

Priscilla gathers up the little strength she has left. "It's still an issue, Wendy. No matter what Astrid did. The gun shouldn't have been there."

"Look, maybe if I get elected, I can tackle this again, but gun control is a tough issue for Americans—and Astrid's story . . . isn't the one that's going to rally people."

"Of course gun control is a tough issue. That's why we have to tackle it head-on."

"There are lots of vested interests."

"You mean the NRA?"

"They have a great deal of influence, yes. And the polls suggest—"

"The *polls*?"

"It's not a good issue to run on."

"So, let me get this straight: you're giving this up because it's not helping your campaign? It has nothing to do with Astrid's involvement—not really. You've just decided that the issue's not going to get you enough votes."

"If I don't get elected, I won't be able to do anything, Priscilla. You're an intelligent woman, I'm sure you understand how politics works."

Wendy holds up a hand to her PA, who has been lurking at the bottom of the hallway, signaling that she's ready to move on. Then she looks back at Priscilla.

"Go and spend some time with your daughter. She needs you."

The words slam into Priscilla's chest. That's what all this had been about. That Astrid had needed her—and that she hadn't been there.

"Maybe we can talk again in a few months," Wendy says.

And then she walks off, her PA coming to join her at her side.

When Wendy's gone, Priscilla stands in the middle of the long, empty hallway.

She stumbles to one of the chairs lining the hallway: beautifully carved wood, silk upholstery. And then, very slowly, she sits down.

Words swim around in her brain. *Astrid was as involved as the rest of the kids . . . We will have to talk to Astrid. To tie up loose ends . . . your daughter joined the game . . . initiated the game . . . she loaded the gun . . .*

Peter, Lieutenant Mesenberg, Wendy—they were all saying that it was Astrid's fault.

And maybe they're right.

Maybe Astrid did have a role to play in what happened.

And maybe Priscilla should have stayed home to watch her.

But couldn't everyone see that it was more than that, too? That parents get things wrong and kids play stupid games and girls like Astrid look for trouble because it's in their nature—or because their mothers have failed them. But it doesn't mean that anyone needs to get shot. They want her to sit back and give up, just because there are reasons why the accident happened, but the biggest reason is still there, isn't it? That there was a gun in the house. How can she let go of that?

CHAPTER

50

9 a.m.

In the small bungalow on Main Street, the one with the brown clapboard and the weeds growing as high as a little girl's knees, Eva sits on the sofa, wrapped in a blanket. There's frost on the inside of the windows from where the seal has broken.

All morning, Lily and Will have been worrying over her. Making her buttered toast and tea, asking her if she needs anything. Finally, she told them she needed to sleep, persuaded Will to go and catch up on some work at the university and sent Lily off to Bryar's for a few hours.

As soon as they left the house, she'd reached for her laptop.

There are several windows open on her screen.

She's been writing e-mails for the last hour.

To the parents of her students in Middlebrook—the few of them who haven't cancelled her lessons—to say that she's going to take a break from teaching.

To the head of Lily's school back in London, to ask if there's still a place for her.

To the agency that's renting out their flat in Ealing, to ask if they can give the tenants warning that they'll need to vacate soon.

To her parents in Dorset, saying that she'd like to talk—that she's got some news to share.

And when she'd written all those e-mails, she opened a new window and clicked onto the British Airways website.

Eva has weighed up what Yasmin said but it doesn't change her mind: she wants to go home.

Yasmin sits on the couch, looking through the big glass doors leading out into the garden. She has opened them wide, wanting to feel the morning air flooding her body. The numbing cold. The newness of another day.

The twins are sleeping in, as though, having told the truth about what happened in the stable, they're able to rest at last.

She hears a key in the lock and then Ayaan's footsteps in the hallway. He goes into the kitchen and pours himself a glass of water. He's been up at the building site since dawn, making sure everything's on schedule for the big opening this afternoon. Or that's the reason he'd give, if he were asked. Really, she knows that he needed to get away from her and the twins: he couldn't bear even looking at them.

He walks into the living room and goes over to close the glass doors and then he turns around and notices her.

"You scared me, Yas—why didn't you tell me you were in here?"

"I didn't think you'd want to see me."

He comes and sits beside her; she feels the couch shifting under his weight.

For a while, they stay silent. Then Ayaan says, "I've been thinking. I know that you and the twins didn't mean to get mixed up in this. If we focus on the opening of the mosque—and on presenting a good face—I think we can move past this—"

"I don't want to move past this."

When Hanif and Laila told them what happened, she'd felt Ayaan's embarrassment. He'd been so sure that his children weren't involved in the shooting. He'd looked at her, waiting for her to join him in his disappointment. But she wasn't disappointed. In fact, she was relieved—glad, even—that for once, the twins hadn't stood apart from the other children; that they'd had the courage to make a mistake.

"You don't want to move past this? What's that supposed to mean?" Ayaan says.

"It means I'm not sorry."

"You're not *sorry*?"

"I'm sorry that Astrid and Wynn got hurt. Of course I am. But I'm not sorry that I took the kids to the party. And I'm not sorry that Hanif took the gun off Astrid. He was trying to do the right thing."

She feels him go quiet beside her.

"I want to make my own decisions. I want to be part of this community on my own terms. I want to get to know America properly. The way things are done here. I'm tired of standing out—"

"You think that being loyal to our heritage is standing out?"

"I think we can each be loyal to our heritage in our own way. The mosque means a lot to you, I understand that—"

"It means a lot to both of us—to our whole family."

"You're not listening, Ayaan."

"Okay then, tell me."

"I want the time and the freedom to work out who I want to be." She looks him straight in the eye. "To work out what I believe."

"What you *believe*?"

"You've known all along—from the moment you met me in New York, you knew that our faith didn't sit right with me. That I couldn't follow it, not like you could. Or my parents. That I wanted to find my own answers. But you pretended not to see it. And I pretended, too. Because pretending feels easier—in the short term, anyway. But I can't do that any more." She takes a breath. She has to say the next words quickly or she'll lose her nerve. "I'm not coming to the opening of the mosque this afternoon. I can't."

He looks struck. And, for a moment, she feels sorry for him and she wants to take it all back, to save him the hurt. But she can't do that, not any more. It wouldn't be fair to him—or their kids. Or to her.

He leans forward and takes her hand. His eyes are wide and vulnerable. She gets a flash of the young man he was when they were at Columbia. She was the one, then, who'd given him the courage to step out into the world.

"I know I've been busy," he says. "That I've left you alone too much, that you've been carrying the weight of the twins—"

"It's not that."

"Well, what is it, then? This—the mosque—it's our dream—"

"It's your dream, Ayaan."

He looks at her, even more wounded than before. And, for the first time in months—maybe in years—she feels a tenderness for him.

"But the mosque was our whole reason for coming here—it's why I got the visa," he says.

"It was your reason. But now I need to find my reason for being here. And the children need to find theirs."

"We're a Muslim family: the face of the new mosque. I need you there, Yas. You've always been so loyal—and now, all of a sudden, you're turning your back on me—on us? I don't understand."

"You can do this on your own. The mosque is beautiful. And you're right: it's going to make a huge difference to our community. To how Americans come to understand Islam."

"So why not be part of it?"

She shakes her head. "I can't."

"What about the twins?" he says. "Have you turned them against the mosque too—against me?"

"Of course not. I'd never do that. But I think you should talk to them. Ask them what they want to do."

"They don't know what they want. They're kids. They're confused. You saw what they just did."

"Hanif was trying to please you."

"He shot Astrid Carver to *please* me?"

"He intervened because he was trying to be brave."

"And Laila—hiding the evidence, who was she doing that for?"

"For you too, Ayaan. To protect you. To protect us as a family. To protect her brother. She knew how it would look if anyone ever found out that he'd shot Astrid."

He shakes his head. "So it's my fault."

She reaches out and takes his hands. "Remember when you met me, at Columbia?"

"Of course."

"Do you—I mean, *really*?"

"Of course I remember. Wasn't I the one who followed you around, begging you to go out with me—trying to get you away from that football player? From the moment I first saw you, I loved you, Yas."

"But the person I was back then wasn't who I am today. That girl was strong and independent. She loved the freedom of being in America. She didn't go to mosque any more or keep up with her prayers. She didn't write to her parents. She didn't wear a salwar kameez."

"But that was different. We were students—"

"To me, it wasn't about being a student. It was about becoming who I knew I was meant to be. And then, when we went home, that me disappeared again. And when we came back to America, I really hoped things would be different. That I'd find that young woman again—the one who wasn't defined by Lahore or Pakistan or Islam or her parents." She looks right at him. "The woman who was happy. The woman you fell in love with."

"So, since you met me, you've been unhappy—is that what you're saying?"

"No, of course not. We've shared times of great happiness: I love you, Ayaan. And having the twins—being a mom—has made me happier than anything I could ever have imagined. But I can't find her any more: the person I was when I first lived here." She pauses. "I've felt so lost."

"I know," he says, gently.

"I kissed Ben Wright." She takes a breath.

His body stiffens. "What?"

"It's not what you think. I don't like him—not like that. And it was just once. I was overwhelmed. He was helping me. I'm the one who kissed him. He was shocked and embarrassed—he didn't kiss me back. And I didn't want to kiss him again. It was just that I had to do something to feel like I was alive, like I had some control over what was happening to me."

He stands up. "So you kissed another man."

"It didn't mean anything. He's a friend, that's it. And he was so kind. He just reminded me, for a second, of the girl I used to be."

His eyes are glassy. "No wonder you won't come to the mosque."

"It's not like that, Ayaan." She stands up and touches his arm. "You're my husband. We can work this out together," she says. "You, me the kids—in a way that doesn't compromise any of us."

"So, let me get this right: kissing Ben didn't compromise you but coming to the opening of the mosque this afternoon would?"

"Kissing Ben didn't mean anything."

"It means something to me."

He sits back down, leaving a gap between them that feels like an ocean.

They look out through the glass doors to the garden. The sky is getting lighter. She wants to reach out to him, to let him know that it's going to be okay, that she'll do what he says, because that's what she's always done. And because it's easier. But she knows she can't play that role any more. That everything is different now.

In the small cabin in the woods, True Bowen sits on the edge of one of the mattresses, next to his three sleeping children.

Wynn is curled up against Skye: True can hear his snuffly-nosed breathing.

He can feel the warmth of his children's bodies, so close to each other.

He looks down at Phoenix. Even when he's sleeping, his lips curl up, suggesting mischief. And that was his lot, wasn't it? That, wherever there was trouble, people traced it back to him. Because he looked the part. Because he liked to skulk in the shadows and hide up in the trees. And because he loved guns—because he was desperate for True to take him hunting.

But it turns out that he was the only kid in the stable that afternoon who didn't even touch the gun. And then he hid Astrid's phone to protect her—to protect all the kids.

He leans in toward his son and whispers, "I'm sorry, buddy. I'm sorry."

Phoenix opens his eyes briefly and looks right at True, but he's not awake, it's just a brief intermission in his sleep. He blinks, his brow furrows and then he closes his eyes again.

When Phoenix wakes up, he'll let him know how proud he is that he made his own decision. And he'll promise never to doubt him again.

True kisses Phoenix's forehead then stands up and walks out through the door of the cabin and sits on the steps, under the dark, starlit sky. He looks at the moon, almost full.

I'm going to do better, Cedar, he says. *I promise, I'm going to do better.*

In the rectory, Avery stares at the blank piece of paper on which she'd intended to write the speech for the opening of the mosque this afternoon. When Ayaan had invited her to say a few words—to show how different faiths could come together and support each other—she'd jumped at the chance. Avery has dedicated her life to bringing people together, but after everything that's happened, she doesn't know what to say.

She looks, again, at the wedding photo of her parents sitting on her bedside table. Mum wearing her Marine uniform. Dad in his clergy collar. They made a funny pair. A beautiful, funny pair.

And then she shifts her gaze to the gun safe she'd had installed to house the pistol her mom had always carried around with her as a Marine. She puts in the code, opens the door and pulls it out.

Growing up, Avery had never talked to her parents about guns; they were just part of her life. Her mom believed it was her duty to keep people safe and, in her world, that meant being armed. But in the end, no one had kept her parents safe, had they? No one had been able to stop their car from driving over a roadside bomb in Afghanistan when Avery was sixteen years old.

If there's one thing Avery regrets, more than anything, about her parents not being around in her adult years, it's the missed conversations. Talking to them about what they believed and why, about the choices they made—about who they were, as adults. And that, in all these years, she hasn't been able to come to them for advice. When things were hard. When, like now, the world stopped making sense.

Sometimes, she finds herself praying to them rather than to God. But all the prayer in the world has never filled the gap they left.

What would they think of her now?

It was her job to take care of them and she put them in danger.

She hadn't taken Priscilla's arguments seriously. Because she'd been raised to believe that there was no contradiction between living with firearms and being good parents—good people. And the Wrights were good people, weren't they?

Ben, in particular, reminded Avery of her mother: his unwavering sense of duty; his love of his country; his determination to keep those he loved—and the wider community—safe. And he, too, was a godly man. One of the godliest she'd ever met. Sometimes, she felt that his faith was stronger than her own.

Avery's mother—and Ben—proved that it was possible to be an American who upheld the Constitution, who believed in the Second Amendment, and still be a person of great faith.

But Abi and Cal were vulnerable, she'd known that from the start. And the fact that she hadn't even questioned that she was doing it, that was the worst part. She'd been too proud—too sure of her own convictions—to see it.

When her parents had died, she'd been carted from one foster home to another until she was considered an adult and could take care of herself. She wanted better for the kids she fostered. She'd hoped to adopt Abi and Cal. To look after them long after they were considered adults in the eyes of the law.

Maybe I don't deserve to have them, she thinks. *Maybe I'm not cut out to be a mom.*

She looks back at the photo and searches her parents' faces, longing to find some answers.

And then she thinks about what her mom would always say when she was a little girl, struggling through a problem. *You can work this out, Avery, I know you can.*

And then her father's voice comes in to join her mother's: *Why don't you ask the Lord, my love? He's always listening.*

Self-reliance and reliance on God. Another contradiction that she'd been brought up with. But isn't it the contradictions that tell the truth, in the end?

Yes, maybe that was what had come from everything that had happened in the past week: that life is lived in the tension between two opposing truths.

She puts the pistol back in the safe and picks up her pen.

In the stable, Kaitlin brushes down the side of Lucy's long gray neck. She's been in here since 6 a.m., trying to avoid Ben.

Ever since Lieutenant Mesenberg called round to say that she was closing the investigation, he's been so happy—as though now, everything is going to slot back to being how it always was.

She leans her head against Lucy. "What am I going to do?" she whispers.

She feels the warmth of Lucy's body; her blood pumping through the vein that runs down her neck.

"Katie?" She hears Ben opening the door to the stable. "Are you in here?"

And then he's standing in front of her, wearing his border patrol uniform, his pistol shining in its holster.

Her stomach churns.

"You're going back to work already?" she says.

"Just for a few hours—to catch up on what I've missed." He's smiling, his back straight, his head held high. He needs this, she thinks. His job. To feel like he's making a difference.

He comes over and kisses her. She doesn't pull away but she doesn't kiss him back either. Not that he seems to notice. He's too happy. Too sure that everything is okay again.

"I'll be back for the mosque opening," he says. "We can go together."

She draws away from him and goes back to brushing Lucy. "You think that's a good idea?" she says, not looking at him.

"Of course. We need to support the Sayeds. We need to come together as a community. To show that this hasn't changed who we are or what we do."

He really believes it, she thinks. That they can just switch back to how things were and pretend this week never happened.

"Katie?"

When she doesn't answer, he touches her shoulder. "Is it still bothering you—that Priscilla didn't want to talk?" he asks. "You know, it'll take her a while to come around."

"Her daughter was shot, Ben. I don't think she's going to come around anytime soon."

He kisses her forehead. "It's been a heck of week. We're all tired. We need to give each other time."

She has to tell him that it's not about being tired or about having more time. But she can't. Because he looks so happy. Because he believes that they're okay. That the twenty years they've been together matter more than one incident in their stable six days ago.

He checks that the top button of his shirt is done up, that his belt is looped right. He glides his hand over his holster. She's watched him doing it a million times. Making sure that the outer man mirrors the neat, ordered, dependable man he is on the inside.

She's always loved seeing him in uniform but none of it feels real any more. It's like he's just dressing up for a part.

"I'd better go—I don't want to be late." He kisses her once more, on the lips. "We'll have some time together soon, just the two of us. I promise."

She watches him walk through the stable and out of the door. Hears him getting into his truck and switching on the engine.

Lucy shuffles her hooves behind Kaitlin and nudges her with her nose. Kaitlin's heart hammers.

"Ben!" she calls out and starts running.

Across the valley, she sees Priscilla's cottage, shining white in the morning sun.

She catches up with his truck halfway down the drive.

"Ben!" she yells. "Ben!"

Finally, he hears her, stops the car, and winds down the window.

She comes to stand alongside him.

"What is it, Katie?"

She looks at him and she can feel it, even before she says anything—what the words she's about to say are going to do to them.

"I can't do this any more," she blurts out. "I can't—" Her voice breaks.

"Katie?"

"I want them gone, Ben. The guns. All of them."

After her confrontation with Wendy, Priscilla went home to have a shower and change her clothes. She'd wanted to go straight back to the hospital but she had to find a way to calm herself down before facing Astrid.

She meets Peter at the bottom of the stairs.

"How did it go?" he asks.

"You were right. About Wendy. About everything."

"I'm sorry." He touches her arm.

She looks up at him. "Are you?"

"Come on, Cil, you know that she was in this for herself—"

She shakes him off and walks past him.

"What matters is that we have our little girl back. That we're both here for her," he calls after her.

She turns around again. "For how long?"

"Sorry?"

"For how long are you going to be here for her?"

"For as long as you need me."

They look at each other. And then she hears a car slowing on the road that runs past their house and looks down the driveway—the driveway they'd fallen in love with before they even visited the house. The way it curved round, concealing the cottage until the very last minute.

And then the cottage itself: an old shell that needed to be gutted and rebuilt. But that was what had excited them. They had similar tastes; they knew how they wanted to live. Priscilla had loved those long evenings when they'd sat together at the kitchen table, looking over the plans, building their lives together here in Middlebrook, forgetting the case she'd run from. It had felt like the chance for a fresh start.

Maybe they can have that again, she thinks. They can't go back to the beginning, of course. They'll have to live with all these years that lie between them, the decisions they've made—the mistakes they've made. But they can try again. Try better.

"Why don't you come with me to the hospital—we should both be there for Astrid right now," she says.

She hears the sound of a car again. But this time, it's drawing closer.

And then they both see it. A rental car pulling up the drive. And sitting behind the wheel, the woman who took her husband away.

CHAPTER

51

10 a.m.

PRISCILLA SWERVES INTO the hospital car park, parks in the first spot she finds and runs to the entrance.

God, I'm stupid! she thinks as she follows the signs toward the pediatric ward.

Stupid to believe that anyone really cared about what happened to Astrid.

Stupid to think that Peter still loved her—that he was even thinking of staying.

Stupid to believe that she could depend on anyone other than herself.

"Priscilla?"

She looks up. It's Kaitlin Wright.

"I thought I made myself clear last night," Priscilla says.

Kaitlin stands up. "You did."

"So why are you here?"

"I want to talk to you. Properly this time."

"Maybe we could sit down?" Kaitlin suggests, indicating a couple of armchairs in the family room.

"I'm fine standing, thanks."

Priscilla regrets having agreed to this. There's nothing she wants to hear from Kaitlin Wright. Not now. Not ever.

Blood rushes to Kaitlin's skin. "I—I understand why you don't want to see me."

"Look, if you're here to apologize, just get on with it. I hope it will make you feel better. Then be on your way so that I can get back to my daughter."

Kaitlin takes off her coat and sits down in one of the armchairs.

Priscilla stays standing.

"Maybe you're right—maybe I'm here to make myself feel better. I don't know. I'm too confused by everything to work out what my motivations are. But I know I have to talk to you about what happened."

Priscilla wants to tell Kaitlin what she can do with her soul-searching or her confession or whatever it is she's trying to accomplish. She's done with listening to people and trusting people and believing that they're ever interested in anything other than themselves. From now on, it's just going to be her and Astrid. They don't need anyone else.

"Please hear me out," Kaitlin says.

Priscilla wills herself to move but something holds her back. Maybe it's tiredness. Maybe she actually feels sorry for Kaitlin. Maybe a little part of her is curious to hear what bullshit excuse she's going to come up with to justify why Astrid got shot.

"Okay. But I don't have long." She sits down.

"Ben and I grew up together," Kaitlin starts.

"If you're here to defend your husband—"

Kaitlin swallows hard. "I'm not."

"You're not?"

"No. But I need to start from the beginning—to help you understand." She takes a breath. "Like I said, Ben and I grew up together in El Paso, Texas. We went to the same high school. We were in the same grade. Our parents socialized. My dad's ranch was next door to the farm that belonged to Ben's family." She pauses. "We were meant to be together."

"Am I meant to find this romantic?"

Priscilla can't bear this. Sitting here, listening to what a wonderful marriage the Wrights have, all the time knowing that her own husband's girlfriend has just parked her car in their driveway.

Kaitlin continues as though Priscilla hadn't spoken. "Ben and I met when we were kids. When our lives were tied up with our families. We didn't question where we came from or what we believed or whether the choices our families made were right or wrong—we were too young or too naïve or too plain stupid to ask questions. But you see, part of why we fell in love was because we were so familiar to each other—because we lived next door to each other, because we shared the same experiences and understood each other's worlds."

"You're saying you married Ben because it was easy?"

"Maybe. I don't know. What I do know is that I love him. That, along with Bryar, he's the most important person in my life. That nothing makes sense without him." She looks at Priscilla. "And I believe he's a good man."

"So, you *are* here to defend your husband?"

"No. What I'm trying to say is that because Ben and I grew up together, we didn't question each other, not in the same way that you do when you fall in love as adults."

"I'm not sure what all this is leading to."

"I'm sorry. I'm not making much sense. I'm only just working it out for myself. I guess what I'm saying is that it's taken this week—with Astrid getting shot and Wynn getting hurt and our children being investigated—for me to wake up."

"To wake up?"

"To question the way things have always been—or how I've let them be."

Although every part of Priscilla wants to look away, she keeps her head up, her eyes locked in.

"And I've realized that you're right."

"I'm *right*?"

"Yes. You were right to keep kids away from the party."

Priscilla looks at Kaitlin's bright green eyes and her frizzy red hair and her flushed cheeks. "Go on."

"And you're right to blame me," Kaitlin says. "More than any of those kids who were in the stable on Sunday. More, even, than Ben. The kids didn't know what they were doing. And as for Ben, guns are part of his life—and his work. He's thought it through. But me? I just went along with it. I never questioned what I really thought or wanted. And you know what? It turns out that I don't want those guns anywhere near my home. That I never did. Even as a kid in El Paso, seeing my dad's guns around made me nervous—like they make Bryar nervous. I hated how they looked. I hated the sound of them and the smell of them when they were fired. I think that I knew, then, deep down, that I didn't want to have anything to do with them. But I went along with it because I didn't think I had a choice." She takes a breath. "But I see things differently now—that's what I came to tell you. Now, every time I even look at the safes in our home or at Ben's trophies or the pictures of him and his grandfather on the wall, it makes me feel sick to my stomach that I never did anything about it. And that makes me most guilty of all, doesn't it?"

Priscilla sits back. There were many emotions she'd prepared herself to feel for Kaitlin Wright, but admiration wasn't one of them. She'd underestimated her.

But then she remembers those first days, when she and Peter had just moved to Middlebrook. How she'd look across the valley at the house opposite theirs and wondered who lived there and whether they'd be friends.

"So, I get it now," Kaitlin goes on. "Why you cut off contact—after what happened to your dog. And why you feel like you do now." She pauses. "How you must hate us. Hate me."

Priscilla looks out of the window. After all the rain, it's turned into one of those bright September mornings that seem to wash everything clean.

"You know that Astrid loaded the gun," Priscilla says.

"Yes. But if there hadn't been a gun in the stable—or ammunition in the house—she wouldn't have had a gun to load."

Priscilla turns back at Kaitlin. She was the last person in the world who Priscilla thought would understand.

"What does Ben think about all this?" Priscilla asks.

"We're not really talking about it." Kaitlin's voice chokes up. "I guess I've let him down too. I was meant to be on his side."

Priscilla looks over at Kaitlin. "I don't hate you, Kaitlin. And I don't hate Ben either. Or Bryar. And Ben shooting my dog—that wasn't the real reason I cut off contact between us. Astrid was wrong to take Jake out: he was a difficult dog. He'd had bad experiences in his previous home. Astrid should have known he'd freak out when he saw the horses." She moves her eyes back to the dark window. "It just brought it all back."

Priscilla notices a reflection of herself and Kaitlin in the window pane. She'd always thought that they were so different.

"You know why I stopped practicing law?" Priscilla asks.

"You used to practice law? I thought you were always an academic."

Priscilla laughs. "No. I looked down on academics: locked up in their ivory towers making up grand legal theories without a clue about what goes on in the real world. Before Peter and I moved to Middlebrook, I was a named partner in a law firm in Boston. I was one of the most successful young female attorneys on the East Coast."

Kaitlin smiles. "I'm sure you were."

"I specialized in defending the rights of women locked into abusive marriages. I wanted to give them and their children a way out. The courage to extract themselves. Enough money to start over."

"That's amazing work."

"It was. It is. And I was good at it. Really good. You wouldn't have wanted to come up against me in court."

"I can believe that."

"But then I went too far."

"Too far?"

"Pride—isn't that what gets us all in the end? I was representing a young woman in her late twenties. She had three children—an eight-month-old, a two-year-old and a five-year-old. Her husband was former military. He'd served in Syria and suffered from PTSD. He was out of control. Drank too much. Spent all their money on liquor and cigarettes. Refused to get help. He'd have such big flare-ups of anger that she'd lock herself and her kids in the bathroom to get away from him. Once or twice she packed her things and moved to her mother's house but he always persuaded her to come back." Priscilla looks up. "She loved him, you see. Felt sorry for him; found excuses for his behavior."

"So, what happened?"

"I fought hard. I wanted her out of that marriage—for good. I wanted her to have a fresh start: a new home in a new neighborhood. New schools for the kids, regular childcare checks. No visiting rights until Dad had gotten himself on some kind of treatment program."

"You didn't win?"

"Oh, I won. I always won."

"That must have been so satisfying—knowing that you'd helped her."

Priscilla nods. "Sure. At first. She was safe—and she and her kids had a future."

"So, what was the problem?"

Priscilla buries her head in her hands. She doesn't know why she's telling Kaitlin all this. No one here knows, not except Peter, and even they haven't talked about it in years. But she feels she has to tell her.

"The night after the case closed, the woman went back with her kids to her mother's house. And later that night, her husband broke in."

Kaitlin's fingers flutter to her throat. "Oh God."

"He brought his pistol with him. One of the many he had in his home. He shot his ex-wife. Then the kids, who were sleeping. Then the grandmother. And after that, he shot himself."

A silence falls between them.

Priscilla thinks that Kaitlin is going to leave. Now that she knows what Priscilla is really like, she'll realize that whatever she might have done differently in her life, no matter how sorry she is for what happened in the stable, none of it compares to this—to how Priscilla destroyed a whole family.

Kaitlin stands up and comes over to Priscilla's chair. She kneels down next to her and takes her hand. "Thank you for telling me."

Priscilla stares at Kaitlin's hands, rough and callused from her work with the horses.

"I don't know how you survived a case like that," Kaitlin adds.

"I didn't. Peter and I moved to Middlebrook. I started the law faculty here. Hid away behind lectures and books. We had Astrid. And I tried, in my way, to fight for gun control—to make myself feel better about what happened. But none of that really worked, did it?"

"You know it wasn't your fault, right?" Kaitlin says.

Priscilla's throat contracts. "I pushed him too hard. He was suffering. And he had a gun."

"It would have happened regardless of the case, Priscilla. You can't make someone do that. He was sick. He needed help. You stood up for his family—you did your job. You couldn't have known what he was going to do."

"It still feels like it was my fault."

"What would you have done differently—if you could take the case all over again?"

"I . . . I don't know."

"You did your job, Priscilla. And you did it really well. And this horrible thing happened—and I understand why it made you feel like it did—but it's not on you."

They remain silent for a while. Then Kaitlin stands up.

"I'd like to help you," she says.

Priscilla looks up at her. "Sorry?"

"I'd like to make it my cause too—to fight for gun control. To make sure that America is safer for our kids."

"But—what about Ben?"

"I don't know. I haven't worked things out that far. But I can't ignore it any more—how differently Ben and I feel about guns. I can't go along with it just to keep him happy." Kaitlin goes over to the chair and picks up her coat.

"But you said you loved him—that you were meant to be together?"

Kaitlin turns around. "How can we be together with this hanging over us? He doesn't want to see it. Now that the investigation is over, he thinks that we can go back to how it was. He doesn't understand that everything's changed for me." She puts on her coat. "I should leave you to get back to Astrid—I've taken up enough of your time."

Priscilla stands up and catches Kaitlin's arm. "Listen," she says. "You're right—to be worried about the guns. And I'm glad that you came and talked to me. And I do think we can work together. I'm not sure how yet, but we can try." She presses her arm. "And you were right about something else too."

Kaitlin looks up at her.

"Ben's a good man."

Kaitlin's eyes fill with tears.

"I worked for long enough prosecuting men who had no right to be with their wives or their families, to get a sense of what a good man looks like," Priscilla goes on. "And Ben's one of them. Don't lose sight of that." She pauses. "I did. I let go of Peter. I didn't realize that he wasn't happy any more."

The two women look at each other and, for the first time in three years, an understanding settles between them: of how fragile marriage is.

Kaitlin sniffs. "But being good isn't always enough, is it? To make a marriage survive?"

"It's a start," Priscilla says. "A good one."

Before Kaitlin turns to leave, she looks at Priscilla once more. And as the women stand there, in this hospital room, they both feel it: that something has shifted between them.

CHAPTER

52

Midday

In the small bedroom of the house that looks over the stable, Lily and Bryar sort through pieces of granite. It surprises Lily that you can find them on the ground here—these stones that look like a night sky full of stars. Bryar had explained to her how, in the ice age, glaciers swept over the landscape of New Hampshire, revealing its stone foundation—that it was then that the granite came to the surface. She wonders what else is down there that we don't know about yet.

It feels easy, sitting next to him, without even needing to say anything.

She notices him snatching glances out of his bedroom window. And she knows what he's looking at: the white cottage across the valley.

She can tell that Bryar's been thinking about her—the girl with the pale hair and the sunburnt skin who, a week ago, came into the stable and changed their lives for ever.

She swallows hard.

"Why don't we go and see her?" she says, the words at odds with her heart. "At the hospital."

He looks up at her. "Really?" he asks.

"Really."

"You think she'll be allowed visitors?"

Lily shrugs. "It's worth a try, isn't it?"

The corners of his lips turn up and his cheeks flush pink. "Okay. But how are we meant to get there?"

"I'll get Dad to take us."

"He'll be okay with that?"

"Okay with me doing something nice for his boss's daughter? You bet he'll be fine with it."

"You've got it all planned, haven't you?"

"Yep."

Part of her wishes that they never had to see Astrid again, but she knows that's not an option. She's in their lives now. And it will help Bryar to see her.

On the driveway of the house with the big marble columns, Laila and Hanif climb into Dad's truck. He's taking them to the mosque: they have to be there early for photos.

Mom stands on the doorstep in a sweatshirt, her hair hanging down her back.

Dad doesn't seem surprised that she's not coming.

Is it their fault? the twins wonder. Is it because of what they did at the party, that their parents don't love each other any more?

As Dad turns the car, they wave at Mom but she doesn't see them; her gaze is far away.

In the old house next to the church, Abi and Cal sit at the top of the staircase. Bill's come back. He and Avery are talking in the kitchen.

It's hard to hear with the door closed, but they catch enough of the words to work out what's going on.

I've had to pull a number of strings for this . . .

I know—thank you.

And Cal defacing the mosque like that—and stealing the spray cans from the art room at school—

I know. But we've talked. He's promised never to do it again. And I've discussed it with his teacher too. She wants to give him a second chance.

It's not the first time he's gotten in trouble. The same for Abi . . . The fact that she took the safety catch off that pistol . . . It really doesn't look good, Avery.

But they weren't actually involved in the shooting—that should count for something, right? And you heard about Astrid: that she was the one who loaded the gun. They all made stupid decisions that day. It wasn't just Cal and Abi.

And you're sure Mr. Sayed isn't going to press charges against Cal for the graffiti?

No. He's been good about it. Cal's going to do some jobs for him to pay him back. A kind of community service, I guess.

There's a silence. They can hear Bill letting out a loud, deliberate sigh.

If there's even the smallest hiccup between now and Christmas—

Cal and Abi look at each other. This was the bit they'd been waiting for. To hear whether they'd get to stay. And for how long.

There won't be. I promise.

I'm not sure it's something you can promise, Avery.

It is. There's a pause. *They're meant to be here, Bill. They want to be here. We'll work this out together.*

Well, we'll see about that.

The scraping of chairs.

The kitchen door opens.

The brother and sister dash back to Cal's room. They stand at his window and watch Bill getting into his gray Subaru, the one that brought them here two months ago. They still remember the smell: of coffee and greasy burger wrappers and old smoke; of the other children who'd sat there before them.

Beyond the car park, Cal notices Skye, walking out of the woods with her dad and her brothers. She looks up at the house and he wants to open the window and wave at her, like he used to earlier in the summer whenever he saw her walking past the church. But he's scared that she's still angry with him. He was the one who suggested they leave the stable that afternoon. And maybe she's angry too, at what he did to the mosque.

In the pediatric wing of Colebrook Hospital, Astrid sits in bed, rubbing her eyes, wondering whether she's still half-asleep or whether he's really here, standing next to her bed.

"I had to pretend I was your cousin, so they'd let me see you," he says. "I told them my dad was finding a parking spot and that I went in ahead of him."

"What?"

"If you're related, they let you in," he says.

"And they believed you?"

He smiles. "Yup." Then his eyes dart around. "Is your mom here?"

"She went home for a bit. I'm meant to be sleeping, but I'm scared to close my eyes . . . in case . . ."

"Yeah," Bryar says. "I get it."

Her face softens.

"I came to say sorry, Astrid," he goes on, looking at the bandages across her chest.

"*You're* sorry?" she says.

He nods.

"But I'm the one who made you open the safe. And get the ammo. I'm the one who loaded the gun and made everyone play that stupid game. You didn't want to do it."

When she told Lieutenant Mesenberg everything that happened at the party, she was sure that Mom was going to be angry with her, but Mom just held her and said it wasn't her fault.

"You're wrong," Bryar says. "I did want to do it."

"What d'you mean?"

"I didn't want you to think I was a loser." He swallows. "I wanted you to like me again." His eyes are shiny.

"I never stopped liking you, Bryar."

"You didn't?"

She shakes her head. "I was just angry at Mom for keeping us apart—I was angry at everyone." Her voice goes thick and choky. "And I wanted Dad to come home. I thought that maybe if I did something bad enough—if I got hurt—he'd wake up and realize that I needed him." She tries to lean forward but it hurts too much. "I should never have come to the party, Bryar."

He looks her right in the eye. "I'm glad you came."

She raises her eyebrows. "You are?"

"I mean—I'm not glad that you got hurt." His cheeks go pink. "But I'm glad you came."

"Me too," she says.

Because they both know that if she hadn't run through the cornfields that day, if she hadn't gone to the party, then they wouldn't be in this room together now, feeling like maybe they could be friends after all.

"Are you going to be okay?" Bryar asks.

She nods. "I think so."

"Does anything hurt?"

"It hurts to breathe. And to move."

He frowns. "So basically, everything does."

"Basically, yeah. But it's okay. I'll get better. That's what the doctors are saying. And, in the meantime, I get to miss loads of school." She smiles. "And I won't have to join in with PhysEd, which is always a plus, right?"

He smiles. "Yeah, it is."

"And when this is over, I'll have a pretty awesome scar too." She strokes the bandage across her chest.

"Like a superhero?" he says.

"A pretty screwed-up superhero, but sure, if you like."

They both laugh.

"We were all so scared that you might not make it." He pauses. "I'm really glad you're okay."

"Yeah, me too."

And she realizes it's the first time she's said it out loud—or let herself think it. That she's happier to be alive now than she was before she was shot. That something's changed. Between her and Mom. Between her and the world.

He glances toward the door. "I brought someone with me."

Her heart skips a beat. "What?"

"I think you'll like her—if you give her a chance."

Before she can stop him, Bryar walks over to the door. "It was her idea—me coming here," he says. "She got her dad to take us. And saying I was your cousin was her idea too. She noticed that we looked alike. And she knows that we used to be friends—really good friends." He looks right at Astrid. "She understood that I had to see you."

And then she's standing there at the door, the English girl with the tangled brown hair and the brown eyes; the girl who'd made Astrid feel so angry—like she could just sweep across the ocean and replace her.

"Hi, Astrid," Lily says.

An old voice pushes to the front of Astrid's throat: it wants to say something mean to make her go away, so that it's just her and Bryar again. But she presses it back down.

"Are you meant to be my cousin too?"

Lily smiles. "I don't think I'd pull it off—at least you guys look alike, right?"

The girls lock eyes.

"So you just snuck in."

"Dad's talking to the nurses—he's good at keeping people talking. They didn't notice me go past."

"Thanks," Astrid says. "For getting Bryar to come."

Lily nods. "Sure."

"And for coming too."

Maybe, Astrid thinks, *just maybe there can be room for both of us. Maybe we could even be friends.*

CHAPTER

53

1 p.m.

A GOOD CROWD HAS turned out for the opening. Locals. A few from further afield. Reporters. Photographers. There's a podium and a microphone set up for the speeches. A red ribbon flutters in front of the main doors to the mosque.

At first glance, everything looks like it's supposed to.

But on the stage, there's an empty seat beside the Sayed twins where their mother should be.

And there's another empty seat too, a little further along with a reserved sign for Dr. Priscilla Carver.

And in the audience, Kaitlin and Bryar sit without Ben. Kaitlin had hoped that he'd be back from work in time for the opening—that he'd *want* to be here, but it looks like he's not coming.

Will, Eva, and Lily Day sit beside them. Eva should have stayed home to rest, but she wanted to be here for Yasmin, though she can't see her.

At the end of one of the rows, so that she can get out easily for her speech, Avery sits with Abi and Cal. The three of them stare at the marble wall of the mosque: someone's put up a sheet to cover the gray shadows left behind by Cal's words.

Near the back, Skye stands next to Phoenix. Wynn is sitting on True's shoulders, so he can see what's going on at the front. Every now and then he pokes a little finger under the cast on his right arm to scratch at a bit of dry skin.

Skye looks over at Cal, the boy with the thick blond hair that she'd run her fingers through when they kissed outside the stable a week ago. It was her first kiss and it had been better than anything she'd ever dreamt of. And a few seconds later, Astrid got shot and Wynn got hurt.

It had felt like a punishment—as if someone was saying to her that she wasn't allowed to have anything just for herself. So she'd tried to block the kiss from her memory. And whenever she missed Cal, she forced herself to feel angry at him instead: for distracting her; for allowing her to forget that her job was to look after her brothers. But the harder she tried to forget—or to feel angry—the stronger it came back, the memory of his soft lips against hers.

So, when Cal turns around, though she knows she should look away, she can't.

You're still here, her eyes tell him. *Despite everything, you haven't been taken away. And I'm glad.*

At the front of the audience, the imam of the new Middlebrook Mosque walks across the stage and taps the microphone. Then he leans in and says, "Welcome, everyone."

On the side of the road that leads up from Middlebrook, a few yards from Woodwind Stables, Priscilla sits in her car, looking at the row of maples. She and Peter had their honeymoon in New Hampshire: they'd walked for hours under trees like this, dreaming of retiring here. And then, after the case that left Priscilla certain that she never wanted to set foot in a courtroom again, it was Peter who suggested they move north, to the countryside—that they start over.

But now, she doesn't know where to go or what to do.

She can't go home, because all she'll feel is the emptiness of him not being there any more.

And she can't go back to the hospital. Because then she'll have to look Astrid in the eye and tell her that she'd gotten it wrong: that her dad's never coming home to them. That she's messed up again.

She's failed. As a wife. As a mom. As a human being. It was obvious to her now that those things Astrid did at the party—they were her fault.

She looks at the steering wheel. At the ignition button. And then down at the pedals. She doesn't know how to do it any more. How to drive. How to keep living.

There's a knock on the window.

"You okay?"

She looks up and sees him standing there: Ben Wright in his border patrol uniform.

They look at each other, feeling the weight of the past week—of the past three years—hanging between them.

She winds down the window.

"Just checking you haven't broken down," Ben says.

"Broken down? No . . . I was just . . ." She feels her throat thicken. "I was just taking a break."

He nods, like he understands.

"I can't seem to . . ." she starts. "I can't seem to get myself together." She reaches into the glovebox for some tissues and tries to sniff back the tears.

"It's okay," he says. "It's okay."

She balls up a tissue and dabs at her eyes. "I'm tired, that's all."

"I understand," he says. And then he leans in toward her. "Look, I realize that I'm the last person you want to see right now, but if there's anything I can do—"

"I'll be fine in a minute."

She waits for him to leave but he keeps standing there.

"I was heading home for a shower—and to get changed," he says. "I might be a bit late, but I wanted to show my support."

She doesn't understand what he's saying.

"Maybe—you'd like me to drive you?" he says.

She looks up at him blankly.

"To the opening of the mosque? I thought that was where you'd be heading."

The opening. She'd forgotten.

Priscilla looks up the valley and thinks of the beautiful, white stone mosque she'd been so keen to support. All the money she'd raised. The planning meetings with Ayaan Sayed. The speeches she'd given. She closes her eyes. She's not that person any more. Maybe she never was.

She opens her eyes and looks at Ben Wright, standing next to her. She doesn't want to be alone right now.

"Okay," she says.

"Okay?"

She nods.

He opens the door for her and she steps out and together, they walk to his truck.

She waits for him in the living room. She'd only been in the Wrights' house a few times before Ben shot her dog and she cut off contact.

She'd forgotten how cozy it was. How although nothing really matches—not like in her house, where every tiny detail is planned—this feels like the kind of home you'd want to come back to: the handmade quilts on the back of the sofa; the scratches on the hardwood floor; the family pictures on the wall; the big old grandfather clock in the hallway, ticking away.

And then she sees it, sitting in the corner in the back. The gun safe. Her conversation with Kaitlin comes back to her and she realizes how absurd it is, her standing here, in this house, after everything.

She turns away—she'll wait for him outside—but a picture catches her eye. She walks up to the black and white print of an old man with a young boy, a hunting rifle in each of their hands.

"My grandfather," Ben says.

He's wearing jeans and a red flannel shirt. He smells of soap.

"My dad was so busy with the farm that I spent most of my time with my grandfather. He taught me how to shoot." He looks over to the safe. "Most of the rifles I have here are from him."

In that moment, looking at the picture, Priscilla realizes how much more complicated people's lives are than their opinions. And how little we often know about those we disagree with.

"Kaitlin came to see me," Priscilla says.

"I know. She said it didn't go so well—"

"She came back—a second time."

He smiles. "Katie's persistent like that."

"Yeah. She is."

"She told me about the argument you had."

"She did?"

She nods.

He feels it too. How strange this new world is, in which Kaitlin would come and confide in her.

"It seems that she's come round to your way of thinking," he says.

"I'm sorry."

He looks up at her. "Are you?"

"I'm sorry that it's gotten between you."

He looks back at the picture of his grandfather.

"I think you'll work it out," Priscilla says.

"I'm not so sure."

"She loves you, Ben. That hasn't changed, just because you don't agree right now."

Priscilla thinks about Peter and Kim up at the cottage. How Kim has travelled thousands of miles for him, because she's certain that Peter belongs to her now.

"Some people are meant to be together. Like you and Kaitlin." She swallows hard. "Others—maybe we just got it wrong from the start."

"Peter should never have left you," Ben says.

"I made other mistakes too. I wasn't paying attention to our marriage."

Ben goes quiet for a while. Then he asks, "Is he going to stay for a bit, to make sure Astrid's okay?"

"I don't think so. He's got work. And someone to go home with."

"I'm sorry about that. About everything."

"And I'm sorry about the things I said about Bryar. And about you."

They lock eyes.

"It's been a hell of a week, hasn't it?"

She nods.

"You really think things are going to work out—between me and Katie?"

The openness in his face—the willingness to be so vulnerable—stops her breath.

"Yes. I do."

"Thank you for saying that."

The grandfather clock chimes. They both look up.

"You still want to go to the opening?" he asks her.

She doesn't know what she wants to do any more or where she wants to be. But the thought of turning up in Ben's red truck, after everything that's gone down between them, strikes her as so absurd that it makes her smile.

"Yes," she says. "Let's go."

The audience watches Ayaan Sayed walking across the stage to the microphone. He takes his speech from his jacket pocket and looks out at them. A few times he opens his mouth and they think that he's going to start, but still, he doesn't say anything.

Behind him, Governor Warnes uncrosses and re-crosses her legs and then looks at her watch. As soon as this is over, she has somewhere else to be.

The imam leans forward and whispers something to Ayaan, but he doesn't seem to hear. He's so distracted, it's like he's not even here.

The audience members shuffle in their chairs, waiting.

When Ayaan looks round at his twins and then back out at the audience, everyone thinks that now, at last, he'll start.

But still, he stays silent.

That's when Avery stands up from her seat at the end of the front row. She walks up the steps onto the stage, pats Ayaan on the back and then leans in to the microphone.

"I think we got our order of service mixed up, didn't we, Ayaan?" She smiles at him. "I was meant to go first, remember?"

She says it with such conviction that the audience believes her.

Ayaan looks at Avery and nods. He heads back to his chair, next to the twins, and everyone expects him to sit down, but he keeps walking. Past his children. Past Wendy Warnes. Past the imam. Down, off the stage. Along the rows and rows of chairs and out toward the parking lot.

People keep twisting around, looking, but then Avery's voice comes through the microphone and they turn back to the stage.

"It's an honor to be standing here today," Avery says. "What a special moment for our community: one we should all be proud of." She looks out and waits until everyone's with her. "I'd like to tell you about two people who taught me a great deal about how complicated—and beautiful—life can be." She pauses again. "I'd like to tell you about my mom and dad . . ."

Before Yasmin sees him, she feels his footsteps, the sway of the dock under her body.

And then he's sitting beside her, in his silk sherwani, a sheen of sweat running along his hairline from having run through the woods.

He takes off his shoes and socks and puts his feet into the cold, rain-swollen water. Their toes brush against each other.

"Shouldn't you be somewhere else?" she says.

He shakes his head. "No." And then he adds, "I'm sorry for forgetting."

"Forgetting?"

"Who you were. Who you wanted to be." He pauses. "I'm sorry for making you so unhappy."

"I'm not unhappy—I have you, and the kids. We have a beautiful home—"

"Please don't pretend. Not any more."

She nods, slowly. "Okay."

"I was scared that I'd lose you again," he says.

"Again?"

"When we were first together—in New York—you were so free. So good at making friends. At adapting to life here. I was scared that you'd leave me behind."

"But I loved you—"

"I know. But I was still scared. In Lahore, things felt easier. You seemed less distracted. You felt closer." He pauses. "And you picked up your faith again. I thought—"

"I did it to please my parents. And you. And, I suppose, because it felt familiar. But my heart wasn't in it, Ayaan."

"So I've been blind for even longer than I thought."

She puts her hand over his. "You said you found things easier in Lahore—why did you want us to come back to America, then?"

"Because I thought it would be different. We were married. We had kids. We had a project to get behind—the mosque. And we were older. I told myself that this time, when we came here, I'd be enough for you. That you'd be proud of me."

"I've been proud of you since the day I met you, Ayaan."

He goes quiet. They look out at the pond, so still today that the trees are reflected like in a mirror. Soon, the leaves will turn orange and red and gold.

"How did you know where to find me?" Yasmin asks.

"You remember the dock—in New York. Off 79th Street?"

She nods.

"When we went on our walks, that's where you always led us. Standing on the water, looking across the city."

She closes her eyes and smiles. "I loved it there."

"Me too."

On long Sunday afternoons, they'd take a break from studying and walk for hours along the Hudson.

"And I followed you out here—a few times," he says.

She opens her eyes. "You followed me?"

"When I came home from work and couldn't find you. When you left our bed, early in the morning, before the kids were awake."

"I didn't think you noticed—"

"I've been blind to a lot—to most things, as it turns out. But I did see it: how you were pulling away from me."

"Why didn't you say anything?"

"Because if I said it out loud—if I admitted it to myself, then I couldn't pretend any more."

"Pretend?"

"That everything was okay. That I wasn't losing you." He holds her hand tighter. "But I get it now," he goes on. "That by holding you back—by holding the twins back—I've been pushing you away." His voice breaks. "It's my fault you kissed Ben Wright."

She looks down at his hand, still gripping hers, and brings it up to her mouth. She presses her lips against his palm.

"I want you to be happy, Yasmin. That's all I've ever wanted. I've just got it wrong—"

"You have to trust me, Ayaan."

"I know. I was just so scared of losing you."

"I love you, Ayaan." She pauses. "You'll never lose me."

He nods. "I'm going to try really hard to believe that."

She looks at him, sitting on the dock, his feet dripping, the hem of his silk trousers wet, knowing that this is the moment when she gets to decide whether their marriage is going to survive.

And the truth is, she doesn't know, not for sure. Whether they'll be patient enough with each other to make it work. Whether he'll allow her to become the person she needs to be. Whether she'll find a way to stand by him without losing herself. But he's right. They should try.

She stands up and holds out her hands. "Come on," she says.

He looks up at her, confused.

"People will be wondering where you've got to."

He bows his head. "I don't think I can go back."

She reaches down and takes his hands and pulls him onto his feet. Then she hands him his shoes and socks and starts putting her own shoes back on.

"You okay with me looking like this?" she says, pulling at the old sweatshirt she's wearing.

"You're coming with me?" he says.

She leans in and kisses his cheek, feeling the warmth of his skin under her lips. "Yes, I'm coming with you."

Yasmin walks with Ayaan onto the stage. She sits down next to the twins and they look at her, wide-eyed.

"You came, Mom?" they whisper together.

She smiles. "Yes."

Ayaan leans into the microphone. "Thank you for your patience."

The audience falls silent.

"I have many people to thank today—and rightly so," Ayaan goes on. "Hundreds of you have helped, in big and small ways, to make this possible." He sweeps his hand to his right where the mosque stands, gleaming in the sunlight. "But there's someone I haven't thanked yet. Probably because it's easy to take for granted those who are closest to us—and who do the most." He turns toward Yasmin. "Yasmin Sayed, my wife, has more of an understanding of what the word 'community' means than I ever will. I might be good at designing buildings—at understanding how marble and cement, glass and steel work together—but Yasmin understands about joining hands, about bringing people together. Without her, I wouldn't be standing here today, watching this dream come true. Yasmin has taught me that we all have to respect the journey of faith that we're on. That there is no clear path. That sometimes we have to move backward to step forward again. That sometimes, we need to stop and rest. That sometimes, we're just walking in the dark." He squeezes her hand. "She's taught me that this building isn't enough—that it's going to take a great deal more to heal the divisions in our community—and in our country. But I believe that today is a start. And that's why I want her to be here, at my side."

"This mosque is the beginning of a conversation. It's the beginning of a new way of understanding how we relate to each other as human beings and through our faith. It's the beginning of being okay with how we're different from each other."

He turns to Wendy Warnes, who looks furious that so much of her time has been taken up by delays she could never understand.

"As you know from the publicity for this event, Governor Warnes was going to cut the ribbon—to officially open our mosque. And we are grateful that she made time to be here today. But I'd like to change that plan."

Cameras flash. Reporters bend their heads and type furiously into their phones. He notices Wendy Warnes's cheeks burn red. She turns to her aides, as though they could fix whatever it is that is going wrong right now.

Ayaan looks over to Yasmin. She feels hundreds of other eyes on her.

"She may not be a political figure or a religious leader. Many of you may never have seen her before—though that's going to change from now on." He looks back round at the audience. "But, years ago, she's the one who saved me from myself. And she's saved me many times since. She's also the most incredible mother. And if there's one thing we've all learned this past week, it's that the mothers—and the fathers—from different backgrounds and from different places in our country and in our world, with different beliefs and priorities and hopes and fears, the mothers and fathers who get it wrong, terribly wrong sometimes, but still show up, day after day, for their kids—they're the people who unite a community like ours, more than a church or a mosque or any other religious building ever could."

Yasmin's eyes well up.

"So, I'd like to ask my wife to honor us by cutting the ribbon."

People start clapping—a deep, warm clapping that tells him that, even though they might not know who Yasmin is, they feel it too: that she's the right person to do this.

Ayaan takes Yasmin's hand and, together, they walk off the stage to the front of the mosque.

Yasmin picks up the scissors from a table set up to the side of the ribbon and then she walks over, takes Ayaan's hand and joins it to hers.

"I want us to do this together," she says.

After it's been cut, the red ribbon floats in the breeze and there's a silence, as though everyone's holding their breath. And then, it drops to the floor.

Two months later

Thursday, 28th November

Thanksgiving

PRISCILLA AND ASTRID climb off their bicycles and prop them against the sign for Woodwind Stables.

They've been going on short cycle rides together to build up Astrid's strength. In fact, they've been doing more together than they have in years. Priscilla's taken a few months off work. Last night, they baked pies for the Thanksgiving party at St. Mary's. They stood together in the kitchen of the cottage, their faces dusted in flour, until the last pie came out of the oven.

The pies are packed into the basket of Priscilla's bicycle.

"See you at the church in an hour or so?" Priscilla says.

"Yes, Mom."

"And you won't push yourself too hard—you'll get off and wheel the bike when—"

Astrid rolls her eyes but she's smiling. "I'm going uphill or if I feel tired or if my chest hurts. I know, Mom."

Priscilla steps forward and tries to give Astrid a kiss but their bicycle helmets bump against each other. They step back, laughing.

Priscilla looks over her shoulder, up the drive. She sees Bryar and his parents standing in the front yard. She gives them a wave and they wave back. The Wrights are coming to the Thanksgiving party too. Most of Middlebrook is. It was Avery's idea to bring everyone together rather than people eating their turkeys in their own houses.

Priscilla looks over at Astrid one last time and then turns back to the road and freewheels down the hill that leads into Middlebrook.

As he cycles down the driveway, past the maples, bare now, Bryar fixes his eyes on the girl standing by her bicycle at the end of the driveway. He gets a flash of the eight-year-old friend he used to know: the friend he thought he would have for ever, and then lost—and now, miraculously, has found again. She nearly died, because of him. And he got to start over. This time, he's not going to let anyone take her away.

He brakes hard and his bike skids to a stop next to her.

She turns around.

"Ready?" he says.

She smiles. "Ready."

They cycle next to each other, the wind whipping their cheeks. They can feel something changing in the air. The sky feels closer. And brighter. And colder. After all the rain in early September, October was beautiful. The brook shrank down again. Soon it will freeze over for winter.

When they get to Main Street, they stop in front of the brown bungalow opposite the Sayeds. There's a to let sign in the front yard.

"I wonder who will move in next?" Bryar asks.

"Mom says they're not going to use it for the university any more, not until they do it up."

He remembers the first time he came here to visit Lily. How Mom had dragged him out of his bedroom, saying there was someone she wanted him to meet. That it was their neighborly duty to welcome new people into the community. He'd hated the way she dragged him out, forcing to socialize when he just wanted to be on his own, but then it turned out that he liked Lily. More than liked her. When it felt like things would never be good again, she'd made life bearable. And she was the one who brought him back to Astrid.

"Hey! Bryar! Astrid!" Laila calls from across the road.

She and Hanif are sitting on the doorstep of their house.

"I like the clothes," Astrid says as she gets off her bike.

"Thanks," Laila and Hanif say at the exact same time.

They look down at their sneakers and their jeans and the Patriots sweatshirt Dad got them for today. The Pats are playing in one of the Thanksgiving games and he said that, now that they were true New Englanders, they should show their support. Ben Wright's been coming over to teach Mom and Dad the rules of football: he says it's the key to understanding everything they need to know about America. Dad's totally taken to it.

And it's more than that. The twins feel comfortable in these clothes. Like they can be one of the other kids.

"Dad got us all sweatshirts," Hanif says. "Even Mom's wearing one."

Hanif and Laila look up at the scaffolding where their parents are standing in their navy sweatshirts and yellow hard hats.

"So, run this by me again," Astrid says. "You're tearing down a mansion to build a house that looks like all the other houses on the street?"

"That's the idea," Laila says.

A few days after the opening of the mosque, Dad announced that they were going to do some remodeling on their house. They wanted it to blend in a bit better with their neighbors, he said. A smaller house with fewer rooms. A house that looked more like it belonged here.

He and Mom have been working on it ever since. Dad's taken a break before starting on his next project. Sometimes, late at night, when the twins tiptoe out of their bedroom and stand on the landing, they see Mom and Dad sitting on stools at the kitchen island, their heads bent over plans for the house.

"Still seems crazy to me," Astrid says. "I'd love to live in a massive house with big columns and marble floors."

"Mom said it never felt like a home," Laila says.

The twins hadn't really thought about it before, not until she said it. But then they realized that she was right. That it had always felt a bit echoey and cold.

"This house is going to be better," Hanif says.

"I think it is too," Bryar says.

The two boys exchange a shy glance. Hanif's gone over to see Bryar a few times at Woodwind Stables. Bryar's been teaching Hanif about his rocks. Sometimes, Hanif likes spending time with Bryar even more than he likes spending time with Laila, though he'd never tell his twin sister that.

"Ready to go?" Bryar says. "If we're going to make it back in time for the Thanksgiving pot luck, we should leave now."

"Ready!" Laila and Hanif say.

Astrid and Bryar laugh. "You guys are totally twins."

"Yeah," they say. "We are." They look at each other. They know that they both messed up: that Hanif should never have grabbed that pistol from Astrid or shot it; that Laila should never have tried to hide it. But they also know that sometimes good things come out of bad decisions. They really let Dad down, but it helped him understand them better—and it made him slow down and notice them again. So, in some twisted way, it's all been kind of worth it.

"We'll see you at St. Mary's!" Laila calls up to Mom and Dad.

"See you there," Mom and Dad say.

The twins look at each other and laugh at how Mom and Dad said the same thing at the same time, like they usually do.

Bryar and Astrid lean their bicycles up against the fountain, hang their helmets from the handlebars, and the four children walk up Main Street to St. Mary's.

Abi stands back from the HAPPY THANKSGIVING banner and smiles. "It looks awesome, Cal," she says.

Everyone had been really surprised when the art teacher, Mrs. Tillman, agreed to let Cal take some paints home over the holidays. They'd been even more surprised that Cal plucked up the courage to ask her. After everything, they thought that maybe Mrs. Tillman would ban Cal from the art room. But she said that every artist needs to go through a rebellious phase—and that now it's time to learn how to channel his art in a way that helps people rather than hurting them.

Abi remembers how she felt when she looked at the graffiti on the mosque: how the words made her feel sick to her stomach. But at the same time, she remembers thinking how beautiful they were. The colors. The shape of the letters. And she knew that he'd done it out of love, to protect her.

Cal gets up off his knees and stares at the banner. His hands and hair and sneakers are streaked with paint. He might be learning to channel his art but he still makes a mess.

"Not too cheesy?" he says.

He's drawn turkeys and pumpkins and squirrels and chipmunks around the edge of the banner.

"What's Thanksgiving without a bit of cheese?" Abi says. "And anyway, you've given them an edge—a cool take on Thanksgiving."

Even when things were really bad with Mom, they'd still celebrate Thanksgiving. They'd have turkey sandwiches rather than a proper turkey, and the pie was from the frozen section at Walmart, but it still felt special. It was the only time they remember ever sitting down and eating together.

"Cool banner!" someone calls from across the road.

They turn around to see Skye walking toward them, along with her brothers.

"Thanks," Cal says, blushing.

It took a while, after what happened in the stable, for them to find a way back to each other. But then, after school one day, Cal went to find Skye in the woods and asked her whether she'd come to the art room with him to look at what he'd been working on. After that, she started visiting most afternoons. The art teacher didn't say anything. Now, Skye and Cal are always together. Abi's never seen Cal let anyone get so close. Until they came to Middlebrook, he always said that it was just a matter of time before they'd be moved on again, so making friends was pointless. But Skye's more than a friend. And this time, he doesn't want to move.

Cal and Abi are trying to forget that they're on a trial period until Christmas, which is when they'll have a court hearing about the fact that Avery wants to adopt them. Bill said that the judge is going to need to see some signs that they've made a real effort to settle in. And that Avery's been able to keep them out of trouble. They have to prove to everyone that Middlebrook is meant to be their home.

It's more than they could have hoped for, especially after the news got out about Cal and the graffiti and about how Abi had taken the safety catch off the pistol. But Avery's speech helped. There was a reporter from the *Boston Chronicle* at the opening of the mosque and she'd asked Avery's permission to print it.

Abi thinks about those things Avery said about her parents and how she grew up surrounded by guns and how that didn't make her a bad person—or her parents either. And she'd talked about Cal, too, that although he did a horrible thing when he wrote those words on the wall of the mosque, he had his reasons. And that it would help us understand people more and to blame them less. *Cal wanted to protect his sister,* she said. *And he wanted to stay in the first home where he's felt safe. He was scared that they'd have to leave—and fear makes you do stupid things.*

No one had ever tried to understand Cal like that. Or Abi.

After the article, Avery got lots of letters of support. And some other letters too, that weren't that supportive. But she didn't seem to mind. *People are never all going to agree about everything,* she'd said. The main thing is that we're talking to each other.

Anyway, they're trying really hard to make it up to Avery and to show Bill and the judge that keeping them here is the right thing.

If there's anything Abi's learned over the past few weeks, it's that no one's family is perfect.

You might have this amazing dad who loves you more than anything in the whole world—but no matter how awesome he is, he'll never be able to fill the empty space left behind by your mom.

You might have parents who end up splitting up because one of them falls in love with someone else and takes off because being with that new person is more important to them than staying with the person they married—and even their own kid.

You might have parents who look like they're really close but they keep secrets from each other, big secrets, like the fact that they're pregnant, and who never tell their secret until something bad happens, like nearly losing the baby.

And you might have parents who have loads of money and a big house and fancy cars and who give you nice clothes to wear—but none of that stuff makes them really happy and they have to tear down their big house and put on new clothes and say they're sorry to each other to make it better.

Having your mom taken away because she was a drug addict who shot someone to get her next fix is a pretty shitty deal to get as a kid, but it's not the only shitty deal.

Skye walks away from Abi and Cal and goes to the back of the church. She kneels in front of Mom's grave and clears away the old mulchy leaves.

Wynn and Phoenix are there already. Wynn's collecting the few leaves that are still a nice color, which he places on top of the grave, like bright flowers.

It was Wynn's idea that the children should get together like this, before the Thanksgiving party. *Last time we did this, it made people happy, and Thanksgiving is about making other people feel happy, isn't it?* he said.

Skye looks back at Mom's grave. *You put a whole lot of you into Wynn when you left, Mom,* she thinks as she brushes over the letters of her name: *Cedar Grace Bowen*.

Dad's always going on about how, when people pass away, their spirit lives on in nature—in the trees and the flowers and the sky and the earth. But Skye thinks that people live on in those they loved. She sees bits of Mom in Dad and Phoenix every day—but most of all, she sees her in Wynn.

She pulls Wynn onto her lap and hugs him. He snuggles in against her chest.

"Pssst—!"

Skye and Wynn look up into the oak tree next to Mom's grave.

"What is it?" Skye asks.

"Don't move," Phoenix says. "I'm coming down."

Phoenix still does his disappearing thing sometimes. Like before, you're still more likely to find him in a tree than on the ground. But he's been spending time with them too. For ages, they felt guilty about assuming that he was the one who'd fired the gun. And Skye had felt bad that she hadn't set everyone straight. But Phoenix brushed it off, like it didn't matter.

I'd have thought it was me too, he said once.

Which made Skye realize that he was way smarter than people gave him credit for.

She'd asked him about Astrid's phone that Dad found under his mattress. About why he'd taken it from the stable that day and kept hold of it.

I reckoned that Astrid had already paid enough for what she did that afternoon. She didn't need people watching that video.

So, you were protecting her?

Astrid's like me, Phoenix had said. *People don't get us because we don't do what they expect us to. And we get stuff wrong without meaning to. And even when we mean to do the bad stuff, there's a reason for it, even if that reason doesn't make sense to anyone else.*

Skye realizes that she'd been one of those people that Phoenix talked about. That she'd assumed that Phoenix was messed up because he did things differently from the rest of them. And she'd thought the same about Astrid too.

Without making a sound, Phoenix climbs down from the tree and stands next to them. "They're here," he says, his eyes sparkling.

Skye and Wynn crouch beside him.

"Look!" He stretches out his arm toward the woods.

A branch snaps.

They can hear soft, heavy footsteps padding through the dark bit of the wood.

Wynn gasps. "It's them!"

He darts forward but Phoenix grabs his sweater and yanks him back. "Just watch, Wynn."

Wynn stumbles back. The three of them watch and wait, holding their breath, as a big bear, her fur a mix of brown and gold, like the leaves in Wynn's bucket, walks under the trees, followed by her three cubs.

And then, as quickly as the bears came, they're gone. For a second, Skye wonders whether Wynn's stories actually wished them into existence.

There are more footsteps but this time they're accompanied by voices. The three Bowen children turn around and see the others walking toward them.

Cal comes over, grabs Wynn from behind and swings him round and round. When he lets go, Wynn stumbles around, dizzy.

"Hey, careful of his arm," Skye calls out. But really, she's glad. That Cal likes Wynn so much. And that he likes Phoenix too. That he's not just hers—that by loving him, he now belongs to all of them.

Cal goes over to Phoenix and looks up into the tree. "I saw you jump down—is it a difficult one?" he asks.

"No, you could totally do it. You just need to find the good foot holds." Phoenix says.

Even though he's the younger one, Phoenix has been teaching Cal to climb some of the coolest trees in the woods behind St. Mary's. Before Cal came to live in Middlebrook, he said that He'd never climbed a tree in his life. Now, when you look up and see a figure sitting in a tree somewhere in Middlebrook, it could as easily be Cal as Phoenix. It turns out that some people are happier off the ground.

"Do you have them?" Wynn asks Bryar.

Bryar nods and taps his backpack.

"I think we should go to the pond before it gets dark," Wynn pipes up.

The kids look at each other and smile and, without anyone having to say it, they take off through the woods behind the cemetery toward Middlebrook Pond. Bryar trails a little behind the rest, turning every now and then to look over his shoulder through the bare trees.

The FOR SALE sign that stood, for over a year, outside the old house at the end of Main Street has gone now.

It's the house past the church and the library and all the other houses, the one that stands on its own, just before the crossroads that leads out of town.

It's an old house, but it's been looked after well. It's got a red roof and white clapboards and a wrap-around porch. It's a house that looks like it's stood here for ever.

Whenever she passed it, the house made Eva think of home: its oldness; the rose beds in the front garden, like at her parents' house in Dorset.

There's been a buzz around Middlebrook about who'll be moving in.

Lily and Will stop walking.

And then they look at each other and smile.

"What's going on?" Eva says.

"You got it?" Lily asks Will.

"Yep." He digs around in his pocket.

"Got what?" Eva asks.

He holds two closed fists out to her. "Which one?" he says.

"Seriously?" she laughs.

She taps his left hand. He holds out an empty palm. "Try again."

She taps his right hand. He unfurls his fingers. A key sits in his palm.

"What's this?" she says.

He smiles. "A bribe."

Lily laughs. "A bribe?"

"To make you stay," Lily says. "Or to make you think about it, at least."

After coming home from hospital, Eva had spent days looking up flights back to the UK and making plans for their return. But then, as things settled down, in the weeks after the shooting, she stopped checking so often. And then she stopped talking about going home. And after a while, she stopped thinking about it too, in that way that time has of making you forget the things that once felt so urgent. Though not altogether. There are days when she can feel it pushing up under her ribs—that longing for home. But maybe that's just how it will always be.

And now it's Thanksgiving. Soon, it will be Christmas. And then the baby in the spring.

"You bought a house?" Eva says. "But we don't have the money—"

"The bank has the money though, doesn't it, Lily?"

"Yep!"

"Lily's been in on this?"

"Of course. It was Lily's idea. I think I had the idea too, but she likes to take the credit, don't you, Lily?"

Lily punches Will's arm playfully. "It was *totally* my idea, Dad."

Eva looks back at the house. "It's an upgrade from the eighties bungalow," she says.

"Yes it is. It will need work though," Will says.

"I'll help," Lily adds.

"It could be nice—to make somewhere our own," Will says.

"You're assuming that I'm going to say yes," Eva says.

Will gives her a sideways smile. "Wasn't that how I got you to marry me?"

Eva smiles. "Maybe."

"I'm going before you two get all slushy." Lily climbs onto the bike. "Promise you'll give it a chance, Mom?"

"*Mom!*" Eva and Will say at the same time.

"If you start calling me *Mom*, we're definitely going back to England," Eva says.

"You're the one who wanted me to integrate."

"Not that much." Will laughs.

Lily clips on her helmet.

"I'll give it a chance," Eva says.

"You'll love the inside," Lily says. "We've decided which room should be the nursery, haven't we, Dad?"

Will nods.

"Oh, so you've seen the inside already too?"

"Yep!" Lily puts her feet on the pedals. "See you later, *Mom* and Dad!"

And then she's gone.

As they watch her pedal away, Eva thinks that this, more than anything, would make her stay: that her little girl is happy, that she has friends. That in the last two months, she's come to see Middlebrook as her home.

"If you decide against it, it would make a nice holiday home," Will says. "We could come back for vacations."

"Since when did we become the kind of people who can afford a holiday home?"

"Well, whatever you decide, I'm sure we'll work it out, my love."

"We will, will we?"

He smiles and hands her the key.

Together they walk up the porch steps. Eva opens the screen door and slots the key into the lock.

Lily pedals as fast as she can down Main Street and then along the narrow path behind St. Mary's, the one that runs along the brook. She cycles past the cemetery and into the woods and she keeps going until the path gets too bumpy. She leans her bike up against a big oak tree, takes off her helmet, puts it in the basket and walks the rest of the way, through the thick part of the wood, until she gets to the pond.

And then she stops and looks at the children standing on the dock, holding rocks between their fingers, and writing on them with paint markers. They're writing the things they're thankful for: the good things that have come through the bad things they've had to live through since the shooting.

She watches them crouch down on the edge of the dock and, one by one, they drop their rocks into the water. She imagines the heavy rocks sinking into the soft, wet soil at the bottom. They're going back to the earth, she thinks. And maybe, thousands of years from now, they'll wash up on the shore and other children will find them.

As she looks out across the pond, Lily's eyes blur in and out of focus as she thinks about how different it will look soon, when the temperature drops and it freezes over and the water stops moving. Bryar's told her how the whole town comes out to skate and how fishermen drill holes into the ice. And then, in the spring, there's a famous polar bear swim when the bravest people from Middlebrook jump into the freshly thawed water. Spring. The baby will be here then. She can hardly believe that she's going to be a sister.

She blinks, her eyes refocus and she looks back at the pond as it is now, today, and how the ripples from where the children's rocks went in, spread out and overlap and then dissolve.

"Lily!" Bryar's noticed her. "You made it!" He's standing on the end of the dock, waving at her. His face is beaming.

She waves back.

Then she looks over at Astrid. Their eyes catch, and they smile.

Bryar comes over and hands her a rock.

She already knows what she's going to write on it. Clem—short for Clement. The name of the baby brother she's going to have in the spring, the name she'd chosen with Mum and Dad. And, on the other side, she'll write the name of the boy she got to know here, in this town, thousands of miles away from London; the boy who made her feel like this could be home, after all.

Kaitlin carries the turkey into the main hall and looks around.

She walks past Priscilla, laying out her pies on the dessert table, and True, setting up the projector and screen at the far end of the church so that everyone can watch the Patriots game.

She puts the turkey down on the table and walks to the far end of the church where Ben's untangling a strings of fairy lights by the altar.

It hasn't been easy between them—to change a lifetime of doing things the same way. They've removed the gun safe from their bedroom and the one from the living room. But there's still one in the basement for his hunting rifles. She doesn't go down there any more and sometimes she can't bear it, the thought of those guns in her house. Because once you see something—once you believe something—you can't unsee it, or unbelieve it. But they both know that they have to meet each other halfway. That marriage doesn't survive absolutes.

He's wearing his border patrol uniform. He won't be staying for the Thanksgiving meal; he likes to take the holiday shifts so that his colleagues can be with their families. And she doesn't mind: it's part of who he is. Doing things for others. Putting them first. He's a good man. Maybe the best she's ever known.

She watches him pulling at the fairy lights, the knots getting tighter the harder he works at them.

"Here, let me help," she says, holding out her hands.

He looks up at her and smiles.

"I'm making it worse," he says, handing her the lights.

She shakes them loose and then eases her fingers under the knots. She feels him standing close to her: the smell of his skin—the warmth of his breath.

When the biggest knots come loose, the smaller ones give way. She hands the string of lights back to Ben. "There—I think they're good now."

He kisses her forehead. She puts her arms around him, leans her head against his chest and listens to his heart. They hold on to each other for a while, the lights trailing on the floor between them.

Avery looks around the church, filled with friends and neighbors. She came here when she was twenty-three, straight out of her ministry training. Her parents had been gone for five years. The town was suspicious of her, being so young and a woman. Preaching about a religion that included everyone. They'd never thought of faith like that before. Sometimes, she'd feared she'd never win them over. But now, here they are: her congregation.

She notices a shaft of sunlight falling in through the stained glass window with the picture of the Virgin Mary. And then something else, too: a gentle white fluttering, like blossom.

Excitement shoots through her. Growing up in the Middle East, she'd never seen snow. It was one of the things she loved most about living in New Hampshire: how you could rely on the fact that, come winter, the sky would open up and the world would turn white.

"Snow!" she calls out.

And then she runs out through the main church doors and looks up at the sky. It's a brilliant white. And it's cold. So cold she can feel it biting right down to her bones. But it's a good cold. It makes her feel alive.

She tilts her head to the sky, closes her eyes, and feels the first light flakes falling on her cheeks and her eyelashes.

Others press out of the church behind her: they want to come and see the snow too. No matter how many times they've seen it, no matter how hard and long and cold the winters are here, the first snowfall always feels like a miracle.

As Priscilla stands in the snow outside the church, her phone goes off.

"First snow," she says, before he even has time to say anything.

"Wow, I miss that."

"Then come home."

There's a silence.

"You know, I think I might."

Things aren't going well with Kim. Apparently, they argued on the drive back to California. Something about him not keeping in touch while he was away.

She made it sound like I was on a business trip, Peter said.

Priscilla should have found it strange, how her husband had called her the night he got back to California and confided in her about the first big argument he'd had with the woman he left her for. She should have found it strange that he'd call her at all. And she should have hung up. The audacity of it—after what he'd put her through—to expect her to sit there and listen to him talking about his girlfriend problems.

But she didn't hang up. Because hearing his voice felt good. Familiar. She missed him. The week they spent together had felt longer, somehow, than their whole marriage. The way they talked in the long, silent hours, sitting next to Astrid's hospital bed. How they'd spent an afternoon, back in their old bed at home, their bodies curled into each other. And how, together, they'd watched their little girl coming back to life.

So instead, she'd said, *You want some advice for free?*

You're going to give it anyway, aren't you?

I can hang up if you want.

No, don't hang up, he said quickly, scared that she might. *Please. What's the advice?*

A pause. And then: *You should go back to your wife.* Another pause. *Your wife never nagged you about staying in touch.*

And he'd laughed. And she'd laughed too. And strangely, things had felt better.

And then he called again. Over and over.

And they fell into joking with each other. Because it was easier, for now. Joking about them getting back together. Joking about him not getting on with Kim. Joking about how the divorce papers were still sitting on the front passenger seat of her car, unsigned.

And here he was, calling again.

"She left," he says.

Priscilla's heart jolts. "Oh."

"So now I'm stuck in sunny California, on my own, longing for snow."

"Poor you."

"Yes, poor me."

A beat.

"So, can I come home?" he asks again.

"We're doing quite well, you know, Astrid and me—just the two of us."

And it was true. Since coming back from hospital, she and Astrid have gotten along better than—well, ever.

"I should stay here, then? Do my penance? Is that what you're saying?"

"Sounds like a plan."

A hesitation. Sometimes, it's hard to know when the joking has stopped.

"You don't mean that."

"It's presumptuous to assume you know what a woman *means*. And anyway, I think we get on better on the phone than in person, don't you?"

Another beat.

"I sometimes feel I can't read you any more, Cil. I don't know whether you're kidding around—"

"Well, why don't we keep calling each other for a bit longer. Work at getting to know each other again. See how things pan out. And who knows, Kim might come back, and then you'll need some more relationship advice."

"She's not coming back, Cil."

"How do you know?"

"I know."

Priscilla's heart jolts again.

Don't let yourself hope, she tells herself. *Not yet.*

"Maybe I could visit for Christmas, then? The snow will still be around, won't it?"

"Can't guarantee it—not these days, climate change and all that," she says.

"Our president doesn't believe in climate change."

"Our next one might," she says.

Another beat. Longer this time. Maybe she's pushed him too far.

"Christmas could work," she says, her voice wavering.

"It could?"

She nods, even though she knows he can't see it. "I'd better go—the party's about to begin."

"Give Astrid a hug from me," he says.

"Will do."

"And Cil?"

"Yes?"

"I love you."

Her heart stops. They haven't gone there. Not once since he left last February.

"I love you too," she says, and hangs up.

As Eva walks toward the church with Will, she hears laughter coming from the woods behind the church. And then the sound of branches snapping and heavy footsteps.

The grown-ups, standing outside, look up.

And then she sees them. The children running toward the church.

Some of them holding hands, some pushing past each other, racing to be first, others with their arms stretched wide, trying to catch snowflakes as they run.

Lily is at the front, with Bryar and Astrid. She tilts her head up to the sky and tries to catch flakes of snow on her tongue.

As the children draw closer, Eva sees the small trail of footsteps stretching behind them on the thin, new layer of snow.

ACKNOWLEDGMENTS

THANK YOU TO all the magical people who made this book possible. My faithful writing friend and first reader, Margaret Porter. Katharine Woodman-Maynard for the incredible map at the beginning of the UK edition. Michael Herrmann for your friendship, support and beautiful bookstore. Barb Higgins, for making it possible for us to stay in the US.

Thank you to Lieutenant Sean Ford, Curtis Arsenault, Dan Feltes and Jim Murphy for helping an English girl understand guns in America.

Thank you to the whole team at Little, Brown, for getting this book out on both sides of the Atlantic, in particular Rosanna Forte, Thalia Proctor, Kate Hibbert and Andy Hine. And to my US publishing team at Crooked Lane Press.

Thank you, as always, to my family who put up with all the highs and lows of having a live-in writer: Mama, Tennessee Skye, Somerset Wilder, Willoughby Walden, Valentine, Septimus, and Sonnet. And of course, the biggest thank you of all to Hugh, my heel-ball-and-toe mate to the end.

And finally thank you to the great, beautiful and complex continent that I now call home; one that I have grown to love deeply: America. Thank you for welcoming me, an immigrant, and my family, with such warmth and kindness. And thank you for sharing your incredible stories with me. I hope I've done you justice in this novel.